Out of the Darkness

Zoe woke in a daze. No windows. A strange room. She was in—oh, right, the tomb. Because people were trying to kill her for no good reason.

She stumbled to the bathroom door and opened it. The sight of a naked male body woke her as no intravenous espresso shot ever could. Water dotted Rand's broad shoulders and dripped down the indent of his spine and over a tight, sweet derriere. Because he was drying his hair with a towel, he hadn't heard her open the door.

The hand towel went flying off the shelf, causing him to turn around to look at her and then behind him to where the towel landed on the floor. The familiar horror at losing control of her crazy energy filled her. The worse part, the absolutely terrible part? She couldn't stop staring! His arms were extended above his head, bulging his biceps. Fine blonde hair dusted the ridges of his stomach. His thatch of hair was dark blond, and a glimpse of …

He hadn't moved since her entrance, but he finally said, "This wasn't quite what I had in mind when I said we were sharing a bathroom, but hey, it's fine with me. Clothes are overrated anyway."

By Jaime Rush

OUT OF THE DARKNESS
A PERFECT DARKNESS

Coming Soon
TOUCHING DARKNESS

JAIME RUSH

OUT OF THE DARKNESS

AVON

An Imprint of HarperCollinsPublishers

This is a work of fiction. Names, characters, places, and incidents are products of the author's imagination or are used fictitiously and are not to be construed as real. Any resemblance to actual events, locales, organizations, or persons, living or dead, is entirely coincidental.

AVON BOOKS
An Imprint of HarperCollins*Publishers*
10 East 53rd Street
New York, New York 10022-5299

Copyright © 2009 by Tina Wainscott
Excerpt from *Touching Darkness* copyright © 2010 by Tina Wainscott
ISBN 978-0-06-169036-5
www.avonromance.com

First Avon Books paperback printing: October 2009

Avon Trademark Reg. U.S. Pat. Off. and in Other Countries, Marca Registrada, Hecho en U.S.A.
HarperCollins® is a registered trademark of HarperCollins Publishers.

Printed in the U.S.A.

10 9 8 7 6 5 4 3 2 1

To RJ Newton, nephew and U.S. Marine.
We're so proud of you!
To great friends, Jeff and Gretchen Naidenhoff.
To my soul sisters: Rachael Wolff,
Sandra Palin, and Mary Olderich

CHAPTER 1

"This would go a lot easier if you'd stop screaming in pain," Zoe told the muscular man lying beneath her.

"Nobody told me this was going to hurt so much," he said in a strained voice.

She arched one of her dark red eyebrows. "What did you think a tattoo needle was going to feel like?"

"Just finish already."

She gave him a sympathetic smile and decided not to point out the girl who actually looked bored while getting her tattoo. "It'll be over before you know it."

A line of people waited to get their tattoos at Creative Ink, and her three artists, RJ, Rachael, and Michael, were all busy doing one of three tattoo designs she'd limited the event to for efficiency. Nothing was more beautiful than the sound of all their tattoo machines buzzing through the shop. Zoe could hardly enjoy the fact that her charity event for SafeHouse was a success. She struggled to maintain control, a mega feat considering how many freaking things had gone wrong so far.

1

She absolutely could not let frustration bubble to the surface. Especially with the news cameras rolling. When she lost her temper, crazy things happened. Embarrassing things.

She'd arrived an hour early, psyched to find about sixty people already waiting. She was totally not psyched about the cop demanding to see the owner. That would be her. Apparently she hadn't set up proper crowd control. Heck, she hadn't expected a crowd. She'd made arrangements to get the velvet ropes that nightclubs used for their overflow lines. Relief. She'd enjoyed that for about five minutes, until the power died for a half hour.

RJ's car had broken down, making him late. Rachael had a cold and had barely dragged herself in. She wore one of those respiratory masks and complained how ridiculous she looked.

"You look like a world-class surgeon, Rach," Zoe called out. "Work it, babe."

Rachael's eyes crinkled in a smile as she lifted one of her blue-glove-clad hands and gave her the finger. A photographer snapped the picture. If that made it into the paper, Zoe was going to—calmly—kick Rachael's pretty little ass.

The hot day spiked impatience levels. Ugly black clouds threatened to dump rain on the people waiting in the line that snaked around the block.

And now this six-foot-two bodybuilder was whimpering in pain before her needle even touched him.

"Key West," Zoe said between clenched teeth. "St. Barts. St. Martin. Nassau." She looked at the poster of Aruba that she'd pinned up next to her station. The tack at the right corner trembled.

Breathe.

"Jamaica."

"Say what?" the guy asked.

"I recite island names for stress relief. You know, visualization, imagining the salty breeze fluttering through my hair, hearing the ruffle of the palm fronds." Someday, when she could afford a vacation, she was going to experience those sensations firsthand. She lowered the needle to his chest.

He screamed like a little girl, and she almost dropped her machine. The photographer walked over to capture the moment. The guy in the chair pasted on a tough-guy smile. *What a bozo.*

Zoe took advantage of the situation and leaned forward to finish the tattoo. The guy jerked when the tip touched his skin. "Look," he said, "I'll give you the money for the shelter's playground but no more of this torture."

She placed her hand on the center of his chest. "You are *not* walking around with half a tattoo telling people that Zoe Stoker did that to you. Buck up, 'cause I'm finishing it."

With a sigh, he slumped into the chair again. She had to hide her grin when he said, "Nassau . . . Paradise Island . . ."

At least she had music. The Russian rock tunes she dug pounded through the shop. They no longer reminded her of Vladimir, the sexy Russian college student she'd superficially fallen for years ago. She didn't have his gorgeous body or his hot temper around, but she had his music. Cued up next was some local rock band RJ liked, where the lead singer screamed the lyrics to every song. Luckily, RJ didn't sing along.

The phone rang off the hook. She couldn't afford a shop manager; she was still making payments to the guy who'd sold her the shop. For today, she'd hired a friend of Rachael's to man the phones and collect money. Breanna kept the coffee brewing, filling the shop with the scent of it. She walked over, her body language giving off vibes of not wanting to disturb Zoe.

"Cyrus Diamond is on the line. He says it's life-and-death important."

Cyrus, the CIA guy helping her to dig into her father's past?

Twenty-one years ago, Jack Stoker, respected Army and family man, walked into the office where he worked and started shooting people. He killed three and wounded four more before taking his own life. He had been working in a classified program. Her mother refused to discuss it, choosing to push the ugliness into the distant past. Or even worse, acting like he never existed at all. Zoe had tried pretending the same thing for a while, too. God, her father had killed people.

Then one day, in a fit of anger, her mother screamed something that struck fear and curiosity in Zoe: *He had something in him, something that made him crazy at the last part of his life. And you have that inside you, too!*

Zoe *did* have something in her. Her mother called it evil, but Zoe didn't buy that. But this thing inside her was interfering with her life. Would it make her crazy, too? What her mother refused to see was the connection between what her father was involved in during those last years and his mental illness. Was there a connection at all? What might have triggered a rage so out of character for him? So she had begun a long and tedious journey into the labyrinth of the U.S. government.

After getting the runaround, she'd finally connected with someone who at least could verify that her father had worked for the Army and that his assignment was classified. The man promised to look into it. When he didn't call her back, she called him, and he'd told her he'd been mistaken. Her father's file couldn't be found. The next person she tried said there was no record of her father's employment with the Army at all.

Then, out of the blue, Cyrus Diamond contacted her, having learned of her inquiries. He also had questions about a friend who had worked with her father. So far, he'd found out very little. So what could be life-and-death?

"Relax," she told the guy as she pulled off her gloves. "Be right back."

She walked to the corner, where posters showcased a selection of flash, her shop's stock designs. The one filled with old horror movie monsters was all hers, as were most of the tropical tattoos.

"Cyrus, what's up?"

"Zoe, I'm sorry to lay this on you. You may be in danger because of our snooping. I'm afraid we got the attention of someone who doesn't want us to find out the truth."

"In danger? From whom?"

"The U.S. government."

His breathless warning seemed so bizarre, she could hardly compute it. "Cyrus, this doesn't make any sense."

"Stay somewhere else tonight. They know where you live. Beware of strangers."

"What about the police? Can't we go to them?"

"*No.* You go to them, and first of all they'll think you're crazy. I can't back you up. I'm being watched. I'll be killed immediately, and they'll make it look like an accident. I can't help you if I'm dead."

"Are the police involved, too?"

"They're not involved, but if a powerful agency claims jurisdiction, they have to cooperate. I know how it works. You'll be taken somewhere for questioning, and no one will hear from you again. I've got to go. I'll call you as soon as I can and explain everything. Be careful, Zoe."

For a moment, she couldn't breathe. His fear was as solid as the phone she held. Now it was her fear, too.

One of the posters jumped off the wall.

No, not now. Control, Zoe, control. St. Thomas. Kitts. Fiji, Fiji, Fiji.

She looked at the line of people that wound out the door and the cluster of lookie-loos crowded at the window peeking in. She was freaking surrounded by strangers!

Cerulean oceans. Balmy breezes. Sand between my toes.

She returned the phone to the front desk. A pencil flew off the counter. Damn! She picked it up and set it next to the message pad, glad Breanna hadn't noticed.

"Are you all right?" Breanna asked. "Bad news?"

What could she say? Zoe gave her a halfhearted shake of her head. She returned to her chair and couldn't even muster up annoyance that her wussy-boy had fled. Surely, Cyrus was paranoid. Except that he hadn't struck her as being high-strung. She looked at the line, and a man took that as the signal to walk over. She pulled the plastic sheet off the chair and replaced it with another while they talked about design and placement.

She prided herself on giving clients one hundred percent of her attention, but damn, how was she supposed to do that now? She tattooed robotically while he chatted about the grouchy guy who'd done his last tattoo. She kept pausing and looking at the crowd.

What had her father been involved in that their inquiries would piss off the government? Would someone actually *hurt* her? Or, like in the movies, just threaten her to keep her nose out of it?

This is crazy thinking.

She worked in a fog for the next hour. When she finished the umpteenth rose, she looked up. Her heart jumped. A guy at the window was looking at her, and not with either the amused or morbid curiosity of the others. He had a rigid expression, and his brown eyes were cold and empty. He was well dressed and not bad-looking, but he gave her the heebie-jeebies.

"Are you done?" her client asked.

She realized she'd been patting his arm with the paper towel for probably a whole minute. "Yes. Thanks for participating."

She pushed back her fears and tried to focus on her work. She owed that to her clients and the kids who were benefiting. Every few minutes, though, her gaze went to the window. The man was still there. She turned away, whispering more island names as she prepared for the next client. He was watching her; she could feel his eyes on her back. She shivered, fighting not to turn around. Maybe he was just a weirdo or your run-of-the-mill stalker and not some government agent out to get her.

And that's supposed to be a comforting thought?

"Nice tat."

The voice, along with a finger tracing across her back, made her scream as she jerked around. The man had a face to match his sultry voice, but she was too annoyed to be charmed by his smile. First, he'd used the word *tat*. Second, he'd touched her.

"So, does your tat mean you're a she-devil?" he asked, that smile edging into a leer.

She glanced in the mirror at the sexy she-devil tattoo that spanned her lower back just above the hip-hugging waistband of her black jeans. "Are you here to get a tattoo?"

"You betcha, babe." He indicated muscular biceps. "Set me up with a tiger, right here."

He already had several tattoos, so he knew the drill. He settled onto the chair, that smile still in place. "I like redheads. The black streaks are hot, too."

Oh, brother. Sometimes she felt this strange obligation to tell people who commented on her hair that she hated the soft red curls she'd been born with, but her pale complexion looked terrible with blond or brown hair. She gelled the curls straight and spiky, to match her personality, one ex-boyfriend had said. Precisely why he was an ex.

"And legs all the way up to your armpits," he continued in a dreamy voice. "And you've got that way of walking chicks have when they know what they want and who they are—"

She pressed her gloved finger over his mouth. "What *I* want is for you to be quiet so I can concentrate. I am totally not interested in dating anyone right now."

She prepped the area with antiseptic and glanced to the window. The stalker had been there for twenty minutes now, and he was always watching her. Even more disconcerting, he never looked away when their eyes met.

"Whoa, what was that?" the guy in the chair asked as a plastic ink cup—thankfully empty—went flying across his chest.

"Air just kicked on." She settled on the stool and began to tattoo.

Zoe, get yourself under control.

Even though the press wasn't there at the moment, she still didn't want people talking. No one knew about her crazy energy, the term she'd given it. She'd gotten good at keeping her emotions under control. It was hardest with people she saw every day, like her employees.

Having her mother think she was possessed by evil spirits was bad enough. She'd sort of mostly gotten used to that once her mother had given up with the exorcisms and holy water and crosses everywhere. Her granddad was the only one in the family who didn't look at her as though she might sprout horns or spew vomit as her head spun around.

Granddad had explained about people being energy and that thoughts and emotions were energy, too. Her energy was stronger than most, and that was why it affected nearby objects, which were also energy. She wasn't sure if she believed it, but she loved that he accepted her.

After graduating from high school, Zoe had gone

to New Orleans and met a man she now considered her onetime guru. He taught her to meditate and visualize, like she did with her island names, and corroborated her granddad's theory of energy. One day, during a long meditation, she connected to a presence she could only describe as God. The most divine joy, love, and above all, acceptance, flowed into her. No way could she have evil inside her when she could feel God.

To celebrate releasing that burden, she'd gotten her she-devil tattoo and a taste of the art of tattooing. When she'd returned to Baltimore, she apprenticed and practiced on melons and greasy pigskins, transforming her love of art into a profession.

She turned her attention back to the man before her. She never forgot how privileged she was that people trusted her to put something permanent on their bodies.

Four hours later, the crowd was gone. So was the heebie-jeebie freak. Except she still felt him watching her. She looked out the large glass window to the street beyond. It was dark now, nearly midnight. People wandered down the sidewalks and in and out of the bars in the area, but she couldn't see their faces.

Someone across the street could probably see into her shop, though.

She shivered.

"Thanks!" she called out to the last guy as he walked out the door. Breanna relocked it after him. "And mad thanks, guys, all of you. You rock."

"Glad to help," Breanna said.

Zoe saw the same feel-good tiredness on their faces that she felt. Except they weren't worried about some guy stalking them. She kept hoping Cyrus would call back. If he didn't call that night, she'd go crazy. Fortunately, she was so damned tired, she'd at least get some sleep.

Somewhere. Not at her place.

She counted the receipts as the others cleaned their stations. "Are you guys ready for the total?" A grin spread across her face. "We made sixty-six hundred freaking dollars for SafeHouse tonight. Plus another three thousand in separate contributions."

SafeHouse gave shelter to abused women and children, and for reasons Zoe couldn't name, she felt compelled to help.

RJ put his arm around her shoulders and squeezed. "The kids are going to get their playground. Nice job, Zo. You put a lot of work into setting this up."

Her eyes watered only because she was so tired. "Nice job to all of you." She handed the bank bag to Michael. "Could you make the drop tonight?"

As RJ started to pull away, she tugged him back, and whispered, "Stay for a minute, 'kay?"

"Sure." He must have picked up on her fear because his expression turned serious.

It killed her to need someone or impose, but that was a lot better than going home alone. She gave them all a hug of thanks before they left while RJ bought time by organizing his station. His mop of shiny brown hair hung in thick strands as he reached for a wayward ink cup.

When they were gone, she said, "Could I crash at your place tonight?"

He raised brown eyebrows in surprise. "Anytime. Is something wrong?"

She glanced at the window. "There was a guy out there for the last few hours watching me. It made me uncomfortable."

No need to get into the rest of it. Then she'd have to explain about her dad, and that was something she wanted no one to know about. Then she'd be poor Zoe, whose dad went on a shooting spree, instead of Zoe who didn't talk about her family. She had told them that her father had died, plain and simple. There was no way for anyone to find out more, including her. She'd Googled her father's name but found nothing. Of course, the shooting spree had happened before the Internet. And no doubt the government had covered it up.

"You know I got your back, babe."

"Cool. I need to go by my place and get some things."

He was still looking at her with an odd expression. "What?"

"I think this is the first time in the two years I've known you that you've asked for help on a personal level." He smiled. "It's good."

She didn't smile back. "I'm just self-sufficient, that's all."

"Everyone needs help sometimes, Zo."

Not her. Zoe Stoker kept her world under control. Zoe Stoker did not need help.

They walked out, and she locked the door. Even with RJ, who was tall and muscular-lean beside her, she felt vulnerable out in the cool night air. She pulled her leather jacket over her black leather bustier and stayed close to RJ.

Fifteen minutes later she walked into her apartment, RJ behind her. She stopped, her body going still.

"What's wrong?"

She looked around the small living room filled with stuff from her life: Halloween masks of Frankenstein and a zombie with a rose clenched in his teeth, cardboard cutouts of Godzilla and King Kong that she'd positioned to kiss each other. "Would I sound crazy if I said I knew someone's been in here?" She saw him taking in her artifacts. "All right, crazier than you already think I am?"

"How can you tell? Nothing looks out of place."

"It's something you can feel; the same way you know when someone's watching you. It's like the energy in here has been disturbed."

He looked around at her old horror-movie posters, all framed in black metal, against the backdrop of dark red walls. "Maybe it's just all the creepy stuff."

"I've had some of those posters since I was a kid. Those monsters are my friends." She decided not to try to convince him. "I'll be out in a sec."

She packed up some of her favorite clothing, her splurges. The urge to pack a few things, not just enough for one night, worried her. Like that nesting urge that pregnant women were supposed to feel right before the baby came. She threw in her iPod and her CD mix of Russian pop music. She carefully folded a few of her Salvage tops, her Brazilian black jeans, and her platform shoes with the inlaid silver-and-wood heels. She went to her filing cabinet, tucked in the back of her closet, and pulled out the stash of cash she kept in her WOMEN'S HEALTH folder.

Just in case . . .

In case of what? She'd talk to Cyrus soon—*please, any minute now!*—and find out he was overreacting or mistaken. She put the cash in her sling purse and hoisted her duffel bag, then went into the bathroom and opened her makeup drawer. Since she didn't drink or smoke or do drugs of any kind, mostly out of fear of losing control, she allowed herself other vices, like makeup. Her current favorite brand: Urban Decay. She scooped out a handful of products and stuffed them into the bag.

The girl looking back at her from the mirror was as frightening as any monster. Her thick black eyeliner was smudged more than she'd artfully done that morning. Her pale complexion looked gray. Her eyes were bloodshot. The scariest part was the fear in her brown eyes and the tightness of her jaw.

Unable to stand it anymore, she called Cyrus on her cell phone. It rang and rang and finally went to voice mail. She didn't leave a message. He'd see the missed call and know it was her.

Come on, Cyrus. Call me before I go mad freaking crazy.

Gerard Darkwell picked up the ringing cell phone. It showed a Baltimore number on the screen. He pulled up Zoe Stoker's profile. Yes, it was her number. He let the call go to voice mail. She didn't leave a message. Too bad.

He made a call of his own. When the man answered, he said, "It's Darkwell. Diamond definitely told her something. Keep a close eye on her. Grab her if you can; take her out if you can't."

"She's suspicious. She took one of the men from the tattoo shop home with her, and they're leaving again.

My guess is she's staying the night with him, and I don't think it's a romantic rendezvous."

If only they could have heard what Diamond told her. Either way, she was now a liability, one that needed to be dispensed with.

"I'm on her, sir."

"Make it clean."

Clean and quick. That was the way he liked it.

CHAPTER 2

Zoe was in the bathroom putting on her makeup when RJ knocked. "Cindy and I are heading out for breakfast. Wanna come?"

She traced a line on the inside of her lips to make them look smaller. She could hear her mother's voice about wearing too much makeup, but that didn't stop her from adding another streak of red blush to her cheeks before she opened the door. "I'm not really much of a breakfast person. Go ahead, I'll be fine."

"Are you sure?"

"Absolutely." She didn't want to impose on them any more than she already had.

He gave her a grin. "You're not rearranging the bathroom, are you?" To Cindy, he said, "She's anal about being organized. At her station and in the supply closet, everything is in alphabetical order, all lined up perfectly. She's always sorting the pens and pencils at the front desk."

Out of their sight, Zoe pushed the row of lined-up bottles back out of order. "I'd have to be a real control freak to organize someone else's stuff." She heard her phone ringing. Charging out of the bathroom, she raced to the living room, where she'd spent the night on the couch, and fished her cell phone out of her bag.

"Zoe? It's Cyrus." She had to strain to hear him over the sounds of traffic in the background.

"Thank God. You give me that freaky message, then leave me hanging all night."

"Sorry about that. I've been tied up. We need to talk in private. I'm not all that familiar with Baltimore. Where's a good place we can meet?"

Uh-oh. It didn't sound like a meeting where he would tell her he'd overreacted. "Tell me what's going on now. I can't wait another second."

"It's not something I can explain over the phone. Believe me, I'm not being melodramatic here."

Her breath tightened in her lungs. "I believe you. You found out something, didn't you? About my dad and your friend?"

"Yeah. Big stuff."

"Meet me at my shop. It's not open until noon." At least that was a place that felt under her control.

"I'll be there in half an hour."

She hung up, a knot in her chest. She hated not knowing what was going on and especially hated surprises. Her staff had found that out when they'd thrown her a surprise birthday party and she'd stomped off. She'd slunk back ten minutes later, after composing herself.

"What's going on?" RJ asked, his cute, blond girl-friend draped around his waist.

The sight of them shot a pang of envy through her. Oh, to have someone to love and support and protect her. She'd been in shallow relationships, but a long-term one was not on her possible list. It was kind of hard to explain that if she got emotional, things would start flying. And being in a relationship and not getting emotional, impossible. She'd tried.

"Loosen up," they'd coax. *"You're too rigid."* Then it eventually changed to, *"Zoe, you're a damned ice cube."*

Or her favorite: *"Ice bitch."*

The damned of it was, she loved sex, but she didn't want to just have sex.

"I've got to meet a friend. Go, have fun," she said, when RJ looked concerned. "See you at the shop in a few hours."

Thirty minutes could not get there fast enough. She wasn't known to be patient in the best of circumstances.

She arrived at the shop, picked up the paper she subscribed to for the waiting area, and unlocked the door. She shook the paper out of the plastic lining and let it drop onto the chair, all the while looking out the window for Cyrus. He had about ten minutes.

Antsy and anxious, she organized the front desk. She noticed a chip in her red nail polish and did a quick fix on it. Silver rings adorned her fingers, except for her wedding-ring finger; she'd had a ring of flowers tattooed on that one. She told her friends she was marrying herself, and they thought it was a joke.

She grabbed a duster and walked over to the sign Michael had given her in honor of buying the shop: NO DRUNKS, NO DRUGS, AND NO ASSHOLES. She smiled. Just like his cutting sense of humor. A collection of framed pictures of her employees covered the wall behind the desk. She kept a fence around her, out of necessity, and allowed RJ, Rachael, and Michael cracks through which to reach her. That they did touched her deeply. She smiled at their goofy faces as they hammed it up for the camera.

She heard a sound in the storage room where the rear exit was. Cyrus! Made sense that he'd come in the back way, where no one would see him if he was being all sneaky-like.

She turned to go to the back when the newspaper caught her eye.

"What the . . . ?"

Cyrus's picture. She snatched up the front section, the others falling to the floor. CIA OFFICER KILLED BY MUGGERS AT PARK.

She gasped. Her eyes lit on different words in the article. *Quiet Waters Park. Two bullets. Last night. Dead.*

Cyrus, dead. Last night.

Which meant he hadn't called her this morning. Hadn't set up a meeting at the shop . . . alone.

Wasn't in the back.

She ran to the front door. Heard a sound just behind her. A hand grabbed her arm. She inhaled to scream. Another hand slapped over her mouth so hard her teeth cut into her lip. She was yanked backward toward the storage room. Someone was dragging her to the back. Through the cracks between his fingers, she smelled sweat and stale cigarettes.

Fear radiated through her body. This couldn't be happening! Bottles of ink flew everywhere. A poster frame fell with a *crack*. She twisted around to get out of his grip and saw his face: the guy who'd been watching her last night. God, he still showed no emotion. Stone cold. Stone-cold killer.

He dragged her into the dark room, one hand smashed over her mouth and the other around her throat. She tried to plant her feet, but he had her at the perfectly wrong angle, and, hell, she was wearing platforms. She grabbed for the sides of the door, fingers clutching at the frame.

He jerked her free with a violent twist and slammed the door shut. Darkness swallowed them. Her eyes adjusted and, in the dim light that crept beneath the door, she saw his snarl. "You girls are sure feisty bitches. I'm going to finish you right here."

You girls? No time to wonder what he meant by that. She was too scared by the meaning of the last part, which was crystal clear. He was going to *finish her*—kill her.

Please, no! I'm only twenty-three, and I haven't gone to the islands or Transylvania or anywhere hardly! I haven't done anything to deserve this!

His arm jackknifed around her throat, pressing against her windpipe. She grabbed at him as she gasped for breath, digging her nails into his arm so hard that she had to be drawing blood. It didn't deter him. Black spots pulsed in front of her. Her body was weakening.

Got to find a weapon before I lose it. She looked where the shelving units lined the walls. *I can't see anything!*

But she knew exactly where everything was . . . in alphabetical order.

She raised her foot and jammed her thick black heel down on the top of his foot. He grunted, but the son of a bitch still didn't let up. She lifted her foot again, and he rammed his knee into the back of hers. She buckled, letting gravity and momentum pull her down. He struggled to fight the fall and keep control. She hit the floor, jerking out of the hold he had around her neck. Gasping for air, she crawled toward where she knew the shelving was. *Bad move.* He straddled her, crushing her into the concrete floor, hands around her throat from the back. Now he had total control over her, pinning her to the floor. She only had one thing going for her—she'd gone from scared to pissed.

Things flew off the shelves and hit the wall. Something hit him, but it didn't faze him. She tried to get to her knees, but he pushed down harder. His arm shook with his effort to strangle her while her nails dug into his flesh. With a burst of adrenaline, she pulled his arm to her mouth and bit down hard.

He held on for a second, spewing curse words she hadn't heard since high school. She tasted his warm blood as he screamed in pain and pulled back. She shoved him away and lunged for the shelving unit, fumbling in the dark for the box of scissors. He ran toward her, following the noise she was making. No box! Her crazy energy must have sent it off somewhere. She grabbed a spray bottle instead. Disinfectant.

He clamped her arm. She pumped the bottle's trigger, aiming in his direction. He hissed in pain as his hand batted the air. It knocked the bottle out of her hand. She crawled away. He still came at her. She wedged her fingers behind the shelving unit and pulled it away from the wall. It crashed down with a clatter. Things shattered and skittered across the floor. Most importantly, she heard an *oof.*

She got to her feet, ankles wobbling on her heels. Her shoes slipped on something that had spilled, but she held her footing. She heard him climbing out from beneath the shelving. She ran for the door, flinging it open and tearing through it, taking only a second to slam it shut behind her.

She heard the man kicking things aside. She grabbed up her bag and reached for the door. Pulled it. Damn! It was locked. Two posters dropped to the floor.

She heard the storage-room door open. A whimper escaped her throat. *Don't look! Just get out!*

She flipped the lock with blood-slicked fingers. Footsteps ran toward her. She pulled the door open. Breathing behind her. She slipped out and pushed it shut again, coming nose to nose with the man's fierce face on the other side of the glass. Blood was smeared on him and now on the glass.

She ran, unsteady on her platforms. She reached her Jeep. No solid doors to keep him out. Gasping for breath, she fumbled with the keys, sticking in the one with the peace symbol design before realizing it was the wrong key. She started the engine and only then looked back. He wasn't there. Wasn't at her shop's door. Wasn't anywhere.

She threw the Jeep into drive and tore out, her whole body shaking. Her gasping breaths turned into sobs. She covered her mouth, trying to stifle them as she drove. Her hands . . . covered in blood. His blood. She looked in the rearview mirror, searching for a car behind her. No one.

The area catered to businesses that opened during the latter part of the day, like skate shops, music stores, and bars. It wasn't busy yet. She pulled into a gas station that had exterior restrooms, parked in the back, and ran into the women's room. Seeing her reflection scared the hell out of her. Dark red hair flattened on one side, sticking out on the other. Red marks around her throat that were tender to the touch. Lipstick smeared across her cheek and black eyeliner smudged in streaks. Blood dripped down her chin like the Halloween costume she'd worn last year. If only she'd had the vampire teeth glued onto her incisors. Then she could have really torn into him.

Anger. Yes, anger was good. Anger was better than fear.

The mirror rattled.

Anger also made things fly. She took several deep breaths.

I'm calm now. I'm no longer in danger. Turks and Caicos. Antigua. Very calm.

Yeah, tell that to my heart.

The mirror stopped shaking. She washed the blood off her face and throat.

"What do I do now?" she asked her reflection.

"Go to the police. That's what you do when you're attacked. Except Cyrus said not to talk to the police." And he was probably right. Just like he'd said, his death was covered up. She had no doubt why, even though the paper called it a mugging. The government wanted to keep its secret at any cost. She'd watched movies about this stuff, but she kind of hoped that was all fiction.

And she was next.

Where did she go? What did she do? Only Cyrus knew the answers, and he couldn't help her now.

"I need time to think. I have to sort all this out."

She cracked the door open and looked for any suspicious vehicles. She didn't even know what the guy drove. He probably knew what she drove, though. She had to get another vehicle. Her yellow Jeep wasn't exactly inconspicuous; she'd had the bright yellow surface painted with the name of her shop, Creative Ink, along with some of her designs.

"This is not real. This is totally not real."

Despite that statement, she dashed to her Jeep. The guy had been at the tattoo shop the evening before, which meant he probably knew where she'd spent the night. She couldn't go back to RJ's or home. She drove through the city, taking a circuitous route, cranking her Russian music.

A buy here–pay here car lot caught her attention. Not the kind of place she'd ever think of buying a car, but it gave her an idea. When an old friend had come in for a tattoo last week, he'd told her he was selling his car. She couldn't remember what kind of car it was, but he'd asked her to keep her ear open for anyone needing a car.

Her client's art studio was several blocks away, and it took her ten more minutes to find a nearby parking garage. She took a spot in the far corner and watched the cars that pulled in soon afterward. None were driven by a man missing a chunk of arm.

When a family alighted from their SUV, she got out and followed them down the stairs, staying as close as possible without violating their space. The father kept glancing back at her. A tattooed woman with black-streaked hair and shirt with skulls on it, not what he wanted too close to his precious white-bread children. He gathered them like chicks, putting himself between her and them.

Zoe cherished being different, even being an outcast. Why, at this moment, when she had much more severe things on her mind, did the father's actions bother her?

She didn't give herself time to worry over it. Once they reached the sidewalk, she split off from them, headed around the back of the building to the rear entrance, and knocked hard. All the while she kept looking around, fully paranoid.

Finally, the sound of a lock disengaging, and the door opened. Ronald Frundmeir stared at her curiously, his long, stringy hair framing a long, stringy face. "Zoe? What are you doing back here?"

She pushed past him and closed the door. "I need to buy your car."

He blinked, at the bluntness of her statement or the desperation she was oozing, who knew? "Uh . . . sure."

She let out a breath of relief. He still had it. "How much? I can give you a deposit now and have RJ withdraw the rest from the business account. And you can't tell anyone about it."

That made him cock his eyebrow.

"Don't ask," she said, raising her hand at the question in his expression. "It's better that you don't know."

"Uh . . . okay." He nodded to the right. "Come on, I'll get the paperwork."

She followed him down the short hallway, her stomach turning at the smell of burnt coffee. Two other offices contained employees who looked at her curiously, the chick who had banged on the back door. Zoe gave them a smile as she closed Ronald's door.

He turned down the Grateful Dead tune and opened a drawer.

"What kind of car is it?" she asked.

That halted him. "You don't even know?"

"I don't even care. I just need transportation. Oh, jeez, it's something really lame, isn't it?"

His body stiffened. "It's not lame. It's a 1976 VW Bug, the best car ever made. I've had it for ten years. I need the money for the business, which is the only reason I'm even selling her."

"Cool. How much are you asking?"

"Three thousand."

"It runs, right? If I take it on a long trip, it won't break down on me?"

"I've taken loving care of her since the day I bought her." He paused as though he wasn't sure, after all, if Zoe deserved such a car.

"I'll take good care of her, too, Ronald. Here's two hundred. I'll call RJ—" That's when it hit her; she'd have to explain all this to him, including the blood and the mess at the shop. She cleared her throat. "I'll call him, and he'll get you the rest. You trust me, right? I mean, we've known each other since design class in high school."

"I do trust you. It's just that this is so weird. You're usually so . . . cool. Composed."

"I know. I'm not into anything illegal."

He laughed. "I know you wouldn't be into drugs. You wouldn't even drink a beer with us at the party spot."

Nothing that would loosen her absolute control over her emotions. She flashed him an innocent smile.

"Exactly. I'm just in a bind right now, some bizarre stuff I can't get into."

He hesitated.

"I love Bugs," she said. "Does . . . she have a name?"

His tense expression softened a bit. "I call her Betsey."

"Betsey it is." She gave him a bright smile, but he wasn't buying it. She dropped the smile. "Look, I need the car, and you need the money. I'll take good care of her, I promise."

He nodded, opening his file drawer and rifling through the hanging folders.

"How fast does she go?"

He stopped.

She waved her hand. "Not that I'm planning to go really fast or anything. Just curious."

He shook his head slightly but continued to look for the paperwork. "If I didn't need the money . . . she's not a speed demon, but she'll get up and go when she needs to."

Zoe glanced around his cluttered office, papers everywhere, a collection of postcards tacked haphazardly to the walls, no order to anything. Before her fingers started twitching over that, her gaze fell on one of the postcards. Most were of vacation spots or of motorcycles with chicks draped over them. The one that had caught her eye was of the Duval Street sign. Not long ago she thought she was going to die before she'd ever seen the islands. Now she needed a place to go to get her thoughts together. By damn, she was going to Key West.

She handed him two hundred dollars as he signed the bill of sale. She wasn't going to freak him out any further and tell him she wouldn't be registering it anytime soon.

Speaking of time . . . it was after eleven. She called RJ on his cell phone. "Hey, it's Zoe. Ronald Frundmeir's coming in today. Give him twenty-eight hundred dollars out of the company's account in cash. I'll explain later."

She hung up, took the registration and keys, and said, "Thanks, Ronald. For the car and your trust. And your confidentiality."

He tapped his chest and held up two fingers at her, love and peace. "Take care of yourself."

She mirrored the gesture. "You bet."

She'd already fought off an assassin. That was pretty good so far.

Ronald's directions led her to the Bug, which was parked in a small lot. "Oh . . . wow." So much for inconspicuous. Its lime green paint job could be seen by freaking satellite. Once in the car, she called RJ. "Hey, me again. Can you get to the shop early? I need to explain what you're going to find there."

"I'm already here. I had to drop Cindy at work, which is one street over, so I figured I'd come in and clean up a bit." Why didn't he have three thousand questions?

"And you didn't quite expect that much of a mess."

"It's only a mess by Zoe standards. The newspaper was all over the waiting-area floor, but other than that—"

"What about the storage area?"

"Yeah, that's a mess, all right. Nothing's in alphabetical order. I guess we were all in a bit of a rush whenever we went back there yesterday to get what we needed."

Her mouth dropped open. "Everything was on the shelves?"

"Of course."

"The shelving unit was standing upright?"

"Yeah," he said, drawing out the word.

He hadn't mentioned blood. He would mention blood, right? That wasn't a normal thing to see, and it would catch his eye. So she wasn't going to mention it.

This meant that the assassin had cleaned up the evidence of the assault in case she had gone to the police, which would have made her look like a loony.

"Zoe?"

She blinked. "RJ, I have a huge-assed favor to ask. I need you to manage the shop for a while."

"Zo, what's going on?"

"I can't . . ." Her throat tightened as her fingers curled around the steering wheel. "I can't explain." *Because I don't even know what's going on.* "I have to disappear for a while."

"Does this have anything to do with that guy you were freaked out about last night?"

"Yes. And I can't tell you any more than that. It's better if you don't know, trust me."

"I trust you. But if you're in trouble, let me help. Let's go to the police—"

"No!" She took a breath, inhaling the smell of old vinyl. "He has connections to the police. Look, I have to get out of town for a bit. I'm sorry to dump this on you, especially without being able to explain why." Yeah, government conspiracies, CIA agents being killed, and the public being lied to about it, that would sound sane and reasonable.

"Don't worry about me. It's you I'm concerned about. This isn't normal for you."

Neither was being chased by assassins. "I'll be fine. I just need to get away for a bit and figure out what to do."

"Promise you'll keep in touch and let me know if you need help."

"I will. Bye. And thanks."

Hanging up felt like severing the cord to her life. Her business and apartment meant everything to her. Her employees were as close to family as she had. She took a deep, ragged breath and started the car. On the upside, if the assassin had been busy cleaning up, he hadn't been following her.

Unless someone else had.

"Glass half-full," she admonished. "If there had been two of them, they would have both been at the shop."

She had one place to go before leaving town: hospice. Though the cancer ravaging her granddad's body left him with fewer and fewer lucid moments, she had to tell him that she wouldn't be there for a while. The thought of it crushed her heart. Even worse, she didn't know what might happen before she could come back.

CHAPTER 3

After a day and a half, Zoe finally believed that they—whoever *they* were—hadn't followed her. She'd been careful during the long drive down, sure that no one pulled off the two-lane highway leading down to Key West whenever she did. She'd crashed for twelve hours at the little bed-and-breakfast where she was staying, then carefully crept out, more concerned about suspicious-looking men than enjoying the scenery. She paid cash for everything.

Zoe had gone to an Internet café and looked up the newspaper article on Cyrus. It gave little information. He'd supposedly been mugged and shot in the Quiet Waters Park after-hours. No one knew what he'd been doing there, though a CIA spokesperson said he wasn't there on CIA business. He'd been hit by two bullets, the fatal one piercing his heart.

On her second night, she actually dared to enjoy herself for a while, needing to push away thoughts of dying and figure out how she was going to keep that from happening. She paused under a lamppost and watched drag queens play badminton in the street in between traffic. As soon as the cars cleared, someone yelled, "Game on!" and a guy pulled the net across the street while the queens, in shoes higher than her own platforms, batted the cone back and forth. The bubble of laughter that came out of Zoe's throat felt so good.

The night brought out the serious partiers and ripened the smell of beer and fruit drinks spilled on the sidewalks. Most of the lightweights and families were back at their hotels. The breeze had picked up, sweeping away some of the humidity an afternoon storm left behind.

She'd eaten out on the patio of a nice restaurant and even treated herself to a Guinness—in honor of her Irish granddad—to take off the edge. Now the edge was definitely off, and she breathed in the scents of the street as she walked: fruit from the smoothie stand, the occasional waft of perfume, and the gorgeous aromas from all of the restaurants lining Duval Street. She loved the older buildings in their pastel colors with balconies that reminded her of New Orleans. She wandered into art galleries and boutiques, and bought a couple of fun tops. In a darker moment, she bought a pair of sneakers and stuffed her platforms into her large leather bag. *Just in case*, a voice whispered in her mind.

She hardly ever wore sneakers, and even the rhinestone-studded ones felt odd on her feet. She never wore normal clothing. She wasn't normal and didn't want to be. Of course, no one would guess how not normal she was.

Live music drew her to the Hard Rock Cafe, where Marker 24 was playing a charity gig. Being a sucker

for charities, Zoe joined the small crowd on the patio.
Jimmy Buffett favorites pumped up everyone, mixed
with jokes and some kind of margarita blender
powered by a lawn-mower engine. It was nearly
midnight, and even without having a drink, Zoe
found herself getting into the mood. Tomorrow she
would sit out by the pool at the bed-and-breakfast
and figure out her next step. Not knowing what was
going on, she didn't want to think about how few
options she had.

She stood at the far edge of the patio, tucked
against the planting beds, with palm fronds tickling
her back as she moved to the music. For a while she
could lose herself in the party that was Key West. For
a while—

A cold, eerie feeling crawled up her spine like a
furry caterpillar. As a gale of laughter rose from
the crowd, dread filled her chest with deadweight.
She relaxed her expression as though she were just
taking everything in. She looked for the man who'd
tried to kill her in her shop. She'd know his face anywhere. Her eyes locked onto another man standing
by the entrance. He wasn't looking at her, was in
fact watching the band. Except he didn't smile like
everyone else. He was nice-looking, of perhaps Latin
descent, but something about him didn't belong
there. A drink tipped over on the table beside her
though no one noticed.

Calm down. Think about it.

No way could these people, whoever they were,
find her. She'd left no paper trail, and if by some miracle someone had followed her, why had it taken him
so long to come into her orbit? Still, her instincts were

flying the danger flag, and she wasn't one to ignore them. So now what? She was cornered, nowhere near the entrance. She would have to walk past him to get out. She twisted around to the planting bed behind her, pretending to move the palm frond that tickled her. The bed was at knee level, and there were spaces between the plants to duck through.

Just in case.

When she looked toward the entrance again, he was gone. Her heart jumped. She scanned the area and found him. He was only three tables away, watching the band and ignoring the old woman who was knocking her hips against his in drunken glory. He was moving closer.

Her heart went into hammer mode. He was still between her and the exit. If she was just being paranoid, he would think nothing of her climbing through the bushes. Worst case, those nearby would think she was skipping out on her bill.

She glanced out to check the surroundings. An alley made of red bricks led back off the street. Ducking out of sight seemed the best option.

One, two, three . . .

She clambered through the gap between the small palms. Her feet pounded across the uneven bricks. The alley led back to buildings that closed it in. Crap, no outlet. Why hadn't she studied the maps and familiarized herself with the layout of the town? A sign announced the *Vagina Monologues*. A theater then, but obviously no play that night since no one was around. Only two lights illuminated the small parking area that contained two cars.

Thankfully, the music covered the rasping of her

breath and her footsteps. She ran up the ramp toward the theater's entrance and tried the door. No luck. She slid into a narrow gap between the railing and a wall, edging through the thick layer of dead, damp leaves. The scents of decay and earth filled her nose. The passage jogged and continued toward the building, latticework on one side and a rickety fence on the other. She couldn't see what was on the other side of the fence or if the passage opened out or dead-ended. Hopefully, it wouldn't matter.

I'm going to feel really silly in a few minutes when no one comes after me.

In a crouch, she watched through the horizontal slats of the lattice.

A man walked into view.

She didn't feel silly. She was scared to death.

He was definitely the man she'd seen, the second man to give her the heebies—and he was definitely looking for her.

A man stepped out of a door at the other end of the building. "Can I help you? The theater's not open tonight."

Zoe had to hold back her gasp when her hunter slid a gun out of his waistband and held it behind him.

Was he going to shoot the man? He's just an innocent bystander. Wait a minute! I'm innocent! Fear tightened her throat. Who was this guy? Who were the people he worked for?

"My dog got off the leash and ran back here," he said. "You happen to see a black Lab?"

"No, sure didn't."

Keeping the gun by his thigh, he turned and started

searching around the bikes and bushes. "Here, boy." He whistled, ruffling his hand through the palm fronds, his face dark in the shadows.

The door closed behind the theater guy, and her pursuer dropped the lost-dog ruse. Unfortunately, he didn't put the gun away. Fear pounded through her, making her breath come in shallow pants.

He walked over to the cars parked next to the ramp. "Come on, let's finally score one for the good guys," he muttered as he knelt and peered beneath them.

The good guys?

Those at the bar whooped and hollered when the band launched into "Margaritaville." She needed the music to cover any noise she might make, though it wasn't as loud back here. Any movement would stir the leaves beneath her feet. She dared to look to her left, but it was too dark to see where the gap led. She swiveled her head and looked between the slats of the old fence but couldn't make out what lay beyond.

She turned back to the parking lot. To the man hunting her.

He was on the other side of the parking area. Looking for people in hiding was obviously something he was used to doing. He meant business.

It was only a matter of time.

She had to move. The crowd broke into applause. Careful of what might be lying on the ground, she took a step. Her knee jammed on a large piece of glass. She hissed in pain, but luckily she'd hit a blunt edge. She took another step and knocked her head into a metal box mounted on the side of the building. Grimacing in pain, she felt her way around it.

The music stopped. Faintly, she heard the lead

singer thanking everyone for coming, and applause broke out. Then . . . silence.

Even swallowing the hard knot in her throat sounded so loud she was sure her hunter had heard it. She still had no idea how much farther she could go or where it led. Now she couldn't see the guy either.

But she could hear him. He was walking up the ramp. How obvious was her hiding place?

Probably obvious as hell. *She'd* found it.

Suddenly she saw a dark figure leap sideways over the short fence . . . feet from her. With a yelp she ran back, feeling the fence like a blind person. Then nothing.

Nothing!

She saw an open space with white gravel and cars. She ran toward it, his footsteps right behind her.

He's got a gun.

She darted behind the cars as she ran. A street! She was on one of the side streets. People walked nearby, laughed, only silhouettes to Zoe. Remembering how her pursuer had been about to shoot that man at the theater, she couldn't chance approaching anyone. Same with going up to the cottages that looked so cozy and safe.

She ran to the right, keeping to the shadows, then to the left. Her best bet—hide. If he couldn't find her, he'd give up, at least for the night. Did he know where she was staying? What she drove? How the hell had he found her?

She looked behind her and saw him coming up fast. Ahead, where Caroline Street crossed Simonton, the streetlights left her vulnerable. She clutched the bag slung over her shoulder and turned back toward

Duval. He hadn't come around the corner yet. She dropped behind a car parked along the street, tucking herself as close to the rear as possible.

A flash caught her eye. She looked down. The rhinestones on her sneakers glittered in the faint light. *Crap.* She slid out of them.

Footsteps scraped on the concrete. Just once. He was light-footed as he passed. A predator. She rose just enough to see through the windows of the car in front of her. He reached the bright lights of Duval and looked both ways, then turned to the left.

She crossed the street and headed to Duval, too, ducking into a store at the corner. She peered out the window but couldn't see him in the flow of people.

"Can I help you?" a man of Middle Eastern descent asked with a smile.

"I need some clothes."

He pulled a swath of beautifully patterned fabric in her favorite colors of cinnamon and clove from a rack, oblivious to her strained breathing. "These are wrap dresses. Very popular. See how easy it is to change your whole look?" He wrapped it around himself, twisted the top, and secured it around his neck. The fabric draped down to his blue Crocs. "Very nice, yes?"

"I'll take one. And a hat. Tie it on me." She lifted her shoulders, still looking out the window. "Over here, by the mirror."

He wagged a finger at her. "Ah, I see. You try to ditch boyfriend. Happens many times."

"Just tie it," she said through gritted teeth.

He did, turning her toward the mirror. "Now take a look, see how beautiful."

She planted a straw hat on her head. As far from Zoe Stoker as she could get. "How much?"

"Forty dollars. But a special for you, twice as much." He grinned.

She shoved the money at him and started to head out. *Wait!* She turned back. "I need sneakers."

Twenty more dollars, and she sported brown canvas sneakers. She sailed out of the shop and tried to pull off the charade of the year: not looking like someone who was afraid for her life.

And stopped dead.

The man stood to the left of the store's entrance, cell phone to his ear. His words chilled her: "It's Steele. She gave me the slip."

A shirt that was hanging outside the shop jumped to the ground.

Costa Rica. Green Turtle Key.

He turned around, and she launched out of the doorway and down the sidewalk.

Steele's frustration level threatened to explode. He had taken out diplomats surrounded by bodyguards and terrorists expecting a hit at any time. But these freaks—women, no less—were sneaky.

He was considered an asset by government agencies that needed certain matters taken care of without being implicated. For a tidy sum of money, he did just that. Even though he'd retired, his boss had offered him an even tidier sum to return to work.

He bumped into someone on the sidewalk, paying no attention to the flow of people, no one but Zoe Stoker, who had given him the slip.

Eventually, she would return to that old car of hers.

He could wait for her there, but that parking area was busy. And he didn't want to wait. He wanted her done so he could move on to the others. It was becoming a matter of pride.

He called his employer as people streamed on either side of him, paying him no mind. "It's Steele. She gave me the slip."

"Gave you the slip?" Darkwell said, his voice reeking of disappointment.

"She made me. I don't know how. I couldn't exactly climb through the bushes after her and not attract attention. When she shows up dead, people would remember some guy crashing through the plants after her."

"Why didn't you just take her out from a distance?"

"I can't just go shooting in the streets of Key West. It's a busy place, lots of cops, too." *A lot of everything,* he thought, as two brightly dressed men walked by holding hands. He hated having to explain himself, and even more, pushing out the words, "Can your freaks tell me where she is? Just give me a clue, and I'll take care of her. She's not going to leave Key West alive, that I promise."

"I'll call you back in a few minutes."

Steele wandered to the left, watching the streets. If only he'd seen in which direction she'd gone, he would have had her. Dammit, the dark alley had been perfect. He clenched his fist. If he'd shot her where she'd been hiding, no one would have even found her body for a few days. He'd have been long gone.

He kept looking for her, hoping he wouldn't need the help he resented having to get, especially given the source.

Darkwell got on the line. "There's an aquarium—"

"I know where it is. I'll be in touch."

He hung up and headed toward the waterfront. He made it a point to know where everything was in whatever town his assignment took place. Now he would make it a point to kill Zoe Stoker.

CHAPTER 4

Zoe staggered past the aquarium, which, like the stores down by Mallory Square, was closed. Lights twinkled out to sea, on the exclusive island offshore and a cruise ship. A few people wandered in the distance, appearing in the dim lights, then disappearing like ghosts, their voices and laughter floating through the air. People having fun. In control of their lives. It was beyond comprehension that Zoe Stoker, who owned Creative Ink and minded her own business and kept her life under tight control, was in Key West not living out a travel dream but running for her life.

She might have melted into a puddle of hysteria if not for her instincts, which, thankfully, were on high alert and driving her actions. She was almost sure she'd lost Steele—she'd heard him on the phone—but then again, she'd thought she lost her enemy before. How had he found her, among all the places in Key West, all the people?

She watched for men walking alone. If she spotted him in time, she would go into a crowded bar.

She didn't think he would shoot her in a crowd. Remembering his cold face, she couldn't be sure.

The heebie-jeebie feeling made her spin around. No one. She strolled down the sidewalk, still trying to look like someone not scared down to her bones. She ducked into the Memorial Sculpture Garden, a fenced-in square containing royal palms, benches, and busts on pedestals that lifted them to roughly her height. Landscape lighting dimly lit the small area. *What a great place to hide.*

She stood behind one of the statues at the far corner and watched, leaving the second entrance in sight. With all those silhouettes of heads, the only way she could tell if one was actually a person was movement.

After a few moments, she was sure she was alone. The question was, for how long? She waited. Listened. She needed enough of a head start to get back to her car. Then go where? She couldn't endanger her employees or her family.

Focus on this moment for now.

She stepped out from behind the statue . . . just as a man walked into the square. Her gaze darted to the second entrance. Her heart jumped. She could just make out a man's silhouette there, too, lingering in the walkway between the garden and the darkened Cuban restaurant.

Not two of them! No, she would have seen them. Except maybe it was the guy he'd been talking to on the phone.

She looked toward the first man. Where was he? Between the statues and the trees, he was hidden. Did that head just move? *Damn, this is a terrible place to hide.* At least she was camouflaged, too. Very slowly she moved toward the entrance through which she'd come. One step. Two. Three. Still no movement to give him away.

Him. Somehow she was sure it was Steele. What about the other man? She could no longer see him from her angle, but the fact that he was lurking didn't bode well. She took another step, aligning herself behind a bust, eyeing the palm tree she would slide behind next. The entrance was only a few steps from there.

Something shifted a few yards away. She blinked. Her eyes were playing tricks on her. Not helping matters, her heart pounded so hard it made her peripheral vision pulse. She stared at the place where she'd seen movement. There! The slightest shift. Steele was moving around to her right, between her and the first entrance. Like a life-and-death chess game, each moved one square closer to the other. She looked to the second entrance. Oh, God, the other man had moved closer, too. Each man closed in on her one step at a time.

She was done. *No, don't give up.* But she was trapped here in this garden. *A beautiful place to die.*

She looked toward the second man. He was a shadow among shadows, and yet she felt him. Something about him tingled along her skin and raised the hairs at the nape of her neck. Then he stepped out of the darkness. His shadow shimmered. Her breath caught as his silhouette liquefied and reformed into something low and sleek and completely different.

I'm seeing things. Or going crazy.

A low, ominous growl came from a black panther

slinking closer. Its eyes glittered in the dark. She could only stare. Even when she heard a sound behind her, she couldn't pull her gaze from the creature. She felt more than saw its body tense, contract, and jump at her.

The scream caught in her throat. A hand grabbed her shoulder from behind. The panther knocked her to the side, also knocking the hand away. She fell, watching the panther land on Steele and throw him backward onto the bricks. She felt the fur brush her skin, the tail flick her arm.

"What the f—?" Steele's words were cut off as the panther pressed its paw to his throat.

Amazingly, it turned and looked at her.

Go!

That word was not her own, and yet she'd heard it in her head. She ran, daring one last glimpse back to see the panther's head lowered to the man's, a warning growl keeping him there as much as the panther's weight.

A panther. In Key West.

Not just any panther.

She ran down the street parallel to Duval, back toward her car. What the hell had happened back there? Was adrenaline and fear driving her totally insane?

Blood pounded in her ears as she ran. Her legs ached, her heart hurt. *Have to get to the car. Get out of here.*

People stared at her, those few she encountered off the main drag, but she kept racing down the narrow street.

Wait.

That voice again! Oh, jeez, she *was* going crazy. Just

like her father. Had he seen men turn into panthers? Was that why he'd walked into his office with the shotgun?

Zoe, stop!

She turned around, her body coming to a stuttering stop, her breath gasping as she searched for the source of the voice. As the panther stepped from the shadows of a lushly landscaped yard, it morphed into a man, a man with dark wavy hair that fell to his shoulders. That he wore black jeans and a tight black shirt, normal clothing on a body that had just been an animal, was even more bizarre. That whole scene had kind of creeped her out, to put it mildly. He was breathing heavily, too, as he came closer. He had attacked her enemy, but that didn't make him friend.

"You can't go to your car. They know what you're driving." He took her arm and led her around the corner of the building while his gaze checked the street.

"They . . ." She could barely put thoughts and words together.

"How do you think he found you here in Key West, and at the statue garden?"

"I don't know. How? And who are you? How did you do . . . whatever it was that you did? Is that guy dead?"

"No. I just bought some time. I'm Cheveyo. Come with me. I'll take you to people who can help you. People like you and me. They'll tell you everything you need to know." He grabbed her hand and pulled her across the street.

She stopped, tugging him back. "People like me? I don't understand. What the hell is going on here?"

"There's no time to explain. We've got to get back to

Maryland. Now." He met her gaze. "You have to trust me, Zoe. Right now, I'm the only one you *can* trust. When I take you to the others, they'll explain everything."

She let him lead her farther into the residential area. "Why can't *you* explain it?"

"It's not my place. I will deliver you to safety and leave you in good hands."

"Leave me? Aren't you one of these . . . people like me?"

He looked back at her. "I am, but I am not part of the group and cannot be."

Before she could ask more, he came to a stop at a black motorcycle parked behind the bushes between two small, clapboard homes. He easily straddled the seat and handed her a helmet.

"No way." A laugh bubbled out of her. "All the way to Maryland on this? No freaking way."

"Have you ever ridden a bike before?"

"Once. An ex-boyfriend took me for a ride, and, when I told him I wasn't going to have sex with him, he tried to scare sex out of me."

His mouth quirked. "Did it work?"

"No. It just pissed me off, and I never talked to him again."

"Okay, he was a dumb bastard. I don't want to get involved with anyone, and no offense, but you're not my type, so you're safe with me." When she didn't move toward the bike, he said, "It's not like we have a lot of choice here. Besides, I can maneuver up the Keys much better on a bike. I know it's not exactly the most comfortable ride, but it's all I have. I didn't have time to make other arrangements; I had to get down here immediately."

"For me?" The words squeaked out. "You came down here just to save me from that creep?"

"Yes. I intervene with the others when necessary. And if we don't want that son of a bitch to catch up with us, we have to go now."

With a resigned sigh, she took the helmet and pulled it on. He helped secure it, then put on his own. Both matched his bike.

"Have you ever climbed on a horse?" he asked.

"No, but I've seen it done in the movies." She wrestled out of the wrapdress thing.

"That's how you climb on the bike."

He inclined his head, and she climbed on behind him.

"You can hold on to me until you're comfortable. Then sit back and relax. Lean into the turns; don't fight them. If you need to stop, let me know, but keep it to a minimum. We have to get out of the Keys as fast as we can. We're trapped down here. Not the best place to run off to, by the way."

Before she could protest that she wasn't exactly an expert at this running-for–her-life stuff, he started the engine. She wrapped her arms around him, and they were off. She had to smile at his assurance that he wouldn't try anything. He wasn't her type, either. But she was damned glad he'd come down to save her.

Steele washed the four long scratches on his cheek, wincing at his reflection in the restroom mirror. Anger surged inside him. He'd had it with these freaks. Not only were they making him look incompetent, they were pissing him off.

He called Darkwell. "Who is the freak that changes into a damned cat?"

"Don't tell me she got away?"

"Just tell me, which one changes form? I didn't even know they could do that."

"None that I know of." Darkwell paused. "Wait a minute. Cheveyo Kee. Has to be. His father was Native American, the only one who could change his energy into animal form. He was a hawk."

"I remember him. Quiet, eerie." He fisted his hand. "I had the girl. I was seconds from taking her down, the place was perfect, no one around—or so I thought—and then this man shows up and changes into a panther before my eyes, like an acid trip. He pounced on me, and the girl ran off."

Darkwell stewed in silence for a second. "Cheveyo. I haven't been able to find him. Now it seems he's joined up with the enemy. Dammit. Wait. Let me see if we can spot them."

Steele walked outside, his eyes scanning the area. He wanted these freaks of nature gone. Give him an ordinary terrorist any day. He headed toward his car, ready to move.

Darkwell came back on the line. "We can't see them. It's the same kind of block we're getting when we try to see where they're hiding out, which makes me wonder if Cheveyo has something to do with that. All right, come back. They won't stay in Key West, not now. He'll bring her back here to the rest of them. See if you can find them on the way. If you do, just follow them. They'll lead you to the others."

CHAPTER 5

"Time to go."

Cheveyo's voice pulled Zoe from a dream of a black panther about to bite her neck. Her eyes snapped open. He was leaning over her, impatience on his features.

Why was she still so dog tired? She looked at the clock on the nightstand in the rathole hotel in Florida that they'd stopped at when she couldn't hold on anymore. "I've only been asleep for two hours!"

"Two hours longer than we had. If I hadn't been worried about you falling off, I would have pushed on."

"We wouldn't have this problem if you had a car. My butt hurts. My body is still vibrating."

"Let's go."

The man had no sense of compassion . . . well, other than saving her life. She pulled herself off the bed with a groan, grabbed her bag, and went into the bathroom. "I need a shower."

"No time," he said. "Don't make me go in there and drag you out."

By the stern look on his face, he meant it.

"You took a shower." She didn't even try to curtail the whine in her voice.

"And you slept. We make our choices. Move it."

With a petulant look, she slammed the door shut. "Ohhh," she said when she saw her reflection in the mirror. Yuck. She went to the sink, washed her face, and started applying makeup.

A bang on the door made her drop her eyeliner. "What's the holdup?"

She opened the door with narrowed eyes. "I'll be right out."

"We don't have time for getting pretty."

She finished her other eye and slapped on some lipstick. "I need this. Just a speck of normalcy." A speck of control would be nice, too. She slung her bag over her shoulder and walked out.

"You'll be giving up normalcy for a while."

Those words darkened her heart. "Please, tell me what's going on. I need to know."

He walked to the window and peered out. "No time for that, either. You'll find out everything when you get to Annapolis. Let's move."

She wanted to scream. Whenever they'd stopped, she peppered him with questions. He kept telling her that this group of people would answer everything. He had told her very little about himself, about why he'd saved her, how he even knew where she was. Just as Steele had found her twice, Cheveyo had also found her. Now he was taking her to people who were supposed to be like her, whatever that meant. It wasn't as comforting as he obviously thought it should be.

"Wait. How many of these people like us are there?"

"I don't know how many altogether. There are five where I'm taking you. Seven, including us. But there are others."

"How did you do that . . . that panther thing? That's the least you can tell me." Because that was just plain freaky.

He reached for the door. "I change my energy. Manipulate it."

"Can you change into anything?"

"Just a panther. It's my animal spirit." He walked to the bike.

She followed. "You're Native American?"

"Part Hopi."

"How will these people feel about you dumping me on them?"

"I think they'll be fine. You're one of them."

"Did you say you think? What does that mean, you *think*?"

He shrugged. "I don't know what their reaction will be. I've never met them." He started to put on his helmet, but she grabbed his arm.

"You're dropping me off with people you don't even know?"

"You'll be fine, as long as they don't shoot first and ask questions second." This time he did put on his helmet and started the bike.

Great. That would give her plenty to think about for the next several hours.

Petra Aruda woke in the night. She sat up in bed, looking around the darkness. No windows, no way to tell whether it was day or night. Like sleeping in a damned coffin. The clock read 2:28, and she was pretty sure it wasn't in the afternoon. She slid out of bed and pulled on pajamas she'd ordered from Victoria's Secret. As she walked down the hallway, the cool air tickled her bare stomach. She ran her hand across her skin, not sure why she was even up or where she was going.

"Hey," a male voice whispered from the kitchen, startling her. "Everything okay?"

She spun to find Rand Brandenburg pouring a glass of water. With his spiky hair and piercings, he was . . . well, interesting. If you liked punk-rocker-looking guys. "I'm going outside. I need fresh air and open space."

When the words came out, she knew that was what had driven her out of bed. The need to get out of the bomb shelter, the tomb, as she called it, crawled through her like a swarm of ants. It was a great hiding place, except for being underground without any windows.

He studied her. "You're not sleepwalking, are you?"

She laughed. "Lucid as can be."

"Be careful," he said.

Well, duh. Like I don't know that already. "I'll only be a few minutes."

She unlocked the thick steel door and walked down the tunnel, then climbed the ladder and pushed open the trapdoor in the old shed, their secret entrance. She stepped outside and took a deep breath. *The world!* Stars and the moon and the breeze that moved through the nearby line of bamboo like the patter of rain. The steady hum of traffic and the sky glowing from the town lights as though it was twilight. It was heavenly, delightful, and—

A hand pressed against her mouth. An arm slipped around her waist, and she was pulled against a hard male body. A voice whispered next to her ear: "Don't scream. I brought you outside because I have an Offspring who needs your help."

She twisted and tried to kick, panic welling up in her throat, but the man held her in a tight grip. She was going to die! Or get strapped down and injected with some terrible substance. She would never see Lucas and Eric and Amy again!

A woman almost as tall as Petra stepped out from behind the shed, and her anxiety was clear, even in the moonlight. "He's all right. We just didn't want you to scream. He saved me from some guy named Steele who was trying to kill me."

Petra could hardly grasp the woman's words; she felt a heat that verged on fire where her body met the man's. He smelled of fresh air and sweat, all male and oddly arousing. Really odd, considering the circumstances.

Get a grip. What did the woman say? Some guy was trying to kill her? Steele? The same Steele who'd come after them? And had he said "Offspring"?

He whispered, "Petra, we're not the enemy. Understand?"

His breath tickled her ear, sending chills down her neck. She nodded. He released her, and she spun around to face him. She put her hand to her heart to calm its racing.

They weren't grabbing her and dragging her off somewhere. She cleared her throat. "Let's go into the garage."

They followed her to the small, detached building. She squinted in the harsh light, taking in the two strangers, who looked road weary. He was gorgeous: thick, dark hair and a muscular body. The woman's dark red hair set off creamy skin; she was lean, with few curves, and yet there was something sensual about her. She had a ring tattoo, a dark red shirt with a skull on it, black jeans, and brown sneakers. Her arms were wrapped around her waist in a protective gesture, her expression wary.

"I'm Cheveyo," he said, capturing her attention. "This is Zoe."

Zoe was pulling her fingers through her thick hair, a grimace on her face, when she realized he'd introduced her. "Sorry. It feels like there are scorpions in my hair. Having that helmet on for hours sends prickles all over my scalp."

Petra turned to Cheveyo. "You know my name." She just now realized that.

"I know a lot more than that."

"What do you mean?"

He waved that away. "That's not important." His hair was in a ponytail that fell beyond his shoulders, and he had blue-gray eyes with an exotic slant to them. She guessed he was of Native American descent, though not completely. His gaze took her in, making her aware she was wearing midriff-revealing PJs. She flattened her hand on her bare stomach.

He leaned against the Toyota, arms loosely crossed in front of him. "Sorry about the whole grabbing-you-in-the-dark thing. Like Zoe said, I didn't want to startle you and draw attention."

There was something about him. She couldn't put

her finger on it, but it crackled through her body like sparks of lightning.

"It's . . . okay," she said, trying to push past that distraction. Of their own volition, her hands starting working, cracking her knuckles. She remembered something. "You said you brought me outside."

He nodded. "You woke with an indescribable urge to go outside. I summoned you."

"You . . . *what*?" That hit her in several different ways. Freaky and annoying and confusing ways. But he was right; she had been compelled to go outside for no logical reason.

"That's not important. Take Zoe in, get her up to speed on what's going on. She'll be an asset to your group. And she needs help."

Petra put her hand to her throat, panic welling. "How do you know about us? How did you know we were here? No one's supposed to know about this place. Who else knows? Oh, jeez, we have to get out—"

He put his hands on hers. "Calm down. I know because I'm an Offspring, too."

She blinked at that. "Why haven't you approached us before?"

"I watch you from a distance. Intervene when necessary. I put a shield on your shelter so they can't find you. I don't know how long it will keep them out, though. The enemy keeps getting stronger, just as you do. The more Offspring you gather, the stronger you'll become."

He pushed away from the car and stepped closer, looking into her eyes. "When you feel them remote-viewing you, close your eyes, get in a calm place—

don't freak out." He gave her a knowing smile. "Get a very clear picture of a golden shield all around you. Imagine things bouncing off it. Lock it in your mind for several seconds, without fear, without distraction. They'll see you during those seconds but not afterward. It will buy you time to get out of wherever you are."

Petra nodded, understanding that but not much else. "How did you . . . summon me?" She shivered. "How did you get into my mind like that?"

Zoe was leaning against the car, watching them intently. "I heard words in my head that weren't mine." She turned to Cheveyo. "That was you, wasn't it?"

He nodded.

Petra said, "But I didn't hear any words. I just felt this urge. Like you were controlling my mind."

"I communicate psychically." He touched Petra's chin, holding her attention with his eyes. "With you I can suggest . . . influence. We have a psychic bond, the way Lucas and Amy do."

That intensified the electricity inside her. "How do you know about Lucas—?"

"Except I will remain at a distance."

"Why?"

Instead of answering, he said, "You did well at the asylum."

She blinked in surprise. "You . . . saw me?"

"I was keeping an eye on you. I knew you'd be all right." Again, he nodded to Zoe. "I knew she wouldn't, so I intervened."

He walked toward the side door they'd come through but stopped and turned. "That shield works to keep you from absorbing other people's energy, too.

Use it whenever you need it." At her questioning look, he said, "That's how you heal others. You absorb their energy, their injuries. It's why you're uncomfortable when you touch people. But be careful about healing mortal wounds. The amount of energy they require could eventually destroy you."

"Destroy me?" The words squeaked out.

"Psychically. It could also disable the person being healed." He reached for the door. "Stay safe."

"Wait a minute." She walked over to him. "How do I know I can trust you? She could be a plant."

He gave her that knowing smile again, holding her with his gaze. "You just do." Though the energy in the garage changed when he left, she still felt that tingle inside her. He *knew* her. Knew she freaked out when she got scared and that she was uncomfortable touching people.

"Who is he?" Petra asked no one in particular, still staring at the closed door.

Zoe pushed away from the car and stepped up beside her. "I don't know, but he saved my life. And if I told you how, you'd probably never believe it."

Petra turned to her. "I believe in a lot of things I never knew existed." She laughed without a speck of humor. "Everything I believed in has been turned upside down. Did he tell you what's going on?"

"No, infuriatingly enough. Only that he was taking me to people like me, whatever that means, and that I could trust you. That you would tell me what was going on. *Please* tell me what's going on."

"What about him? What do you know?"

"Not much more than his name and that he very definitely is a loner. He's a gentleman. He held doors for me, saved my life, of course, and let me sleep for two hours when he didn't want to stop at all."

Petra caught herself rubbing her chin where his hand had been. She'd been jealous of Amy and Lucas's connection, chagrined to find that the one she had was with the enemy. She apparently had a much more interesting but hopeless connection with a sexy, mysterious loner. Figured.

"I guess you'd better follow me. We have a lot to tell you."

Zoe scooped up a big hobo purse and slung it over her shoulder. "Thank God."

CHAPTER 6

It annoyed Zoe that a part of her felt she'd passed some kind of acceptance test. Like those awful days in school when she didn't get picked dead last, only second to dead last. When the Goths accepted her because she sure as hell didn't fit in anywhere else. She'd never really fit in with them, either, but at least she wasn't sitting by herself in the cafeteria under the condescending scrutiny of the jocks and cheerleaders. She had company. That was when she'd come to embrace her uniqueness . . . well, except for the crazy energy.

She followed Petra down a dimly lit passageway. "What is this place? It's creepy, like the sewers."

"This is the passageway to what I call the tomb. It's actually a bomb shelter built in the fifties, when the country was all worried about nuclear decimation."

Petra reminded her of one of those girls Zoe had hated in high school: pretty, clean-cut, probably a cheerleader. Zoe would try not to hold that against her.

Intermittent lights left shadows and dark patches

where she imagined creatures lurked. Not like Dracula, but dog-sized rats and mutant slime.

Zoe strained her eyes to see into the shadows. "Do you ever worry about . . . something hiding in here?"

"Only the bad guys." They turned a corner, their shoes thudding on the damp concrete floor. "If you jumped out and had a gun to my back, you still couldn't get into the shelter."

Zoe heard a sound up ahead, her breath holding in her throat at the thought of what Petra had just said. They were about to walk into a better-lit area, and she stepped up her pace to reach it.

A shoe scraped on the floor—and it wasn't hers or Petra's. Before Zoe could open her mouth, someone grabbed her. Petra gasped. Zoe screamed as the man threw her to the floor, his hard body landing on hers. He pinned her wrists to the floor. His breath came heavy, pulsing at her neck. She could see his outline against the faint light behind him that put his face in shadow.

Then his voice, next to her ear. "Petra, get inside! I've got him."

"Rand?" Petra's voice quivered. "Is that you?"

"Yes, it's me. Now go, get to safety. Tell Eric and Lucas to bring guns. I've got the guy."

Petra stepped into the light, her eyes wide. "Rand, that's not a guy! Let her up!"

"What?"

"She's one of us. Let her up."

His weight was crushing Zoe into the hard, cold floor, but he wouldn't relent. *Petra knows him. She's telling him to let me up, which means she thinks he'll listen. Which means maybe he won't kill me.*

His voice boomed next to her ear. "But you said

something about a having a gun to your back. I thought you must have heard me and were letting me know you were in trouble."

Petra let out a strangled laugh, and only then did the man on top of Zoe ease up. "Rand, we were talking about someone lurking in the shadows. I didn't think anyone was actually there."

Before he fully released her, though, he said, "You're sure she's not dangerous?"

"She might be now that you've thrown her to the floor and won't let her up."

Zoe pushed against him and felt bare skin. He wasn't wearing a shirt.

Finally, he moved off her, and his hand reached for hers. "Here, let me—"

She jerked away. "I can get up on my own." With a groan, she pulled herself to her feet. In the light, she could barely see the guy who'd jumped her, a little taller than her, his 'do mussed. She tried to put her weight on her ankle and hissed in pain.

He said, "Look, I'm sorry. I thought Petra was in trouble. I thought you were—"

"A guy!" Zoe finished. "You scared the hell out of me, branded a dozen bruises on me, and . . . and . . . you thought I was a guy!" The outrage, the insult, and the adrenaline pumped her up. She lowered her voice. "Belize. Haiti. Saba."

"What are you calling me?" he asked.

"I'm not calling you anything. Not out loud, anyway. Nervous habit. I name the islands I want to go to. It calms me."

"She-it, I'm sorry," he said again, reaching for her. "Are you all right?"

She waved him away. "I'm fine. What'd you call me? A she-it?"

"No, that's just the way I say 'shit.' "

Petra brushed dirt from her back. "He didn't mean to hurt you. We're a little paranoid, and . . . well, we look out for each other."

"And it's dark," Rand added. "Now I can clearly see that you're a woman."

"Uh . . . that's good to know." She wasn't sure quite how to take that. Zoe had to admit that she was probably a teeny bit sensitive because of her lack of curves.

He was assessing her for damage as they continued down the tunnel, but she tried to ignore him.

"You're limping," he said. "Did you twist your ankle?"

"I'll be okay."

He swooped her up, his arms strong. He didn't grunt in exertion, thank God.

"You don't have to—"

"Yes, I do."

Oh, no, he really didn't. Strange things were happening to her body. First, she'd forgotten all about her ankle pain. The side of her breast rubbed against his hard chest, and her hip was pressing his six-pack stomach. Her hands, curled around his neck, brushed against the ends of his hair. In the dim light, she saw the bulge of his biceps, but his face was still in shadow.

It had to be all that motorcycle vibration. It had a, uh, stimulating effect. Except that after a few hours it had a numbing effect instead, but now it was back to that stimulated level. The faint scent of soap she smelled on him wasn't helping. She loved the smell of clean male, no cologne to interfere.

A few minutes later the tunnel dead-ended in a wall. Petra punched a code into a keypad, and the "wall" became a door that would keep out hordes of gladiators. It slid to the right, opening into a chamber.

Petra turned around with a sheepish look. "If you think Rand's bad, you'll love my brother, Eric."

"Why, what's wrong with him?"

"Oh, you'll see." She opened the door and gestured for Rand to go first.

Finally, she was going to get answers to all of this craziness. She was going to find out why people were trying to kill her, why they'd killed Cyrus. She was going to find allies. For some reason, she felt nervous. Being carried wasn't helping. She was pretty sure she hadn't been carried since she was a child. One thing was for sure, she didn't feel like a child. Even worse, her nipples were tight; *gawd, I hope no one can see them through my shirt.*

He carried her into a large room, illuminated only by the lights in a kitchen.

Petra waved toward a hallway that led out of sight. "I'll get the others."

"Can I freshen up first?"

"Sure."

Zoe turned to Rand. His face was covered in yellow-and-purple bruises and a few healing cuts. "Did that—are those"—she gestured to his face—"from back there? 'Cause if so, you got it a lot worse than I did."

He let out a laugh. "No." He turned his arm and

showed her a red scrape along his flexed biceps. "This is my only injury from the accidental tackle."

She was studying his bruises, a sympathetic wince on her face, when she realized she'd been staring at him. She cleared her throat. "Please put me down. I'll be fine."

He walked through the front part of the room, which held a huge dining-room table, past a desk, to a burgundy pit-group couch like she hadn't seen in anyone's house since she was a kid.

"I'll put you on the couch." He didn't give up easily. First at letting her up, and now at setting her down.

"Really. I'm okay."

He gingerly set her down on her feet, lightly settling his hands on her hips in case her ankle gave out. At least she thought that was why he'd done it.

Now that she was used to his bruises, she took a better look at the man himself. His dark hair had blond tips, and the blond strip of a goatee ran from below his lower lip to his chin. A spike pierced his eyebrow, and a bar lanced the top of his ear. He was compact, muscular without looking artificially built, and she'd felt every inch of him, thank you very much. His previous beating had been contained to his face; his torso was perfectly unmarred. And in blue jeans and nothing else, he looked absolutely yummy.

His gaze swept her again, and he lifted her hands and inspected her arms. "No scrapes? Bruises?"

She looked, too. "I don't know about bruises, but I don't see any scrapes."

Their gazes met, and she felt the oddest swirl in her stomach. What was going on inside her? She'd been around delicious guys before and never felt like this. She turned and looked at the room instead. Each wall was a different, vibrant color, and an equally vibrant painting adorned each one. An artist's easel filled the other corner.

"Who the hell is this?"

She followed the source of the harsh voice to a man advancing out of the hallway with narrowed, icy blue eyes and dark brown hair. She turned to Petra. "Let me guess: your brother."

"Bingo," Petra said under her breath. "Eric, this is Zoe. She's an Offspring."

He blinked in surprise, and Zoe almost wanted to laugh at the dumbstruck expression that juxtaposed his beefy fierceness. He aimed that look at Petra. "Explain."

"I went upstairs for some fresh air."

He raised his eyebrow. "Wait a minute. You go up for fresh air and come back with an Offspring." He looked at her. "A hot-chick Offspring, no less. Just like that?"

Petra did laugh. "Yeah, kinda funny, isn't it?"

"'Funny' isn't quite the word I'm thinking right now. 'Weird.' 'Bizarre.' 'Suspicious,' to start with." He looked at Rand. "Where do you fit into this?"

"I tackled her. I thought she was one of the enemy."

"A male enemy," Zoe added.

Rand let his gaze slide down her. "I won't make that mistake again."

Eric was also looking at her. "Man, you thought she was a *guy*?"

"It was dark!"

"Which still doesn't answer my initial question."

Zoe raised her hand. "Uh, can I use the bathroom, please? I really want to clean up."

"Sure, this way." Petra led her down a hallway to the third door on the left. "Do you need any clothes?"

"I bought a few things in Key West." She tapped her bag. "Be out in a few minutes."

Questions crowded her mind as she showered, found a hair dryer in the cabinet, and did a quick dry. At least it looked as though these people would give her answers, unlike Cheveyo.

She grimaced as she looked in the mirror. She had no gel to slick her hair, so it was all soft curls, which made the black streaks look strange. She ran some water back through it again and grabbed her makeup bag. Dark red lipstick, matching rouge, powder . . . yeah, she'd have to remove it before she finally crashed into sleep, but no way was she facing these people without it. She pulled out the stretchy top with bleeding roses on it, along with black lace panties, and bit off the tags. She slid back into her black pants and the platforms she'd stuffed in her bag. She needed to be *her.* Zoe Stoker. Different. Separate.

She emerged and followed the murmur of voices into the large, well-lit room . . . and stopped. Their conversation stopped as well. Five people, all in their midtwenties like her, took her in curiously, assessing. She felt like the new girl in class, simultaneously craving their acceptance and trying not to care.

Petra and Eric sat on the couch with their legs propped on the coffee table.

Petra said, "Everyone, this is Zoe."

She waved for her to come into the room, making Zoe feel pretty lame lingering in the hallway like a scared rabbit. With a nod, she walked over to the desk and perched on the surface, keeping a bit of distance between herself and the others.

"That's Amy and Lucas," Petra said, pointing to a couple sitting by the easel. Amy also had short hair, though hers was brown and frizzy. Lucas had dark, wavy hair and incredible, blue-gray eyes that reminded her of Cheveyo's. Amy sat on his lap, and his arms loosely circled her. *To have someone hold me like that, especially now . . .* Zoe pushed away the thought and nodded to them.

Petra's mouth quirked. "And you've met Rand."

He sat on the carpet with his arms propped on his knees. Despite his bruised face, he was gorgeous, with high cheekbones and sea-green eyes. This was so totally the wrong time to be revved up on a guy. So why did she feel the kind of spark she'd witnessed between Petra and Cheveyo?

No way was she going there with anyone here. She just wanted answers.

Eric leaned forward, aiming his attention at her. "What's your story, morning glory?"

Before she could ask the same back, Amy lifted a hand. "I remember how frustrating it was when you and Petra kept me in the dark, while I answered all your questions." She gave Zoe a sardonic grin. "Not to mention being kidnapped and drugged, which at least you get to avoid." She looked at Eric again. "Tell her what's going on. She's not the enemy; she's one of us." She gave them a mysterious nod.

Zoe simultaneously felt a glow at Amy's defense of her and a chill at being one of them. She didn't even know who these people were, what they were. "All

I know is that one minute my life is normal, and the next, some guy is trying to kill me in my shop. I go on the run down to Key West, and no way could anyone find me, then some guy who turned into a panther saved my ass from a second guy who was about to annihilate me, and after a thousand hours riding on the back of a motorcycle, I'm here . . ." The power of her voice gave way to a tremble. "Yeah, I want answers." She looked at Amy. "And I want to know about this kidnapping and drug stuff, too."

Petra's eyebrows furrowed. "Panther?"

Eric shot Amy a look of annoyance. "Lucas, keep your little woman in line. We don't know who this chick is. What if they sent her here?"

Petra said, "Cheveyo brought her here. I know he's not an enemy, and if he's not, then she's not either."

Zoe met Eric's suspicious gaze head-on. "I think we've just got to trust each other. This guy went to a lot of trouble to save me and bring me here without asking for anything in return. He supposedly put some kind of shield over this place. Sounds like he's looking out for all of you."

Rand was watching her, and she felt a tingle go through her body as his gaze drifted down her long legs to her shoes. "I say we trust her. Besides, we want to find more Offspring; well, one just got delivered to our doorstep."

Eric scowled. "And how does this guy know where we are?"

Petra said, "He's protecting us. Besides, if he wasn't on our side, Darkwell would have found us already."

"I still don't like it. He knows too much, he's supposedly on our side yet he won't talk to us." Eric settled his hard gaze on Petra. "Except you. And he's another mind controller." He clamped his hand over hers. "Stop." To the others he said, "She's a crack addict. Cracks her knuckles when she's uptight, which is most of the time."

Petra tucked her hands between her thighs.

Zoe let out a breath. "So tell me already, what the hell am I involved in here? Two different men have tried to kill me, and frankly, it's pissing me off."

Amy grinned. "She'll fit in just fine." She faced Zoe. "Without really knowing anything about you, we know that you lived near Fort Meade about twenty years ago, your mother or father died in an odd way, perhaps suicide, and you have a psychic ability that you may not even realize is psychic or an ability."

The blood drained from Zoe's face. For the first time in her life, she said the words, "My father walked into the office where he was working and killed three people and wounded four more. Then he killed himself." *And I may have inherited that,* she couldn't say.

Amy covered her mouth. "That was *your* father? Cyrus told me about that. Cyrus is—"

"Cyrus *Diamond*?" Zoe asked.

Amy leaned forward, her eyes wide. "Yes. You know him?"

"He was helping me find out more about my dad's shooting spree. He called me last Thursday and said his digging had put us in danger. The next day I saw in the paper . . . he'd been killed."

Amy turned to the others. "Zoe Stoker, one of the names on his speed dial. He told me she was one of his Offspring."

"I was one of *his* Offspring?"

Amy got up and walked closer. "Let's start from the beginning. Twenty-five years ago, two men created a top secret program called BLUE EYES that recruited people with psychic abilities to help win the war against terrorism. Their goals were to spy psychically on the enemy and find hostages. It's called remote viewing." Amy chuckled. "Yeah, I probably had the same look on my face when Cyrus told me about it. It's the ability to see a place that is remote to you. Or, as we've found out, the ability to find someone so you can send an assassin after them. That's how the guy who tried to kill you in Key West found you. And probably how Cheveyo found you."

Amy leaned against the desk chair. "Darkwell, one of the men heading BLUE EYES, gave the subjects— our parents—some kind of 'nutritional' cocktail that boosted their powers. We don't know what was in it, maybe pharmaceutical substances or illegal drugs. What we do know is that it also had another side effect: it made the recipients go crazy."

"And sex-obsessed," Eric added, and as though to illustrate, his gaze raked down her.

Amy waved away his comment. "Each of us had a parent in that program, which is why we're called Offspring. That's why your father went berserk and shot people. Why my dad killed himself, why Eric and Petra's mom set herself on fire, and maybe why Lucas's mom got into a fatal car accident."

Rand added, "Maybe why my father embezzled money from the government, then shot himself when he was found out." He didn't look as though he believed that, though.

Zoe dropped the pen. "You're saying my dad—that

we all had parents—who died because of this program? It wasn't just . . . normal craziness?"

Amy gave her a watery smile. "It's a relief in a way, isn't it? For a long time I thought my dad just didn't care enough to stick around."

"And it was because of this cocktail?"

"That and probably the stress of what they were doing."

Lucas spun the chair he was sitting on and leaned against the back of it. "When your dad went berserk, the program was closed down and covered up. The government paid each family involved a big sum of money to appease their curiosity."

Zoe ran her fingers through her hair, so stunned by all this she could hardly cringe at the fact that her hair was now dry and curly. "My dad had psychic abilities? And it was this program that made him crazy, not something psychological. So . . ." Did she dare voice the next part? "That means I couldn't inherit that craziness since it came from something outside of him." The relief at that!

Except Amy was shaking her head. "We inherited our parents' enhanced ability. We don't know about the crazy part."

Zoe's shoulders sagged. And then—"Wait a minute. We inherited a psychic ability? That's what you said before, that I had an ability. But I don't. I can't see the future or . . . what did you call it? Remote-view?"

Eric pushed to his feet, grabbed up his empty milk glass, and walked toward her. He stopped a foot in front of her. "What makes you different from everyone else?"

She raised an eyebrow. "What makes you think I'm different?" She didn't like people seeing through her.

"You've got 'stay away' written all over you."

"Sexy but don't touch," Rand added, with a glint in his eyes.

Zoe bent one leg and propped her arm on her knee. Yes, a physical shield. Maybe they were right, but their assessments made her uncomfortable.

Amy was less confrontational. "We see it because we all have it."

"What is crazy energy?" Rand asked. "Oh, you didn't say that yet. Sorry."

Zoe slid down from the desk, hands out to push them back. She aimed a look at Rand, whose pupils had dilated to pinpoints. "How did you know about my crazy energy?"

"I can see ten seconds ahead. I saw you saying the words."

She took them in. "You're all a bunch of freaks."

Petra grinned. "And so are you, my friend."

Zoe narrowed her eyes. "Can you . . . read minds? Or, like Cheveyo, mess with someone's thoughts?"

"Not that we know of," Amy said. "We're all kind of feeling our way around this. Cyrus told me that we have powers we might not even be aware of."

Eric walked into the kitchen. "One of the things we suspect the Offspring have in common is some kind of bioenergetic ability."

"Bioenergetic?" Zoe asked.

He poured milk into his glass without even looking. "Psychic. The ability to change energy." He stopped pouring a millimeter before the glass would have overflowed.

Amy waved her hands a few inches above Zoe's head and shoulders. "I see glows, colors around people that indicate their mood or intention. Offspring have a mix of all the colors, which is how I knew you were one of us. I thought that was strange enough, but now I've discovered I can talk to dead people. Or at least Cyrus."

Zoe's eyes widened. "You've talked to Cyrus after he died?"

Amy nodded. "He helped us once. It's not an ability I particularly like, though."

She glanced at Lucas, who said, "I used to get dreams and draw sketches of something that was going to happen in the future. Then Darkwell's guys nabbed me, and he shot me up with that Booster stuff he gave our parents. Now I get this storm of images that feels like an electrical charge going through my brain."

Zoe said, "They nabbed you?"

"It's a long story, but they kidnapped me and took me to an old insane asylum. They were going to keep injecting me and testing my abilities until I died."

Amy's fingers twined together. "He was supposed to die after getting the fourth round. Thank God he never got that shot."

Zoe's hand went to her mouth. She felt as if she were in a horror movie.

Amy said, "Cyrus gave me enough information to help find Lucas."

Lucas nodded toward Rand. "They got him, too."

"Hauled my ass right out of a casino," Rand said.

"So that's what happened to your face." Zoe could now see that his nose was slightly crooked.

"No, the casino dudes did that. Big and Beefy and Tall and Mean." He shrugged. "I use my talents in ways that the casinos don't particularly like. They caught onto me, roughed me up, then Darkwell came in and took me away. They gave me LSD to see if it would expand my skills." He shivered at the memory. "Waked me out big-time, but I don't think it did anything for my ability."

"Waked you out?" Zoe asked.

"Freaked. Wigged." He nodded toward Lucas. "These guys broke in and rescued him, then they came back and got me." He gave them an affectionate smile. "Crazy bastards."

Zoe, however, was still horrified at the part before that.

Petra had traded one nervous habit for another, braiding her long hair, undoing it, then braiding it again. "I have extraordinary hearing. Now I've discovered I can also heal. When we went in to rescue Rand, things went bad. Lucas got shot. I had this overwhelming urge to touch his wound, and I healed him." So much emotion crossed her face as she spoke. "But at a price." She turned to the others. "Cheveyo warned me that I have to be careful about healing mortal wounds. It could destroy me psychically. And he also said that whoever I healed could lose their powers."

Lucas stiffened. "I don't have powers?"

Amy said, "You haven't had that storm of images, but it's only been, what, twelve hours since you were shot and revived."

Lucas asked, "Is this lack of power permanent?"

Petra shook her head. "He didn't say. I got side-tracked by his warning about healing people. I wished I'd had the presence of mind to ask him more. Before I knew it, he was gone."

Eric walked back out into the living area. "Yeah, we need to find out more about that guy. I don't trust him."

"You don't trust anyone." Petra went into the kitchen.

"I think he may be right," Lucas said. "I've felt . . . different since Petra healed me. Lighter. As much as I hated it, I would hate not having it. Not being able to protect my people." Lucas's gaze went to Amy, and Zoe shivered at the intensity of love and fear she saw.

Zoe met Eric's eyes. Even in her platforms she was still a few inches shorter than he was. "And what do you do?"

His mouth quirked. "I set people on fire."

"Okay, then." A tingle of bizarreness at the situation flowed through her.

Petra took out a piece of bread and slathered peanut butter on it. "His other less glamorous ability is to remote-view."

Zoe looked at Eric. "So you're not the guy to piss off."

Petra's laugh was more like a snort. "Yeah, good luck with that."

Rand came to his feet. "So, what's crazy energy?"

They'd shared with her; and hell, if anyone would understand, it would be these people. *My people.* Those words startled her. She'd never belonged to any group, really belonged. "Whenever I get emotional, things start to fly around. Glasses, books, pens. I'm also bad around small appliances. They sort of blow up."

Eric walked into the kitchen and poured another glass of milk. "Telekinesis."

This weird thing about her, and he had so casually tossed out a word to describe it. "What?"

"The ability to move objects with your mind."

"Well, if I actually had control over it." She looked at Rand, who was standing just a little too close. "Can you control that seeing ahead thing?"

"Yeah, but it's so natural, sometimes I don't realize I'm doing it." Their gazes locked for a moment. He cleared his throat and walked into the kitchen. From a more comfortable distance, he asked, "So you rode all the way here from Key West on the back of a motorcycle?"

Without even thinking about it, Zoe rubbed her behind, which was still sore. "Yeah."

"Cool. What kind of ride?"

She cocked her eyebrow at him. "I didn't exactly notice."

Rand asked, "Want something to drink or eat?"

She walked into the kitchen, too, and nodded toward the bottle of beer Rand pulled out. "One of those would be good." Heck, she deserved it.

Soon everyone stood around the kitchen, washed in yellowed, fluorescent light. Amy tossed some kind of chocolate balls up into the air and caught them in her mouth. Rand poured Zoe's beer into a mug and handed it to her. When their fingers brushed, she felt a jolt. At the blink of his eyes, she guessed he had, too. Great, just what she needed.

She shifted her attention to someone—anyone else. "All right, so maybe I inherited this crazy energy from my dad—"

"Oh, you did," Amy said.

Zoe's chest tightened. "So why are these people after me? Why are they kidnapping us and trying to kill us if this program existed so long ago?"

"I told Cyrus, who was like an uncle to me, about seeing glows. He was worried that if I had inherited my dad's psychic ability, maybe I'd inherited the craziness, too. He mentioned it to Darkwell, who had apparently been really bummed that his pet project got tanked . . . never mind that people died.

"Anyway, when he heard that I'd inherited Dad's abilities, he started wondering if the offspring of the other subjects did, too. Extrasensory abilities do run in families, but what if we'd inherited the enhanced abilities? He saw the resurrection of his program." Amy popped another chocolate into the air and caught it. "Darkwell assigned three CIA agents to track down the Offspring. Cyrus was reluctantly dragged back into the new program, called DARK MATTER, as one of those agents."

Zoe took a cold sip of beer and wiped the foam from her upper lip with the tip of her tongue. "What is the program about? What does he want to do?"

"The thing is, what Darkwell's trying to do isn't all bad: he wants to use us, our abilities, to save hostages and find terrorists. But he's going about it the wrong way."

"Well, *yeah*, kidnapping us, injecting us with stuff." The memories of the men trying to kill Zoe were way too vivid.

Eric grabbed Petra's hands again to still her cracking. "They're doing that to us because we're the Rogues. We're onto them, and we won't join. We're looking for other Offspring so we can find out what happened to our parents. They don't want us to find the truth, so they're trying to take us out."

"How can the government do such a thing?"

"You'd be surprised what they've gotten away with," Eric said. "But DARK MATTER isn't officially CIA or government. Darkwell's hidden it under legit programs."

"Cyrus helping me with finding out about my dad . . . that was a ruse?"

Amy gave her a sympathetic nod. "Afraid so. Darkwell probably found out about your inquiries and had Cyrus approach you. What he was really doing was assessing your psychic skills."

"Then why did they try to kill me? Cyrus called to warn me, then this guy tried to kill me at my tattoo shop."

Amy said, "They probably wanted you dead because Cyrus called you. They figured he'd told you enough to make you a liability." Her expression darkened. "They got Cyrus's other Offspring for the same reason."

"Got . . . as in killed?"

Amy nodded. "I tried to talk to him, and I guess he started looking into it. The next thing we knew, he'd killed himself. But I don't think he committed suicide."

"Killed like they killed Cyrus? They did kill him, didn't they?"

Amy nodded, her face shadowing. "He and I were close. He was telling me everything and they . . . two agents took him out and tried to take me out, too."

Eric's shoulders broadened a bit. "Until I intervened."

Amy narrowed her eyes at him. "Let's not go there just yet."

Zoe leaned against the counter, the reality of all this, the days of fear and hours on a bike catching up to her. "I need to get this around my head. I mean, my head around this."

"Believe me, I know the feeling, but there's something else," Amy said in a gentle voice that told Zoe she wasn't going to like it. "They have recruited at least two Offspring, a man and a woman. We don't know their names. He can find Petra; apparently he's got a connection to her. And he can get into our heads."

Eric's expression was grim. "Or at least mine."

Zoe slid down to the floor, clutching the sides of her head. After a moment she looked up and found them all watching her with varying degrees of empathy. "What do I do now?"

Rand knelt beside her. "The way I see it, you've got two choices: you go back out there and get killed. Or you join us."

CHAPTER 7

"I'll take her downstairs." An hour later, Rand walked over to a bookcase and pushed it aside to reveal a hidden stairway. "Seeing as I just went through this a few hours ago."

Zoe stared at the small opening, a combination of wariness and disbelief on her face. The same expression, he'd noted, when she'd first seen his face. He didn't blame her on either account. Course, he'd just jumped her . . . sheesh.

"My room is *down there*?"

Amy shrugged. "Sorry, the three rooms on this level are already taken. There are four more downstairs."

"It's only a little claustrophobic." Rand was amused at her reluctance. "I'll keep you company." Now even more reluctance colored her face, and he was less amused. "I only look like a monster. And I promise I won't jump you again."

Judging by the continued trepidation showing in her expression, none of that seemed to console her. She was a looker, but not in any traditional sense.

Which appealed to him even more, oddly enough. Her creamy complexion was covered in makeup as much as his face was covered in bruises. He bet she looked prettier without it. She had a tall, lean build and long legs that he imagined wrapped around his hips at the very second that she looked at him, and said, "It's not you I'm worried about."

Well, that was a dash to a guy's ego. Then again, he shouldn't be imagining anything. Now was not the time to get involved with anyone. Forget the way she'd run the tip of her tongue across her upper lip to erase her foam moustache.

"I'd take off those shoes before you go down the stairs. Might be a bit dicey."

She leaned against the wall and stripped off her thick-heeled shoes, wrapping her finger around the straps.

"Get some sleep," Petra said. "We can talk in the morning. I want to hear more about Cheveyo." She cleared her throat. "Out of curiosity."

Zoe stepped into the stairwell. "Like I'll get any sleep."

Rand followed her, noting the slender line of her back, a small but shapely behind. He admired the fact that she'd escaped an assassin twice. They'd all listened intently when she'd told them about her two encounters.

"The two rooms on the right are stuffed with supplies," he said, as they walked through a large room that mirrored the space above, only this one had a smaller kitchen and a gym set up in one-half of the living area. "My room's here." He pointed to the first door on the left and pushed open the door in the middle. "We'll share this bathroom; there are doors from our rooms, too." He walked to the third door and opened it. "This is your room."

She stepped inside and checked it out. She looked tired and disappointed and a little scared. The last tugged at him, pulling him inside the room, too, when he ought to have been saying good night.

"I'm sure you can get Petra to decorate it for you," he said. "She's the one who painted the walls upstairs and picked the paintings."

She grimaced.

"Okay, maybe not."

She climbed across the bed like a cat, so tired she could hardly move. He saw an intriguing tattoo across her lower back. When he leaned forward to see it better, she dropped onto the bed and twisted around to face him. Their gazes met, and his heart *stopped* for a second. *What the hell was that about?*

She wrapped her arms around herself as though she were cold. "This all seems so unreal. You just came here, too? Just learned all this?"

He sat on the edge of the bed. "Yeah. The five of us"—he gestured upstairs—"spent some time together when we were real young, but I haven't seen them since. I rep them big-time."

"Rep them?"

"Respect them. They saved my ass. I wasn't making it out of that asylum alive. We barely got out of there. I'll tell you the whole story sometime. Eric's a bit waked out, not sure what to make of him. Lucas is a cool cat. His loyalty rocks. When I asked him why he risked his skin to get me out of that place, he said, 'You're one of us.' Being part of a group, that's . . .

well, it's not me. But loyalty is something I can understand."

"Not being part of a group, well, you sort of get
that way when you're a freak."

Her wounded soul tugged even harder on him. She
wore her freak identity like a shield to keep others
out. He noticed another tattoo around her ankle, a
ring of flowers and dragonflies, and a smaller ring of
flowers around her wedding finger. "Makes life sim-
pler, too."

"Oh, sorry to interrupt," a female voice said by the
door. Petra looked as though she'd come upon them
in an embrace. "Zoe, did you need something to sleep
in? I've got a nightshirt and pajamas." She held up one
in each hand.

"That's okay, thanks. I just sleep in my panties."

Great. Just what he wanted to know. He gave both
women a wave and headed to his room. He stretched
out on his bed, listening to the water running in the
bathroom and imagining Zoe washing off all that
makeup, combing her hair, doing all those things
women did when they got ready for bed.

Sleeping in her panties.

Probably lacy panties.

Probably lacy thong panties.

She-it. He rolled over to face away from the bathroom. It was just his body complaining about the lack
of female companionship lately. His lifestyle didn't
lend itself to a long-term relationship or being around
quality women. Women in casinos didn't tempt him;
most were married and looking to score in more ways
than one. Others wanted to hook up with the guy who
was making money.

Women who just wanted sex didn't appeal; most were skanky. Women who wanted relationships were out, too. If he didn't object in principle to paying for a date, he could see the appeal of hiring an escort.

What he needed was a visit to Fiona, the rich divorcée in Atlantic City who distrusted most men but liked him because he didn't give a damn about her money. It was empty sex but pleasurable.

That's all it was, the horny gremlin at work. So why did the memory of Zoe's scared face bother him more than the sight of her delicious body?

Zoe woke in a daze. No windows. A strange room. She pulled herself out of bed and oriented her mind. She was in—*what had Petra called it? Oh, right, the tomb.* Because people were trying to kill her for no good reason.

The room was sparsely furnished, just a bed, nightstand, and dresser. Gray carpet and gray walls. She stumbled to the bathroom door and opened it. The sight of a naked male body woke her as no intravenous espresso shot ever could have. Water dotted Rand's broad shoulders and dripped down the indent of his spine and over a tight, sweet derriere. Because he was drying his hair with the towel, he hadn't heard her open the door.

A hand towel went flying off the shelf, causing him to turn around to look at her, then behind him to where the towel landed on the floor. The familiar horror at losing control of her crazy energy filled her. The worst part, the absolutely terrible part? She couldn't stop staring! His arms were extended above his head, bulging his biceps. Fine blond hair dusted the ridges of his stomach. His thatch of hair was dark blond, and a glimpse of what stood at half-mast was more than she'd seen on the few men she'd seen naked and fully erect.

He hadn't moved since her entrance, but he finally said, "This wasn't quite what I had in mind when I said we were sharing a bathroom, but hey, it's fine with me. Clothes are overrated anyway."

His words, along with his knowing grin, finally snapped her to attention. She slapped her hand over her eyes and closed the door, murmuring, "Sorry," followed by a groan of embarrassment. Which was when she realized that she was also naked but for her black lace panties.

From the other side of the door, he asked, "Was the towel flying your crazy energy?"

So he'd noticed. "No."

"Interesting," he said.

"It's *not* interesting."

She dropped onto the bed and buried her face in the blanket. She couldn't, however, bury her body's reaction to the sight of a gorgeous naked man. *Come on, Zoe, this is nuts. You just met him, and you've got a lot more things to think about than that.*

He knocked on the door. "All yours."

With another groan, she wrapped the sheet around her and opened the door. He was in the opening to his bedroom, a devilish grin on his face and a towel wrapped around his waist. Her pulse jumped, and she yanked his door shut and locked it.

He chuckled. "Hey, doll, at least we got that 'seeing each other naked thing' out of the way."

Doll. The word tickled through her. She found a

pile of washcloths beneath the sink. "Are you teasing me or trying to make me feel better?"

"Maybe a little of both."

She liked the sound of his voice, sexy and fun, filled with a smile she knew was teasing even though she couldn't see him.

She stacked the washcloths on one side of the cabinet and washed her face. How long was she going to be here, hiding from these awful people? She needed her stuff: clothing, toiletries, and hair gel. She used the men's deodorant that was on the counter, then lined that up with the soap pump. She picked up the towel she'd sent flying. One toothbrush sat in a holder, and she was about to ask where he'd gotten it when he called out, "In the back of the cabinet."

"How did you know—you jumped ten seconds ahead?"

"Yep."

She brushed her hair and frowned at the softness the curls gave her face. Curls hadn't adorned her head since she was twelve, when she chopped them all off in a fit of ire. She got dressed, made her bed, and returned to the bathroom to brush her teeth when a thought hit her.

Just then he knocked on the door. "You decent? I forgot to put on deodorant. Got a bit, er, distracted."

She opened the door to his room, her eyes narrowed. "Did you know I was going to walk in on you?"

He gave her a totally innocent look as he walked in wearing just jeans. Damn, did he *know* what that did to her? "Of course not. I would have warned you."

She couldn't tell if he was being honest. She'd met

guys like him before—well, not exactly like him. Playful, flirts, too good-looking for their own good. As much as she liked to flirt, too, she usually kept her cool with guys who actually stirred her senses. Rand was definitely one of those guys, even with the faded bruises on his face.

"Look, just because we"—she waved her hand to indicate the naked thing—"you know . . ."

"Saw each other naked?"

"Yeah. Just because . . . that, doesn't mean . . ."

He waited patiently for her tongue to untangle the words in her head.

"Don't get any ideas."

He merely grinned. "Yes, ma'am." He swiped on deodorant and was about to leave when he looked at her.

She wasn't wearing any makeup. No one saw her without makeup, and now she was naked in another way. She dug out her bag and pulled out her foundation.

He crossed his arms in front of his chest as he watched her. "You look better without all that stuff."

"No, I don't."

It gave her a funny feeling to have him watch her as she used her puff to layer on Urban Decay mineral powder.

"You don't look like a tattoo artist."

She stopped midrub. "What's that supposed to mean?"

"They're usually Gothish, covered in tats—"

"Tattoos. We don't call them tats." She went back to rubbing in foundation.

"And scary-looking." He leaned against the counter, making himself comfortable. "You're too whole-some. You look like that cute redhead who acted in all those eighties films—"

"I do *not* look like Molly Ringwald. And I'm not cute."

"You even sounded like her when you said that!" He put his hand over his heart. "I had such a crush on her when I was a kid."

She thickly lined her eyes in black, trying and failing miserably to ignore him. "Don't stereotype tattoo artists. There's a lot of diversity in the profession." But the thing was, she didn't really fit in there, either, despite her statement. Most artists *were* covered in tattoos, a tribute to their passion; she only had four. Her employees were always trying to get her to adorn herself more, but she felt that too many tattoos detracted from the beauty of each one. Natch, she wouldn't tell her customers that.

After swiping on lipstick that matched the bleeding roses on her shirt, she flexed her nails and bared her teeth at him. "Boo. Scary now?"

"Very." With a grin, he pushed away from the cabinet. "Ready to head upstairs?"

What was he smiling about? Did she want to know? Probably not. "Yeah, I'm ready."

She preceded him up the stairs. The others were standing around in the kitchen, and Zoe's stomach perked at the smell of toast and coffee.

"I thought breakfast would be long over," she said, gratefully taking the mug Amy handed her.

"We just woke up," Amy said. "I'm a night owl anyway."

Zoe poured coffee into her mug. "Me, too. That's

why being a tattoo artist is the perfect profession. Not many people wanting to get tattoos in the morning, thank goodness."

Petra's eyebrows rose. "I'd been thinking of getting one . . . before all this craziness started." She wore a ruffled teal top, black pants, and high heels that matched her top. Pretty fancy for the tomb.

"Let me just go in and take the bastard out," Eric said to Lucas where they stood at the far corner of the kitchen, obviously immersed in a discussion. "Burn the whole place up with everyone in it. Then it's done."

Lucas pressed his hand flat against the counter, impatience tensing his handsome features. "After we find out the truth. We can't go back to our lives until we find out what happened and what's in us."

"You think that guy's going to tell us anything? You think he's going to let us waltz in and look through his files?"

"Eric, don't go off half-cocked again. You almost got us killed last time. In fact, you very nearly got me killed. You deviated from the plan. It was stupid and dangerous."

Zoe could see anger seething in waves off Eric; Lucas wasn't too happy either. She grabbed a piece of toast and walked over to them. "If this man had anything to do with my father going in and shooting those people, I want to know the truth."

Amy walked over, too, sliding her arms around Lucas's waist. "Eric, you can have your revenge later. We need answers first. We have to find out what they injected into Lucas. We've got to approach this logically. Carefully."

Eric slammed his mug on the counter. "What, you all ganging up on me?"

"If we have to," Amy said.

Eric's body tensed as he took them all in. Finally, he relaxed. "We take a couple of days and regroup, research. But then we make a move."

Petra rolled her eyes. "The last time we were going to chill for a few days, we jumped right back into the fire to rescue Rand. Amy and I were held at gunpoint, Lucas was shot, blood—" She took a deep breath when she realized everyone was looking at her. Cracked her knuckles. "I'm not buying it this time."

The need to find out why her father had done what he did grew inside Zoe. "Seems like we need to work as a team."

"Exactly." Lucas gave Eric a pointed look. "There are six of us now."

"And more of them," Eric said.

Zoe leaned back against the counter and took a bite of toast. "How many are there?"

Amy poured more coffee into her mug. "Two men run the project: Darkwell and Robbins, his second-in-command. Cyrus told me that the two men who headed the program are dangerous and powerful, and all they care about is their cause at any price. But Robbins appeared reluctant about what they were doing to Lucas. He even helped him, brought him a toothbrush and deodorant. From what we can tell, Robbins is our best chance to get information. He doesn't seem as dangerous as Darkwell."

"So how do we approach him?" Zoe asked.

"We kidnap him and see what we can get out of him."

Zoe blinked. "Kidnap? As in, take him by force?"

Eric said, "That's usually what kidnap means."

Amy nudged Eric with her bare foot. "I know, it sounds crazy and insane and totally bonkers, talking about kidnapping people when just a few days ago your biggest worry was paying your bills or running out of toilet paper. Nine days ago I was sleeping in my cozy bed in my cozy life when a sexy stranger broke in and told me about being an Offspring." She glanced at Lucas. "My life will never be the same again. To be honest, I don't want it to be."

Zoe shook her head as she lined up four spice jars on the counter in alphabetical order. "I do. I want to walk into my tattoo shop and bitch because my two o'clock canceled and get on Michael's case about keeping his station clean and . . ." She leaned against the counter and pinched the bridge of her nose, despair washing over her. When she looked up, Rand was watching her with an intense look on his face. He quickly looked away. "I want my life back."

Amy's expression softened. "Yeah, I felt that way, too."

Zoe said, "But then you met this gorgeous guy who obviously loves you. At least you got something good out of the bad."

Amy tilted her head in sympathy. "I'm afraid you don't have a choice, at least for the time being."

One of the spice jars tipped over. Zoe took a deep breath. "Puerto Rico. Montserrat." She crossed her arms over her chest. "Where does that leave us? What does it mean for our future?"

Rand leaned forward, obviously wanting to hear the answer to that, too. "We can't hide here forever. Nothing personal, but I'd rather them take me out than have to hide down in this hole for years."

Petra's eyes widened. "Years? No, I can't be here for years. I won't be able to shop and so what if I do have cute clothes if I'm stuck down here and—?"

Amy put her hands on Petra's shoulders. "Right now we have to focus on our next step. We find Robbins. Unfortunately, we don't have a clue as to how to do that. We need someone who can find people. None of us can do that. We have the names of two more Offspring. I say we try to find them, add to our ranks. And to our skills."

"We need someone who can see into the future." Lucas nodded to Rand. "No offense, but for longer than ten seconds. I hated those images, but at least I had a clue as to what was going to happen."

Amy pressed her cheek against his back. "They were also tearing you apart."

He gave her a look filled with fear. "It's worth it if it saves your life."

It was obvious that she didn't agree. The depth of their love was so palpable, it twisted inside Zoe's chest.

Rand was watching them, too, an odd expression on his face. She shifted her attention away. "These people, are they so ruthless that they'd hurt our friends or family? Would they go to my tattoo shop and threaten my employees? My mom? My grand-dad?" The thought tightened her throat.

Lucas looked at Amy. "When they were holding me at the asylum, they used Amy to coerce me into cooperating."

Petra's eyes widened. "When I was hiding at the asylum—" She turned to Zoe and Rand. "When we went in for Lucas, I got stuck there and had to hide out for a day. I overheard Darkwell talking about you, Rand. He said he'd found out you were close to your grandmother, that you sent her money."

Rand's body stiffened. "How the hell did he find that out?"

"He's got government resources even if the government doesn't know what he's up to. He was going to use her to get you to cooperate, too."

"I need to check on her. Warn the staff. Something." Rand jerked his fingers back through his hair. "I've got to do that today." It warmed Zoe that he obviously cared about someone, and even more so when he said, "What about your grandfather? Where is he?"

"Hospice, in Baltimore." The saltshaker toppled over. She wrapped her fingers around it, hoping no one noticed her crazy energy. "He's . . . dying of cancer. But I don't want those bastards doing anything to him." She set the shaker on the counter. "I'm going with you."

She thought he was going to object. His mouth opened, and he had *No* written all over his face. Then he looked at her eyes. "All right. But I don't have a vehicle."

Petra said, "We've got a car."

"I want to get my wheels. But I—we need a way to get to Baltimore."

Eric shook his head. "Is your car still at the casino where they nabbed you? They might be watching it."

"I've got another set of wheels in a friend's garage.

They'll have no idea where to find it. Getting there's the issue."

Amy lifted a finger. "I'll call Ozzie. He's my neighbor and friend, and he sort of but not really got involved. He knows I'm caught up in something, but he thinks I saw some files on a hard drive I was recovering that I wasn't supposed to see. I only tell him what he needs to know to keep him out of this as much as possible. The funny thing is, he wants to help in the worst way, and besides, I need to get my parrot."

"Parrot?" three of them said at once.

Eric held out his hand. "No parrot."

Amy stuck her tongue out at him. "Lucas said I could have one. So there."

Eric nailed Lucas with a harsh look and a grunt. "Woman's made you weak."

Lucas pulled Amy against him and nuzzled her neck. "Weak is not always a bad thing, my friend."

Zoe was absolutely sure these people were going to drive her nuts. At least when her employees bickered, she could stop them. She was in charge. She could order them to clean up or could organize things herself. But this wasn't her place, and these weren't her employees.

Obviously she wasn't the only one feeling the strain of the chaos. Rand said, "I've got to get out of here."

Amy said, "Let me call Oz, see if he's up for a little adventure. He'll do anything if I take Orn'ry out of his hair."

"Orn'ry?" Zoe asked.

"That's the parrot."

Eric frowned. "I was afraid you were going to say that."

"You won't even know he's around." Amy walked over to her purse, which was sitting on the desk. "Except when he cusses, which is cute because he doesn't do it right." And in a lower voice, "Or when he screeches or has hissy fits. I'll have to take a ride and call Ozzie. We can't risk calling from here in case Darkwell's monitoring his phone. We should give him one of our untraceable cell phones."

Eric got up and waved her toward the hallway. "I've been doing some research. If we call from the computer, it's a lot harder for anyone to trace. We unplug it, so it runs off the UPS, which is the uninterrupted power supply. It's still got to be a quick call, though."

He pulled up the software, unplugged the computer, and dialed the number. Immediately the UPS started beeping, signaling the loss of power.

When a man answered, Amy said, "Oz, it's me."

"Are you trying to give me a heart attack, not calling for days? I can only take so much, you know."

Zoe whispered, "Sounds like your mother."

Amy snorted. "Oz, you know I can't call just to give you updates. But I'm fine, thanks for caring. You up for a little adventure?"

"Does it involve giving you the parrot back?"

"Yes, and a quick trip to Baltimore."

"Deal."

Eric groaned. "He's way too eager to get rid of it."

Petra leaned forward. "Did you get the 'Cuda, Oz?"

"Who's that?"

"A friend," Amy said.

"Yes, I got the car. A friend is storing it in his garage, and he thinks it's stolen, which is just too cool."

Amy grinned. "I'm proud of you. Thanks."

Lucas leaned toward the phone. "Yeah, much appreciation, man."

"All right," Amy said. "Here's the plan . . ."

CHAPTER 8

"This bird's going to be a pain in the ass, isn't it?" Lucas asked as he drove to the drop location.

Amy shook her head, but said, "Yeah."

Zoe felt like she was on a double date, sitting next to Rand in the back of the Camry. They'd arrived at the rendezvous site early and waited for their target. The bright green Toyota Prius pulled behind the shopping center. They waited ten more minutes to make sure he hadn't been followed.

"This is how it's going to be, isn't it?" Zoe asked. "Being afraid of someone following me, waiting for an attack at any moment."

Amy turned around in her seat. "Believe it or not, you do kind of get used to it. A little."

"I don't believe it."

Rand ran his fingers down the strip of his goatee. "When you've got a good reason to run, you get used to it out of necessity."

Zoe wasn't sure she wanted to know how he knew that. He hadn't been running from this Darkwell long enough to get used to it yet.

Amy pulled a garage-door opener from the glove box and handed it to Zoe. "Use this when you get back."

Lucas started the car. "Let's move in." He drove around the back, where the Prius had gone.

A short, wiry guy with a big nose jumped out of the car, taking in Amy the way someone who hasn't seen food in a week takes in the sight of a hamburger. He gave her a hug with such abandon, eyes squeezed shut and all, it made Zoe smile.

Ozzie's hair was so shiny and perfect, he reminded her of a Ken doll. When he opened his eyes and saw Lucas, he pushed back from Amy so fast she stumbled. "You're okay. I've been really worried, and these government men have been questioning me, though of course I haven't said anything, and . . ."

"What have they been asking you?"

"If I've heard from you. If I know anything about what you're involved in. For a while they were following me, but I think they finally realized I'm in the dark as much as they are." He looked at Lucas. "This must be the guy you were talking about."

"This is Lucas." Amy nodded toward them. "And this is Zoe and Rand, the two you're taking to Baltimore."

Rand stepped forward and gave the guy a shake of the hand. "Thanks for having our back, dude."

"Uh, yeah, no problem . . . dude."

Zoe also shook his hand, which felt a bit limp. "Yeah . . . what he said." She frowned. Something was making an awful racket. "What's wrong with your car?"

"That would be Orn'ry." Ozzie ran back to his car and opened the rear door.

Amy followed, the only one wearing a smile. The breeze blew her frizzy hair in her face, and she pushed it out of the way as she leaned in the backseat. "Orn'ry!"

The racket stopped, and Zoe heard a long whistle. Amy pulled out a medium-sized cage half-covered with a bright orange blanket. She put her mouth to the wires, and a cockatoo walked over and did some kind parrot-kiss thing. It made clicking noises Zoe took for happy sounds.

Lucas took the cage from her. "I hate to break up happy reunions, but we've got to split."

Orn'ry ran across his perch and tried to bite Lucas's fingers as he carried the cage to the back of the Camry.

Lucas scowled at him. "Hey! Bad bird."

"Kill the bird, kill the bird," Orn'ry said, no doubt mimicking something somebody had said quite often. Obviously not Amy, who looked at him like a mother might look at her child.

Lucas put the cage into the backseat, and Amy followed with a PVC pipe perch.

She gave Ozzie a hug. "Thanks again. For taking care of him and driving our friends to Baltimore . . . for everything."

"I like being involved. Other than taking care of that thing."

Rand held the passenger front door open and waved his hand toward it. Zoe climbed in, and he closed the door for her. So he was a gentleman.

A freaking sexy-as-hell gentleman, a naughty voice whispered, throwing that memory of him naked into her mind.

Ozzie got in, Rand got into the back, and off they went. Men's cologne filled the car. Ozzie turned to her. "So, what do you do?"

Now she knew why Rand let her sit in front. He was tuned out in the backseat, stretched out sideways with his head resting against his crossed arms, eyes closed.

She hated small talk. "I stick people with needles." Waiting a beat she added, "I'm a tattoo artist."

After small talk that studiously avoided details of what he called "the conspiracy," Rand directed Ozzie to an area of town unfamiliar to her. He'd borrowed Eric's cell phone until they could get more untraceable ones, and he made a call. "Hey, Maggie. How are you? . . . Good. How's Chloe? . . . Excellent. . . . Yeah, I know, I haven't been around lately. Look, can you unlock the back entrance? . . . Thanks."

He directed Ozzie to a four-story brick building. "While I'm in Baltimore, I want to get some of my stuff."

"What if they're watching your place?" Zoe asked.

"They can't link it to me. I'm subletting it from an acquaintance who skipped town when the creditors started coming after him. Ozzie, pull around to the back of the parking lot. Never hurts to be careful, though." Rand jumped out. "Be right back."

A curvy woman with blond waves opened the rear entrance. He gave her a kiss on the cheek, and they disappeared inside.

"Is he your boyfriend?" Ozzie asked, making Zoe realize she was staring at the glass door with narrowed eyes.

"No freaking way. I only met him last night."

A few minutes later Rand walked out with two duffel bags. The woman walked out as well, concern on her expression. He handed her something that looked like a wad of cash, and they hugged again before he headed back to the car.

She didn't care about the woman or Rand's love life. So why did the words, "Who was that?" come out of her mouth the moment he got into the car. "Just curious," she added with a shrug, working a little too hard to look casual.

"My neighbor. Her daughter has leukemia. Nice lady, cute kid, damned shame. I'm going to miss them."

Nice lady didn't indicate a romantic attachment. Giving her money was odd, but she wasn't going to comment on that. It was none of her business.

"What's in the bags?"

"Clothes, stuff."

"No fair. I want to go to my place and get my clothes and stuff." She affected a pout because she knew damn well that was impossible. "I know, don't even say it. They *do* know where I live."

Ozzie was paying attention to their conversation and trying hard not to look like he was.

Rand said, "We'll stop at a store, and you can get what you need."

She closed her eyes in bliss. "Hair gel, girl deodorant, clothes . . ."

Rand gave Ozzie directions, and a few minutes later they were in another neighborhood with small houses and nice, normal people living nice, normal lives. "You can drop us here. Thanks, dude."

"No one's ever called me 'dude' before." Ozzie smiled, but it faded. "I think that's good, right?"

She patted his arm. "You're the shit, man." She tried to hide her grin when his expression really got confused. A laugh escaped anyway. "It's all good. Thanks."

"Do you need me to do anything else? Score something for you? Make a drop?"

"We're all set." Rand pulled his bags out of the car.

She followed him around the side of a garage, where he set the bags down and felt along the top of a window frame until he produced a key. He opened the door and again waved for her to precede him.

Okay, he was sort of a gentleman.

She stepped into the gloom. "This place is creepy." Stuff she didn't dare identify piled up to the ceiling, and the whole place smelled musty. The car sitting to one side would only run if God Himself touched His finger to it. She wasn't even sure what kind of car it was. "Uh, how long ago did you leave your car here?"

He laughed when he saw the pile of scrap metal. "That's not mine." He walked over to a dark corner. "This is mine." He pulled on a cord and a bare lightbulb lit the space.

"Oh, no. No freaking way am I getting on that thing."

A motorcycle. Of course!

Rand unlocked the garage door and hoisted it. "I thought you just spent a day on one of these things."

"I just spent like almost *two* days on one of those."

"Then you'd better catch Ozzie and hitch a ride back with him. These are my wheels, doll."

She darted to the street in time to see Ozzie's car turn the corner. With hunched shoulders, she trudged back into the garage. "Can't one thing go my way?"

"On the contrary, it's your lucky day. You get to hang on to me."

Her heart jumped into her throat, and a little vibration spiraled its way down her stomach. He was straddling the bike, looking very James Deanish with a rogue grin, even more roguish considering his bruises.

She cleared her throat, but even so, her voice came out hoarse. "Nice bike. For a bike."

The metallic blue paint flared upward into misty silver accents that reminded her of wind.

"Thanks." He started it and let it run for a few seconds, cocking his head and listening to the engine. It was the quietest bike she'd ever heard. Then he killed the engine.

"You asked what Cheveyo rode. It was a Harley. And no, his wasn't bigger than yours." She gave him a devilish grin of her own. Oh, jeez, she was flirting! She liked flirting when it was fun and not serious. What bothered her was that it felt different with Rand.

Like it might actually go somewhere.

He grinned. "You know how to make a guy feel good."

She wasn't kidding, either. Rand's bike was big, with storage in the back and a comfortable seat for two. "What is this? Not that I know anything about bikes."

"It's a Honda ST1300, what they call a sport touring bike. I call her Blue."

He pushed the bike out of the garage, and after she followed, closed the door. He unhooked one of the helmets, set it on her head, then moved close to secure the strap. She swallowed hard as his fingers brushed the soft skin beneath her chin. "Let's roll, babe."

He put on his helmet and climbed onto the bike. She got on and wrapped her arms around his waist. Her thighs snugged on either side of his hips. Cheveyo hadn't been bad to hold on to. Rand, however, gave her a tingly feeling as their bodies melded together.

"Ready?" he asked.

She rocked her hand. "Ish."

He started the engine and pulled out of the driveway.

This was different from the grueling ride up from Key West. She wasn't scared to death, so that was probably a factor. The guy she was holding on to hadn't turned into a panther before her eyes. The bike itself was a big difference, too. It rode quiet, even when going fast, though the engine had a space-age whine when it accelerated. The windshield kept the wind and bugs from beating her up.

It felt odd being out in the open on a bike. The fresh air and sunshine were nice, though. Not so much the smell of exhaust fumes. Or the feeling of her butt coming off the seat whenever they hit a dip in the road. For all those hours on the back of Cheveyo's bike, she'd seen mostly the back of his helmet and his ponytail. The neat part was watching the reflection of the road falling away.

When they stopped at a light, she asked, "Are you driving like an old lady on my account?"

He turned toward her, and their helmets bumped. "I always drive safe when I've got someone on the bike."

She glanced down and saw their shadow on the

asphalt. Two riders who had been strangers not very long ago.

A few minutes later he pulled into the parking lot of an assisted-living facility that almost made Zoe want to be old. Flowers bloomed everywhere, and people strolled through the gardens and sat on benches beneath trees and played chess. It looked . . . safe. She never thought she'd want a safe, normal life.

She remembered Amy's words: *My life will never be the same again. To be honest, I don't want it to be.*

Pressed against Rand, their bodies damp where they touched, Zoe felt—just for a second—what Amy was talking about. Then she came to her senses.

He pulled around to the far right of the parking lot and tucked the bike into a clump of trees. Wariness replaced his earlier playfulness as he searched the surroundings before removing his helmet.

"I just want to eyeball Gram. I don't want her to see me. I'm not in the state of mind for that right now. But I do want to talk to the manager and let them know . . ." He ran his fingers through his hair, now flattened by the helmet. "What? If some government agent comes in, not to let them talk to her?" Frustration tightened his face.

"I'm going to have the same issue with my grand-dad. We could tell them . . . we could say there's some trouble in the family, and that our uncle Guido has Mafia connections."

He raised his eyebrows at that. "Might work."

Before giving it enough thought to stop herself, she touched his cheek. "If she sees you, she's going to want to know why your face is bruised."

"Oh, crap. I didn't even think about that."

"They're fading but still visible."

He leaned down into the side mirror. "She'll see them. She misses nothing."

She dug into her purse and produced her makeup bag. "Look at me." She held his chin and rubbed on foundation. His green eyes locked onto hers, because at that distance he couldn't really look anywhere else. She tried to focus on the task at hand, which was rubbing her finger along the ridge of a cheekbone most women would kill for. She fought the urge to run her finger down that strip of blond hairs on his chin.

"Randall? Thought I saw your bike come in. What are you doing hiding over there?" The voice came from a distance. A small woman with a slightly hunched back was marching right at them.

Zoe dashed on one more swipe of foundation over the healing cut on his lip and stepped aside.

His grandmother's face brightened. "You brought a girl!" She turned her head and shouted in a voice Zoe couldn't imagine coming from such a small woman, "Randall's got a girlfriend! Nancy, Al, Joe, get over here!"

Rand groaned, lowering his face into his hand. Just before his gram got there, Zoe whispered, "On the contrary, it's *your* lucky day," mirroring his words. "I think this is going to be fun."

A small cluster of old folk came over with as much vigor as his gram did. Rand pulled himself together and stepped forward to give her a hug. "Hi, Gram. This is Zoe. Zoe, this is Ruby."

Ruby took Zoe's hands in a firm hold and gave her a brilliant smile. "This is the first time Randall's ever

brought a girl here. You must be something special."
She looked at Rand. "Why were you hovering over
here? What, you ashamed of your girlfriend? So what
if she's got tats? She's beautiful. Looks like that gal
who played in all those teenage angst movies back in
the eighties."

Rand burst out laughing at that. Maybe this wasn't
going to be as much fun as she thought. He was supposed to be in the hot seat, not her. Zoe forced a smile
because she wasn't going to argue with an old lady.
But Rand was right; Gram missed nothing. In seconds
she'd spotted both her ring and her ankle tattoos,
which made Zoe realize her pant leg had hiked up
during the ride.

Ruby turned her hand to look at her ring tattoo.
"This is going to compete visually with your wedding
ring, you know."

"Ah, I wasn't really planning on getting married."

"Nonsense. Come on, Randall, let's get to know
your girl."

"Uh, Gram, we really don't have—"

Zoe looked back as she was pulled toward the table
where the others Ruby had summoned were heading.
"I was thinking of getting a tattoo right here, Zoe."
She pointed to a spot just above her right breast. "I
want it to say 'Go screw yourself' backward. Then if
someone pisses me off, I can tap it, send 'em the vibe,
or get a mirror."

"That's what I happen to do," Zoe said, grinning at
Ruby's tattoo idea and the impish spark in her eyes.

Ruby's eyes lit up. "You're a tattooer?" She turned

to the others. "She's a tattooer, Randall's girlfriend. Can you believe that?"

Zoe pulled up her other pant leg, and Ruby gasped at the lifelike Dracula tattoo on her calf.

One of the men said, "Oh boy, Rand won't be bringing us any more porno movies."

"Or sexy massage therapists," a tall, Italian man said. He waggled his eyebrows at Zoe. "He always brings us things to liven our spirits."

"And brings prizes he's won for meeting sales quotas that we use for our poker games," Ruby added, pride in her voice.

Zoe turned to Rand. "Sales quotas?"

"For my job at the *communications company*, of course," he said with a pointed smile.

Ah, he wanted her to play along. Interesting. She was pretty sure he didn't work for anyone. Why was he lying?

Ruby patted his shoulder. "He's the top producer in his division. He's always winning all these prizes, and he shares them with us."

Zoe felt a pang for a different reason this time, the motherly pride and affection she saw in Ruby.

"I'm sure he told you that I raised him since he was twelve. Have you met his mother?"

Zoe shook her head.

"Don't blame him for that. Woman's good for nothing, crawled into the bottle after his father died and stayed there. I'm ashamed to even call her my daughter. Randall started hanging with troublemakers, out all hours, and his mother was too stoned to even notice. That's when I stepped in."

"Gram, I need to talk to you . . . alone." Rand nodded away from the group.

She followed Rand and Ruby to another table several yards away.

Ruby took them in with glowing anticipation. "You're pregnant!" She eyed Zoe's flat stomach. "Well, if you're pregnant, then you're getting married. No kid of mine's letting his baby be born without his name."

"No, Gram, it's not that."

Zoe noticed he hadn't corrected her assumption that she was Rand's girl. Then again, how would he explain her presence in his life?

After all, you have seen each other naked, that voice whispered.

She could see Rand's mind working to come up with a story.

"Gram, there's been some trouble at work. Someone was playing with the numbers, and I turned him in."

"Oh, honey . . . like your father? Taking money?"

"Something like that." He was a good enough liar to meet Ruby's eyes, but Zoe could see he didn't like doing it. "The guy has Mafia connections that reach to the government. They know about you, so if any agents come asking about me or telling you stuff—"

"They can go to hell." Her tough expression faded, and she put her palm on Rand's cheek. "Is that why you're beat-up?"

Rand cringed. "A little. But I'm okay. They were just trying to scare me, that's all."

Her eyes narrowed. "What's going to happen if they get serious?"

"I'll be fine. I'm just worried about you."

"I'm a tough old broad. What are you going to do about this business?"

"We're going to be careful, Gram. We'll be fine."

She jerked her thumb back toward her friends. "Joe's got connections, too. I can—"

Rand waved his hand. "No, I don't want anyone else involved."

She looked as though she were going to say something else but released a breath instead. "I know you're capable, and too damned independent, you ask me. But check in, let me know you're okay." She took the two of them in. "So, no other announcements?"

"No, that'll do it. We've got to go. I'll be in touch."

Ruby took his hand in hers, gripping it. "Do that. And be careful. Nothing's worth dying for."

Rand's face softened for a moment, and she could tell his mind had sped off in some other direction. He gave her another hug. "Bye, Gram."

"No 'byes.' Just *see you laters*." Ruby surprised Zoe by giving her a hug, too. "Take care of each other."

They waved to the group and headed to the bike. He gestured to his face. "Thanks for the quick fix. I should have figured she'd spot it."

She paused. "What were you thinking about, when she said nothing's worth dying for?"

He stared beyond her. "I saw Lucas throw himself in front of a bullet for Amy." He shook his head. "I can't imagine that kind of love."

"Wow. Me either." She felt that ache again, remembering how the two shared such a deep connection. It made her uncomfortable. "So what's this about your sales job?"

He tilted his head back. "I knew you weren't going to let that slide."

"I can't." She gave him a grin. "I'm your girlfriend, after all."

He leaned against the bike with a sigh. "It made Gram happy to think I had a girlfriend. Doesn't hurt her to believe in something that makes her happy."

"Like you having a sales job with perks?"

He looked over at Ruby, talking with her friends. "Yeah. It's not that I'm ashamed of gambling for a living. I'm who I am. I'd never change for anybody. I just want to be ambitious and successful for her. It makes her feel good."

"You want to be the good guy."

He looked at her. "I just want to *pretend* to be the good guy . . . for her."

"You send her money. And I saw you give money to your neighbor."

"It's the casino's money. I figure they're due for some giving for a change."

She crossed her arms in front of her and tilted her head. "You like being the hero. Robin Hood."

He took her helmet and settled it on her head. "Not me. I'm the lone Musketeer. All for one, and all for me." He put on his helmet and straddled the bike. "Tell me where your granddad lives."

She climbed on behind him, leaning against his warm back. Who was the real Rand? The one he pretended to be or the one he wanted to be?

CHAPTER 9

DARK MATTER had started rather simply: find Offspring and offer them contracts to be government consultants while he tested their abilities and a bonus if they'd live on-site for the duration. He'd managed to procure a couple of CIA agents who were considered trigger-happy and, therefore, dangerous to put in public situations. He'd had to hire security people with his own money. Gerard had had some success . . . until the Rogues became a problem. Dammit, they were sucking his resources and his patience dry. He'd lost several of his men through death or injury. Instead of having his Offspring move ahead on tactical missions, they had to find the Rogues.

One of his recruited Offspring had zeroed in on Randall Brandenburg earlier. Just a glimpse, but he'd pinpointed his location in Baltimore, and Steele was on his way there to be ready if his subject got more information.

As much as he wanted to blame Steele for letting Zoe Stoker get away, he knew that wasn't fair. These kids were wily, and they had skills Steele didn't. But he would get them. It was only a matter of time.

His phone rang. It was his assistant. "Yes?"

"The program just got a hit. At hospice, where Zoe Stoker's grandfather is."

Some casinos were equipped with facial recognition technology that matched gamblers to a database of faces containing known felons or terrorists. He had plugged Brandenburg's face into their database. That was how he had found Brandenburg in Atlantic City, just before the casino's thugs pummeled him to pulp. Now Gerard had that technology. He was pulling out all the stops, saving his subjects' resources for the important tasks.

He rubbed his lower lip. Stoker and Brandenburg together. That meant she'd hooked up with the Rogues. They kept growing their numbers while his dwindled. His fingers curled. Oh, yeah, he wanted Brandenburg. That would show the Rogues. They'd gone to all that trouble to break him out, and now Gerard was about to nail him. Getting Zoe would be sweet, too, for giving him such a hassle. Mostly he wanted Eric Aruda and Lucas Vanderwyck. And he wanted the mysterious Offspring who'd rescued Stoker.

"Thanks." He hung up and called Steele. "I've got an address. It's a two-for-one."

When Amy saw Petra's relief that she and Lucas had returned to the tomb, she tried to make light of it. "Back safe and sound, no assassins or nothing."

Orn'ry was sitting on her shoulder, and Lucas carried the stand and cage.

Petra was standing on the back edge of the couch, holding the bottom edge of a large painting as she tried to hook it onto the hanger. Uh-oh, she was re-arranging the décor again. "Just like the good old days, leaving on an errand and coming back un-scathed. Except that we're living in a bomb shelter and can't go out and shop, and, oh, people want us dead."

The strain in Petra's clipped words was clear. Amy was sure that seeing her and Lucas together wasn't helping. Petra had accepted that the boy who had grown up as part of her family, but for whom she had harbored romantic feelings, wasn't going to be more than a brother. Still, it probably stung.

Orn'ry hunched in on himself as he took in his sur-roundings. He made a long, humming sound, then nipped her on the nose.

Amy tapped his beak. "Stop that. I know you're pissed at me for leaving you, but you're just going to have to get over it."

Eric burst out of the hallway, his expression hard and tight. "I went to the asylum."

"What?" Lucas said.

Orn'ry squawked at the sudden movement, flap-ping his wings and sending bird-scented air across her face.

He took in the parrot but didn't comment. "Remotely. I wanted to see what was going on. I checked out the rooms, Darkwell's office, everything."

"I thought they had a shield over it."

"They don't need a shield. They're gone."

"Damn." Lucas rubbed the back of his neck, a pained expression on his face. "They probably hauled ass because we knew where they were."

"They're good at finding us," Amy said. "Can't we find them?"

Eric's face reddened. "I don't know how to remote-view without knowing their location. But I'll work on it."

Amy took a deep breath. She was comfortable seeing glows, but communicating with the dead . . . not so much. "I'm going to try to contact Cyrus. After sleeping much last night, I'm tired enough to crash. I'll see if Cyrus knows where Robbins lives. And if he has any ideas where Darkwell might have moved his operation. I want to find out more about the scientist who created the Booster, too. If we find him, we can find out what's in it."

"Do you want me to sit with you again?" Petra asked.

Last time Amy tried to contact Cyrus, Petra had kept her company.

Lucas put his hand on her shoulder. "I'll take care of her."

Petra's expression dimmed. "Good luck."

Amy doubted that Lucas had any inkling how Petra felt about him. Amy sure as heck wasn't going to tell him. She grabbed up the stand and set it in the corner of the bedroom.

Lucas looked ambivalent. "Damned bird's tried to bite me a dozen times."

Amy gave him her sweetest smile. "He'll come to love you just as I do."

He made a grunting sound that she took as *I'm sure he will* because, hey, she was optimistic these days. She nudged Orn'ry into the cage and put his orange blanket over it. "That should quiet him for a bit."

She stretched out on the bed, and Lucas sat beside her. "You look good there."

She recognized the hunger in his eyes, felt warmth spread between her legs. She reached up and ruffled her fingers through his thick, dark waves. "We could—"

"Do this first. I don't want your mind on anything but me and how your body feels as I'm ravaging it with my tongue."

A growl erupted in her throat, mirroring the one deep in her soul. "Deal."

"How does this work?"

"It happens when I go into the hypnagogic state of sleep. Most people have minidreams at that stage. I hear voices, snatches of conversations, words. I don't mind that so much, but sometimes I'll hear my name. When I realized the voices were trying to talk to me, that creeped me out. Cyrus said I'm a channel. That's how he gets through. Unfortunately, that's how others can get through, too. Last night, Gladstone came in. With Zoe showing up, I haven't had a chance to tell you."

Gladstone was the agent assigned to evaluate Lucas, Petra, and Eric, and his hatred of the Offspring would have led to their deaths if Eric hadn't killed him.

He took her hand in his, obviously seeing her fear at that. "What happened?"

"He said, 'You will all be annihilated. I see your destruction.' I was able to shake him off, but . . ."

"But what?"

"With all of this stuff, we just don't know the boundaries."

He rubbed his thumb over her lower lip. "I'll be watching you. If it looks like anything is happening, I'll bring you out." He shook his head. "I hate not having my ability."

"Try coming to my dreams once I fall into REM sleep. Maybe Cheveyo's wrong."

Four months earlier, Lucas had used his dream-weaver ability to seduce her in her dreams. But her optimism only made his eyes darken.

"Lucas, what's going on in your head?"

"Too much." He kissed her nose.

"It has something to do with your captivity, what Darkwell did to you, doesn't it?"

"I don't want to talk about that. Are you ready?"

She let out a long sigh of frustration and hurt. Why wouldn't he share his darkness with her? At least now that the storm of images was gone, she didn't fear that he'd go insane. She knew that was his darkest fear. Once he'd heard about Zoe's father shooting people, Lucas feared he would go crazy and hurt them. She'd overheard him making Eric promise to kill him if he ever showed signs of that kind of instability. The thought of that tightened her throat. Eric wasn't the best judge of mental stability.

She settled back on the pillow and closed her eyes. Lucas stroked her face with his fingertips, lulling her into sleep.

She fell swiftly, and the whispers came. Random words. Nothing scary.

Cyrus? Are you there?

Amy! Is everything all right?

We're surviving. We've got Zoe now.

Thank goodness. I hated dragging her into this, almost as much as I hated dragging you in. It's all my fault—

Cyrus, we don't have time for that. There's a man named

Robbins who works in the program. Do you think he'd tell us what's going on?

Yes, maybe. He got pulled in like I did—reluctantly. If you can get him outside of Darkwell's influence, I think he'd help you.

What can you tell us about him? Where he lives, what he drives?

Years ago he lived in Bethesda, Maryland, but I don't know the address. He drives a black Hummer, the smaller version.

That'll help. Darkwell has moved his operation. Do you have any idea where he'd go?

He's got personal resources; the Darkwells are loaded. Maybe a family property.

You said a scientist created the Booster. Where is he now? What's his name?

He disappeared after the program was dismantled, went into hiding, I suspect. No one's heard from him since. He's probably dead by now. Amy, there's something I need to tell you. It's about your dad. He had an affair with a woman in the program. You remember I told you about the side effect of the Booster, how it ramped up everyone's sexual appetite? So it wasn't strictly his fault. He admitted that he'd gotten her pregnant but wouldn't tell me who it was.

So that means . . . I have a half sibling?

Yes. And, Amy, it might be Lucas.

The shock of that nearly catapulted her out of her dream state. She held on. *No. That can't be.*

There were two men and two women in the first stage of BLUE EYES. Eric's mother was one and Lucas's mother was the other. Both women were pregnant at the time.

What about the second stage?

Darkwell kept them separate. Especially when the side effects became evident.

Cyrus's voice got fainter. Another voice pushed through, taunting and evil, drawing out her name.

Amy. Wait until you're here with me. You will be here, you know. All of you freaks will be here, and I'll be waiting for you!

His anger was so ferocious it pushed her out of sleep. She came to a sitting position, inhaling breath into her tight chest.

Lucas pulled her against him. "What happened? Talk to me."

She squeezed her eyes shut, all of it bombarding her. "Gladstone broke in again. That's why I woke up."

He held her tighter yet. "Are you all right?"

"Lucas . . ." She pulled away and looked at him. The words tumbled out, thick with emotion. "We might be related."

"What?"

"Do you know anything about your birth father?"

He shook his head.

"Cyrus told me my father had an affair with someone in the program, got her pregnant. It's either your mother or Eric and Petra's." She couldn't get her mind around it, that this man she was totally in love with might be her half brother. Her hand went to her mouth. "Maybe that's why we have this connection."

He pulled her close again as her eyes filled with tears. "Shhh. We'll get a DNA test, okay?"

She looked at him. "We can do that?"

"Sure. It's all by mail, so we'll send off for a kit. One of my employees at the art gallery found her birth father, but she wanted to be sure. It was simple. We don't have to tell anyone. We'll have it mailed to the gallery upstairs. They know to stash all pertinent mail in the back room. We'll sneak up through the hidden entrance like Petra does when she trades out the artwork. And until we know . . ." He laid his hand against her cheek. "We'll play it cool."

"I don't want to play it cool. I want you inside me, I want . . . oh, gawd."

She fell against him, feeling the weight at knowing the truth lift off her chest. And feeling it return at the thought of keeping her hands off Lucas until the results came.

Rand rubbed his shirtsleeve over his face the moment they got off the bike.

"What are you doing?" Zoe asked.

"I'm getting this makeup off me." He lifted his helmet. "Look. There's *makeup* on the padding."

She crossed her arms in front of her. "You just thanked me for trying to save you from having to answer some squirmy questions."

He looked at her, tall and lean, not one curve really, and yet sexy galore in her own way. She wore a black, knit top with lacy holes at the shoulders that went to mid-thigh. "I know, but now I'm going to be my bruised self."

He unlocked the bags on his bike and felt around inside one of the duffel bags. He pulled out a light, black jacket and slid it on. Then he knelt again and grabbed hard, cold steel. Glancing around to make sure no one was in sight, he tucked it in the back of his waistband.

"What was that?" she asked in a low voice that indicated she had an idea what it was.

"Just in case."

"I'm beginning to despise those words. Have you ever used it?"

He stood and faced her. "On someone, you mean?"

"Well, that would be good to know."

"No. I've aimed it at a couple of toys pulling beef, though." At her puzzled look, he realized he'd slipped into street jargon. "Kids causing trouble, wanting to fight. I spent a lot of time on the streets before I went to live with Gram. Not sleeping there, thankfully, 'cause I always had someplace to stay. I hated being home. I crashed with these older dudes, spent the night on the couch or the floor. I scored the gun when I was fifteen, unregistered. Crazy to think it now, but I felt like I could handle it. It's good to have some power. I've practiced enough to hit a static target. A moving target, that I don't know. I never tried to shoot someone running away."

"Gee, that's comforting."

She turned toward the hospice building, and he saw her take a deep breath. "Okay, I'll be back in a few minutes."

"Back?" He hooked his helmet to the bike. "I'm going with you."

"You are?" A mix of surprise and relief colored her expression. "You don't have to do that. It's not a fun place."

"I'm not doing it for kicks. When we go out, we stick together. Just in case."

Wait a minute. Was that a protective feeling washing through him, giving him no choice but to accompany her into that building of death?

She-it, it was.

She gave him a soft smile and turned toward the

building. He followed, enjoying the sway of her hips and the little slice of skin that showed between the slits cut into the back of her dress. He could see bits of her tattoo, and he had a stomach-twisting vision of her lying naked on the bed while he explored every line of that she-devil and every inch of those pale long legs.

Seeing her naked had been a kick-ass way to start the day, but it was buggin' on him now, taunting him. It wasn't helping that she'd been wrapped around him on the bike, her breasts pressed against his back, pelvis snugged up against his lower back.

Now this protective feeling, which had nothing to do with being horny, was even more buggin'. At least being horny was a normal state of mind; feeling protective—no way.

And he felt vaguely degenerate walking around with an erection in a building where people were dying.

Yep, he was going to hell.

He expected the place to smell like a hospital, but mostly he picked up on the scent of cooking food. Scattered along the hallways and near the front door were people in wheelchairs. Each room bore the name of the person inside, and in many there were family members visiting. The colors on the walls were clearly meant to be calming: beiges and pastels. When they walked into the section where her grandfather was, the plump woman with pink cheeks smiled. "Hey, sweetie." Her smile softened to one of sympathy. "It's not a good day. He's pretty gone on morphine right now."

He actually ached at the sight of Zoe's pain. She obviously visited her granddad often if the nurse called her that endearment.

"I just want to see him for a few minutes." Zoe leaned against the counter. "There hasn't been anyone come to see him other than the usuals, has there?"

"Nope."

"What happens if someone does come in who's not family?"

"They can't see him. Visitors have to be on the list."

"Even if it was someone, say, from the government?"

Though the woman's curiosity was piqued, she only said, "I would tell anyone that he's not up for visitors. Most of the time that's true anyway."

Zoe's body relaxed. "Thanks." When the woman looked up at Rand, Zoe waved her hand dismissively. "He was in an accident."

She pulled him away from the desk. The woman seemed just as curious about him as she was about Zoe's questions.

She slowed down as she reached the room on the end. Her hand slid out of his, and she took a deep breath.

"I'll stay here," he said.

She chewed her plump bottom lip and, with a nod, walked into the room. Rand found a wall and leaned against it. From there, he could see Zoe walk up to an emaciated man on the bed. He couldn't hear what she was saying; her voice was softer than he'd ever heard it. She, in fact, looked softer than he'd ever seen her, especially with her curls and doe eyes. Vulnerable. He shifted his gaze away, but invariably it slid right back.

He couldn't tell whether her granddad was awake

or not, but she stroked his hand around the IV and tubing and continued to talk to him. Seeing her raw pain gave him an ache worse than the one he'd had when he'd been challenged to a hot-salsa-eating contest—and won. This was why he kept his distance. Now he wanted to go and fix her pain, and dammit, he couldn't take away her granddad's cancer or her pain.

When she said goodbye to him and turned toward the door, Rand looked away. She walked out of the room, wiping her eyes, and killing him . . . just killing him.

"I want to tell him that his son wasn't a crazy murderer," she said, emotion tightening her voice. "I need to tell him that it wasn't Dad's fault. It broke his heart, knowing his son had done that. I need to find out more, so I can relieve him of that before he goes."

Rand thought of his father. If he had embezzled money because his brain wasn't right, which Rand wasn't convinced of, he wasn't sure his mother would ever be sober enough to process it.

After a deep, shuddering breath, Zoe continued on. She kept her focus on the floor, her arms wrapped around her waist. She didn't want him to see her tears or her vulnerability, and he didn't want to see them either. Her chin quivered with the tears she was holding in. Every muscle in his body strained to touch her, to put his arm around her shoulder or, even worse, pull her into his arms.

Cut that out. You do that, then you'll be wanting to do a lot more and you'll get attached, which is going to suck for you and her when you hit the road. Remember how much you hate sympathy. Maybe she does, too.

Don't look at her. Just focus on those ugly sneakers of hers and don't think about her wedding-ring tattoo. Don't look at her face or the way her body is hunched in pain.

He stepped up beside her, his arm brushing ever so slightly against hers. Their gazes met for a moment, and he gave her a smile. The sad little smile she gave him back yanked his lungs right out of his chest.

He looked away as they headed toward the entrance, focusing on those doors sliding open. Then, as they walked out under the portico, on the front tire of his bike peeking out from behind the van he'd used as cover.

Then on the guy in dark shades standing several yards from the bike, talking on the phone . . . the guy watching the entrance.

"I think we got trouble." Rand took her hand and pulled her around to face him so she wouldn't look over and give away their suspicion. He did just as he'd wanted to do earlier, pull her into his arms and give her a consoling hug. "Pretend I'm comforting you, you're all sad, boo hoo. Stay here for a few seconds and let me scope the guy out."

Her voice was warm against his neck. "Is he tall, a bit on the thin side, with brown curly hair? Looks Middle Eastern."

"Yeah. He's got scratches on his face, like a big cat swiped at him."

"Steele. The guy who tried to take me down in the Keys."

Rand wanted to kill him right there but he couldn't just pull out his gun and take aim when he wasn't absolutely sure it was the guy.

"Lean and Lethal's between us and Blue. Let's stroll

this way, see if he follows." He slung his arm around her shoulder, and they walked away from the bike. "I'm pretty good at eluding people. I guess you're pretty good, too. You've ditched these guys twice."

He heard the tremble in her voice when she said, "I got lucky. But how long is my luck going to hold out?"

His arm tightened on her involuntarily. "Remember, it's your lucky day."

That got a smile out of her, albeit a nervous one. Her gaze shifted over his shoulder. "He's coming."

"I saw him." A mix of dread and pressure filled his chest. "What's around the back of this building?"

"A courtyard. Bushes. Old people sitting in the sun."

"Will we be trapped?"

"No, there are spaces between the buildings."

"We need to go around, get out of his sight, and get to Blue. As soon as we turn the corner, he's going to be on us. Are you ready to run?"

Fear tightened her pretty face. "I'll do whatever I need to. I kind of like being alive."

He shot ahead ten seconds.

The zing of a bullet. Zoe's cry. Blood.

No!

He threw his body against hers, twisting to the side so he wouldn't fall on her. "He's shooting at us. Going to shoot at us." He scrambled to his feet and pulled her up.

A bullet chipped the corner of the building.

With her hand still clutched in his, he said, "Time to haul ass."

CHAPTER 10

When Amy and Lucas emerged from the bedroom and walked into the kitchen, he poured two glasses of juice and handed one to her. Their gazes never left each other.

"I'm going to see if I can find anything on Robbins." He went into the office, and she suspected he was also going to look up DNA testing. She could not, would not, believe that they were related.

Petra picked up on their tense mood. "What happened?"

Amy had her arms around herself, and she dropped down onto the couch and tucked into a corner. "Gladstone broke in again. He's becoming more invasive. I don't know how much longer I can communicate with Cyrus before Gladstone becomes dangerous. Cyrus did manage to tell me that he thinks Robbins would cooperate."

Petra said, "Wouldn't that be great, to find someone who could tell us everything."

Eric scowled. "Yeah, right before he shoots us. What about the location?"

"Darkwell's family has a lot of money. They may have homes elsewhere that he could use."

Orn'ry was screeching, and Eric slid a slit-eyed glance toward the hallway. "Chicken, anyone?"

"He'll get used to being here. He's been through a lot, you know," Amy said.

With a grumble, Eric stalked into the kitchen and opened a beer. "We need to get online and find out everything we can about the Darkwell family. With the great war-hero brother recently dying, we should be able to find something."

"Shhh!" Petra lifted her hand as she turned to the television. They all tuned in when they heard Zoe's name.

Zoe and Rand tore through the courtyard, their hands still linked. That connection made it difficult to maneuver around the tables and people, but it gave her a bit of security. She wasn't alone this time.

"That's definitely Steele," she said between gulps of air. "We need to get away from these people. I don't want them shot."

Just as they turned the corner, she glanced back and saw Steele running after them. A nurse yelled something and stepped in front of him.

Zoe's chest hurt with exertion and fear. "Can we make it to Blue?"

"Too open. He'd have a clear shot at us. We need to give him the slip."

He ran to a large, empty pallet leaning against the wall up ahead. They edged between the bushes and the wall. He pressed as close to the wall as he could. She edged in front of him, the pallet scraping her back. Any second Steele would come bounding around the corner.

Rand leaned to the side. "No good. Down."

They dropped to their knees, him guiding her to the ground and squeezing next to her. He was so close she could feel his pounding heartbeat as though it came from her. Their bodies, now damp and heated, pressed against each other from hip to chest. Her legs straddled his, thigh to thigh. She felt a long, hard ridge pressed into her hip. Was that—? No, had to be her imagination.

Steele's footsteps crunched through the grass.

Something nearby fell to the ground. Her face was tucked into the crook of Rand's neck, her head tilted upward so their eyes locked. She saw the question in his eyes: *Your crazy energy?* She shook her head. *I don't know.*

Very slowly, he moved his other hand around to his back. The gun. His eyes widened. He looked to his left. She followed his gaze . . . to where the gun lay several feet away. It must have fallen when they'd slid against the wall.

Steele slowed his steps. "I know you're here, you crazy bitch. My watch is going whacked."

She squeezed her eyes shut. *St. Thomas. St. Martin.*

She couldn't see through the bushes, but she glimpsed movement. Rand's fingers tightened on her back, pressed against the flesh between the slits of her dress. It was only then that she realized her hands were on Rand, too, gripping him. She relaxed her fingers.

Steele's footsteps moved past them. Rand swiveled his head a fraction of an inch, perhaps eyeing a gap in the bushes. Was he gone?

Another sound. Yes, probably her crazy energy.

Got to control it. Come on, you're the control freak.

Lean and Lethal, as Rand had called him, spoke from a few feet away. "It's Steele. Put your viewer to work. They're hiding here somewhere."

Viewer! Petra had said they had the ability to spy psychically. Someone was going to see them. They'd be trapped. No way could Rand get to the gun before Steele would take them out.

His eyes were as wide as hers. He knew what that meant, too.

Wait. Cheveyo had told Petra about putting up a shield. What had he said?

"You see them?" Steele said. "Good. Give me a clue."

A golden shield. Things bouncing off it. Hold the image.

For those seconds, though, until the shield took effect, their enemy could still see them.

Stay calm. Don't freak out, that's what he told Petra. She closed her eyes, laid her cheek against Rand, and concentrated. The smell of his body heat filled her senses.

Golden shield.

"Wood? Like stacks of wood? Looks like they're doing some kind of construction around the back."

If the viewer saw the pallet, they'd be done for.

Things bouncing off.

Bouncing.

Ten seconds.

"What do you mean, you lost them?" His footsteps moved away. "Get them back."

Rand leaned a little to the right. "Get ready." His pupils shrank to pinpoints. "He's going to walk around the corner in six seconds. We're going to get up, and I'll grab the gun. We'll go back the way we came."

She nodded, brushing against his chin.

"One. Two. Three."

They climbed out, he grabbed the gun, and they took off.

They rounded the front corner. With a glance behind them, they sprinted across the parking lot in a crouch. They crossed the far section of the lot, ducking behind the row of vehicles at the outer edge.

She'd never been so happy to see a motorcycle.

"Put your helmet on," he whispered, as they took the last steps to it. "If he chases us, we've got the advantage of mobility. But we're vulnerable out in the open."

So much for comfort.

She pulled on the helmet and climbed on as fast as he did. He kept an eye on the corner of the cluster of buildings where Steele was. His pupils shrank again.

He started the bike and rode on the strip of grass at the edge of the lot to keep out of sight. As soon as he reached the end of the row, he darted right and gunned it to the entrance. She dared a look back. No sign of Steele.

Rand didn't bother stopping at the entrance to the parking lot. He rolled right into the stream of traffic.

An oncoming car screeched its tires, making a U-turn. A coincidence?

No way. The black sedan was coming up on them fast, cutting off a truck to pass another car.

"Hold on, babe," Rand yelled.

She hadn't even caught her breath from the last escape, and here came another one. The man behind the wheel wore sunglasses. Something about him and the way he drove meant business.

Rand jerked the bike to the left and shot down the center line. He reached the intersection ahead. Traffic going in their direction stopped for the red light. He cut in front of the car to their right and tore down that road. She peered over his shoulder. He was going eighty. Eighty-five. *Ninety.*

She looked behind them. No sign of the car. Why was he still screaming down the highway? His body was hard as a rock. She held on tighter, burying her face against his back.

Two more minutes flew by as he raced down the highway, passing cars, running yellow lights.

No one was behind them.

Finally, she screamed, "Rand, why are we still going like a bat out of hell?" When he didn't respond, she patted his stomach, as far as she dared remove her hand from him. "Rand!"

His head jerked as though he'd come out of a trance. She felt his body loosen. He stopped at a light, the first one in several minutes. He looked behind them.

"We lost him years ago."

Without a word, he turned into the shopping center on their right. He pulled behind the building and came to a stop. She jumped off, removed her helmet, knelt, and kissed the asphalt.

When she got up and wiped asphalt crumbs from her lips, he still hadn't moved. The engine was running, his legs bracing the bike.

She walked up to him, leaning in front of his face. "Are you all right?"

He stared ahead.

She waved her hand in front of him. "Rand?"

He killed the engine, but he was much slower in

taking off his helmet. He set it on the ground, running his hands through his hair. He sucked in deep breaths, just staring into the distance. Finally, he looked at her. "You all right?"

"Right now it's you I'm worried about. You were in a trance."

He shook his head. "I got waked out. All I could think about was getting away. Just going and going and going. With you on the bike. Dammit, stupid, reckless . . ." He slapped himself on the head.

She put her hand on his arm. "Stop it. You got us out of there."

"Yeah. I did." A ghost of a smile hinted at the corners of his mouth but just as quickly faded. "But I almost got you killed, too."

"I'm okay." She lifted her arms. "See?"

His gaze looked hungry as he did, indeed, see her. An answering hunger tingled through her body right down between her legs.

She had to know. "Rand, when we were pressed against each other . . . I thought I felt . . . did you . . ." *Hell, just say it.* "Were you *aroused*?"

His mouth quirked. "You know how things fly when you get excited? Like whatever you were sending to the ground? Whenever there's risk or danger, my energy goes elsewhere. Has since I hit puberty. I used to bug about it big-time, especially when I realized other guys didn't have such an extreme reaction. I got used to it. Eric told me it's a side effect of the Booster they gave our parents. It makes us hypersexual." He took a step closer, heat in his eyes. "Does danger jump you up?"

Oh, yes. She'd been aware of his body pressed

against hers. If she'd been a guy, would she have had a hard-on? "I don't know." She took a step back.

"Can you have multiple orgasms? I guess it's not all that unusual for girls—"

"Can you?"

"Yeah." He smiled. "I can go all night long. How about you?"

It was hard to think about her last sexual relations with Rand so close. "I . . . I don't think I'm hypersexual. I like sex when it's done right, but having sex is more personal than I want to get with someone." She wanted to make love to someone she had feelings for, but because of her freakiness, she couldn't let herself have feelings. A cruel paradox. "I'm not into casual sex so much." But sometimes the urge, the hunger, overcame her. "Maybe it does jump me up, as you put it, but I control it." Most of the time. "I have to control everything, or I'll have some explaining to do."

Rand edged closer. "So it's not only anger or fear that sets off your crazy energy?"

"It's joy, extreme physical pleasure—"

"Orgasms?" he asked with a lift of his eyebrow, making his spike glint in the light. He let loose with a grin that tickled her stomach. "I'll bet having sex with you is wild."

Her face flushed. "Not for me. I've got to hold on so tight to control my passion, worrying about something flying."

The green of his eyes were as liquid as the sea in one of her Caribbean posters. "You know, with me you wouldn't have to—" His pupils dilated for a second, then shrank. "She-it!" He flung himself away and snatched up his helmet.

"What was that about?"

"Let's get back to the tomb."

She grabbed his arm just as he was about to jam his helmet back onto his head. "Not until you tell me what that was about."

He leaned down into her face. "You really want to know?"

"I wouldn't have asked if I didn't."

"I saw us in a serious lip lock. In ten seconds we'd have been tongue dancing."

She blinked, backing up a step without even thinking about it. "That's crazy." No, it totally wasn't. Her body had been leaning, actually *leaning*, toward him as he spoke those last words, and she didn't have to see the future to know what he was going to say. With him, she wouldn't have to hold back. He understood what her crazy energy was about. And more tantalizing yet, he was okay with it.

A pit inside her stomach yawned open, like a cat wakening from a long sleep. It was awake, and it was hungry. *Meow.* It wanted to growl and scream and completely let go.

"Crazy," he agreed, "and foolish and has *bad* painted all over it in cherry red."

"Well, I wasn't going to go that far."

He walked to his bike, twisting his hand around the grip. She saw something on his expression, though, as he stared at the highway beyond, something fierce and afraid. Like he wanted to be there—away—more than anything.

Without looking at her, he said, "I work alone. That's how I like it. I don't want this . . . this thing happening between us. I don't want to be responsible for someone, to worry about them, to do stupid things to risk their life." He looked at her finally. "I am reckless. I'm a risk taker. I never involve anyone else in that, though. I *never* put someone else at risk. That's why I work and live alone."

It scared him that he'd put her at risk. She could see that in his eyes and the tension in his face. "You were just getting us out of there."

He wasn't buying it. He was mad at himself for putting her at risk. And it hit her. He was mad at himself for caring about her safety. For wanting to kiss her. Even worse, it scared him in a way that flying down a highway going ninety miles an hour on a motorcycle didn't.

He straddled the bike, his jeans pulling tight over his thighs. "I owe these guys my help. They pulled me out of that asylum. But after that, I'm out of there. I can't be locked up in some bomb shelter." *Or tied to one woman.* He didn't say it, but she knew that's what he was thinking.

She crossed her arms over her chest. "Look, I don't want anything . . ." She gestured between them. "I may not be able to control my ability, if that's what it actually is, but I can damn sure control my feelings and my body. I've been doing it for a long time. There will not be a kiss, so don't look so worried about it."

"I'm not worried about it."

"No, you weren't worried. You know what's funny? You weren't afraid when we were hiding from an assassin or running for our lives, but it scared the hell out of you when you almost kissed me. You tell me you're a risk taker, but kissing me is a cliff you can't jump off. Why is that, Rand?"

He yanked on his helmet. When he started the bike, she thought he might just leave her there. She stood, waiting to see what he'd do. He gunned the engine, pulled up the kickstand, and tensed his body to go.

Her heart was thumping, but not out of fear that he'd take off. A can skidded across the asphalt and bounced off the building. *Calm down, Zoe.* She couldn't believe she'd said what she'd said to him. She couldn't believe that he was getting to her. She wanted to engage him, force him to face his demons, to stand naked before her . . . metaphorically speaking.

And otherwise. She wanted to have wild, crazy, mating-panther-claws-out sex with him.

A piece of cardboard lifted off the ground and spiraled through the air. There wasn't a lick of breeze.

He looked at her. Their gazes held, though through the plastic shield she couldn't see his eyes clearly. He waited. She held her smile in check and put on her helmet in a much calmer way than he just had. She didn't exactly take her time, but she didn't rush. Their bodies melded when she climbed on, damp and hot, and she wrapped her arms around his waist, fingers splayed over his stomach. It felt right. Too right.

He drove like a little old lady again. He cared about her, but he sure didn't want to. That went two ways. She didn't want to feel anything toward him either. The physical aspect was easier to face up to. She could still feel the imprint of his arousal against her hip, still feel the tingle at the thought. Was it only the danger that had stimulated him, or did it have to do with being pressed against her?

CHAPTER 11

F reedom. The word loomed large in Rand's mind as he and Zoe thudded down the dimly lit tunnel toward the tomb. An appropriate word, that. He'd never been tied down in any way. Now he was hiding belowground and—he glanced over at her silhouette walking beside him—feeling a pressure in his chest he'd never felt before.

Claustrophobia closed his throat.

The crinkle of bags Zoe carried echoed off the walls. She'd asked to stop at a shopping center on the way home so she could buy stuff. After what she'd been through, he could hardly refuse.

Only one of the things that ate away at him. He'd always been able to say no. Twice she'd gotten him to give in, and without even resorting to crying, a blackmail tactic he despised. No, she'd just looked at him with those big hazel eyes, and he'd crumbled.

"What is in there that's clinking?" She pointed to his duffel bags.

"Cans of hair spray."

"Really? Boy, you use more product than I do."

Petra was waiting by the big slab of a door. Her gaze went right to the bags. "You went *shopping*?" That last word was a mix of accusation and longing.

"I needed clothes and hair stuff."

Petra pouted. "No fair! That cute little Novelties boutique just right up there is having a sale, and I can't go."

Rand rolled his eyes. He'd had to endure Zoe buying panties, and the woman didn't buy those cotton ones with roses on them. No, she had to buy black lace and pink-with-ribbons *thongs*. Having seen her in one didn't help.

"Didn't Lucas and Amy come back?" He'd been concerned to find the car still gone.

"Yes, but they went back out again. She needed bird food, and they weren't exactly in a fun mood, so I didn't tag along."

Rand had to admit, though, that Petra had done a lot to make the tomb homey, or at least interesting. The vivid colors brightened the big space, as did the paintings. Eric lounged on the couch, feet on the coffee table, watching a soccer game. And from somewhere in the back, the racket they'd heard coming from the car: the parrot.

"We had a run-in with two of Darkwell's thugs," Rand said, capturing their attention.

Eric sat up, scanning them for injuries. "You're all right?"

Zoe dropped her bags by the stairwell and stretched out on the gray carpet. "Rand did some kick-ass motorcycle riding."

He chafed at the compliment, still pissed at himself for getting waked out with her on the bike. He let her tell them what happened, watching her expression and the sensual way her body moved as she acted out some of the motions. She left out the part about him zoning; all he heard was her praise of his riding skills.

Even while he trashed his recklessness and reminded himself that he'd be on his own again soon, something else crept in, too. Her earlier accusation that he wanted to be a hero echoed in his mind and reverberated through his body. He'd helped save them. He'd ridden well enough to get away from their pursuers.

Don't go there. These aren't your people. She's not your girl, no matter how natural she felt riding with you today.

Thankfully she also left out the bits about him having a hard-on and her challenge that kissing her was a cliff he couldn't jump from. He wasn't scared of much beyond being tied down or locked up. Yet, it had never occurred to him to haul ass or do anything but keep Zoe with him. To protect her. For several moments back at hospice, his fear centered on not what might happen to him but what might happen to her. The thought of that scared him more than anything.

Getting attached to someone was a risk he wasn't willing to take. Ever.

Petra wrapped her arms around herself. "So they can remote-view any of us now. That's scary."

Rand pulled out of his dark thoughts. "Apparently. We heard the guy asking someone to view us."

Zoe's face glowed. "And that shield thing Cheveyo told you about worked!"

Rand said, "Whenever we go out, it's got to be a quick trip. This Steele guy's just going to be hanging around waiting for word on our whereabouts.

We have to get in and out before he can reach our location."

Eric's face reddened, and his fists clenched. "We need to take this Steele son of a bitch out."

Petra cracked her knuckles. "But there'll be more of them. There are at least two. Who knows how many more assassins he has? Plus the Offspring. How can we win?" Her voice rose with each sentence, her blue eyes widening. "Eventually, they're going to get us."

Eric shot her a quelling look. "We kill them all, that's how. One by one."

Rand stuffed the tips of his fingers into his front pockets. "One at a time is our best bet, considering how the last infiltration went."

"At least we took out several of them at once." Eric's bloodlust burned in his eyes. "Unfortunately, they seem to have the same shield around their location that supposedly this Cheveyo guy put on us, according to Miss Doe Eyes over here."

Petra flipped her blond hair over her shoulder. "I'm not doe-eyed."

"Every time you mention the guy, your voice gets all gooey, and your eyes get all dewy." He snorted in laughter. "Gooey and dewy."

She crossed her arms and pushed her mouth out in a pout. "I do not get gooey."

Eric kept teasing her, typical sibling stuff, Rand imagined. Even though Eric was now in a teasing mood, Rand would never forget the sight of him pummeling that guard at the asylum, waked out in his own zone. Even harder to forget was the fact that he himself had shot a man. Had he killed him? Enemy or not, he had shot another human being.

He'd hear that gasp of pain in his nightmares for a long time.

Eric, on the other hand, appeared to enjoy the prospect of killing.

Petra picked up one of the accent pillows and threw it at Eric. "Stop!" She dropped down on the couch again, her expression changing to pensive. "Eric, we need to tell Zoe about the news report." She looked at Zoe. "The Key West police found an abandoned VW Bug and traced it to Ronald somebody or another. He, in turn, told them about your hasty purchase and request for him to keep it quiet."

Zoe let out a breath. "What do they think?"

"Apparently they talked to someone at your tattoo shop, and he said a guy was stalking you. You're a missing person."

"Great."

Eric dismissed her concern with a wave. "It'll die down before long, and everyone will forget." He looked at Rand. "Sit down, will you? You look like you're about to sprint."

Eric was right. Rand's body was tensed and ready. He sank to the edge of the couch, his body still unwilling to commit to a comfortable position. Zoe scooted closer to the table, remaining on the floor.

Eric said, "Lucas looked on the Internet for anything on Robbins. He was quoted in an interview, but that's it. He's not listed in the phone directory. I couldn't find anything on Darkwell either. We're going to focus on finding more Offspring who can hopefully help us get Robbins. This guy's a good bet."

Eric pulled a folder from the corner of the coffee

table and opened it. "Amy got onto Cyrus's computer before he died. She saw three profiles. Rand, you were one. These are the other two. We know that a male and a female Offspring work with Darkwell. We've got to be prepared that one of the two men in these profiles could be our enemy. Nicholas Braden works at a marine salvage company and volunteers at Bone Finders, an organization that finds dead people."

Petra wrinkled her nose. "Ew."

"He helps the cops find the remains of missing people. And according to what I've been able to find on the Internet, he's damned good. I bet there's a reason for that."

Rand read one of the sheets of paper. "He specializes in finding bodies and other items underwater."

Zoe shuddered, rubbing her hands over her arms. "I can't imagine anything creepier than diving in water *and* finding a body."

Rand gave a look of understanding. "The guy finds people. Maybe he can find Robbins."

"Exactamundo."

Rand set the sheet back on the table. "So what's the plan?"

Petra said, "Not grabbing him in the dark. Take it from me, it's pretty disconcerting."

"But effective," Zoe said. "If Cheveyo hadn't grabbed you and covered your mouth, you would have screamed your head off."

Eric's eyebrows furrowed. "If this guy dives and does salvage work, I'm betting he's not a weakling. We need to watch him first, make sure he's not one of them."

"I can do that." Rand's body strained to leave right

then. He relaxed his muscles. "Do we know what he looks like?"

Eric shook his head. "Amy saw their profiles, but she didn't have time to get a good look at the pictures. We have an address. He lives in Annapolis."

Rand stood. "I'll go tonight, see who comes home. Then I'll return in the morning, follow him."

If he helped them get more Offspring, he'd feel better about leaving. He glanced at Zoe, who watched him in a worried way. He had to get out of there before something really dangerous happened. Before he started caring.

Rand didn't return to the tomb until nearly midnight. Zoe, passing time with the others, had begun to wonder if he'd return at all. That thought twisted her stomach until she remembered his promise to help the Rogues because they had saved him. She knew he kept his word.

His hair was mussed, as though he'd run his fingers through it to fluff it up after wearing the helmet. His gaze went right to her, but he quickly shifted it to the others in the living area. "I found Braden's house. It was dark, no activity." He dropped down on the floor near Zoe. He smelled of fresh air, of wind and freedom, and she felt a curious pang at not having gone with him.

You hate motorcycles, remember?

Lucas tossed a pen in the air and caught it. "He could be on vacation. Or on assignment. We'll call the salvage company tomorrow, see if we can find out anything."

Lucas and Amy had been acting strange all evening.

Even Eric had asked if they'd had a fight. They didn't share those casual touches, like the brush of a hand across a derriere that Zoe had noticed with longing. Yet Lucas still seemed protective of her, sharing intense looks that seemed to ask, *Are you all right?* Something was definitely up, but they weren't sharing.

Eric asked, "You're going back tomorrow morning?"

"Yeah, early. If he's there, I'll catch him leaving, follow him."

"Don't approach him yet. We've been working on a plan."

Rand sank down to the couch. "Hit me with it."

"First, we need to find out if this guy is actually an Offspring. We need Amy for that."

Amy said, "Remember, Offspring have mixed-color glows."

Lucas put his hand on her arm. "We're going to knock on his door, tell him we've heard about his special skills from a CIA friend, see if we get any reaction to that. Maybe they've approached him, and he's turned them down. If he's working with them already, we should see some kind of response, even if it's as subtle as a twitch of his eye. If he's not working with them, he should be intrigued by our knowledge of his special skill, which is probably locating. We present the facts, the program, his parent, and draw him in."

Rand stretched out his legs, clad in tight jeans. "I'm sure you've got a backup plan in case he's either one of them or being watched."

"You, Eric, Zoe, and Petra are all going to be lookouts, posted in the area. If you see a sign of anything, ring my phone. It'll be on vibrate and in my hand."

"St. Martin, Negril, Montego Bay," Zoe whispered, looking away.

"What'd you call me?" Rand gave her a smile that referenced their first meeting.

She could barely smile back. *Talk of lookouts and bad guys . . . holy crap.*

A popping sound sent everyone's gaze to Petra, who pulled her hands away before Eric could stop her. She started braiding her hair instead. "I don't want to be a lookout. Even when you think it's safe to be outside the action, men with guns show up and the plan goes wrong and—"

Eric pressed his hand over her mouth. "You really got to stop doing that, too."

"I can't crack my knuckles, can't talk—what *can* I do, bossy little brother?"

"Hum. I've heard you sing in the shower. You're good."

Her face flushed.

Eric walked to his room and returned a minute later with a big plastic bag bearing a drugstore's logo. Like a kid with his Halloween candy, he dumped the contents on the table.

Lucas picked up one of the many boxes. "Hair dye?"

"They know what we look like. You and Amy especially need to modify your looks." Eric looked at Zoe and Rand. "You guys have distinctive hair. Even though you're only lookouts, you should change it up."

Zoe grimaced as she picked through the selection. "I've tried different colors, believe me. I don't look good in anything but shades of red."

"This isn't about looking good," Eric said. "It's about surviving."

Petra grabbed a hank of her hair as though someone were threatening with scissors. "I'm not dyeing my hair. I'll braid it, pin it up, whatever, but I'm not messing with it."

Eric made a scissor gesture with his fingers. "How 'bout I chop it off?"

Petra stalked off, holding her long hair as though she expected him to come after her. He rolled his eyes and gestured to the table. "I printed out a map."

Zoe grabbed a box of black dye and pushed to her feet. "I'm going downstairs. See you all in the morning."

They all bade her good night. How freaking odd it was, living with a bunch of strangers, suddenly having a bond with all these different people.

She wasn't tired. She usually didn't stop working until midnight. She needed space. A sense of control. Planning the approach to Braden wasn't her area of expertise, and Eric had shot down the two ideas she'd suggested earlier. She ached to return to her shop, to give some orders, to do tattoos.

She went down to her room and pulled out the pens and notepad she'd bought. Doodling to her was like snacking to other people. It kept her fingers busy and her head clear. Most of her doodles were movie monsters, and sometimes they incorporated her dream of going to the islands. Frankenstein climbed a palm tree, or Dracula floated on a raft.

She sat on the bed, but the room was oppressive with its silence, gray walls, and no windows. She hooked up her iPod to the speaker unit that looked like a dog, and carried them out to the downstairs living area. Opposite the gym area were a couch and coffee table, presumably to give the three families who would be living there post–nuclear war a little space. She was grateful for that.

She curled up in the corner of the couch, her note-pad resting against her thighs, and started to draw. Her favorite music filled the room, and the dog danced along. Doing something familiar gave her such a sharp sense of comfort it nearly brought tears to her eyes. Today she'd almost died; tonight she was in a quiet space doing something she loved.

Her peace of mind didn't last long. Rand's foot-steps sounded on the stairs, and he appeared in the opening. He paused at the sight of her—okay, her cin-namon tank top did dip a bit low in the front—and continued to his room.

She let out a breath, not sure if she was disap-pointed or relieved that he didn't stay and talk to her. She knew where he stood where she was concerned. Really, the last thing she needed was to get involved with anyone, especially someone who had plans to sprint the moment he could.

The problem was she couldn't get his little com-ment about having multiple orgasms out of her mind. The sight of that gorgeous naked body of his, coupled with that thought, was making her restless.

So it was disappointment she'd felt when he'd passed her by. Her heart jumped when he reappeared wearing shorts and sneakers and nothing else. She raised an eyebrow at his lack of apparel, but before she could comment, he walked over to the gym equip-ment and settled onto one of the benches.

Crap, he was going to work out. He was going to get sweaty, and his muscles would be working, and she wasn't going to get any doodling done. Or get any peace of mind.

A piece of mind isn't what you want, kid.

She blinked at the outrageous thought. *Calm it down, or you'll blow up your iPod.* He pulled down on the lat bar, his muscles flexing just as she'd imagined. *Damn.* Her eyebrows were furrowed into a frustrated frown when he looked over at her.

"What are you listening to? Either I'm waked out, or that is not English or Spanish."

She smiled. "Makes perfect sense to me."

He waited her out. She added nothing but an ingenuous look.

"Seriously, what is this noise?"

"No need to get testy. It's Russian."

"Russian?" He pulled down the bar for several more reps. Then he stopped and looked at her again. "Russian?"

Her mouth curled into a smile. "I dated this Russian guy, and he turned me on to his music. This was what was popular on the radio at the time."

Now *his* eyebrows furrowed. "Dated? You're not seeing him anymore?"

"No, that was a couple of years ago."

He lifted an eyebrow. "And you're still hung up on him? That's sad."

She wrinkled her nose. "I still love the music. I like not having the words to distract me."

He did another set before moving onto the biceps curl station. *Great. Biceps.* She loved biceps, bulging, well-defined, tanned biceps. And something she'd never admit to anyone: she liked armpits. Nice, clean, with soft hair, and that creamy length of skin just beneath it.

Zoe, you're salivating.

A pen sitting on the end table moved.

"Russian guy," he muttered, shaking his head as he grimaced in exertion.

She set her notepad aside and propped her leg up on her knee, pen clenched in her teeth. "He was hot, too."

His pace stepped up just the slightest bit.

She continued. "I think Russian men are better lovers than Latin men."

His jaw tightened, and his face reddened.

"His name was Vladimir. And boy, he was well . . ." She let that hang for a moment, and then finished. "Off. Had lots of money."

The weights dropped with a thud. He turned to her very deliberately. "Stop talking. You're distracting me."

Back at ya, babe.

He moved on to leg lifts, purposely ignoring her.

She couldn't help the grin on her face. God, she loved flirting. She supposed she was a bit of a tease since she rarely followed through. Still, it felt good now, giving him a bit of frustration back. Because damn, he had nice legs, too, dusted with golden blond hairs that caught the light.

She pulled her notepad back, scratching loops, but with a better idea in mind. She let him sink into his thoughts and pretend to ignore her even though she saw his gaze slide her way every so often.

She focused on the small towel he'd slung over the back of one of the benches. It lifted slightly. Fell back.

She tried again. All it did was shift over an inch. She blew out a breath and tried again.

Feeling him looking at her, she met his gaze and gave him a bland smile. He must have sensed she was up to something because he narrowed his eyes at her. She went back to her notepad and waited for him to detach the lat bar and replace it with a rope thing. He grasped each end of that and pulled down. Then she stared at that towel harder than she'd ever stared at anything.

It jumped! She went at it again, and it popped off the seat and onto the floor. Rand hadn't noticed, so she stifled her whoop of triumph. He finished his set and rested. The triangular piece with the handles was still swaying from when he'd released it. She focused on that. Though it already had momentum, she saw it twist against its natural rhythm.

He grabbed it again and did another set. She got momentarily distracted from task by the sound of his labored breathing. Wouldn't he sound like that while thrusting into a woman—not her, of course—and perhaps even grimacing like he was, and . . .

The pen fell off the table.

Focus!

He let go of the piece, stood, and stilled the movement. As he began to step out from the machine, she sent a blast of energy toward it.

It swung over and knocked him in the temple. He stared at it. Zoe held in the snort of laughter that so wanted to escape. His gaze slid to her just as she held the notepad in front of her face.

She coughed, covering the sound of her laughter, and managed to give him yet another innocent look. "Is the music bothering you?" She tilted her head. "I've polluted it with the image of me and a hot Russian guy going at it, haven't I?"

He choked at that, pounding his fist against his chest.

"Here, I'll switch it if it bothers you that much." She changed to another play list. The Pussycat Dolls started singing "Don't Cha."

Oh, yeah, she was evil.

In a good way, she quickly added, thinking of her mother.

Berlin started the next song with a whispered, "Sex . . ."

Zoe averted her gaze to her notepad, pretending to concentrate on the scribbled mess on her page. From the corner of her eye she saw him staring at her, but damn, she was good; she kept her gaze on the page. So she'd accidentally picked the "Sex Me Up" playlist. *Oopsie.*

Just as he started working on pull-ups, she sang along with the song here and there. "I'm a bitch . . . I'm a virgin . . ."

His groans of exertion grew a little louder. Oh, yes, his body was responding. She held up the notepad when her smile threatened to break loose, though she managed to maintain it because she had exquisite control over her physical body.

Well, most of the time.

Rand had an effect on her, and this teasing was just one symptom. What made it safe was knowing that he wouldn't act on his desire, not after what he'd said that day.

She studied the gym equipment, wondering what else she could practice her skills on.

I wonder if I could pull his shorts down.

She almost lost it at that.

He picked up the towel, wiped his face, and tossed it over a nearby bar. He climbed up for another set of pull-ups.

The towel jumped straight up, making him jump, too.

He swung around with a look of such consternation, she did burst out laughing.

"I'm practicing my skills," she said, before he could possibly suggest *she* was the one who was aroused.

"On me."

She nodded, another gale of laughter overtaking her. He stalked over, but she was helpless to regain her composure. He reminded her of Cheveyo in panther mode, his eyes narrowed, his body moving fluidly as he closed in on her.

He stopped in front of her, his legs against hers, and leaned down in her face. He planted his hands on either side of her. She expected that he'd tell her off.

He kissed her instead.

Oh, not just any kiss, either, but a full-on, lip-lock, tongue-dancing kiss with just a touch of aggression.

She wasn't laughing now.

Her body had done a somersault, going from delirious to delirium in one second flat. Her mouth wasted no time in switching gears, taking in his tongue with hers. He tasted of toothpaste, fresh and minty. Her hands slammed against his slick skin, pressing against his chest but no, not pushing him away. She loved the feel of a man's body, the ridges of his chest, the soft skin on his sides, all hard and firm and muscular. Her thumbs brushed his nipples, and his breath hitched. She couldn't help grinning at the power of doing that to him.

Until he did it to her. He caressed her with one hand, then he slid it beneath her shirt and let out a sound of surprise when he found that she wasn't wearing a bra. That touch sent a direct line of heat straight down between her legs. He kneaded her breast, a firm but gentle pressure that she involuntarily moved into. He traced her nipple with his thumb, and suddenly she couldn't breathe. Just like that she'd lost control.

And speaking of . . . her notepad jumped off the couch.

She slid her hands around to his back and down to the waistband of his shorts. Her fingers dipped beneath the band, teasing along the edge. He squeezed her breast a little more hungrily. And the things he was doing with his tongue, teasing along the rim of her lips, nibbling . . .

Then her pen went flying. She had to get back in control of herself and this situation. She jammed her hands all the way down his pants, grabbing on to his cool, tight butt. He groaned, a soft, low sound that reverberated in her mouth. His hand went lower, across her stomach and down to the waistband of her shorts. *Oh, hell.* The way she was throbbing, if he even so much as brushed her clitoris, she was going to lose it. She moved her hands around to the sides of his hips, then to the front, her splayed fingers touching the edge of his springy hairs. His fingers were already burrowing into her pubic hair, moving closer, closer . . .

How far did she want to go in this game? Would the one who lost control really be the loser?

He pulled back enough to look at her, his green eyes heavy with lust. "I just jumped off the cliff." His breath came heavily. "How deep do you want me to dive?"

This wasn't teasing anymore. A hungry glint lit his eyes, and he knew he had the upper hand now. *Damn him.*

As Outkast sang "The Way You Move," she tried to catch her breath as she met his gaze.

"As deep as you want to go." Where had those words come from?

He obviously hadn't been expecting that response. She saw his mind working, weighing, agonizing, then he pushed away. "You're not into casual sex, and I'm hitting the road before long."

He returned to the machine and focused on sit-ups. Totally focused. His expression was fierce, and so were the ridges of his stomach as he relentlessly pulled up and down, up and down.

He was pissed. Because she'd called his bluff? Or because he hadn't gone diving?

CHAPTER 12

Zoe woke, blinking in the darkness. She hated not knowing the time by how high the sun was. The digital clock read 10:00. Rand was supposed to head out early and monitor Braden's house that morning. Was he back?

She hoped so. Waiting for him to return, only because she was concerned about his safety, was hell. She pulled herself out of bed and turned on the light. Though she'd had fun teasing him last night, she didn't want to push him too far.

"Get having sex with him out of your mind," she muttered as she threw on a robe and made her bed. "Going there is a bad idea."

She turned on her iPod dog and carried it to the bathroom. With her hand paused at the doorknob, she knocked.

No answer. She opened it and clicked on the light, smelling the lingering scent of men's deodorant and hair dye. Stained gloves, empty bottles, and the box were all stuffed into the garbage can. The door to his bedroom was slightly open. Her gaze, of course, went right to the opening. She had to close the door anyway, and if her gaze strayed into his room, it just couldn't be helped.

She sensed that he wasn't in there. Which made it even more tempting to peer in.

"What a slob." Her gaze scanned clothing on one lone chair and on the small dresser before settling on the rumpled bed. He must toss and turn as much as she did; the sheets were half-hanging off, pillows askew. Her bed was neatly made, just as she liked it, but somehow his looked more inviting.

On the nightstand was a stack of books that he'd bought when she hit the clothing stores. Vampire books, and from the hot chicks on the covers, sexy books. With a sigh, she closed the door and went through her morning routine. She sang along to Ida Maria's "I Like You So Much Better When You're Naked."

Fifteen minutes later, she went back to her room and picked up her box. Ugh. She'd never dyed her own hair.

"This is going to be fun. Not."

When she was done ruining her hair, she turned off the music and was about to open her bedroom door when she heard rock music and a sound that stopped her.

Moaning.

Groaning.

Someone having sex.

Her heartbeat did a little dip when she imagined Rand and . . . who? Petra, perhaps, going at it in the living area. What did she do now?

She cleared her throat loudly and opened the door. Coughed.

The moaning continued.

She closed her door with a loud thud.

The groaning kept on.

Then Petra's voice. "God, you're loud."

Petra and Rand. When had they hooked up?

Who cares?

Another voice whispered in her head, *You do.*

Who cares? Who cares? Who cares?

"Hullo," Zoe said as she walked down the hall.

She steeled herself for a sight she wasn't going to like and walked to the open area. All she could see were Petra's bare calves, slightly spread, coming from the right side of the living area. Zoe stepped out of the hallway.

Petra was lying on one of the gym benches, pushing up the chest press bar. "Morning," she said, not looking the least bit happy at being there.

Eric sat on another bench, pulling down the lat bar. His hair was a shade lighter, and his face was red, veins sticking out at his neck. He gave her a nod and pulled down the bar again, along with a huge stack of weights.

It wasn't relief cascading through Zoe, because it wouldn't have mattered if Rand and Petra had hooked up.

The groan Eric emitted sounded a lot like Vladimir when he came, long and breathy. The thought of sex and sounds and Rand's rumpled bed shivered through her body, especially since he'd gotten her all worked up the night before. Talk about a tease!

She didn't recognize the band, but she knew the music was heavy metal from the eighties.

Petra let go of the bar. "I hate working out."

Eric rolled his eyes. "If you say that one more time, I'm going to kick your butt out of here."

Zoe leaned against the wall. "Then why are you doing it?"

"Because I made a promise that if I got out of the asylum, I would get into shape."

"To who?"

"God. Me. I don't know, but I keep my promises." Petra sat up and grabbed a bottle of water. "I was running through the woods, and these guys were after me, and I could hardly breathe. Running for your life requires being in good shape. Trust me on that."

Zoe's chest tightened. "I should probably work out, too. I remember thinking the same thing when I was running from that creep in Key West." Before she could stop the words, she asked, "Is Rand back?"

Eric dropped the stack with a crash. "Not when I came down. He checked in, though, eyeballed a guy he thinks is Braden at the house. I called the salvage yard this morning. Apparently Braden quit recently to start his own business. The plan is on for tonight, so be ready."

After her run-in with Steele only the day before, she was totally not ready.

Pushing down her worry, she went upstairs to forage for food. Her gaze searched for Rand the moment she entered the upstairs living area.

The scent of coffee and something sweet lingered in the air. Amy was eating what looked like a Pop-Tart with yogurt on top.

Amy lunged for a piece of the tart that broke off. "He's not back yet." Her previously brown hair was now a dark blond and slicked straight.

"Oh, you mean Rand?" It unnerved Zoe that it was obvious she was looking for him. She shrugged. "I'm sure he'll be back when he's ready."

Lucas, his nearly black hair now several shades lighter, sat at the table with a printed satellite map of Annapolis. "That's the problem with him. He's too edgy, too restless. The longer he stays out there, the higher the odds go that they grab him."

Zoe couldn't hide her fear at that. Flashbacks from their recent escape filled her mind. She saw Rand tearing down the highway on his bike, in that adrenaline trance, bad guy on his trail, traffic, going too fast. . . .

"What the fluck?"

She turned at the sound and spotted Orn'ry, scooting sideways from one end of his perch to another.

"Popcorn!"

Amy pointed at Orn'ry. "You've already been fed, piggy."

The door slid open, and Rand stepped inside. Relief transformed Zoe's face into a smile, which she quickly ditched when he looked at her. She let out a bark of laughter. "You're a redhead!" His hair was nearly the same shade as hers had been. Even his eyebrows, though he'd shaved his goatee. He looked different without it: less punky, more sexy.

He took in her jet-black hair, and for a second his pupils dilated. Hm, did that mean he liked it?

He wasn't saying. He dropped into the chair next to Lucas, eyeing the map. "We're all set for tonight?"

"Yeah, but you need to stay closer to home, man. I know you don't like being shut up down here." Lucas gave him a knowing look. "And after what we went through, I understand why, but it's risky going out."

Rand scrubbed his hand through his hair. "It's not just from being locked in that asylum. I've been roaming since I was kid. It's hard staying in one place for any length of time. I appreciate your concern, but I can handle myself."

Zoe couldn't imagine being locked in a room at an asylum. Just the thought of Rand being held a prisoner, given LSD, made her want to pull him into her arms. At least he hadn't been given the ominous Booster that Lucas had.

She slid into the chair opposite Rand. "You said you were good at eluding people."

"Yep." When he realized everyone was waiting for more of an explanation, he added, "I spent time hanging on the streets."

Lucas asked, "In a gang?"

"Nah, I'm too much of a loner for that." He obviously had no intention of further explaining himself since he looked at the map. "I'll return to Braden's house at four, keep an eye on him until we're ready."

Remembering that Rand liked being reckless, Zoe said, "Don't do anything crazy until the rest of us get there."

Lucas nodded in agreement. "For now, you *are* part of a team. Eric went off on his own mission when we rescued you, and look what happened." His expression darkened. "Anyone who has his own agenda risks our team."

Rand looked just as fiercely resolute. "Agreed."

Zoe knew he'd never put anyone in a dangerous situation, at least not on purpose.

Lucas said, "Even when Amy determines that Braden is an Offspring by his glow, we still can't let down our guard. The enemy could be watching him. They know where he is, too. That's how we found him."

"Making plans without me?" Eric's hard voice came in shards from the stairwell. Petra followed him up, her neck damp with sweat, hair swept up in a knot on her head.

"Just going over the plan again," Lucas said, not responding to his suspicious tone.

Eric took in the group with a scrutinizing gaze. It dissipated when he accepted that they weren't plotting without him. "Any images, Lucas?"

He shook his head. "I hated them, but now it's killing me not knowing."

"Which reminds me." Eric nodded at Lucas and Amy. "There's nothing we can do about you two, but we can't afford to let this romantic shit tangle us up." He pointed to Petra. "Not you, Miss Gooey and Dewey." He shot a look at Zoe, then at Rand. "Or you two. If you get a hard-on, I've got some *Playboy*s you can borrow."

Zoe put her hands to her hips. "And what about us girls?" She glanced at Petra, who put in, "Yeah."

"Girls don't get the itch like guys do."

Zoe started to object but thought better of it. Did she really want to argue about who was hornier?

Zoe turned to Petra. "Guess he told us, huh?"

Petra giggled. "Kinda like having a dad."

Zoe's smile faded. "I wouldn't know." For some reason, her gaze went to Rand. For a moment, their eyes locked in empathy. He didn't have a father, either, and according to Ruby, his mother was a drunk. He turned away, his eyebrows furrowing at her sympathy.

Eric walked to the fridge and pulled out a bottle of water. "Tell you what, Zoe. If you get the itch, I'm glad to oblige. I have a feeling you and I wouldn't get emotionally involved."

"Because you're a bonehead?" Zoe asked.

Petra giggled.

Rand's eyes narrowed. "That's out of line, dude."

Eric lifted his hands. "I was just being a nice guy, offering to take the edge off."

Rand's defense of her took her smart-assed retort right out of her mouth.

Lucas stood and faced Eric when he came out of the kitchen. "After what you pulled at the asylum, you don't get to make rules."

Eric's broad shoulders tightened. "I got you out of there, didn't I, bro? And Rand."

Amy said, "And nearly got Lucas killed."

He leaned down in her face. "And you think that's my fault?"

"Yes, I do."

Orn'ry must have picked up on the tension, or threat, to his mistress. He started flapping his wings and squawking, "Kill the bird!"

Eric narrowed his eyes at Orn'ry. "Love to."

Rand held out his hand. "Let's agree to focus on the mission and only deviate when necessary. I agree that we don't need to muddy the waters by getting hot and bothered. I may not be a team player, but I do know that we've got to sync up before we go out tonight. We go out, make contact with this guy, and return as planned."

Zoe heard the unspoken: *And then I'm outta here.*

Eric said, "Let's get some shooting practice in. The girls need to learn to be comfortable around guns."

The girls. Zoe tried not to be annoyed at that. She stood. "Where are we going to practice?"

"There's another level below yours that's a big open space with more canisters of food. They make for great target practice. You ever shoot a gun before?"

"No." She took in Amy's and Petra's trepidation. "But I'm not afraid of guns."

Eric nodded toward Amy and Lucas. "We've only got four muffs, so you guys can practice after us."

They went down the small stairwell to the second level, then walked through yet another doorway and down more steps to the large room Eric had described. He knelt and pulled out three guns and the earmuffs.

Rand had gone to his room on the way down and now came in with his gun. "This one might be better for Zoe to use. It's got less recoil."

Eric reached for it. "I'll show her—"

Rand pulled the gun back. "I'll handle it, dude. My gun, my . . ." The way his gaze slid to her, Zoe heard the words *girl.* "Responsibility."

Eric paused, seeming to assess Rand's intentions. He handed out the muffs. "Zoe, some basic rules of handling guns: always treat them like they're loaded. Never point at anything you don't want to shoot. Never put your finger to the trigger until you're ready to shoot."

Rand added, "And never eyeball the barrel to make sure it's clear."

"Well, duh."

Eric cocked an eyebrow at Rand but said to Zoe, "In a real-life situation, always keep in mind what's behind what you're shooting at."

They faced the stacks of white buckets. Someone had drawn angry faces on them at head level, which made Zoe smile.

Rand stepped up beside her. "Have you ever handled one at all?"

She turned with an ingenuous look, and in a coy voice said, "I've touched one once. It was hard and cold and felt very dangerous."

His mouth twitched. "Yeah, okay." He cleared his throat. "Put your hands around it like this, hold it steady." He molded his hands over hers.

She started to put her finger on the trigger but remembered Eric's admonition and stopped. "This feels comfortable. Lemme shoot at something."

They put on their muffs, and she faced the buckets. Rand came up behind her, his arms over hers and hands guiding hers. He smelled good, wind and cologne, and he felt even better. Maybe it was best if he did leave soon. She was losing control of her tongue, and worse, her body. Tingles shimmered down her backside where their bodies connected, and she fought the urge to wiggle just a little, to tease, to flirt. She didn't even need to wiggle. She felt him hardening against her butt, and the knowledge zinged through her veins.

He leaned forward and guided her finger to the trigger. "She's got a kick, but you should be able to handle it." His body tensed, ready to brace her.

Damn. It would be better if she could believe what he believed, that he was selfish and didn't care about anyone but himself.

He pushed her finger into the trigger. The gun did kick, sending her into the brick wall of his body.

"Not bad," he called out next to her ear. "Try it on your own."

He remained behind her but slid his hands from hers to rest on her arms. She pulled the trigger. The bullet went into the buckets close to where the first shot had gone. She squeezed off two more shots.

"If you like it, use it tonight." He moved away. "I'll use one of the .357 Magnums."

She tilted the gun in her hand. "Does this mean we're going steady?" She smiled and added in a sing-song voice, "Kidding."

"Doll, there's nothing steady about me."

And nothing about him made her steady, either, but she kept that tidbit to herself and aimed the gun at the buckets. *Time to kill your libido, Zoe.*

CHAPTER 13

Homes lined one side of Braden's street, commercial buildings the other. The area was quiet, with most folks tucked in their cozy beds in their cozy, narrow houses. The commercial side, which was closed at this hour, gave the Rogues nooks and crannies in which to hide. For the moment they were together, walking down the sidewalk in front of Braden's house, but soon they would split up.

Zoe shivered at what Eric had said about that: *Then, if things get really ugly, at least some of us will get away.*

Amy was trying to look into Braden's front window. "I can't see his glow at all."

Zoe said, "I thought everyone had a glow."

"They do, but if someone is very controlled, it's too close to their body for me to see." Amy looked at Zoe. "Yours is that way most of the time. When someone is agitated or emotional, their glow expands and sometimes becomes jagged. I see that on Petra and Eric a lot."

He merely grunted.

"Because we've learned to control our emotions, to

keep ourselves apart from others, Offspring can have those controlled glows." Amy looked at Lucas. "We need to go in, talk to him. I'll be able to tell close-up. If I still can't see it, I'll shake my head. We'll back off for now, set up an appointment to talk to him about our salvage needs."

Lucas's hand slid to Amy's and locked around it. "We'll keep the cell phone connection on between her phone and yours, Eric, so you'll know what's going on."

Petra said, "I'll be able to hear it, too."

They reached the corner of the street, and Eric faced the group. "We know where our lookout points are. If any of us sees something suspicious, we send out the alert."

Each of them had the number of another Rogue at the ready. Two presses of a button and the phone would vibrate. That person would then call their link on the chain.

Rand pulled out his phone and checked it. "We retreat if possible. Shoot at close range if necessary. We don't want to risk taking out one of our own." He looked at Eric specifically. "Right, dude?"

"Yeah . . . right."

They moved into their spots as Amy and Lucas approached the house. Zoe tucked herself between a trailered boat and a steel building. Her getaway plan was to run to the boatyard around the back. This was crazy. She was holding a gun. A freaking *gun*. Like the cops she'd seen on television, she held it down and aimed away from her feet. Rand was in front of the adjacent building, behind the hedges that ran along the sidewalk. He and the others blended into the shadows, and for a moment she felt very alone.

They're there. A scream away.

She raised her binoculars and watched Amy and Lucas walk up the steps to the front porch and knock. The man inside answered. They talked. Being able to see whether the man had an Offspring glow or not would really help. Zoe stared so hard, her eyes blurred. Did Amy shake her head?

Yes, there it was. She couldn't see his glow.

Damn. Zoe tucked the gun into the waistband of her pants as she'd seen Rand do, pulled out her shirt to cover it, and walked toward the front door. Braden needed to be agitated. She would agitate him. As she neared, she heard Lucas keeping the conversation neutral, giving Amy time to discern his glow. "My boss has a particularly sensitive job, and he doesn't want anyone else involved."

"Nicholas Braden!" Zoe startled them with her harsh voice. "You don't remember me, do you?"

Lucas's and Amy's expressions froze.

Braden, medium height with a shock of brown hair, shook his head.

Zoe injected emotion into her voice. "You sleep with me, tell me you love me, then I never hear from you again. And now . . . you don't even remember me!"

"Look, I've never seen you before, and—"

"Sure you have." Zoe stepped right up to him. "Maggie Bagbaum. You called me Magpie." She punched him in the arm, realizing she'd used Rand's neighbor's name. "How could you forget that?"

He was thrown off, too, rubbing his arm. "You've got the wrong—"

"You told me I was the prettiest girl you ever knew,

that if I slept with you, you'd love me forever, that you'd take me home to meet your mother!" She started beating on him, giving Amy a pointed look.

"Stop!" Braden deflected her blows.

"And that night, that beautiful night, you were telling me to come!"

Amy nodded for Zoe to keep it up.

Braden was trying to grab hold of her flailing wrists. "Get out of here."

Zoe shot a look at Amy. "Is this your new girlfriend? He'll use you like he used me. I'm warning you now."

Amy's eyes lit with fear. "We have to go."

No Offspring glow.

As she and Lucas backed up, a hand grabbed Zoe's arm and twisted her around so that her back was against Braden's chest. His arm came up around her throat from behind and something hard jabbed her in the side. "You're not going anywhere. Get inside, now, or I take her out."

Lucas and Amy froze, indecision flashing in their eyes.

Go, get out of here!

Please, don't leave me!

Defeat shadowed their faces, and both stepped inside. Braden, or rather the guy pretending to be Braden, patted Zoe down and found the gun. He tossed it onto the table and patted down Amy and Lucas, too, finding their guns as well.

"Where's the firestarter?"

Lucas narrowed one eye. "Who?"

"Eric Aruda, the son of a bitch who torched my partner." He nodded toward the door. "He's out there, isn't he?" When Lucas said nothing, Braden punched him in the face. Lucas's head snapped back, and blood spurted out of his lip, but he still said nothing.

Amy let out a whimper, her green eyes filled with terror. Fear spiraled through Zoe's body. She could see Lucas calculating, though, looking for an opportunity.

Braden grabbed a walkie-talkie on an old trunk that served as the coffee table, keeping the gun trained at them. "It's Samuels. I got three of them: Shane and Stoker." He looked at Zoe. "I didn't recognize you at first." He pressed the TALK button again. "And the guy must be Brandenburg 'cause he's not Aruda."

Zoe remembered that they thought Lucas was dead from the last Booster shot he was supposed to have been given.

The man spoke into the walkie-talkie. "I'm sure both Arudas are out there. They'll be charging in for the rescue any minute now. Take out the sister but bring Eric here. I want to put a bullet right in his forehead."

A voice crackled on the other end. "Darkwell has plans for Aruda."

"He didn't watch his friend go up in flames. He didn't smell the burning flesh. Aruda's *mine*." Hatred rolled off him in waves.

The voice crackled again. "Don't go off. That's how you ended up working this detail."

Samuels tossed the walkie-talkie on the table.

"Where's Braden?" Lucas asked.

"That's none of your concern." He smiled at the three of them. "Finally, we get rid of you." He pointed at Amy. "You were there, too. You go first."

Lucas's body tightened, and Zoe knew he was going to throw himself between Amy and that bullet, just as Rand had described. To be loved like that . . .

Movement on the wall caught her eye. She looked at the myriad items mounted in diagonal patterns, including a porthole and a piece of old wood with the word *Astonia* painted on it. A blue glass globe with old ropes wrapped around it hung from the ceiling. It vibrated. She concentrated, and it fell to the floor. Samuels twisted and shot at it with a muffled *whump*, putting a hole in the wall.

Lucas leapt at him, and screamed, "Amy, get out!"

Samuels spun around and cuffed Lucas in the head with the butt of the gun. He fell to the floor with a groan.

Amy and Zoe were halfway to the door when Samuels aimed the gun at them. "Stop. Sit down over there. We'll wait for your friends."

Zoe's heart pounded so hard it hurt her chest. She grabbed Amy's hand and pulled her toward the beige leather couch Samuels indicated. Amy's gaze was on Lucas.

"He's okay," Zoe whispered.

Blood trickled from a cut on his temple, but she prayed he was only knocked unconscious.

Amy faced Samuels. "We had nothing to do with torching your friend. We didn't even know Eric could do that."

"Save your breath, sweetie. Either way, you're all dying."

Zoe concentrated on the gun.

Samuels felt it quiver and thrust it toward them. "Whatever tricks you're playing, stop it, or I'll take you out right now." He pulled a chair from the kitchen table, spun it around, and sat. He kept his dark eyes on all three of them. "I don't know how Aruda set that fire or how you just made my gun move. What are you, Satan worshippers or something?" When they didn't answer, he pointed his gun at them. "If I sense anything weird, I'll just shoot you."

Lucas stirred, his hand slowly moving toward the wound on his head. Samuels watched him, gun at the ready.

It hit her then, that Eric and Rand *would* come rushing in, having no doubt seen what happened. Rand might be shot. He might be killed. She might be killed.

An old green bottle, covered in barnacles, quivered on the coffee table. Zoe's gaze shot to Samuels, who hadn't seen it. If only she could use her skills better, she could fling that heavy bottle right at him. It would probably just fall off the table, then he'd shoot her.

The walkie-talkie crackled. "I've got one of them in my sight. I'm moving in."

Rand watched Lucas and Amy walk up to Braden's door. Through the front window he could see the man moving around in the kitchen, making dinner. Alone.

There was something sad about that, guy by himself, eating alone . . .

Hell, that was him most of the time. And that was how he liked it.

He kept scanning the area and checking ten seconds ahead. No sign of anything suspicious. He understood Lucas's trepidation at having the girls join the mission. He'd had this odd desire for Zoe to hurt her foot or something so she couldn't go. Lucas's love for Amy amazed Rand. The fierce, protective look on Lucas's face dug right into his chest. To love someone like that meant that losing them would rip out his insides.

He chuckled at Eric's rule against sexual involvement—until he thought about his offer to sate her hunger. Chucklehead. And that reminded him of kissing Zoe the night before. He'd wanted to teach her a lesson, but for the life of him, he couldn't remember what it was. As soon as his mouth touched those bee-stung lips he'd been dreaming about, logic fled. It was all he could do to pull back. One kiss, teach her a lesson or something like that, and then out again. As his tongue did its own thing, he wanted to tear off that sexy little tank top and get good and sweaty on the couch.

He glanced down. *Good job, Rand, give yourself a stiffie.*

Eric was right. Caring about any of them meant a brain tangle, and none of them could afford that. From now on, no flirting, kissing, or stiffies. *Focus on what you're doing.* He watched Lucas and Amy talk to Braden.

What the . . . ?

Rand's muscles locked as Zoe stalked across the street. Through his binoculars he watched her make a scene. What the hell was she doing? She was supposed to be over there in her safe hiding spot, sticking to the plan, not pummeling Braden.

He time-shot forward ten seconds. Braden grabbed her, his arm locking around her neck. It felt like someone reached into Rand's chest and tore out his heart. He couldn't breathe.

His body tensed to rush forward. *Stop. If this is a setup, he's not the only enemy around. You won't help them by getting shot.*

He helplessly watched the scene unfold as he'd seen it. The guy had a gun. Rand couldn't see it, but he knew that was why Amy and Lucas were going inside the house.

The door closed.

She-it.

His phone vibrated.

He crept toward Eric's hiding spot behind a company van that was parked in front of the next building. He time-shot forward again. A bullet tore through Eric's shoulder.

"Eric, get down!"

Rand heard the bullet hit the metal building a few yards away. The guy was using a silencer. Had to be; the gun was too quiet. A shadow moved to his right several yards behind him. He had someone on his tail, too, and he'd just given away his position. He fled to the end of the hedges. A silhouette slipped around the corner of the building. His gaze went to the house across the street. Damn, he needed to get over there.

Petra rang his phone. "I just heard a shot coming from the house!"

Zoe!

A bullet whizzed by him. He had to focus, to stay alive if he was going to be able to help them. He raced across a small expanse of asphalt and dropped down next to the van Eric had been hiding behind. His pursuer wasn't a big guy, but he was fast. Mouselike footsteps tracked him.

Rand edged the building to stay in the shadows and ducked behind a bush at the street corner. His finger shook as it poised over the trigger.

Kill or be killed.

Eric called the person on his chain: Petra. "Get back to the car. We're not leaving you behind this time."

"Okay. But Eric, there was a shot inside the house."

"Maybe it was one of us." He disconnected and crept closer to the street. If it was one of them, they'd be leaving the house by now.

A shadow raced across the street toward the house. He narrowed his eyes, imagining the man going up in flames. Wait. What if he set Rand on fire? Dammit, he couldn't take that chance.

He got to the corner of the building. A car drove down the street, two women at the wheel. Not the enemy. Eric crossed the street, using the passing car as cover.

He crouched next to the first house on the street, surveying for enemies. A man crossed the street roughly in the same place he had. His pursuer. Setting him aflame would definitely get the neighbors' attention, though. He shot at him, and the man fell. Eric sprinted around to the back of the first two houses on the block, approaching Braden's house from the rear.

He didn't know whether the man in Braden's house was an enemy Offspring or a CIA guy.

Eric.

He jerked at his name. Cold dread prickled his skin. Not someone nearby, but someone in his head. Just like at the asylum.

Get out of my head, you asshole.

He couldn't let the enemy Offspring get the best of him this time. He had to keep control.

Control? Funny you should say that, Eric. You have no control.

He shook his head, trying to fling away the voice, and crept along the back side of the property. Did they know where he was? Not exactly, or he'd already be dead.

He wanted the guy who'd tapped into his head, wanted to crush his throat in his hands. For now he'd have to settle for the regular guys. He looked in the window and saw Lucas slowly getting up from the floor. A tall, dark-haired man directed him to the couch where Amy and Zoe sat. Lucas had blood on his temple, but he was moving, so it couldn't be a bullet wound.

He focused on the guy holding the gun on his people. *Burn, baby, burn.*

No fire, Eric. Go in gun blazing, blow the guy away.

He looked at the gun in his hand. He could always use his pyrokinesis as backup.

A sound snapped his head to attention.

CHAPTER 14

and heard a shot and saw a man drop in the street. Not a silenced gun. One of theirs, then. The guy started crawling in the opposite direction, injured but not mortally. Quick and Mousy cursed and ran over to him in a crouch. Rand couldn't make out what they were saying. He aimed the gun at his pursuer as he helped the injured man.

Shoot the guy! Do it.

His finger trembled. A dog barked.

He's one of the bad guys. Take him down.

His arm faltered. Shooting a guy in the back . . . man, he just couldn't do it. The guy sprinted across the street toward the residential side. No way could Rand take the chance of killing some innocent bystander.

Once the guy disappeared into the shadows, Rand time-shot ahead. All clear. He followed the guy. Circling around, he crept up to the rear door of the house. He wasn't sure if his heart was thudding from running or fear. He didn't have time for fear.

Lights had come on in two houses after the gunshot. One shot could be a car backfiring. Still, someone might call the police. They had to clear out before the cops arrived.

He couldn't see movement, but he heard the guy creeping through the backyard. He had to get rid of him. He patted the ground and found something that felt like a small rock.

Quick and Mousy walked up the steps to the back door. He opened the door and peered inside, closed it. He looked at the bushes surrounding the rear of the house: a perfect hiding spot. Rand's body tensed as the guy came closer. One step. Two. With a flick of his finger, Rand sent the rock behind Quick and Mousy, who turned at the sound.

Rand leapt out and coldcocked him with the side of his gun. He grabbed him before he hit the ground so he wouldn't make any sound but let him drop the last few inches. He couldn't risk the sound of another gunshot that might disable the guy in a better way, so he slammed the gun to the side of his head again. Then he grabbed his gun.

He looked up to see a gun pointed at him.

He looked farther up to meet the eyes of the guy who was going to trash him—and let out a soft laugh of relief. The gun dropped several inches. Eric.

Eric nodded toward the guy on the ground. "Good job. They're inside. There's only one guy that I can see. I'm going in the front."

"I'll go in this way, cover you from the back."

Eric ran around the corner. Rand launched up the steps to the door. Holding his breath, he turned the knob and stepped inside. A second later, Eric threw open the front door, his gun pointed at the guy holding the gun on Zoe, Amy, and Lucas. It was a standoff. The Braden imposter wasn't backing down.

"Drop the gun!" Eric shouted.

"Pull the trigger, and I'll take at least one of them with me."

Rand slunk down the hallway. The three on the couch came into view, and the sight of Zoe at gunpoint nearly caved him in. She looked up, caught his gaze, and her fear tore him apart. She averted her gaze so as not to give him away. He raised his gun to their captor. This guy he would shoot.

"No!" Eric's face contorted. Slowly, the hand holding the gun shifted. His arm trembled, his teeth gnashed together. "No," he growled.

What the hell?

His head twitched, like it had in the asylum hallway when he said someone had gotten into his mind. His arm kept moving, away from the enemy and toward . . . Zoe, Lucas, and Amy.

"I won't . . ." he gritted out. "I won't do it."

The guy was in his head again. The enemy Offspring was telling Eric to kill his comrades. Rand raised his gun, and God help him, aimed it at Eric. His stomach churned as he watched Eric fight what looked like a ghost.

Even though everyone in the living room watched in horror and confusion, the enemy kept his gun aimed at the three on the couch. "What's he doing?" he asked.

No one answered.

Eric turned his hand inward, his whole arm shaking. His eyes bulged in horror.

Lucas shouted, "Eric . . . come out of it! Dammit, Eric!"

The Braden imposter shoved his gun closer to Lucas. "Shut up."

Rand couldn't say anything without giving away his presence. He kept his gun aimed at Eric, fighting a similar battle. Could he hit Eric's gun?

Eric pulled the gun around, inch by inch, until his intention washed over Rand in a cold wave. The barrel of the gun turned around, aimed right at Eric's face. Rand shifted his arm to the right and shot the enemy, then raced toward Eric. He sailed through the air, aiming for the arm holding the gun.

He reached it, shoving it down. The gun went off. Rand landed against Eric, who collapsed to the floor. Amy's and Zoe's screams sounded as though they came from miles away. Blood gushed from Eric's thigh. The bullet had hit an artery, likely fatal.

Rand dropped to the floor and pressed the bottom of his shirt against the wound. "Someone, get a towel!"

Amy ran into the kitchen.

Eric arched and groaned in pain. He was lucid enough to let out a string of curses.

"Stay calm, dude. Don't move."

Eric sucked in shallow breaths, his teeth gritted. "It's just my leg. It'll be fine."

Rand wasn't going to panic him by telling him the truth. He'd heard about that football player who'd been shot in the leg and died.

Lucas made a call on his cell phone, his voice breathless. "Petra, get to the house *now*. I can't explain, just get here." His voice cracked on those last words, his gaze on Eric.

Rand looked at Zoe, whose face was ashen as she also stared at Eric. "You all right?"

She only shook her head, not shifting her gaze. She was in shock.

Amy dropped down beside Rand and pressed the towel against the wound. "It's too much blood!"

Rand's shirt was soaked in it, and the spill on the hardwood floors kept growing despite the towel. Eric's face was losing color by the second, turning an ashen gray.

Rand looked at the man he'd shot, draped over a trunk in the living room, blood pooling beneath him. His stomach heaved.

No time for that.

He did take the time to grab the imposter's guns and jam them into his waistband. The Camry screeched up the driveway.

Eric tried to sit up, but his head wobbled, and his eyes rolled back in their sockets. Rand grabbed him before he hit the floor. "We lift him on the count of three."

Lucas grabbed hold of Eric's legs, Zoe took some of the weight from the middle, and Rand positioned his hands beneath Eric's shoulders. "Onetwothree!"

They hoisted him up. Rand's wobbly legs staggered beneath the weight, but he gained his balance and pushed on. Amy kept the towel pressed against the wound as they carried him out the door.

Zoe said, "His skin is cold and clammy."

Petra met them halfway down the sidewalk. "Put him in the back! I'll work on him."

Luckily, the fence going up both sides of Braden's property shielded them from view.

Petra helped support Eric's weight the rest of the way to the car. "He's having trouble breathing! Hurry!"

She was right. His breathing was coming in shallow pants.

Once they had him laid out on the seat, Rand closed the door. He shoved two guns at Lucas. "I took these from the CIA dudes. We've got to get out of here. I'll meet you at the shelter."

Zoe grabbed his arm, squeezing tight. "I'm going with you."

Seeing that she teetered on the edge, he took her hand, and they ran across the front yard and the street.

More lights blinked on in the surrounding houses. Two gunshots had definitely gotten their attention.

The Camry screeched away as he and Zoe reached Blue's hiding spot. No time for helmets. He jumped on, and she climbed on behind him, holding on so tight it hurt. He started the bike and raced off.

He rode as fast as he could and still maintain control. He felt spasms moving through Zoe's body. He couldn't tell whether she was crying or what. He squeezed his eyes shut for a second, pushing everything down inside him: the horror of shooting a man, seeing Eric shoot himself, and the bone-deep need to stop and hold Zoe.

He shouldn't be here. Dammit, he shouldn't be in this situation, having to shoot people, running for his life, wanting to scram *and* wanting to pull Zoe and the rest of them closer.

He rode for several minutes, trying to orient himself. Her tremors intensified. He had to stop; she was going to fall off the bike. Where was the park he'd found when he was wasting time before returning to the tomb? He spotted the sign for Truxtun Park. He turned into a deserted parking lot near the tennis courts. The lights were on, but no one else was there.

As soon as he stopped the bike, she jumped off and ran toward an opening in the woods.

"She-it." He killed the engine, put down the kick-stand, and raced after her. In the lights, he could see that it was a path, but once he entered the woods, it was barely discernible. So was she, in her black pants and dark shirt, which had been the point. He followed the sound of her raspy breaths.

"Zoe! Dammit, what are you doing?"

His chest already hurt; the last thing he needed was physical exertion. But here he was, because he couldn't let her get lost or hurt. He heard her gasps and footsteps ahead. The girl could run, but he was faster.

That's what you do, Rand. You run, a woman's voice from the past reminded him.

He closed the gap, reached out, and grazed her shoulder. "Zoe! Stop already!"

"No."

The fear and emotion he heard in that one word did another number on him. He stepped up his pace and grabbed her around her waist. They both stumbled, but he fought to hold their balance. He sure as hell didn't want to tackle her twice.

Pinecones whizzed past him. Her crazy energy. She wriggled, pushing away from him. "I can't do this! I need to get away. Please let me go."

He held on tighter, closing his eyes at the feel of her trembling body and the sound of tears in her voice. "No."

She was too tired to really put up much of a fight, but she was giving it her best. "I need to be alone. I can't . . . can't . . ." She disintegrated into sobs.

He pressed her face to his chest. "It's okay, babe." Tears. They ripped through him. He wanted to take them away, wanted to shush her, but he couldn't do either. "I know. I know."

He did know. He lifted his face to a break in the trees and the night sky, stroking her back and whispering, "I know," over and over, lost in the images of the last hour: Zoe getting grabbed by that thug. Being held hostage at gunpoint. He'd almost lost her, almost lost all of the Rogues.

He didn't even realize he'd started kissing her hair between words. Comforting kisses, calming kisses, along her hairline, across her cheek as she looked up at him. The taste of salt, the moisture of her tears, and the softness of her mouth. The little sound she made, a whimper, then a groan.

Suddenly they weren't comforting kisses anymore. They were desperate kisses, and hell, he was as desperate as she was. Desperate to feel alive, to taste something they'd nearly lost. She gripped his face in her hands and kissed his chin, his cheeks, eyes and the spike in his brow . . .

"Zoe," he groaned. *We shouldn't be doing this. Wrong time, wrong place, wrong reason.*

Instead of saying that, he trailed his fingers into her thick hair and crushed her close for another kiss. He could lose himself in that lush mouth of hers, and

God help him, he was. She pulled off his shirt, then hers. The moonlight hit her pale skin and dark lace bra, reminding him of every sexy vampire he'd ever read about. Especially with her black hair. He tore off the bra and sucked her puckered nipples. She groaned, her fingers kneading his scalp. "Rand . . . more . . . more."

He tasted the sheen of sweat on her skin and needed to taste more of her. He nibbled the swell of her breasts and trailed his tongue over the soft skin, all around the edges, into the indent between her breasts and over to the other one. He slid down to his knees, trailing his tongue down her stomach as he went. His hands slid down to her sweet ass, squeezing her the way she'd done to him. He dipped his tongue into her belly button and circled the perimeter.

He wanted to rip down her pants and bury his face in her mound and feel her bare ass and bury himself inside her, too. He heard her soft, rapid breaths, felt her fingers tensing in his hair.

Dude, don't do this. It's wrong.

He rubbed his face against the front of her pants, fighting sensibility.

I need this, too. Remember, I'm a selfish son of a bitch.

He wrapped his arms around her and pulled her against him, reining in the explosive energy tearing through him. He fought to remain still, to not stroke her or move his face or anything.

"What?" she whispered, fear back in her voice.

God, she thought he'd heard something.

He looked up at her. He couldn't see her face for the moonlight behind her. "We can't do this." Borrowing from his conscience, he said, "Wrong time, wrong place, wrong reason."

He got to his feet as she took a shuddering breath, looking around as though she'd just woken from a trance. He grabbed up her bra and shirt and pressed them into her hands.

"Tell me it was all a nightmare." She sounded so much like a scared little girl who'd just woken up from a bad dream that he couldn't help but draw her close.

"I'm sorry."

He held her, skin against skin, wishing he could just absorb her into his body, keep her safe and warm.

Ah, she-it, don't think thoughts like that. Those are more dangerous than anything you just went through.

He kissed her temple, feeling something open inside him.

"I tried to use my ability to help. I made a glass globe fall down. That's all I could do. Big freakin' deal."

"You did the best you could. You'll get better at it."

She looked up at him. "Do you think so?"

"Definitely."

"What about Eric?"

"Petra can heal him, remember? He'll be okay."

"He was going to shoot us."

"The enemy Offspring got into his head. Had to be. The guy was probably telling Eric to shoot you, and he fought it."

She shivered. "He shot himself. To save us."

"Yeah, I know." He'd never forget that. As much of a bonehead as Eric was, he would take his life rather than take out his comrades.

A few minutes later she stepped back. "How are we supposed to win against these people?" The light cast her face in silvery planes of moonshine and shadows. "They can get into our *heads*."

"We fight because we can't give up."

She buried her face in her hands, still holding her clothing, and took a deep breath. "I'm sorry I freaked out. It was too much."

He touched her chin, lifting her face to his. "It's all right. But we'd better get back."

She clipped on her bra and slid her shirt back on. He roused himself to put on his shirt only when she looked at him.

She was beautiful. Even now, even in this wrong place and wrong time, she was so damned beautiful, it hurt.

He had to get out of there. Despite the thought, he didn't resist when she slid her hand into his as they walked.

She looked around at the shadows surrounding them. "I hope we can find our way back."

"Me, too. I don't want to spend the night here."

"St. Thomas. St. Kitts. Fiji. Paradise Island." She tilted her head. "Calming myself."

It took a lot longer to get back to the bike than it had to race away from it. He slapped at the mosquitoes that had now found them. "I'd better call, let them know we're on our way. See how Eric's doing." *That's what you do when you're part of a group. For now, for a little while, you're part of this group.* He punched in the numbers.

Amy answered. "Rand? Are you two all right?"

These people really cared. "Yeah." He cleared the

hoarseness from his throat and looked at Zoe. "I was a little too buggin' to be riding a bike. We stopped for a few minutes to unscramble our brains. How's Eric?"

"Petra healed him, the same way she did Lucas. But it took a lot out of her."

Relief flood through him. "We're heading back now. See you in a few." He disconnected and relayed Eric's status to her. "Are you all right to ride?"

She nodded, slapping at mosquitoes. "You didn't have to lie to cover my freak-out."

Another sign that he was in big trouble.

Remember, all you care about is yourself. Look out for number one and all that.

He handed her the helmet, avoiding her gaze. "Let's roll."

CHAPTER 15

As much as Zoe didn't like being closed up in the ground, she was relieved to get back to the tomb.

Amy was curled up in the corner of the pit group, Lucas's arms around her. The sight of it reminded her how Rand had held her in the woods, which then led to what had almost happened afterward, and— *screech! Stop those thoughts.*

Relief washed over Amy's features. "Thank God you're back."

"It was me." Zoe grabbed up a pillow and hugged it to her chest as she dropped to the floor. Her gaze went to a new painting on the wall, a multicolored sun with half a happy face and half a sad face. She forced her eyes to them. "We stopped because of me. I freaked." She couldn't let Rand take the blame for that.

He merely raised his eyebrow at her admission while he slumped into the chair as though his bones had dissolved.

Amy's fingers still trembled as she brushed a strand of stiff hair from her face. "It's all right. That whole scene was freaky."

Rand looked around. "Where's Eric? And Petra?"

"In Petra's room. She was out of it when we got back. We carried her in. When we last checked, Eric was kneeling by her bed, watching over her."

The idea of that was such an anomaly for Eric that Zoe was tempted to see the sight for herself. "Did he say anything about what happened?"

"Not much. He's pretty shook-up," Lucas said. "Only that the guy got into his head, and this time he mind-controlled him to shoot us. Thank God Eric fought it. But what happens next time?"

The fear that had overtaken her in the woods rushed back. "How do we win against these people? They have the government on their side, the police, and they have Offspring, powerful Offspring."

A hoarse voice from the hallway said, "We destroy this guy."

Eric stumbled into the living room and collapsed onto the couch. It was unnerving to see the usually strong, brash Eric looking so pale and weak. The right leg of his jeans was cut up the middle and blood stained the denim. Zoe stared at the red welt that replaced the wound she'd seen a short time ago.

He caught her awed expression. "It's a friggin' miracle, isn't it?"

She could only nod. "I mean, I know you told me how she healed Lucas, but seeing it . . . I still can't believe it."

Eric leaned forward and rubbed his hands down his face. "She should have let me die. What if that son of a bitch comes back in my head?" He gave Lucas a grave look, one that held undertones Zoe couldn't interpret. "If I ever point a gun at anyone in our group again, take me down. Because if I killed one of us, I'd kill myself."

Amy said, "Don't talk like that." She looked at Lucas, who shared the same dark expression as Eric. "None of us is killing anyone in our group. Bottom line, you took back your control."

Fear lit his icy blue eyes. "It took everything in me. It was the strongest impulse I've ever felt. I had to shoot someone, and it couldn't be the enemy. The directive was so strong . . ." He pinched the bridge of his nose.

When he looked up again, the fire in his eyes had returned. "I will destroy him. Just like with Gladstone, I have to get him before he gets me. Or any of us."

No one argued with that.

Lucas said, "We need to find out who he is. Maybe it's this Braden guy."

Rand rubbed his finger down his chin, where his goatee used to be, reminding her of kissing that slight indent there. "Can we assume that Braden's one of them?"

Lucas nodded. "Probably. When I asked where Braden was, the guy holding us at gunpoint said it was none of my concern. Then he gave me a smug smile. They obviously knew we were going to approach him and set up this other guy to take his place." He looked at Amy. "You saw Braden's profile when you sneaked onto Cyrus's computer to find information on more Offspring."

"Yeah, but they couldn't know that it was me."

Zoe's voice cracked when she said, "Maybe they have someone who can see into the future?"

Lucas gingerly touched the cut on his temple. "The

damned of it is, they could. We know they have two Offspring working for them, a man and a woman. The guy—Braden maybe—can get into Eric's head and remote-view; maybe she can see the future."

Zoe covered her face with her hands. "Then they know what we're going to do! We're going to die. They're going to get us."

The microwave beeped. Papers on the table fluttered to the floor, and the canvas on the easel fell forward. Three pens flew off the desk, and Eric had to duck to miss getting hit.

"Don't wig out. You sound like Petra." Eric picked up the pen and stared at it, then her.

"Sorry." She pressed her forehead to her knees and took deep breaths. "Montego Bay. Negril. Cayman Islands." She didn't dare look at Rand because she'd think about when she really did freak out in the woods.

At Eric's raised eyebrow, Rand explained, "She does that to calm herself down."

Eric looked at Amy. "What about the other guy's profile that you saw? Jerryl Evrard."

Lucas rubbed the back of his neck. "Do we dare approach anyone else?"

Eric said, "It's a good bet that he's not working with them, at least not yet. The sooner we get to him, the better. First, we've got to make sure he's an Offspring. If Amy can't see his glow, we don't approach, period."

The thought of going on another mission sent a decorative pillow rolling off the couch to land near Rand's feet. She stared at it, focusing her attention on it. *Move, dammit.*

It jumped up and landed on Rand's lap.

"I did that! On purpose. Well, not putting it in your lap, but moving it. I'm going to get better at this." She looked at the three on the couch. "I'm going to get really good at it, so the next time we're stuck at gunpoint, I can send the globe into his head."

Eric gave her a thumbs-up. "That's the spirit."

Rand stretched out his legs. "And I'm going to work on seeing farther ahead. That Darkwell dude seemed to think I could." ·

"Good." Lucas shook his head. "Because I'm still getting nothing. Eric, what about you? Did you lose your skills, too?"

He shrugged. "I'm too tired to light a cigarette with a lighter, much less psychically." But the fear that he'd lost his ability tensed all the muscles in his square face. "I'll try to remote-view tomorrow."

"How's Petra?" Amy asked.

"Asleep," Eric said.

"She looked really pale after she healed you. I saw her holding her leg." Amy turned to Lucas. "When she healed you, she said she could feel your wound."

Lucas lifted his shirt, revealing a muscular chest and a small red welt like the one on Eric's leg. "She's taking on our wounds."

Zoe leaned forward. "Cheveyo warned her to be careful about healing mortal wounds. He said it could destroy her psychically."

Eric waved that away. "What does he know?"

"A lot. He knew I was in trouble in Key West. He knew that you all were here. And he knew that when she heals, the person loses his or her ability."

That killed the argument Eric was about to continue. He let out an agonized breath. "If she dies . . ."

Amy held out her hand to stop him from going further. "Let's not go there. She's going to be fine. But we can't let her heal those types of injuries anymore." She looked at the three of them. "We're on our own."

Lucas brushed Amy's hair back from her face. "We do have one advantage. They think I'm dead. The guy at the house assumed I was Rand."

Eric said, "And now he'll probably think I'm dead, too. We took out three of Darkwell's men tonight, injured if not dead. We need to move in on this other Offspring before Darkwell gets replacements. He may have what we need to find Robbins."

Lucas rested his head against the back of the couch. "We need time to recoup from this one."

Eric's mouth tightened in impatience. "One day."

Lucas held up two fingers. "Petra needs time."

Eric's resolve faltered at that. "All right, two days. Amy, can you talk to Cyrus, see if he knows whether this guy is one of them?"

Her face paled at that, but she nodded. "I'll try."

Lucas turned on the television. "Let's see if there's anything on the news about the shooting."

A few minutes later a breaking-news announcement cut in. The female reporter said, "We are at the scene of the bizarre shooting in Eastport that we told you about earlier. I have Captain Tony Sanchez of the Annapolis Police Department here. Captain Sanchez, can you tell us what's going on?"

A nice-looking Latino man stepped in front of the camera. "The investigation is just getting started, and we don't know yet exactly what we have here. At approximately 10:00 P.M. our 911 center began receiving calls from neighbors about a disturbance, saying they saw people running around this house, and that two different cars were seen coming and going from the scene at a high rate of speed. Some callers reported hearing what sounded like gunshots."

The reporter cut in. "We understand you've found blood."

"Blood was found on the street, but so far no bodies or guns have been found. We're presently trying to contact the owner of the house to get permission to enter. We are also in communication with the District Attorney's Office, discussing the possibility of obtaining a search warrant for the residence if we can't get in touch with the owner. As you can see, this is a very active crime scene as the investigation continues. That's all the information we have at this time."

Cameras panned to a cordoned-off area in the street, closing in on what looked like a blood spill, to the house where police officers worked the yard, then back to the reporter.

"The house belongs to Nicholas Braden, a salvage diver. According to one neighbor, Braden hasn't been around in the last few weeks."

The screen changed to an elderly woman with red, plump cheeks. "Nicholas is such a nice boy, always helps take my trash cans out or fixes the things that get broken. I can't imagine he'd be involved in something like this."

The reporter's face filled the screen again. "We'll keep you informed about what happened here in the days to come."

Lucas turned off the television. "Either Darkwell had more men nearby, or the two weren't mortally injured and were able to clean up and get out before the police arrived."

Eric stood. "I was shooting in the dark, so I don't know where I hit my guy."

Rand rubbed the spot between his eyebrows. "I saw him crawl away. I only coldcocked the guy at the back door. But I probably killed the guy in the house."

Eric held up his fist. "Say that last part with pride, my friend. Too bad you didn't take out two of them."

Rand didn't look proud at all. He looked haunted.

Eric jabbed his thumb back toward the hall. "I'm going to check on Petra. I'll see you in the morning."

"We all need to rest." Lucas helped Amy to her feet. The subtle difference in the way he looked at her, as though he were going to lose her, scared Zoe. Did he know something he wasn't telling?

Zoe struggled to her feet, her legs like rubber. A hand reached down, surprising her. She took it, and Rand pulled her up. He let go as soon as she gained her footing.

They'd gotten too close. For those frantic moments in the woods, she'd wanted to feel alive and safe. She'd wanted something she never wanted before—someone to watch over her.

She still did.

Involuntarily, she glanced over at Rand, who was watching Lucas and Amy with an odd expression, almost like longing. He sensed her gaze and met it before snapping his attention away.

Not him. Besides, she didn't need anyone to watch over her. Just as she'd been doing since she graduated and moved out of her mother's house, she would take care of herself.

He followed her down the stairs. "I'm going to jump in the shower. I'll just be a minute."

She listened to the water running, imagining it sluicing down his naked body. *Zoe, you just need a human touch, that's all. It could be anyone. Well, not Lucas. Eric. Yeah, it could be Eric. Okay, not Eric. Too hard and edgy. But it doesn't have to be Rand. Any strong, sexy male would do.*

You keep telling yourself that, kid.

She inhaled the soap-scented steam that floated beneath the connecting door.

A few minutes later, he knocked. "All yours."

All mine. With a sigh, she opened the door in time to see him go into his bedroom, towel around his waist, tight over his derriere. The sight of that rumpled bed tugged at her. She wanted to crawl into it and feel his body protectively curled around hers.

He glanced at her briefly. "Something wrong?"

She shook her head, need washing over her and pushing the words, *Let me sleep with you tonight. Just hold me,* up her throat. She closed the door.

Lucas had let Amy shower first, and while he showered, she stood at the dresser mirror and stared at her reflection. She should be in that shower with him, running her soapy hands over his body. They shouldn't be acting like roommates, covering their nudity, holding back the need to bury themselves in each other's bodies.

In the mirror she saw the sensuous paintings Lucas had done of their dream encounters. The first time she'd seen them, she'd been stunned. Now they filled her with bittersweet longing.

He came out of the bathroom, wearing only pajama bottoms, and stopped when he saw her. "That shade looks good on you."

Did he think that was why she was staring morosely into the mirror? The dark blond hair looked odd, but she didn't care about that.

She crooked her finger at him. "Come here."

He walked up behind her, draping his arms around her shoulders and looking at their reflection. She took in his almond-shaped eyes, thick brows, and full lips.

Voice hoarse, she said, "Our eyes . . . noses . . . mouths . . . they don't look alike. You don't have freckles. Your complexion is olive, and mine is pale. Your hair is wavy and glossy, mine's frizzy. There's nothing similar in our features."

His expression softened. "No, there isn't."

She stared until her eyes watered. "Not one thing."

"It'll be okay, babe." He turned her around and pulled her close.

She pressed her face against his chest, breathing in the scent of him, fresh and clean and slightly damp. "When we find out for sure that we're not related . . ." She looked at him. "When we make love again, I want you to make noise."

His eyes widened in surprise and curiosity. "Noise?"

"You don't make noise. I don't know whether you're holding it in or just not letting yourself go, but I want to hear you come. Petra said she used to hear you with a girl, you know, making love, and she never heard you make sounds of pleasure. I realized you don't do that with me, either, not even in our dreams."

He smiled softly. "You think I'm not enjoying myself?"

"I know you are. But I need to hear it."

Seeing or perhaps sensing her need, his smile faded. "All right." At her smile, he said, "I'll moan and I'll groan and I'll blow your house down."

He nuzzled her neck as he growled the words, and she buckled in laughter, collapsing onto the bed in his arms. Chills swept down her neck and over her body. It felt so good to laugh, to lose herself in him. Their gazes met, and their laughter died.

He kissed her forehead and sat up. "And I never made love with anyone but you. Anything else was just sex."

She put her hand on her heart, feeling his words fill it with warmth. "Thank you."

He touched her cheek. "It's true." After a moment, he let his hand drop. "Are you going to try to talk to Cyrus tonight?"

She nodded.

"I'll be right here."

She slid under the covers, and he stretched out beside her, his leg touching hers for support. They still slept together, albeit in pajamas. She couldn't bear to sleep apart from him, not after almost losing him twice.

She drifted into sleep, swaddled in corrosive thoughts about the night and the pain of not knowing if she would ever have Lucas again.

With his fingers tracing the curves of her face, she slipped through the veil and into hypnagogic sleep.

Cyrus.

She heard a strange sound, like muffled shouting, and then, *Amy. It's me.*

I can barely hear you over that awful noise.

It's Gladstone. He's trying to barge in, but I'm keeping him at bay.

We'd better hurry. Cyrus, there's an Offspring named Jerryl Evrard. Do you know if he's working with Darkwell?

No. He's on military leave. He wasn't interested in joining the program. He—

She heard Gladstone shouting her name. How long could Cyrus hold him off?

The connection broke, and she climbed out of sleep long enough to mumble, "Evrard's okay," before falling into deep sleep.

CHAPTER 16

Amy watched as Eric used the computer to call the number for Margery and John Evrard, the only Evrard in the book. When a woman answered, he said, "Hi, I'm looking for Jerryl. I served in the Marines with him and got discharged myself, thought I'd try to look him up."

"He's not in right now, but he'll be back this evening. Can I leave a message for him?"

"I'll try him later, thanks."

He disconnected. "So he's staying with his parents. We need to track him, check him out."

Rand raised his hand. "I'll go."

Lucas shook his head. "Amy's got to go, make sure he's an Offspring. And I'm going with her."

"Then we'll all go," Rand said.

Lucas leaned against the rack of batteries, his arms crossed loosely in front of him. "The fewer of us out there, the better. Every time we leave, we risk our lives. Look what happened last time you and Zoe went out."

Amy tilted her head. "I understand your frustration, but Lucas is right. Hang tight, decompress. You'll be out again soon enough."

Jerryl's parents lived in a town south of Annapolis,

a twenty-minute drive. They followed the directions to the Evrard home, which was across the street from a large recreational park. They circled the park and left the car in a distant lot. Looking like a couple out to enjoy the early-summer day, they held hands and walked into the wooded area that bordered the park to the east.

Lucas pointed. "According to the Google maps satellite view, if we head toward the road, we'll be across from the house."

They spotted the house through the trees, small and well kept, with an American flag and a red Marine Corps flag flying from a pole. Amy laid out the blanket she'd brought so they'd look like two love-birds hiding out in private.

Forty minutes later, a brown truck pulled into the driveway. A muscular young man with a cast on his ankle maneuvered his way out of the driver's side. It was almost painful to watch the awkward way he had to close the vehicle's door while balancing a bag and crutches.

Amy heard the excitement in her own voice. "He's one of us."

"That doesn't mean we can trust him. Even if Cyrus did say he'd declined to be in the program." He glanced at her. "I know, I sound as paranoid as Eric. After what just happened, I have to be. Mostly, though, we've got to worry about who else might be watching him, too."

"He's not the guy we saw at the asylum when we were casing the joint to rescue you. A man and woman walked out together. We couldn't see their faces because it was dark, but he wasn't limping." She felt Lucas relax a bit. "We need to take him off guard, like you did with me. But I think he'll be okay."

He nodded. "Not at his parents' house, though. We'll take turns watching him over the next couple of days, get a bead on his routine. He won't be much of an asset physically. Let's see what he can do psychically."

Three nights after the Nicholas-Braden-imposter fiasco, Zoe's dreams were still filled with images of fear and blood and death. And almost as bad as that, the helpless feeling of not being able to help. So she'd been practicing her skills. She spun around in the bedroom and stared at a book of matches she'd set on the dresser. They shot into the air and landed on her perfectly made bed.

With her hand in the shape of a gun, she lifted her finger to her lips and blew off "smoke." She was getting the hang of this bioenergy stuff. She'd be able to help this time. At least a little.

She walked out into the hallway. No groaning, thank goodness. Just music, a sort of punky rock she'd never heard before: "Got to keep 'em separated."

She stepped into the living area. Rand sat in the chair from which she'd mercilessly teased him a few nights ago. He was bobbing his head to the music, absently stroking his chin and completely immersed in her sketchbook. Damn, she'd left it out.

Aiming her energy at it, she sent it flying out of his hands. He jumped, his gaze going right to her. "She-it, you scared the hell out of me."

She scooped up the book. "You should never look at a woman's diary."

"That isn't a diary."

"It's my sketchbook, same thing."

"Then you shouldn't leave it out." He got to his feet. "If you weren't being so snippy, I'd compliment you on your artwork."

She raised an eyebrow. "Really?"

Oh, no, there she went, seeking approval. An old, bad habit. *Don't go asking for more. Just keep it at that.*

And right out of her mouth came, "My monsters?"

"Yeah. But what's the eye thing?"

She flipped open the book. "This?"

"Yeah."

She traced the outline of the eye. "Something I dreamed about one night, so I started playing around with it." It had given her an eerie feeling but not necessarily a bad one. "I realized that the eye could be for BLUE EYES, the project our parents were involved in. The iris could be an O, for Offspring. And the slashes in the pupil look like an R for Rogues."

"That's ill." At her confused look, he said, "Ill. Good." He grinned. "But the monsters are really cool."

She pouted. "I miss my monsters. I've got movie posters all over my apartment. The classics, like *Frankenstein, The Mummy, The Lost Boys.*" She gave the book a shake. "I specialize in monster tattoos."

She felt her heart catch when he grinned. "Monsters, huh?"

She angled her leg out and pulled up the stretch pants to show him her Dracula tattoo. "I didn't do this one, of course, but it's my design."

"I didn't get a good look at it when you showed it to Gram." He lifted one eyebrow. "I couldn't act as though I'd never seen it before if I was pretending you were my girl."

He knelt and studied it, running his finger over the lines. Seeing him down there reminded her of that night in the woods when he'd been on his knees. When he'd been kissing her stomach, pressing his face against the front of her jeans, then he'd stopped and just held her tight.

She felt heat right where his face had been. There was something so powerful about a man kneeling before a woman. Damn, she couldn't let her thoughts go there. She was getting a handle on her ability; why couldn't she get a handle on her heart?

He stood, which put him inches from her. Appropriately enough, the lead singer was singing, "Gotta Get Away."

"Who is this?" she asked.

"One of my fave bands. You'll never guess their name." He waited a beat. "The Offspring."

"Perfect." She tossed her book in her room. "I'm going upstairs. I'm starved."

Rand shut off the radio. "Me, too."

The aroma of coffee and bacon revved up her appetite even more. The television was on, as it had been the day before, so they could catch any more news on the shooting. The story seemed to die from lack of further information.

The four were scattered around the living space upstairs, and all gazes went to her.

"What?"

Amy, who was in the kitchen, poured a mug of coffee and walked it over to her. Uh-oh, this was going to be bad. Petra, looking tired as she sprawled on the couch, set down her *Cosmo* magazine and tilted her head in sympathy.

Zoe wrapped her hands around the mug. "Don't string me along. What's going on?"

Amy said, "There was a follow-up on the missing Zoe Stoker story. The police found a bag of cocaine hidden in your apartment. Enough to charge you with dealing. And now they're saying that you're obviously missing because of a drug deal gone bad."

Zoe felt her mouth melt into a frown. Her voice came out high-pitched. "They think I'm a drug dealer?"

Amy nodded.

"My friends, my family, my employees . . ."

Amy nodded again, sympathy etched on her freckled face. "I'm sorry."

Zoe sank into the nearest chair at the long table. "My mom is going to think I'm into drugs. Would that surprise her? Probably not." She heard the bite in her words. When she realized everyone was looking at her, she feigned a smile. "So I'm not the poor, missing Zoe anymore."

Rand gave her a sympathetic look. "And you won't be able to go back to your life until—"

"Until when?" She swung around on him. "Until Darkwell tells the police that he set me up? Even if we kill them all, I'll still be wanted for dealing drugs. *Drugs*, for God's sake! I've never even *done* drugs!" No way could she let herself get out of control like that.

She looked at Eric. "Now I know why you want to annihilate these creeps."

He threw his hands up in the air. "Finally, someone understands me."

She walked into the kitchen to stir sugar into her coffee. She wasn't hungry anymore.

Rand followed her, and her body strained to feel a comforting hand on her shoulder. He paused next to her but only grabbed a glass from the cabinet. "I've got to take off for a bit," he said to no one in particular. When Lucas started to object, he said, "Look, we approach this Jerryl dude tomorrow, and I may get killed. I'm not dying without one more joyride, one more taste of freedom. I've been down here for twenty-four hours, and I'm beginning to twitch." Rand poured a glassful of water and chugged it.

Lucas tapped his fingers on the table. "I can't stop you, but be careful. Don't stay in one place for long."

"I never do."

"I want to go," Zoe said before even considering the words. She turned to him. "Please."

"Oh, hell." He rolled his head back.

"I need to call the guy who's heading my shop and tell him to take over." Her voice broke when she said, "Maybe even arrange to sell it. And I need to call my granddad. I can't take a chance of doing it from here. Both calls might take too long to make from the computer."

Rand very clearly, totally, did not want her to go.

"Fine." She walked away from him. "I'll take the Camry."

Eric shook his head. "Can't. That car is hot right now. Witnesses saw it leave, and the police may be on the lookout for it."

"We need to get the 'Cuda as a backup." Lucas looked at Amy. "Maybe your buddy can arrange to get it painted, put on some groundwork, spoilers, and stuff so it doesn't look the same. It's too recognizable to leave it as it is."

Rand grabbed his keys and walked to the door. He punched the buttons to open it. Took a step. Stopped. His body stiffened, and he turned to Zoe. "All right."

She crossed her arms over her chest. "Forget it. I don't want you taking me out of pity."

Rand slapped his forehead. "Women. Look, I'm leaving. You can come with me or not." He stepped through the opening.

"Men," Zoe muttered, stalking toward the door.

She didn't say a word as they walked down the tunnel. The smell of damp concrete filled her nose, though every now and then she got a whiff of his deodorant.

He turned to her when they reached the garage. "I'm going to Baltimore. I didn't want to tell them that. I rep Lucas. I know he's concerned about me . . . kind of like an older brother, I guess." His voice had grown soft at that. "But I don't answer to anyone. And the reason I'm telling you is because you're a wanted felon in Baltimore."

"I'm going to have a helmet on most of the time. My hair's black now. I'm not going to my shop or my apartment."

"Your choice." He stepped closer. "And I don't do anything out of pity, got it? I hate pity, hate charity. I wouldn't put that on anyone else."

"Well, you sure seemed reluctant to let me come."

"Because I want to be alone. Because you and me together has bad painted all over it in pistachio green. And because I've got a hobby that's, shall we say, slightly illegal, and I'm fiending for a fix. If you come, you've got to promise you'll keep your mouth shut." His gaze briefly dropped to her mouth.

An illegal hobby? "Well, it can't be any more illegal than dealing drugs. Right?"

"Not drugs. I don't do them either."

"And it can't be any more dangerous than what we just went through the other night. And nothing is going to happen between us. It's just a physical thing, right?"

"Right," he said a bit too fast. "And maybe that horny side-effect thing."

"Yeah, a bit of that, too. We had our little lip-lock thing, and now it's done. So I'm in."

He had tried his best to dissuade her. She wasn't backing down, though. Not only did she need to call two people, but now she wanted to find out what he was up to.

He got on the bike, and she climbed on behind him. And having to hold on to him wasn't so bad, either.

Gerard was sitting at his huge mahogany desk when Pope walked in, filling the room with his presence. At six-foot-five, with a solid frame and well-defined facial features, the man always took Gerard back.

Pope didn't take the chair, though he did take the proffered glass of rare Scotch whisky as he set down his leather briefcase. He walked to the window and looked out to the lawn. The afternoon light reflected off his shaved head in a muted glow.

"What did you tell your family you were doing here?"

Gerard joined him at the window, taking in the well-manicured gardens and the maze his grandmother had loved. "Not much, only that I lost the building I was using for a strategic project and didn't want to cram everyone into one space at headquarters.

My brother, Leon, passed away, as you probably know. They're distracted by that for the moment. Since this estate has been unused for a year, and has been moldering on the market for even longer, they likely won't even think about it."

He wished he'd thought of it earlier. His grandfather, a military man and highly successful businessman, had been paranoid enough to install security around the grounds. All Gerard had had to do was update the system. Even better, it was close to headquarters, yet still surrounded by twenty acres of land.

He wasn't sure if he liked Pope's involvement in DARK MATTER. Having a powerful man with spider ties to the FBI and none of the restrictions of actually working for them had its advantages. Pope had been peripherally involved in the first program, and because of the messes the Rogues had created, Gerard had to involve him again to help in the cleanup. On the other hand, Pope's interest in the Offspring was disconcerting. Gerard had worked hard and invested a lot of his own money in DARK MATTER. He wasn't about to let someone meddle with his baby.

Pope turned to him, his eyes an unusual shade of violet-blue. "Your men are going down like flies in a bucket of frogs."

The expression would have seemed oddly amusing, coming from the always-serious Pope if Gerard hadn't been annoyed. Pope seemed to know everything, and yet, Gerard knew nothing about who he was, where he came from, or what he did.

"We've taken out two of the enemy: Lucas Vanderwyck and Eric Aruda." He didn't want to get into the details, as delicious as they were. Pope was already too intrigued. "That leaves three women and one man, and he can only see ten seconds ahead."

"And how many of yours have they taken out?"

Pope was poking Gerard's wounds with a stick. And by damn, he seemed to be enjoying his failure.

"Three. Most of them were only injured." He looked at Pope. "Are you ever going to tell me what you did to those men?"

"You only need to know the end result. Isn't that what's most important? No one finds out about your program or exactly what you're doing. No one probes."

Gerard swallowed his frustration. "Of course." It made him crazy, wondering. Something else made him wonder, too. "Why are you helping me? You and I have no special connection."

Pope smiled. "But we do. It is our fascination with things that can't be explained. And our desire to protect what others would shut down."

Gerard couldn't help but think there was more, but who was he to push? The man had saved his ass, and his program, twice. If not for Pope, Gerard would be under intense scrutiny, and, no doubt, DARK MATTER would be gone. The three men who'd been killed he'd had to report as missing. Gladstone had been the trickiest; he'd been a good agent, no history of instability. The two others had been on the edge anyway. One of them, also torched by Eric Aruda, would simply be missing forever. Samuels's body might turn up eventually. That both men were friends helped; they were obviously involved in something illicit that got them both killed.

"Why not just let the Rogues be?" Pope asked. "The more you go after them, the more men you lose, the more cover stories we have to concoct, the higher risk that an innocent person gets caught in the cross fire, and the FBI and your superior get wind of it. The media are awfully interested in the shoot-out at Braden's house."

Gerard's mouth tightened. "I can't let them be. They know too much. They're a threat to my program. And I'm damned close to eradicating them. Then I can move ahead without problems." He didn't want to defend his actions. He'd be tempted to say too much. "You said on the phone that you found my missing Offspring."

His chest tightened. He had discovered an Offspring that no one knew about, but finding anything else about the baby that one of the original subjects had given up for adoption led to several dead ends. Dead ends were Pope's specialty. "Where is he?"

"There's good news and bad news. The good is that we know exactly where he is and that his location makes it easy for us to contact him."

Us. Gerard felt that twitch that had started when Pope first became interested in the program. "And the bad news?"

"He's in prison for murder." Pope walked over to the briefcase and opened it. He pulled out a green folder and handed it to Gerard. "Here's his record. He killed a woman by crushing her throat with his bare hands. He was suspected in another woman's murder, but they didn't have enough evidence to prosecute. They barely had enough to get him as it was."

He itched to dismiss Pope, so he could devour every word, but no one dismissed a man like Pope. Not even, he hated to admit, a man like Darkwell. He flipped through the file, his eyes catching words here and there: *assault . . . stalking . . . victim claimed.*

He only had an idea what the man's powers were, but he definitely had aggression and the ability to kill. Best of all, he was an Ultra, born from two of the subjects in the program, twice as powerful. Gerard fairly salivated.

Pope closed his briefcase with a loud snap. "Read his records. You'll agree that he's not an Offspring you want to work with."

"If he's what I need, I can handle him."

"If you bring in this guy, the Rogues will be the least of your worries. Even the warden is unnerved by him."

Gerard bristled at being told what to do. He'd had enough of that, through his childhood, his career. With DARK MATTER, he had no one to answer to. He pulled his gaze from that intriguing folder, finding Pope watching him. "I'll keep your warning under advisement."

Those eyes seemed to reach right into him. "I hope you do."

"Thank you again for your assistance."

Pope grabbed up his briefcase and paused at the door. "Desperate men lose their judgment. If you make the wrong decisions, I won't be able to help you."

Risking Pope's assistance might be worth not having him breathing down his neck. Once the Rogues were all dead, there would be no more messes to clean up, only victories. He would aim his powerful weapons away from the local area. The right people would start dying with no one the wiser.

Pope left, closing the door with a decisive *click*. Gerard felt a shiver go up his spine. From the prospect of adding perhaps the most dangerous Offspring yet to his program? Or a dark omen?

CHAPTER 17

oe held on tight to Rand as he maneuvered through traffic toward the John Hanson Highway. Just before the exchange, he took a side road next to Weems Creek, a wide waterway that flowed in from the Severn River. On the other side of the creek were homes with their docks and boats.

Rand parked just off the road. He let her alight first, then climbed off the bike and set his helmet on the seat. "Call your granddad before we head off to Baltimore. We don't want them to get a bead on us through the cell tower. And remember, we've got to make every stop quick."

She pulled out her cell phone and dialed the facility's number. "May I speak with Marge Connell, please?" Marge answered a moment later. "Hi, it's Zoe Stoker. I'm checking on my granddad. How's he doing?"

The silence actually felt cold, and then she realized —Marge had heard the news about the drugs. To confirm her suspicion, Marge said, "Should you be calling here?"

This was killing her. "Yes, I should. There's been a terrible misunderstanding." Zoe stopped herself from explaining further. The rest would sound even less believable, and she didn't have time. "How's he doing?"

Marge's normally warm tone was rigid. "He's had some lucid moments, been asking for you."

Zoe grimaced at the ache in her chest. She couldn't risk a visit, not now. Not for a long time, probably. "Tell him I'm sorry I can't be there. He . . . doesn't know about the news report, does he?"

"No, and I wouldn't tell him that. It would break his heart."

Like it was breaking hers. Like his son broke his father's heart when he walked in and shot seven people twenty years ago. She had to tell him that her father hadn't been in his right mind. "Can I speak with him?"

She didn't answer for a moment, as though considering whether a wanted felon should be allowed to talk to her dying grandfather. Zoe squeezed her eyes shut and pushed out, "Please.

"I'll see if he's available."

"Everything all right?" Rand asked from beside her.

She stared at the sunlight reflecting off the wind-ruffled water. "The nurse thinks I'm a drug dealer. Thank God he doesn't know."

"Zoe?"

His voice filled her with both love and grief. "Granddad! How are you?" She turned away from Rand, wanting privacy.

"I'm alive," he said, his voice strained. "So far."

Was she going to see him before he died? "I'm sorry I haven't been by in a couple of days. I'm kind of tied up out of town right now. I'll check in as often as I can."

"I'll be . . . all right, sweetheart."

The endearment made her eyes tear up, and she quickly rubbed at them. "There's something I need to tell you. It's about my dad. Your son. About the shooting."

She heard a *clunk,* like he'd dropped the phone. A woman's voice came on. "I'm sorry, but I've got to give him morphine. Please call back another time."

"No, wait! I've got to tell him something."

"Ma'am, he can't talk anymore. He's in a lot of pain. Call back later." The phone disconnected.

"Damn!" She turned to find Rand standing by the bike. "A nurse hung up on me."

She swiped at her eyes, hating that Rand would see her upset again. This time she had the wherewithal to be embarrassed about it. Last time, in the woods at Truxtun Park, she was out of her mind. "I need to make one more call to RJ, who's taking care of my shop. Then we can roll."

A breeze swept in, carrying the faint scent of salt. She punched in the number and felt a pang of homesickness when Rachael answered, "Creative Ink."

"It's me . . . Zoe. Put RJ on, quick."

"Zoe! What's—"

"No time, sweetie. I need RJ."

A moment later RJ came on the line. "Zoe, what the hell is going on?"

"I'm being set up, and I can't explain more than that. You know me; I don't even drink. I like kids. I'd never deal." She took a breath, halting more words of defense. "Please believe me."

"I do, but—"

"No buts. Just listen. I need you to take care of the shop for . . . for a while. Up your salary, pay my rent for a month or two, hire someone else, just please keep my baby alive, okay?"

"Yeah, sure." His confusion was clear in his voice.

"You have to trust me. This is mad-crazy stuff I'm tangled up in. I've got to go. Thanks." She turned to Rand. "I need to talk to my mom."

He glanced at his watch. "Go ahead, but be quick."

"No, I need to see her. I can't tell her this on the phone. She'll hang up."

"Can't do it, not in person. If they were watching your granddad, they'll be watching her, too."

"Except I'm not that close to her. Haven't been in years." She shrugged. "Ever, really."

"If she's not a drunk, you're way ahead of the game."

Her laugh had not a shred of humor. "No, she doesn't drink, smoke, or cuss. She married a preacher. Do you want to know how she met him?" Bitterness crept into her voice. "She was getting every preacher and priest to exorcise my demon. The one that makes me send things flying."

He lifted the back of her shirt and traced his finger along her she-devil tattoo. "Is that why you got this?"

"I went to New Orleans for a few weeks with some friends after I graduated, and the guy whose apartment we crashed at, he was into meditating, vegan, crystal bowls, and stuff. I thought, what a hippie. But the thing is, this guy had such inner peace that before long he was teaching me to meditate. My friends would go out and party, and I'd stay home with Ralph and do guided imagery and stuff. And I felt—you'll think it's crazy—but I felt God. I connected to something so pure, so joyous and loving, I knew it was God. If I could feel God, I couldn't have evil in me. I got the she-devil to celebrate releasing those old beliefs and because I know He has a sense of humor."

Her mouth quirked. "Mostly it was to spite my mother. And, oh, she was spited all right. I got in her face and showed it to her. It freaked her out and pissed her off, just like I wanted it to. I was eighteen, too immature and hotheaded." She let out a sigh of regret. "I've hardly talked to her since except for strained holiday meals where everyone in the family —including my stepsister and half brother, who are perfect and normal—looks at me like I'm a freak."

"Nothing wrong with being a freak," he said, his way of sympathizing, she guessed.

She shook her head. "But I'd accepted that this thing, whatever it was, was part of me. And now I know it's not evil at all. But the thing is, I like the tattoo. It signifies a change in my attitude and taking back my power. And who needed a mom, anyway, right? I had my granddad and my Goth friends at school. But I need to tell her why Dad went off, and why I have crazy energy and, now, that I'm not a drug dealer."

"You didn't need her approval when you got this." He touched her tattoo again, sending chills up her spine.

"I don't need her approval."

"Yes, you do."

Damn, she hated when he was right. "I just need her to know that I'm not what she thinks I am."

"It's too risky."

"It's not something I can do over the phone. With Granddad, I don't have much choice. But she would just hang up. He wants to hear the truth; she doesn't." She took a deep, quick breath. "All right. Let's go."

They climbed on the bike and made the ride to Baltimore.

Deep into a part of the city she wasn't familiar with, he pulled up to a diner. A real greasy spoon, with a long counter and stools that looked like they'd been there since the fifties, and not in that bright, kitschy way that some diners did. She followed him in. He waved at the guy in the kitchen and the waitress. They knew him, but not by name apparently.

She slid the menu to the side. "I'm not hungry." Since she'd heard about the drugs, her appetite had fled.

When the waitress came to take their order, Rand said, "We'll have two hamburgers, fries, and two chocolate milk shakes." He turned to her. "They have the illest shakes here."

Zoe raised her eyebrows. "You're awfully hungry."

"Half of that's for you, doll."

She started to object, but he handed the menus to the waitress.

"You don't have to take care of me."

"It's nothing to do with taking care of you, just common sense. You didn't eat anything this morning. I don't want you to faint dead away on the back of my bike." He wrinkled his nose. "Messy."

That selfish thing might have worked if he hadn't noticed that she'd skipped breakfast.

She forced herself to eat the burger, though the shake went down good. Dark thoughts pummeled her with the faces of all the people who now thought she was a drug dealer.

He glanced at his watch. "Time to fly."

She pulled herself from the booth, hit the bathroom, and off they went.

He rode into what she would almost call inner city. Older buildings, some covered in graffiti, made her think of gangs. Her chest tightened. What was he up to? And could she keep it a secret if it was really bad?

He pulled beneath an overpass, paused, and surveyed the area. With a nod he killed the engine and kicked down the stand. She climbed off the bike, and he followed, unlocking the bags. He pulled out that black duffel that had made the clinking sounds earlier.

He glanced around again and unzipped the bag. Reached inside. And pulled out a can of spray paint. Then four more. He faced the section of the wall that was covered in a mishmash of names and pictures.

"Toy shit," he muttered, shaking the can for a few seconds, then spraying a wide swath of white paint over the mess.

He was in a zone, like the one he'd been in when he'd maniacally ridden the bike.

She could only stare for a moment. "This is your secret? You vandalize public property?"

"I don't vandalize." He nodded to the section of wall that he hadn't painted over. "I buff ugly stuff like that, walls the toys make a mess of. I only do places the city lets go to pot, or derelict buildings. Instead of looking at that"—he pointed to the other wall—"people get to look at a cool burner."

She walked up to the wall he'd pointed to. "Toys? Oh, you mean kids?"

"Newbies, actually. Wannabes." He shrugged. "We all gotta start somewhere. At first you do bubbly throw ups, just wanting to bomb everywhere you can to get your name up. You build your rep. Then you elevate, hone your craft, and start doing pieces—whole walls, big elaborate paintings—and get as hot and crispy and burnerific as possible."

She chuckled. "Burnerific?"

"Good, delicious *art*. You find your own style, then everyone starts jocking it, imitating you. That's when you're the king, the mac daddy. I've been there, but I don't care about being a king anymore. I just want to paint."

She couldn't help grinning. He'd segued into street slang, and even the way he spoke changed, like he was slinging out the words the way the diner cook slung out the orders. He grabbed another can, faced the now-pristine white wall, and started spraying. "I don't have time to do something burnerific, but man, I just need to get up. Seeing your sketchbook made me itch for it. To feel the can's button on the pad of my finger, the smell of paint, seeing something come together where there was just some crappy wall."

"And what if someone paints over your . . . piece?"

"They will. There's a lot of beef around here—feuds. My boys won't paint over my pieces, but the others will, especially the toys."

He painted as he talked. Since he wore a tank top,

she could see his muscles flexing as he moved the can in graceful arcs. He glanced around every so often as he worked, those checks integrated with his movements.

A lightbulb went off. "Ah, *this* is how you got good at eluding people."

"Exactly." An eagle came to life as he painted. "Graffiti is a twin seduction. There's the element of danger, yeah. Cops, thugs . . . nothing compared to the sons of bitches we've got after us now, though." He paused and assessed his piece, then dropped one can and picked up another in a move so smooth, she hardly saw it. "But mostly it's the art. Expressing yourself, getting this stuff that's inside you out, venting, meditating . . . the art, it's in my mind all the time. I dream about it. I breathe it. I do it for me, mostly, but it's nice when my pieces get people talking."

She watched him fill in shading above the eagle. "I have to admit, I never thought of graffiti as art."

"Most of it's tagging, where writers just slap their throw ups anywhere just to say, 'I was here.' Nothing creative about it, though they think so. That's what gives graff a bad name. But there are some dope artists out there, and if you're lucky enough to see the pieces before they get trashed, they'll blow you away. Some of them get published in books or put up on Web sites, though, so they're preserved. Sometimes I'll do a piece at night, and when I come back to look at it in the daylight, it's already painted over."

"I'll bet that pisses you off. I mean, what's the point if nobody sees it?"

"Yeah, I used to get pissed when someone trashed a piece. I craved applause"—he glanced at her—"peer approval. Since the public hates graff, that's the only approval we get. But I got to a point where I realized it's the art itself, what it means to me. This keeps me grounded. It's the only thing I do that really makes me happy."

"What about gambling?"

He shook his head but kept his gaze on the wall. "Just a means to an end. And a small payback for a friend who got sucked into the addiction and ruined his life. Poor son of a bitch threw himself off a bridge."

Rand filled in a luminescent blue sky in broad strokes. He painted with abandon, his whole body moving with his passion. Oh, to be able to let go like that. To open herself and just let go.

A mouse appeared, hunkered down to avoid the eagle's claws.

"Wow, it's amazing! It's like 3-D." She tilted her head. "Are we the mouse? Is the eagle Darkwell?"

He stood back, looking at the piece. "No, we're the eagle."

"Freedom! Dude, where ya been?"

They both turned at the voice that belonged to a tall, skinny black guy with a Mohawk. He and Rand did some kind of hand-slap shake.

"Been rocking some heavy shit," Rand said. "Had to get up, though."

"Heavy shit, huh? Anything I can help with? As much as you've had our backs, the boys'll have yours, too."

"Thanks, man, but I gotta handle this on my own."

The guy's eyes lit with both interest and curiosity when he saw her.

Rand put out his hand as though to present her. "This is my . . . my . . ." He looked at her, suddenly uncomfortable labeling her in his life. "This is Zoe. Zoe, this is my boy, Taze. That's his graff nickname."

Taze gave her a nod as his gaze took her in. "Nice tattoo," he said, tilting his head toward her Dracula tattoo.

"Thanks."

Rand signed his moniker in letters that looked like stylized, three-dimensional squares.

Taze surveyed the new piece. "Not your best, but still a burner."

Rand glanced at his watch. "Don't have time for the best."

"The city buffed your homage, dude. We're going to hit it tonight. You in?"

Rand threw the cans in the bag and zipped it up. "Can't. Paint my tag in for me."

"Homage?" Zoe asked.

"It's nothing," Rand said, but Taze said, "You didn't see it? Oh, man. I got pictures." Taze started digging in his back pocket. "I can show you—"

"No, we gotta run." Rand walked over and unlocked the bags on his bike. He obviously didn't want her to know about this homage. So naturally, she wanted to know.

"I'd love to see pictures."

He patted his other pocket. "Damn, they must be back in my car. Check out my MySpace page, T-A-Z-E, Sly's slide show."

"Gotta go." Rand gave her a pointed look.

"Who's Sly?" she asked, not budging.

"One of my boys." Taze rubbed the back of his

neck. "Kid was just sixteen, poised to be a king. Freedom took him under his wing when he first started, used his crazy knack for knowing when the cops was coming. The kid idolized this guy."

Rand's expression darkened, and his jaw tightened. "He just hung around, that's all."

Taze continued, so caught up in his story he didn't notice Rand's obvious objection. "We was doing a piece—Sly's first. Freedom has that sixth-sense thing, though, and he started running to Sly, telling him to scram. We thought the cops was coming, but this car came screeching around the corner." He pointed, and Zoe guessed it had happened here. "Sly froze, man, just froze like a deer, and Freedom and I, we was screaming, but he didn't move, and the car slammed right into him. The driver freaked, stumbling drunk, crying and shit. Freedom ran over and grabbed him up, but his head was wrecked. He was breathing, gurgling, then he was gone."

Zoe looked at Rand and saw deep grief and self-blame on his face.

Taze went on. "The driver got six months in jail. That's it, six friggin 'months. Freedom let him have it, did one of his satire pieces, a burnerific painting of Sly's face and the words, 'If a poor black kid dies on the streets, and the rich white folks don't hear it, did he really die?' Cut 'em, man. It cut 'em good. It was all over the news."

She put her hand to her mouth. "I saw that in the paper. Wait a minute." She turned to Rand. "You're *Freedom*, that guy who does the controversial graffiti!"

He took her by the arm and pulled her to the bike. To Taze he said, "We gotta run, dude. Later."

He barely gave her time to get on the bike before he took off. She could feel the tension in his body. He rode for several minutes, then he turned down a road leading toward the water and several marinas. He pulled into a parking lot and killed the engine, set his helmet on the asphalt, and walked to the seawall. He stared across the expanse of water toward boat-storage houses and a dock system.

She remained a distance from him after getting off the bike. He radiated a *Stay away* vibe, his jaw tense and expression fierce. She *should* stay away, give him space. She should.

But she couldn't.

She walked up behind him and slid her arms around his waist, pressing her cheek against his back. The salty breeze whispered through her gelled locks, strong enough to lift them.

He set his hands over hers for a second, then peeled them away. His breathing came deeply, as though he were fighting to keep something inside. She dropped her hands, but remained pressed against him.

"You never let yourself grieve for him, did you?"

"He was just a kid, a punk."

"You cared about him."

He spun around. "I don't *care* about anyone."

"Maybe you can convince yourself of that, most of the time. It's easier for you, and for me, to see you as the reckless, selfish rebel. I hate to tell you this, but you do care." She took a step back. "You blame yourself for his death, don't you?"

He looked away and took a deep, shuddering breath. His eyes glistened with tears. "I saw it happen ten seconds before. And I couldn't stop it. What good is this damned ability if I couldn't save his life?"

"It was his time, Rand."

"He was just sixteen years old!"

She cradled his face in her hands. "I know it's not fair. But you couldn't stop it. You tried, you did your best, but it happened. It wasn't your fault."

"He died in my arms. That kid took his last breath in my arms. And no one cared. The cops didn't care, the media didn't care—"

"You cared."

He shook his head, but she kept her hold on him.

"You care, Rand. You hate it, you fight it, you deny it, but you care. You care about that little 'punk kid,' and you care about your gram, and you care about the Rogues, and you can't stand it, but you care."

He looked everywhere but at her. "I don't want to care. I lose everyone I care about."

The emotion in his voice reached right into her chest. "I know. It's easier to detach. I know, Rand. But sometimes we can't detach." She imagined her grand-dad lying in that bed, wasting away. "And sometimes we lose the person we care about, and dammit, it hurts, and we just have to live with the pain. We feel the pain because we feel the love, but the pain is better than being numb." She didn't even know where these words were coming from, spilling from her heart.

"No, numb is better," he said, staring just beyond her.

The sound of a boat's horn filled the air with its plaintive wail. Even the seagulls seemed to be crying.

She turned his face so he had to look at her. "Numb isn't living. I used to believe that, too, until I nearly died. That night in the woods, what happened, or nearly happened between us, was us needing to feel because numb isn't working. Feeling something is scary. Caring is scary because one of us might die, and another one of us might be holding that person when they take their last breath. But if we don't feel that moment and feel that pain, then we are not alive. We may be the one who survives, but we are not living." Emotion tore through her, pouring out in her voice. "And if you hold me as I take my last breath, and you call me some punk kid who meant nothing to you, I will haunt every waking moment of your life."

His face paled. His voice was nearly a whisper when he said, "I won't . . ."

"Then grieve Sly. Honor him in a deeper way than painting his picture and flipping off the people who didn't care. Because *you* care. Honor him with your heart, Rand."

His chin trembled as he still fought the emotion. She pulled him against her, her arms going around his shoulders. He tried feebly to push away, then he locked his arms around her. His body shuddered as his grief poured out. She knew he'd never let himself cry, not for Sly or for his father or himself and all of his losses.

She felt a ball of emotion in her throat. Neither had she. How they had suffered because of Darkwell. How much they had lost. Could they ever get any of it back?

Standing there, holding Rand, she thought: *Maybe. Maybe just a little.*

He released her, looking away as he wiped his eyes. "We'd better go. We're too vulnerable here."

She nodded, following him to the bike. She knew he meant vulnerable because of Darkwell, but she wondered if he'd meant emotionally, too.

As she settled onto the bike behind him, she knew things had irrevocably shifted between them. He would either draw closer to her or back so far away she'd never reach him again. As she leaned against him, she had a feeling it would be the latter.

The thought crushed her. *Don't get swallowed up, Zoe.*

As they sped out of the parking area, a terrible irony hit her: she was finally beginning to gain control over her power . . . but she had lost control over her heart.

CHAPTER 18

Petra was still wiped out from healing Eric. They had agreed that she should stay back on this mission. She hadn't argued, though she knew waiting for them to return from their meeting with Jerryl Evrard was going to drive her crazy with worry.

While they were going over their final plan, she took a nap. She drifted in and out of dreams, memories of their attempt to contact Braden, hearing echoes of Cheveyo's warning about healing mortal wounds.

So when she heard Cheveyo's voice calling her, she thought it must be part of the dream.

Petra . . . careful . . . danger . . .

She tried to come awake to hear the rest of the words. What if it was a warning? Like when he'd summoned her earlier?

She struggled, but her mind slipped back into deep, dreamless sleep.

Zoe was the bait. Somehow everyone had decided that she was the sexy vamp who would lure Jerryl over to her broken-down car, and so here she was, leaning over the open hood just outside the gym where Jerryl went daily. She positioned herself so that her derriere would be the first thing he'd see when he hobbled out the door. She'd be hard to miss, in bright pink, skintight gym shorts and dainty white sneakers, which would have looked terrible if she were a redhead. Only now she wore a long, curly, blond wig.

To ensure he took the bait, she looked up when Rand gave her the signal and met Jerryl's gaze with her pleading one. "You wouldn't happen to know anything about cars, would you?"

His tank top revealed well-defined muscles. He was more bulked up than Rand but in an artificial way. His hair was as short as his five o'clock shadow.

He squinted his brown, feral eyes and walked over. "What's the problem?"

"When I pulled into the lot, it made a really awful noise and conked out. I barely made it into the parking spot."

Rand walked toward the gym door, then headed in their direction, as though he'd just come out of the building and was ambling over to help.

Except he had a gun under his light jacket. When Jerryl leaned over the engine, Rand came up behind him and pressed the barrel to his hip. "Dude, I hate to do it this way, but we've got to talk. Get in the car."

Zoe bit her lower lip as she met his confused gaze. "Sorry. We can't take any chances. We need to talk to you about some serious stuff that has to do with either your mom or dad . . . a top secret program they were involved in twenty years ago."

Jerryl glanced around as though contemplating

either running or flagging help. Rand pushed the gun harder into his side. "In the car."

Jerryl complied, getting into the backseat with Rand. She slammed down the hood, pulled his crutches into the front, then got into the driver's seat. She glanced around but didn't see Eric and Lucas, who were somewhere nearby. Once they made sure no one followed, they would head to the next location on Rand's bike. She had to take the long way to give them time to get into their lookout positions.

Rand said, "I know this seems waked out to you; I know it did to me. But we're the offspring of people who were in this program, and we've each got a psychic ability. We understand that someone from the government tried to recruit you. Despite the fact that I've got a gun pointed at your appendix, we're the good guys."

She glanced in the rearview mirror. Jerryl didn't seem to buy that. "Where are we going?"

"Someplace we can talk without getting shot at. We're trying to get enough of us together so we can figure out what happened to our parents." He wasn't going to get into the annihilation part yet.

Zoe asked, "Did one of your parents die when you were young?"

"Yeah, my mom. She worked for the DIA—Defense Intelligence Agency—and some guy walked in and shot a bunch of people. She was one of them."

She nearly ran into the back of the car in front of her. The blood drained from her face. She exchanged a glance with Rand in the rearview mirror.

He turned back to Jerryl. "The guy who tried to recruit you, he works for the guy who ran the original program. He's got a new program, and he wants to use us because of the skills we inherited from each of our parents."

"Man, this is some pretty crazy shit you're telling me."

"I know. It takes a while to sink in. We'll tell you what we know, and you can check around on your own. If your father is still alive, he probably won't know much about what your mom was involved in. Apparently the government paid off the families involved to keep them quiet. They don't want anyone to know about this, and they'll kill us to keep it that way. That's why we're taking precautions."

Jerryl sat back in the seat, a stunned expression on his face. "Can you lower the gun? You're making me nervous, especially with her looking back here more than she's looking ahead."

She blinked and faced forward.

"She's got it under control." Rand warmed her with his confidence, even if she didn't quite deserve it.

"How many of you are there?" Jerryl asked.

"Not enough."

Nicely evasive, she thought.

She drove back to southern Annapolis to a run-down area with a jumble of faded warehouses. Because of its creek-side location, the area was destined for demolition. The developers of the future upscale shopping area were probably waiting for the economy to resurface. For the moment, it was a good place for clandestine activity, as nothing was nearby. Lucas had told her that he, Eric, and Petra had taken Gladstone, the CIA agent assigned to assess them, here to interrogate him. She'd also learned that Eric, behind their backs, had set the man on fire.

Lucas had done his prescient sketches of a man kill-ing Eric, and Eric recognized that man as Gladstone. Amy, with her crackerjack ability to recover lost data on damaged hard drives, was able to read the agent's journal and confirm Eric's suspicions. The man was going to recommend that Eric be terminated. That Eric had killed Gladstone against the others' wishes was another example of his volatile nature, and that nature worried Zoe almost as much as what Jerryl might do if he was the enemy.

Lucas and Eric had already removed the chain that barred the entrance to what had once been a thriving industrial park. Weeds sprouted through cracks in the asphalt parking area and even grew in the gutters. The once-blue buildings had faded to a powdery gray. Some windows were broken out, and what Rand would probably consider "toys" had left their marks with graffiti tags so stylistic she couldn't read them.

She parked around the back of the building next to the creek. She didn't see anyone but knew that Lucas and Eric were positioned at opposite corners outside the building so they could scan the sur-roundings, weapons ready. Amy was standing on the rim of a Dumpster outside a broken window, where she could communicate with both of them and also listen to what was going on inside. Neither man would make an appearance unless necessary, at least not yet.

She pulled a gun from her purse. Rand insisted she be armed, just in case.

Those words again!

She held the gun by her thigh as they walked into

the cavern of a warehouse, Jerryl slower because of the crutches. Several broken windows let in enough watery light to showcase the dust motes dancing in the musty air. She passed a scorch mark on the concrete floor and shivered. A man had died there. Burned to death. She forced her gaze to a grouping of chairs below the window where Amy was positioned.

Jerryl looked around. "What is this place?"

Rand said, "A private spot to meet. So, if you haven't decided we're crazy, are you ready to hear more?"

"Yeah. Sure."

Rand nodded toward the chairs. Both men sat backward. Must be a guy thing. She bent one knee beneath her and sat.

Between the two of them, they filled him in.

He didn't ask a lot of questions, just seemed to absorb what they were saying. When they were done, he asked, "We all have different psychic abilities then?"

Rand said, "Yeah. What's yours?"

"Sometimes I have a knowing about things. Freaked out my superiors when I mentioned it. I stopped mentioning it." He looked at them. "What about you?"

Rand had said to downplay their abilities, though the bad guys already knew what he could do. "I see ten seconds ahead. Zoe, we're not too sure what she can do yet."

"What about the others?"

Rand shrugged. "A little of this and that. We'll let them tell you, when we're ready. For now we want to give you time to absorb all this. Be careful, though, about digging too much. These guys already killed one of us for doing that."

Jerryl looked at Rand. "You're right; I never heard squat about the circumstances surrounding my mom's death. It was a big secret. Always bugged me."

Rand kept the gun at his side. "What we're involved in here is a war. Except the people we're fighting are the ones most of the country thinks are the good guys. We can't go to the police or the FBI or anyone in the government. We're on our own. And it's dangerous."

Jerryl nodded toward his foot. "Took a piece of shrapnel in the ankle. But the Marines don't want me back. Because I'm different. Because of the things I let slip that I knew were going to happen. I don't know what I'm going to do. But I had gone in for the fight. Sounds like this is a battle that's even more important. I want to meet the rest of you, get up to speed. If what I have is a psychic ability, I want to work on it, master it. Where do I sign up?"

She and Rand exchanged a glance. *That was easy. Too easy?*

"Excellent, man." Rand shook Jerryl's hand. "The next step is to figure out our next step. Right now you're not a target, so it's best to keep you on the outside. We'll get you an untraceable phone so we can communicate."

After Lucas, Eric, and Petra had inadvertently become the Rogues, no one since had joined voluntarily. Amy, Rand, and Zoe had joined as a result of being in danger.

Their plan was to watch Jerryl for a few days and see what he did. Then they'd get him a phone and introduce him to the rest of the Rogues. No one had to explain the reason for being paranoid to her.

Trusting the wrong person could be deadly.

Amy braced her hands against the side of the building for balance and listened to the conversation. Relief flooded through her when she heard Jerryl sign on. Lucas was at the far corner. She smiled and gave him a thumbs-up. Holding on to the edge of the window, she leaned around the edge and spotted Eric at his corner. Thankfully, he was still in place. She gave him a thumbs-up, too.

The moment of triumph shattered when Lucas clutched his head, let out a groan of pain, and collapsed to the ground.

Her first panicked thought: *He's been shot!*

With a fearful cry, she dropped to the ground and, ducking, ran to his side. In her peripheral vision, she saw Eric swinging his gun in arcs as he made his way over.

I don't see blood. There'd be blood, right?

"It's . . . back," Lucas said.

No, no more of the storm of images.

His body trembled, and the veins in his temples and neck stood out. "Jerryl . . . I think . . . he's the Ultra . . . enemy Ultra."

Lucas fell, limp. She tried to revive him, but Eric grabbed her shoulder. "Did he say what I thought he did?"

"He said, 'I think.' We can't shoot Jerryl if we're not sure."

Rage burned in his eyes as he stalked to the door, gun at the ready. "Then I'll make sure first."

* * *

Zoe looked up at the window when she heard Amy's gasp. Both men stood, and Rand reached for his gun. She stood, too, her heart pounding and fingers tightening on the gun she held.

No, not when things are going smoothly for a change.

"What's going on?" Jerryl asked.

The door burst open, and Eric charged through, his gun aimed at Jerryl. "This is the guy who got into my head!"

Amy ran through the door yelling, "Eric, don't!"

A strong arm grabbed Zoe and spun her against a hard chest. Before she could orient herself, she felt the gun torn from her hand and pressed to her cheek. Black spots floated in front of her for a moment. When they cleared, she saw a terrified Rand and to her left, Eric pointing his gun at her—or rather at Jerryl, who was holding her, and so she was looking down the barrel, too.

"I thought you were dead." Jerryl's voice took on a taunting tone. "Didn't you go a little crazy and shoot yourself? This time you're going to shoot your buddy, Randall."

Eric's face paled. He began to point the gun toward Rand, his head shaking back and forth.

Zoe screamed, "No!"

Chairs fell over, and one even skidded across the floor. Her crazy energy.

Eric swung the gun toward her. It went off with a deafening explosion of sound. Her body shuddered. Warm blood gushed down the back of her shoulder. She stared at him in disbelief. He'd shot her.

Wait. No pain. He hadn't hit her. He'd hit Jerryl. But

a second later the gun was again pressed against her face.

"Here!" Eric tossed his gun to Rand.

Rand caught it and faced Jerryl. "Let her go. Your beef is with us."

"My beef is with all of you. And you're all going to die." She felt Jerryl's body tense.

He would shoot them first, using her as a shield.

Not if she could help it. She focused on the gun. *Push!*

Jerryl swung the gun out and aimed at Rand, who jumped to the side. Jerryl's arm trembled. "What the hell?"

She saw him fighting the pull while Rand moved around behind him. She took a deep breath and with a grunt of effort sent the gun flying out of Jerryl's hand. Eric started running toward him, but stopped dead, looking behind her.

Jerryl swung around in time to find Rand aiming the gun at his head. Jerryl dragged Zoe in front of him. "Shoot me and you shoot her."

Rand's face reddened with fear and frustration. He couldn't shoot without risking hitting her. Eric had, but Rand wouldn't.

Jerryl's eyes narrowed. "Right now I can get into Eric's head. Soon I'll be able to get into all of your heads."

Without needing crutches at all, Jerryl hauled Zoe to the door and leaned out. Amy stood there, arms and expression rigid as she held the gun. She faltered when she saw Zoe and gave a helpless shake of her head.

"Set the gun down."

Amy lowered her body as though to set it on the ground, but she twisted and threw it instead. It skidded beneath the car behind her.

Jerryl growled under his breath. He'd probably intended to grab it.

"Get out your car keys," he said to Zoe as he walked toward the car. "Slowly."

She pulled them out of her pocket. *I can't let him have the keys. He'll take me to that awful man who'll shoot me up with the Booster until I die!* She eyed the creek several yards away. *Yes!* She threw them into the water.

"Bitches. You think you're so smart. At least I'll get one of you. This time."

He hauled her backward as Rand and Eric ran out the door. She tripped, but he held her tight. That gave her an idea. She let her body go limp. It hadn't worked with the first assassin, but Jerryl would be too vulnerable if he tried to pin her down.

He grabbed her tighter around the waist, so tight it hurt, and suddenly she felt nothing below her feet. Her stomach clenched as her body fell backward. She saw sky.

He'd stepped off the seawall!

They hit the cold water with a breathtaking splash and plunged below the surface. She twisted, kicking at his legs, but the water rendered her kicks useless. His arm was like an iron band around her stomach. He was a Marine. He could probably freaking hold his breath for an hour.

But I can't!

His shoulder. She reached back and, claws out, grabbed where she thought the bullet went in. She heard his garbled roar of pain even below the water.

His hold on her loosened enough so that she could kick him in the stomach to swim free.

He grabbed her ankle, pulling her back. She turned and kicked at him again. He tried to grab her other foot, but she jerked it free. He was holding her with his injured arm. She pulled hard and freed her foot.

Her chest tightened from lack of oxygen. She swam as fast as she could through the murky water. The glow of light played on the surface above her. She swam toward it. He was behind her. Coming for her.

Don't look. Just swim!

She burst upward and gasped. Through water-logged vision she saw Rand kick off his shoes and dive in. Amy and Eric came into view, running along the seawall with their guns poised. She turned behind her and looked for Jerryl. He didn't have a hold on her, which meant they could shoot him if he surfaced.

Amy frantically waved her over to a dock that had a ladder. "Zoe, this way!"

Rand reached her, his gaze taking her in and then looking all around them. "You all right?"

She nodded, unable to speak. Jerryl was below them. The thought paralyzed her for a moment. Coming up on her. Ready to pull her down. She kicked downward just in case, expecting to hit an arm or leg. Nothing.

"Swim toward Amy. I've got your back."

Her arms felt like rubber as they thrashed through the water. The ladder seemed miles away. Fear underlay Amy's words of encouragement: "Come on, Zoe, you can do it!"

The hell she could. She was breathless, exhausted.

Rand gave her a helpful push the last two feet to

a decrepit ladder. The rung beneath the water was rotted. The one above it was cracked. Amy reached out, and Zoe grabbed her hand and stepped on the sturdier-looking rung. Once she put her weight on it, she heard a *crack*. It gave way, and she started falling backward. Amy's hand squeezed hers hard as she tried to pull Zoe up. Rand's hands cupped her behind and gave her enough of a push so that Amy could pull her the rest of the way onto the dock.

Zoe fell on the weathered boards in a heap. From her sideways angle, she saw Rand pull himself up without benefit of the rickety ladder. Eric still monitored the water, gun ready, but he clearly had no idea where Jerryl was.

Amy knelt next to her. "Are you all right?"

Zoe nodded. "Just . . . need . . . a . . . breath."

"I've got to check on Lucas. He had another one of his storms of images and collapsed. You'll be okay?"

"Yes, go."

Love and fear mingled in Amy's expression, then she ran. For a moment Zoe stared at the stark blue sky. The ache in her chest eased with each gasping breath. Rand's face appeared above her, dripping water onto her cheeks, and she swore she saw the same combination of emotions on his face.

"I'm fine," she said, anticipating his question. "Help me up."

His hand clasped hers, and he pulled her to her wobbly feet. She leaned on him for a second before regaining her balance.

Eric came up to them. "Can't find the son of a bitch anywhere." He took one last survey of the water. "Dammit."

"He's good." Rand scanned the water, too. "He knew we'd approach him, and he went along with the story. Played us. Even used crutches to make us think he wasn't a physical threat." He stepped closer to Eric. "But don't you ever shoot anyone when he's holding one of ours. You could have shot Zoe, for God's sake."

Eric's face showed no regret. "But I didn't. At least I got a shot at him. Unfortunately, it wasn't fatal."

"Did he get into your head again?"

"Yeah, but I reacted as soon as I heard him, pretended he had me."

"Good job getting rid of the gun."

Eric's mouth tightened. "Can't get me to shoot someone if I don't have a weapon in my hand." He turned to Zoe "And you . . . nice job pushing his gun away."

She glowed at the compliment.

"Let's get out of here," Rand said.

They reached the car as Amy helped Lucas around the corner. He looked flushed and weak. "The storm of images is back."

Eric knelt and grabbed the gun Amy had thrown beneath the car. "Your ability is back."

"More intense than ever. It knocked me on my ass. Sorry I couldn't help."

"But you did. You warned us, and you were right. We almost let the enemy into our ranks. If we'd taken him back to the tomb, it would have been the end of us."

Amy's face was pale. "Lucas, you can't take many more of these."

"It's not like I have any choice."

Zoe could see the price of loving someone on

Amy's face. *With the pain comes the joy, and with the joy comes the rain,* as her granddad always said.

Rand looked at her. "You go in the car, Zoe. You're too wet to ride the bike."

Not to mention that he obviously didn't want a cold, wet, shivering-with-fear person clinging to him. Or anyone clinging to him. As they walked to the car, she felt a shiver and looked behind her. She didn't see anyone . . . but he was there.

CHAPTER 19

"Dude, you sound like a porno flick," Rand said as he pushed the chest press bar the next morning.

Eric let out a long groan and let the stack clang down. "A good one, I hope."

Lucas chuckled as he did biceps curls. "He's always been loud."

Rand sat up. "Speaking of women . . . we need to keep them out of anything like what happened yesterday."

Lucas lifted an eyebrow. "Try telling Amy that. She'll deck you."

"It's not that I think they're less valuable or weak. They're more vulnerable." And if he witnessed Zoe being grabbed or held at gunpoint again, he was sure he'd have a heart attack. "Now they know we'll drop our weapons if they can grab one of the women."

Lucas gave him a knowing smile. "Sucks when you love 'em, doesn't it?"

"No, it's not that," Rand said a bit too quickly. "But you know, seeing a woman in a position like that just rips out my chest. Should have been one of us being dragged into that water."

Eric leaned against the preacher-curl pad. "Not you, too. God, I'm surrounded by *couples*. And all I've got are my *Playboy*s." He shook his head in disgust and went back to his groaning and weight work. "Didn't I warn you that getting involved was a bad idea?"

"We are not a couple." Okay, he'd definitely said that a little too emphatically. "I've never wanted what you and Amy have. I think it's great, for you. For other people. Someday, I'm going to hit the road, and I'm going to be alone. Me and my bike."

Lucas regarded him thoughtfully. "I hate to tell you this, but I tried just as hard not to fall. I had noble reasons, too. Good solid reasons. Still do, for that matter. But here I am. Even when she thought I was going to die, she wouldn't let me go. She said she'd rather have love now and lose it than not have it at all."

"Do you believe that, too?"

Lucas paused, then nodded. "Yeah, I guess I do."

Rand went back to his chest presses. His sexual attraction to Zoe, that was one thing. Yeah, a big thing. His mouth had tasted her flesh, her breasts, and damn, he couldn't get that image of her half-naked in the moonlight out of his head . . . or other places in his body. He could chalk all of that up to his libido.

But that scene by the waterfront, when she'd forced him to face his loss . . . that cut deep inside him. He'd never realized how dangerous tenderness was.

Eric dropped the stack and pushed to his feet. "Lucas, your powers were gone for about a week after Petra healed you. So mine should be back in a couple of days. I want another face-off with this guy, Offspring to Offspring. If he can get into my head, then I can get into his. I'll send him to hell. I'll find where they are and torch the whole place. I'll—"

Lucas held out his hand. "I'm about ready to keep you back from the action, too. You're volatile, Eric. You talk about letting emotion get in the way of logic. Love's not your problem, my friend; it's rage and your thirst for revenge. You've gone barging into situations without thinking things through. You put us all into a bad situation at the asylum when we went in for Rand. And yesterday, we could have handled Jerryl without alerting him to our suspicions and risking Zoe." Lucas pressed his fingers against his temples. "We need to be logical, to be . . ." He drifted off, his eyes vacant.

Eric curled his hand into a fist. "When the moment's right, no one's going to keep me from smashing them. I—" He slapped his hands together, and Lucas blinked.

"What?"

Rand said, "Dude, you faded away right in the middle of a sentence. Do you have a headache?"

Lucas seemed to realize he was rubbing his temples. "Just a dull ache."

A fissure of fear crossed his expression. He didn't think it was just a headache. And neither did Rand.

Zoe, Amy, and Petra all reached for different feminine-protection products at the department store.

Zoe rolled her eyes. "Can't ask the guys to pick up this kind of stuff."

Petra giggled. "They'd be all like, 'What's the difference between maxi and mini? And what the hell are *wings*?' "

Amy shook her head, laughing. "They just wouldn't do it."

Petra turned to Zoe. "Lucas would. If he'd take a bullet for her, you know he'd buy tampons." Amy's face sobered at that.

"He would probably consider both equally grievous," Zoe said.

Petra walked over to the magazine aisle. "That's the test of real love, you know. Or even real lust. Ask the guy to run out for pads, especially when he knows he's not getting any."

Zoe hooted. "Rand certainly wouldn't. You should have seen his agony while I was buying panties."

"He would buy tampons," Amy said, "but he'd make a big deal about it to preserve his manhood. You should have seen the look on his face when Jerryl grabbed you. He dove into the water. I think he'd take a bullet for you, too."

Zoe dismissed that with a wave of her hand while her heart leapt at the suggestion. "He'd do the same if any of us got grabbed. It's a macho thing." She walked over to the makeup center and plucked mascara from the rack.

Petra joined her, holding eight magazines in her arms. "Don't take this personally, but you wear a little too much makeup."

Amy threw back as she walked away, "Unlike me, who doesn't wear enough, according to Miss Beauty Expert."

Zoe caught her reflection in a small mirror above the shades display. "I've always worn this much makeup. I remember leaving for school and doing it at the bus stop so my mom wouldn't see me."

"You're very pretty." Petra appraised her. "At least, I bet you are."

Zoe felt that need for approval rise, but she wasn't giving up her makeup. "It feels comfortable. Natural."

"Doesn't look natural." Petra wiggled her fingers like a mad scientist. "You should let me make you up sometime."

Amy said, "You had me looking like a sex kitten. She already looks like that."

Petra's blue eyes glinted with ideas. "That was for a reason. With you, I'd go light and natural, autumn colors. Cinnamon would look incredible on those luscious lips of yours. Do you realize women get injections to have a mouth like that?"

"I hate my mouth." Still, the compliment felt good.

Even though Zoe didn't want anyone messing with her look, something about the exchange felt sisterly. Her stepfather had a daughter about Zoe's age, but they couldn't have been more different: preacher's daughter versus possessed Goth girl, smackdown at eleven.

Standing at the display of condoms, Amy held up one of the boxes. "Is ribbed really better? Lubed or not? Good grief, how many varieties can there be?"

Petra looked at her watch. "Ten more minutes." They were limiting their outings to less than half an hour.

Zoe said, "I need to buy pistachio ice cream for Rand."

Both Petra and Amy wrinkled their noses. "Pistachio ice cream?"

"Yeah, I know. It's *green*."

Amy pushed the shopping cart down the aisle.

"Petra, I'm surprised you're not all over the clothing section."

Petra wrinkled her nose even more at that. "I don't buy my clothes at stores that also sell tampons and lawn mowers." She was, of course, way overdressed.

Amy laughed. "Ah hah, you're a shopping snob."

"You bet I am. The next time I'm out, I'm hitting the boutiques. I need a clothing fix."

A few minutes later they headed out to the car, all watching the parking lot.

Zoe said, "As much as I detest being locked up in the tomb, being out and paranoid isn't much better."

Amy tossed the bags into the backseat of the Camry, her thoughts obviously in a dark place if her frown was any indication. "I know Cyrus wouldn't have betrayed me. He died trying to protect me. He gave me this car. So what happened with Jerryl?"

Zoe slid into the backseat as the other two got into the front. "You said there was another guy who tried to break into your dream."

"Gladstone, the guy Eric killed. That last time, he was screaming, trying to come through, but Cyrus didn't let him."

Zoe ran a finger over her ring tattoo. "What was Gladstone saying? Could you hear?"

"No. It was hard to hear with all the racket."

"Oh, my God," Petra said, looking back at Zoe, whose expression mirrored hers. "Are you thinking what I'm thinking?"

Zoe nodded. "It wasn't Cyrus," they both said simultaneously.

Amy had been about to put the car into reverse. She stopped and looked at them. "Why didn't I think of that? You're right. Yes, you have to be right. It was Gladstone who told me that. He wanted us to contact Jerryl, knowing he was the enemy. And that was Cyrus screaming in the background, trying to warn me." She pressed her forehead against the steering wheel.

"We'd better go," Petra said.

Amy jerked into action, pulling out. A few minutes later she grabbed her cell phone and dialed a number. "Hey, Oz."

On the speaker they could hear him say, "Amy! It's always such a relief to hear from you. At least I know you're alive. You should call in every day so I don't worry."

Petra gave Zoe an amused look and mouthed, "*Yes, Mom.*"

"Oz, I need a favor."

"Great. Fantastic. I've been working out, you know. I've got biceps when I flex real hard."

Even Amy had to tighten her mouth to keep from laughing. "That's good, Oz. This won't require any feats of strength or speed, though. Could you find someone who can change the look of Lucas's car? Dumb it down, maybe even put a different model's nameplate on it so it doesn't have the word *Barracuda* anywhere?"

"I know an IT guy who dabbles in car restoration."

"Perfect. Don't let on that we're trying to hide it from the cops, though. Raises too many questions."

"To which I have no answers anyway." His consternation over that hardened those words.

"For your own good. Give him some story, like a stalker ex-girlfriend."

"I'll take care of it."

"We'll reimburse you for any expense."

"Don't worry about that. What else do I have to spend my money on? And that means we'll have another rendezvous, right?"

"Ah, yeah, I suppose we will."

"I'm on it. I'll let you know when it's ready."

Amy's voice softened with affection. "Thanks, Oz."

"Anything for you."

As soon as she disconnected, Zoe said, "He has such a crush on you. I could see it that day we got Orn'ry."

Amy sighed. "I know. And in a weird way, his semi-involvement in our mess might be good for him, might punch up his confidence."

They were within a few minutes of the garage when Petra gasped. "I've got the feeling!"

"Oh, hell." Amy turned and sped away in the opposite direction.

Zoe looked from one to the other. "What feeling? What's 'the feeling'?"

Petra wrung her hands in nervous flutters. "One of them is remote-viewing us. It's a creepy feeling, like a shiver that starts at your neck and crawls down your spine."

"Yeah, I feel it, too," Zoe said. "Like I did when we were at hospice."

Amy asked, "It's not Eric?"

Petra shook her head. "No, and . . . I'm pretty sure it's not the guy who remote-viewed us when we were getting this car. It's a different kind of energy. Not as heavy."

"Maybe it's the girl we saw at the asylum."

"Put up the shield," Amy said.

"Wait. I want to try something." Petra looked up. "Whoever you are, you're on the wrong side! Darkwell is lying to you. You lost your mom or dad when you were young. They were working for the government or were part of some program that no one can tell you anything about. They died because of that program, and now you're working for the man behind it. He only wants to use you. All *we* want is the truth. Don't you want to know why you have the abilities you do? Don't you want to be on the right side?"

She squeezed her eyes shut. "Golden shield, golden shield." Seconds later, she opened her eyes. "She—or he—is gone. Let's go."

After returning to the tomb and putting away the supplies, all three went downstairs. Petra waved her hand in front of her nose. "Whew-ee, it reeks of testosterone in here!"

Eric let out a groan as he pulled down on the lat bar. "You better believe it, baby."

Zoe found her gaze slipping to Rand. His bare chest was slick with sweat, and the light played off his piercings. Unlike a lot of tattoo artists, she wasn't big into body piercing, but on Rand . . . well, they were growing on her.

Like a kid, he asked, "Did you get my ice cream?"

"Of course."

Petra said, "One of them remote-viewed us." That got their attention, and she went on. "I think it might be the girl. I told her about the people she was working for. Maybe it'll make her start to question things."

Eric released the weight stack. "Good idea. But I'm

still going to blow them away the second I lay eyes on them. Girl or guy. Once an enemy, always an enemy."

The thought of killing someone made Zoe shudder. To change the subject, she asked, "Have we found out any more about Robbins?" Kidnapping a man wasn't quite as bad as talking about killing a person.

Lucas shook his head. "We've been all over the Internet. We're going to have to go to Bethesda and see if we can spot his car. It's a shot in the dark, but it's all we have."

She carried her bag to her room—and dropped it. As she stared at the far wall, her hand went to her mouth. It felt as though her heart was filling with helium.

Rand had painted a collage of monsters: Dracula, Frankenstein, the Mummy. Her open sketchbook lay on her bed. He had painted not only monsters, but *her* monsters. And he'd done a freaking ill job.

Sensing him standing in the doorway, she turned and without even thinking, threw her arms around him. "I love you!" She blinked and backed away. "I mean . . . not *love you* love you, but . . ." She turned back to the wall, her eyes glistening. "I love it. I totally love it."

He shrugged. "Gave me something to do."

He wasn't going to admit he'd done it to be sweet, and maybe he hadn't. She walked closer to the wall, now smelling the scent of paint, and touched the lines. "This is mad cool."

"Whoa."

She turned to find everyone crammed into the door opening, having heard her exclamation.

Rand shrugged. "I do a little painting."

She noticed he hadn't signed it. He was only willing to reveal a tiny bit of his secret to make her room more like home. Still, that he'd done that much nearly made her cry.

"It's cool," Eric said. "Almost as cool as naked women."

Lucas assessed it. "Nice work. Excellent shading, good dimension . . . how did you do this?"

"Aerosol."

Lucas's eyes bugged out. "As in *spray paint*?"

Rand's pride filled his smile. "Yep."

Lucas looked at the wall with renewed appreciation. "That is amazing. You can't even tell."

Petra didn't share their enthusiasm. "Yikes, I wouldn't want to wake up with those looking at me."

Zoe grinned. "What better to keep the monsters away than monsters of my own? I told Rand I missed my monsters; I've got movie posters all over my apartment. So he gave me back my monsters."

She saw Lucas give Rand a curious smile, but she was too touched to think about it.

Eric turned to Rand. "I got a serious art question for you: can you do hot chicks?"

CHAPTER 20

With her hands wrapped around a hot mug of coffee, Zoe dared to check the computer the next morning and see if there was any follow-up to her arrest warrant. She was touched to see that RJ had sworn he'd never seen Zoe so much as drink, much less smoke, and how could a woman who'd just raised thousands of dollars for a playground deal drugs?

Evidence was evidence, the article seemed to sum up. If the drugs weren't hers, why wasn't she coming forward to proclaim her innocence? Why was she, in fact, hiding?

She leaned back in the chair and swiveled around. The small room was crammed with a desk, a rack of car batteries, and security monitors that showed the entrances to the shelter. One of the three entrances was obsolete, though a camera still showed a blank wall. One came in from Lucas's art gallery upstairs and led to his and Amy's bedroom. The frame showed a bookcase similar to the one that hid the stairwell in the living area. The third frame showed the interior of the shed, which was barely discernible in the dark.

Zoe sighed and was about to log out of the newspaper's site when she caught something about her stepfather. The Reverend Harry Withers would be hosting an old-fashioned revival in Baltimore that weekend. Her throat went dry. She knew her mother would be there, the faithful preacher's wife at his side. Zoe also knew she had to take the opportunity to talk to her. Not only to tell her that she wasn't a drug dealer but that she wasn't evil, either. She couldn't tell her all of the truth, but a little bit of it. Maybe she could find out more about what made her father "evil."

She joined the others in the living area. The place was growing on her, which was scary. The vivid colors on the walls made her feel at home, though some of the wild artwork didn't. Lucas was painting, deep in his own thoughts. Amy was sitting on the floor watching him, lost in dark thoughts of her own. Petra was lying on the couch, her feet up on the back, thumbing through a fashion catalog. Zoe's gaze always seemed to seek out Rand, and if that wasn't annoying enough, he usually caught her.

"My mom is going to be at a huge revival in Baltimore this weekend. I need to talk to her."

Eric shook his head. "Not safe."

Rand mirrored Eric's motion. "No way."

Remembering what Rand had said to Lucas, she said, "I'm not asking permission, other than to use the car. It's a perfect opportunity. There are going to be hundreds of people around. I'll slip in the back. If Darkwell knows anything about me, he knows I'm not close to my mother and stepfamily. And I'm not exactly a churchgoer. I'll be careful."

Amy said, "Oz left a voice mail for me. He's already

taken the 'Cuda to his friend, who doesn't think it'll take long to 'de-glam it,' as he put it. Maybe we'll have two cars by then."

Petra gave her a knowing smile. "Or five. He's so eager to please you."

Lucas looked up, one eyebrow arched. "Should I be worried? Will I have to duel this guy for your hand?"

Amy's smile was tinged with sadness. "I've got eyes for no one but you."

Eric nodded to Zoe's hand. "What's that?"

She twisted her hand to give him a better look. "I'm experimenting." She sat down next to Rand on the sofa. "Wondering what it'd look like as a tattoo." She explained the significance of the Offspring eye.

"I want one." Eric lifted his sleeve and flexed his biceps. "Right here."

Eric's enthusiasm made her smile.

Amy leaned over and studied the drawing. "I like it. It could be our symbol."

Rand shook his head. "Not me. I don't do tattoos."

Zoe would bet it was because he didn't want something that tied him into a group. Just like he hadn't painted his walls; he wasn't going to be there long. "When I get to Baltimore, I'll pop into my shop and get my equipment. It'll fit in my pocket." Before they could protest, she added, "I haven't been to my shop in almost two weeks. They won't expect me to go there now. It'll be in and out."

The thought of seeing her shop, even for a few seconds, caused a bittersweet ache in the pit of her stomach. Would she ever be there, working at her station, kidding with RJ and Rachael, again?

Eric propped his feet on the coffee table with a thud. "On the upside, every time we encounter these schmucks, we have a chance to kill one. As long as we're prepared. We've got another field trip to make. When Petra and I went to my . . . father's house to find out more about what our mother was involved in before she died, we found a letter in a box of her stuff." He pulled a wrinkled letter from his pocket. "It's from Calvin Hobson, President of the SPP, Society for Psychic Phenomena, in Washington, D.C., to my father." He cleared his throat. " 'Dear Mr. Aruda, We have just learned of Camilla's death, and we wish to extend our sincerest condolences. She was very special to us here at SPP and will not be forgotten. We were never comfortable with her involvement in the program and continue to have our suspicions. If you wish to discuss any of this, please contact me at the above number.' "

Clearly Amy and Lucas already knew about it, but they listened nonetheless.

Eric said, "Our father denied knowing anything about it, and as it turns out, he's not my father or anyone who will help us. But I've got this, and we can find out more from this SPP, I bet. I looked them up. I was stunned to find that they're still around." His voice got a little softer. "And maybe I can find out who my father really is. My mother apparently met someone in the program. Lucas's mother, too. Hey, Lucas, we might be related."

Amy had gotten pale and quiet. It was obviously a sensitive subject.

Eric waved the letter in the air. "We don't know exactly how the SPP plays into this, but it sounds like our mom was involved with them, and they didn't like her being in the program."

Petra's eyes widened. "Which must be BLUE EYES."

Eric nodded. "And if the SPP didn't approve, they're obviously not connected to the CIA or Darkwell. I poked around their Web site early this morning. I'm going to call and make an appointment."

Lucas planted his hands on his knees. "We have to figure out if it's worth the risk. They weren't involved twenty years ago. But what about now?"

Amy said, "Maybe they'll know what our parents were given. I agree with Eric, amazingly enough. It's worth the risk. And while we're out, we'll go to Bethesda and see if we can find Robbins."

Gerard Darkwell walked the prison hall to the visitor room, with its stark gray walls and floor. He wrinkled his nose at the smell of old coffee. Nobody visited Sayre Andrus, not his adoptive parents, who'd ended up testifying against him and were now dead, not a wife or girlfriend. Sayre was destined to spend the rest of his life in prison, and, according to the warden, he seemed strangely peaceful about his prospects. That was only one of the things that unnerved the warden, the guards, and even the other prisoners.

Sayre was brought in by a guard who, despite his six-foot-five frame, tried his best not to touch the prisoner. They *were* spooked, even though Sayre's hands and ankles were cuffed.

Gerard hid his smile at seeing Sayre. He was exactly as he'd imagined him, except for his eyes. They reminded him of a goat's eyes, flat and shallow. His dark hair was cropped short.

Sayre eyed him curiously as he took a seat. The guard closed the door but remained within sight, watching through the window.

Sayre rattled the handcuffs he wore, and his smile was sharp. "I can't wait to see what the CIA wants from little ol' me." His Southern accent put a twang to his words.

"I'm Gerard Darkwell, Director of Science and Technology. I'm working on a classified program that uses the extrasensory skills of gifted individuals. I suspect you have skills. I want you to do some work for me."

Sayre rolled his head back and let out a laugh so loud, the guard stepped back in to see what was going on. Gerard shook his head—no assistance necessary—and waited for him to close the door again.

"You find that amusing. I'm glad."

Sayre met his eyes, a sarcastic smile still on his lips. "You won't be when I tell you that you can kiss my sweet ass. I don't work for anyone, especially the government."

Gerard's mouth twitched, but he wasn't about to reveal his annoyance at Sayre's lack of respect. "I understand your sentiment. But what I'm proposing isn't standard government work. It's top secret. And it involves sanctioned killing, though if you tell that to anyone, I'll deny it." He smiled. "You like killing, don't you?"

Sayre had never admitted to his crime, and Gerard didn't expect him to. Seeing the interest in the man's eyes, he continued. "I have three women who need to be executed, all beautiful, in their early twenties, like you. You could have fun with them. And you would never need to worry about being prosecuted."

Sayre's pupils flared at that, but he banked his enthusiasm. "What do I get out of it?"

"What do you want?"

"Out of here."

"I can't do that."

Sayre stood, the chains linking his cuffs rattling. "Then we're done."

"Isn't there anything else you want? Money for someone you care about?"

Sayre laughed. "Know who I care about? Me."

"Then I'll pay you."

Sayre waved his arms to indicate the room. "And where am I gonna spend it? I don't do drugs, don't need cigarettes. Can't exactly order in some muff." His expression darkened, which made his smile even more sinister. "And I can already kill anytime I want. Just ask the warden." He rapped on the door.

"Through your dreams?"

Sayre turned around, surprise on his face, as the guard opened the door.

Gerard stood and walked over to him. "I know about the dreams, Sayre. I know more than you think. And I can help you discover more about your talent, about who you are, where you came from." He handed Sayre his card. "Call me if you change your mind."

The guard ushered him out, but Sayre continued to look back.

Later that day, when Gerard returned to his office,

he found Robbins at his desk reading something he'd left out. "What are you doing?" Gerard growled.

Robbins jumped, but he didn't look the least bit chagrined at being caught snooping. He held up Sayre's file. "You are *not* thinking of bringing him in."

"He's got valuable skills."

"He's psychotic."

Gerard snatched the file from Robbins's hand. "He's not interested anyway."

Robbins's eyes widened. "You talked to him?"

He slapped the folder on the desk. "If I ever catch you sniffing around my office again, I'll snap off your pinky fingers. For starters."

Robbins's tongue darted out to moisten his lips. "I . . . I was leaving you a note and saw the file."

"Forget you saw it. For now it's not an issue. I've got to go to Langley." His real job was getting in the way of what he really wanted to do.

Robbins left without saying another word, but recrimination glowed like embers in his eyes. A few minutes later Gerard walked out of his office and locked it. His shoes made hardly a sound on the carpeted treads. When he reached the bottom of the stairs, he caught Olivia, his assistant, and one of his subjects in what appeared to be an intimate discussion. They broke off abruptly, and her cheeks colored. He would have a talk with her. It was bad enough that two of his subjects were romantically involved. He couldn't have one of his staff getting involved with the third subject.

He was tired of feeling as though he needed to answer to anyone. This was *his* program. *His* baby. If he broke a few rules, if he took risks, if he had to eliminate people to protect it, he would, without anyone's conscience getting in the way.

Zoe rode with the rest of the Rogues in the Camry to the SPP in D.C. Rand had taken his bike, volunteering to watch the car from a distance.

Zoe watched the wind ripple Rand's shirt. "He seems to want to believe his dad was a thief. Or maybe he's just comfortable with the idea."

Lucas said, "Some people don't care to know who their fathers are. Or why their dads were the way they were."

Zoe leaned toward the front, where Lucas sat for the leg room and to navigate. Driving was too dangerous given his episodes. "Do you want to know who your father is?"

He and Amy exchanged that odd look again. "Not as much as Eric does."

"I want to know everything about him," Eric said from the driver's seat. "I may have other powers, ones I don't even know about yet." His hunger for that was palpable, but it quickly changed to frustration. "When my powers come back, that is. It's been over a week. Where the hell are they? Lucas's came back after a week." Now fear transformed his gruff expression. "What if they don't come back?"

Amy said, "There are no hard-and-fast rules. Chill out, and they'll come back."

He grunted, not convinced.

They drove into the city, the buildings rising up around them, people walking down the sidewalks, suits and briefcases. It all looked so normal, average . . . boring.

Petra smoothed down one of Amy's gelled locks of dark blond hair. "You missed a spot. You have to check all around in the mirror." Like a proud older sister, she said, "But you're getting the hang of it. Doesn't it look much better without the frizz?" Petra, whose own hair was pinned back in a bun, looked at Zoe's hair with a critical eye. "You know . . ."

Zoe put her hands over her head like a helmet. "I've done enough with my hair, thank you very much."

Lucas directed Eric to a parking garage near the SPP's address. Rand followed them into the multilevel garage.

When they all got out, he was already standing at the edge of the deck, scanning the area with binoculars. "I can see part of the front of the building from here. Not the front door from this angle, but close enough. I'll keep an eye on the car, too."

Zoe wanted to say something to him. He'd put a wall up between them, especially after he'd painted her monsters. Every time she got close, he backed up.

He's a loner. Get that into your head.

She used to think of herself as an outcast, though, and now she wasn't. She took in the group and felt a swell of affection for them. These were her people. All outcasts like her . . . all freaks like her, too.

Eric looked over and caught what must have been a soft smile on her face. "What?"

"Nothing. Are we ready?"

Eric turned to Petra. "Keep your ears on. If someone's making a call, having a conversation, whatever, tune in to it. I gave them a false name, so if they have any connection to Darkwell, we'll take them by surprise. Someone will have to make that call to alert him."

Zoe fought not to glance back at Rand as they walked to the stairwell. And then, just as she descended, she did look back—and caught him watching her. Then he disappeared from view.

Eric led the group down the sidewalk to the unassuming building with the even more unassuming sign that read SOCIETY FOR PSYCHIC PHENOMENA. "I made an appointment to see if I'm a candidate for their programs. I asked to see Hobson, but the receptionist said he doesn't talk to candidates. I did make sure he'd be here, though." He held the carved wooden door open as they filed inside. The lobby was masculine and smelled of leather. The walls were paneled in dark wood, with elaborate crown molding at the ceiling and the doors. Classical music flowed softly from the overhead speakers.

A glass partition reminded Zoe of the dentist's office. A woman on the other side slid the window open. "May I help you?"

Eric stepped up. "My name is Bill Farraday. I've got an appointment to see Paul Ganyon, but I really need to speak with Calvin Hobson."

Her eyebrows rose. "He doesn't take appointments."

"Tell him I'm here to talk to him about my mother, Camilla Aruda. I think he'll remember her even though it's been over twenty years."

She closed the window and made a call. She nodded, hung up, and left her desk. A moment later the door opened. "You can come back." Her eyes widened when she saw the other four, but she didn't say anything. She led them down a carpeted hallway to the office at the end.

Petra slowly looked from left to right as they walked, tuning in to whatever conversations were going on. Zoe saw people laughing in a large room on the right, cards with symbols hanging on the wall.

The man who waited for them near his open doorway was in his seventies, slight frame, and was of Asian heritage. He too looked a bit taken aback by the group coming his way.

Eric shook his hand. "Thank you for seeing me. Us."

"Your mother was Camilla Aruda?"

He pulled Petra forward. "*Our* mother was Camilla. I'm Eric. This is my sister, Petra." He held up the wrinkled letter. "I found this in a box of my mother's things."

Hobson read the letter, his expression tensing. Then he looked up. "Come in." He leaned out in the hallway. "Sandra, bring three more chairs, please."

Zoe let out a breath of relief. He was going to talk to them.

Then again, maybe this was going too easy. She really hated the paranoia, the never feeling safe. She wasn't the only one. The others looked warily around at the many doors, most closed. One bore the sign, TESTING IN PROGRESS.

Sandra brought in one chair at a time, and Lucas took them from her and set them in the room. Hobson's office, which continued the masculine décor, was large enough to accommodate his massive desk, credenza, and two leather chairs. He nodded for them to take a seat when Sandra delivered the last chair and closed the door behind her.

He waited for them to settle before saying, "So you found this and you have questions."

Eric smiled, shaking his head. "You don't know the half of it. I've read about your organization on the Web site, but could you explain what it is that you do here?"

"We are a research facility for all things psychic. We believe that psychic abilities are in the untapped portions of the human brain, and we have been working on proving it since the SPP was founded thirty years ago. We undertake studies, research projects, investigate reports of parapsychology in certain individuals, and try to present the world with an educated view of the extrasensory." He folded his hands together. "I hope you do not think your mother was an oddity."

A tremor of laughter moved through the group. Eric rubbed his face to wipe off his smile. "We're not really in a position to judge. And unfortunately, I don't know much about her. My father won't talk about any of this."

Hobson stood and walked to his computer, where he punched the keys with amazing speed considering that he used only his pointer fingers. He turned the monitor to face them, and they saw a black-and-white picture of a beautiful blond woman with broad features.

Petra gasped. "Mom."

Hobson leaned back in his chair. "Sandra, my assistant, had the bright idea many years ago to scan all the old documents into the computer. I thought it was a waste of time." He gave them a chagrined smile. "Guess I wasn't so psychic after all." He turned to the computer and squinted as he read. A minute later he turned back to them. "Camilla was one of the most talented members we've ever had. You might find her gift hard to believe."

Eric said, "She had pyrokinesis."

"Yes. How did you—" Hobson blinked. "You inherited it, didn't you?"

Eric nodded. "What else could she do?"

"That's all that I knew about. She was just beginning to set fires from a remote location."

"And then she joined Darkwell's program."

Hobson's expression darkened. "So you know about that, too." He shook his head. "It never felt right to me. Richard Wallace was in charge of SPP then, and he was all for it."

"Wallace?" Eric asked.

Hobson punched some keys and pulled up a picture of a man with light green eyes and blond hair so light it looked white. "Richard Wallace, founder of the SPP. Somehow he met up with Darkwell, who became fascinated with psychic phenomena when a fellow soldier saw a vision of an explosion that happened the next day. Darkwell wanted to use psychic abilities for spying and terrorism. I picked up on his aura, as sinister as the one I could see in pictures of Adolf Hitler."

Amy leaned forward in interest. "You can see a person's glow—their aura, I mean—just by looking at their picture?"

"Yes." He narrowed his eyes at them. "Your auras, though, I cannot see at all."

Eric drummed his fingers on his thighs. "Go on."

"Darkwell spent some time here, where he and

271

Richard conducted military experiments with some of our more gifted people. Richard himself was very gifted. Odd, since he'd come from a scientific background. I'm afraid he was seduced by Darkwell's hunger to use psychic abilities for the supposed *good of the country.*" Hobson used his fingers for quote signs. "Richard talked three of our members into joining some top secret program under Darkwell's direction. I never saw them again. One by one they died in unnatural ways. I questioned Darkwell about what they'd been put through after hearing of their psychological problems. He subtly threatened me if I tried to investigate further. I saw his aura, and he meant it." He looked at Eric. "I sent that letter to your father before that conversation. He never contacted me."

"Who were the other two people?" Lucas asked.

"Francesca Vanderwyck."

Amy grabbed Lucas's arm. "Your mom!"

Hobson's stubby fingers poked the keys, and an exotic-looking brunette's picture appeared on the monitor. "She and Camilla were best friends. They met here and bonded immediately." He looked at Lucas. "Have you inherited her ability as well?"

"I can get into people's dreams." He glanced at Amy. "And I get visions of the future that come out in sketches."

Hobson read over the data on the screen. "Francesca was a dreamweaver. She was working with our sleep team, and we were achieving some amazing things with her. She could get into a test subject's dreams and suggest things, and they would wake up and want a beer for breakfast." His face lit up at the memory. "A lovely woman. Very quiet, very serious." He looked at Lucas. "I can see her in your face. But she didn't get visions like the ones you described. However, the third member did."

His fingers jabbed again, and a man's picture came up. "Wayne Blackhawk Kee. Originally from the Hopi Indian tribe, though that's as much as he would ever say about it. Judging by his eyes, my guess was that his father met a white woman, and he was exiled from the tribe. He had many talents, including visions that came out in pictures he had no memory of drawing."

Amy and Lucas looked at each other, their fingers intertwining as though they had a will of their own. A smile broke out on her face. "The full mouth and blue-gray eyes . . . Lucas, he's got to be your father."

Petra pointed to the screen. "That has to be Cheveyo's dad."

"Cheveyo." Hobson looked up in thought. "Yes, I remember his wife had a son." Petra's face glowed as she looked at the picture. "He looks just like that, and he has"—she looked at Lucas—"the same shade of eyes as you do. I knew there was something about his eyes, other than they were gorgeous, but I was too thrown off to connect the dots. Lucas, maybe he's your brother."

Lucas's hand came up to rub his mouth as he studied the picture. "There is some similarity."

Eric said, "Well, Kee's sure as hell not *my* father. I don't have any of his features or ability." He looked at Hobson, who was taking in the scene with curious interest. "Those were the only three who went with Darkwell?"

"Yes, thank goodness. Besides Richard, of course."

"Richard Wallace," Eric said. "Tell us more about

him. Could he remote-view? I must have gotten that from my father."

"He went beyond remote viewing; he could astral project to another location, see what was happening, and actually move objects."

Eric waved his hand back and forth. "Can we go back to Wallace?"

Hobson pulled up his profile, and Eric leaned forward to study it.

Petra looked at it, too. "You take after Mom, Eric. I don't think you'll find any resemblances to your birth father."

Amy pressed her cheek against Lucas's arm, her face aglow. Zoe found her enthusiasm odd considering that Lucas hadn't been nearly as interested in finding his father as Eric was.

Amy said, "You said Wallace was a scientist." She turned to the group. "Cyrus said the guy involved in the project was a scientist. It's probably this Wallace." She turned back to Hobson. "He created a substance, a psychic Booster, that he gave the people in the program. Do you have any idea what it was?"

Hobson shook his head. "I've never heard of anything that would boost psychic abilities."

"Try sensory deprivation," Lucas said in a flat voice.

Hobson tilted his head. "The Ganzfield environment. Yes, it does help, at least with those who can handle it. But this Booster, I have not heard of this. Did it work?"

Amy's arm curled around Lucas's. "Yes, but it made the subjects mentally unstable. That's why they died."

Petra rubbed the back of her neck in quick strokes. "I'm getting the *feeling*."

Hobson looked puzzled. "Feeling?"

"I get a feeling whenever someone is remote-viewing us."

He chuckled. "There's a lot of that going on around here. No privacy at all, though we do have ethical restrictions we ask the participants to adhere to. You'll probably pick up all kinds of vibes if you're sensitive."

She shivered. "I hope that's what it is." She didn't look convinced.

Amy got to her feet. "We have to go. But quickly, what kind of scientist was Wallace?"

"He was a botanist and mycologist."

Her eyebrows furrowed. "Plants and . . . ?"

"Fungus."

Amy seemed to consider that. "Maybe he used either one of those in the Booster. Unfortunately, we can't ask him. For all we know, he's probably dead by now."

"Dead?" Hobson asked.

"He's been missing for over twenty years. He went into hiding when the program dissolved."

"I didn't know that. He certainly disappeared from my orbit. When he stopped reporting the results of BLUE EYES, as was agreed, we severed ties, and he was removed from the SPP by a committee decision. I hadn't heard from him at all until a year ago."

Amy's body stiffened. "You heard from him a year ago?"

"He called, wanting to speak with me. I only wanted to know what had happened to my three people. When he wouldn't tell me, I hung up on him. I haven't heard from him since."

Amy turned to the rest of them. "He could be alive. We have to find him."

Hobson studied them. "If you—I'm assuming you all have psychic abilities, I'd love to talk to you more."

Eric stood, leading the rest to take his cue. "Maybe another time. We've got to go. If you ever hear from Darkwell, you never saw us."

"I wouldn't give the man the time of day."

Amy turned to them. "He means it. I can see his glow."

Lucas paused. "Can we have a printout of our mothers' files?"

"I suppose that would be all right. I can't give you Kee's file, though. Confidentiality and all." He clicked the mouse and the printer whirred to life.

"He's dead, too?" Lucas asked.

"Suicide. His wife was the most upset at that, the most confused. She told me he believed that if you took your life, you would be doomed to eternal darkness."

Hobson handed each man his mother's file though Petra snatched hers. "Your mothers were talented, lovely women. I'm sorry for your loss. And mine."

Lucas asked Petra, "Still got the feeling?"

She shook her head, but anxiety still tightened her face.

Eric checked his phone, making sure he hadn't missed any calls from Rand. All clear. At least for now.

CHAPTER 21

Jerryl reclined in the chair, his eyes closed. "I can see Petra. Wait, the others are there, too."

Gerard Darkwell, who sat beside him, leaned forward. "All of them?"

Jerryl's closed eyelids twitched. "Not Brandenburg. They're in an office, talking to some skinny old guy. He's Asian." He fell silent.

Gerard wanted to ask him more, but he bit his tongue and waited.

"They're talking about someone named Wallace," Jerryl said after a few minutes.

"What about him?"

"Fungus . . . . missing for twenty years . . . the old guy is saying that he heard from him a year ago. And Shane is excited about him maybe being alive. They want to find him."

Wallace alive? Could the man have hidden so well for that long? I'll have to find him first.

"They're walking out of a building. It says SPP on the door. I can't read the smaller writing."

"The SPP. How did they find out about that?" They

were in D.C. Gerard wondered where Steele was. But they were already leaving. They'd be gone by the time anyone could get there. "See if you can follow them to their car."

"And when they get there, I'll get into Eric's head again. I want that bastard bad. I can't believe he's alive. I was sure he hit an artery, and they couldn't take him to a hospital." After a minute, "Uh-oh, Petra's tuned in to me. Damn. I can feel the shield going up." He grimaced in his effort to stay on-site. His face reddened. With an angry exhale, he opened his eyes. "She ousted me. I've got to work on staying there, even with the shield."

"That's all right. We got some valuable information."

Jerryl didn't want pain medication for fear it would dull his senses. Fortunately, even though it was more than a flesh wound, it wasn't serious. Just the kind of man Gerard wanted on his team. He hadn't given up on Sayre yet, either. The man just needed time to consider. Darkwell had a feeling he'd be in touch soon.

The Rogues had planned to find Robbins later in the day, when they had the best chance of catching him. It was a long shot; they knew that.

Zoe wanted to talk to this man as much as any of the rest of them did. He held the answers.

They drove into Bethesda, Zoe riding with Rand, and split up to cover more ground. How hard would it be to find a black H2?

"Got one!" Rand said after they'd been driving around for a half an hour.

Her heart jumped. *Could it be this easy?* She called

the others and gave their location. "We see a man driving, and he's by himself."

"Sounds good," Amy told her. "We'll catch up to you in a few minutes."

Zoe disconnected and held on to Rand as he swerved through traffic to keep up with the H2. They only had a vague description of the man, from Lucas's recollection. They moved closer to the H2, and finally Rand was able to pull up next to him, but the windows were too dark to see inside clearly. The man looked over at them, but even then, they could only make out indistinct features.

A few minutes later he turned, and Rand had to cut through a parking lot to catch up with him. She breathed out in relief when they caught up to him again.

"He's probably going to figure out we're following him now," Rand said.

The H2 took a sharp right turn down a side street.

"I think you're right."

"He's not real good at eluding us, though. If he was CIA, you'd think he'd be better."

She caught a street sign and called Amy to update them on their location. The H2 couldn't go very fast because of traffic.

Rand said, "I'm going to jump ahead and see where he's going. He won't be able to pull a move on me again." At the next light, he stopped two cars behind the H2.

"Do you know your pupils shrink when you shoot ahead?"

"No, I didn't. I've never looked in the mirror when I've done it."

"They get real tiny, like little dots."

He glanced back at her for a second and gave her a grin. "Cool."

She rolled her eyes. *Such a guy!* He moved when the light turned green. They followed the H2 for five more blocks, the driver turning several times in obvious and lame attempts to lose them. Which was why they were so surprised when he pulled into a grocery store lot and parked. A man got out and stood next to his vehicle, his legs slightly apart, his gaze on them.

She and Rand exchanged glances. He didn't look armed or particularly aggressive, and surely he wouldn't gun them down in front of everyone. With these guys, though, who knew?

"Surely it can't be this easy," she said.

"I don't see any danger, but I'll keep checking."

They pulled up beside him. The man wasn't quite as old as Lucas had surmised Robbins to be. He wore a suit, though, with neatly combed silvering dark hair. He crossed his arms over his chest. Not the stance of a man who might shoot them.

Rand cut the engine and got off the bike, Zoe following. Before they could say anything, the man jabbed his finger at them.

"You're not going to find anything. Do you understand me? Not a damned thing."

Of course he would recognize them. Rand walked a little closer. "We just want answers."

"No, you want evidence. I know the game you're playing."

Zoe stepped up next to Rand. "No, I don't think you do. We only want to know what's really going on. Our lives depend on it."

"Well, here's your answer. I'm not cheating, so she's not going get any evidence to use against me in court. She's wasting *my* money paying you to follow me around. I don't give a rat's ass about your livelihood. I've got thousands of dollars racking up in lawyer's fees, both hers and mine, and now yours. I've had it. Do you understand? I've had it!"

She and Rand exchanged glances again, this time with their brows raised. Rand was trying hard to hide his sheepish grin when he said, "Your name isn't Sam Robbins, is it?"

Now his brows furrowed. "No." Relief broke out on his expression. "You're after someone named Robbins? Not me?"

Rand lifted his hand. "Sorry to have bothered you. Wrong cheating bastard with a black H2." He got on the bike, Zoe quickly following him.

"That was embarrassing," she said, once they were heading out of the parking lot.

He shrugged. "We'll never see him again."

She called Amy. "Not Robbins." No need to get into the rest of it.

"Damn. Well, let's keep looking."

But after two more hours of driving around, they found not one more H2.

"Time to pack it in," Rand said. "It's starting to get dark."

She made one last call to Amy. "We're out of here."

"Yep, us, too." Disappointment saturated her voice. "I knew it was a long shot, but damn, I wanted to find him."

"I know. Sometimes it feels good just to do something, anything. But we're going to need help with this. Or else, we're going to spend a lot of time riding around looking for this guy."

She signed off and leaned against Rand, her arms loosely around his waist. Maybe that wasn't such a bad thing after all.

Petra curled up in bed with the pages Hobson had printed clutched in her hand. For the first time she had real knowledge of her mother and not just anecdotes. Had her father known anything about Camilla's abilities? Had he thought her ability to hear extraordinarily well just an extreme physical ability? Had he known about her pyrokinesis?

Holding the pages made her feel closer to her mother than she ever had. She drifted into sleep feeling warm and fuzzy.

She woke with a start, a voice whispering in her head. *Petra. Come to the garage.*

Cheveyo. God, that was freaky how he could get into her head like that. Freaky and intimate. Her heart thrummed as she pulled on a robe, glanced in the mirror at the silky pajamas she wore, then ditched the robe. She slipped into the Jimmy Choo Molly orange heels that matched her jammies.

She had to be quiet and not wake anyone. Eric would insist on coming. He'd bully and chase away Cheveyo with his suspicions. No, she wanted Cheveyo all to herself.

She crept out into the dark hallway. All quiet. She tiptoed into the living area, also dark and deserted. As she made her way down the tunnel, she reminded herself that Cheveyo was probably more of a loner than Rand, and that was saying something.

Petra knew the bone-deep agony of being in love with someone she couldn't have. Though she could clearly see that Lucas and Amy were meant to be, watching them together was still painful.

She climbed up into the shed and opened the door to the night. The cool, moist air snapped on her damp skin. It had rained, and she hadn't heard a thing. Damn, she hated being shut off from the world. She took a deep breath of the earthy air and listened for any unusual sounds over the traffic in the near distance. Raindrops pattered onto leaves and a dog barked. She looked for Cheveyo. Had he brought another Offspring?

He stepped out of the shadows, and in his black jeans and leather jacket, a naughty voice in her head— her own this time—whispered, *Too bad he didn't grab me again.*

"You rang?" she said in a singsong way, though her voice quivered.

"Let's talk in the garage."

They walked side by side, she a bit wobbly on the grass. She lost her balance for a second, and he took her arm to help.

"Heels on grass," she muttered.

"Heels? You're wearing heels with pajamas?"

"They were the first thing I grabbed."

She unlocked the garage, and he waited until she walked in first. A gentleman, as Zoe had described. Petra had tried to squeeze every bit of information out of Zoe about Cheveyo without seeming obvious.

"Don't turn on the light," he said in his soft, low voice.

He leaned against the car in a slice of light coming

from the neighbors' house, his hands braced on the hood. His dark hair was loose and wavy, his eyebrows defined in the dimness. He smelled good, fresh air and the faint scent of cologne. For her?

Petra took the spot next to him, extending her leg so the shoes showed. "Is your father Wayne Blackhawk Kee?"

For a change she took *him* off-balance. "How did you know that?"

"We went to the Society for Psychic Phenomena in D.C. Did you know he was involved in that?"

"Yes."

"Do you know that Lucas is your half brother?"

"Yes."

Okay, her turn to be surprised again. "Why didn't you say anything?"

"No need. Tell Lucas that my father loved his mother. The Booster played with his libido, made him cheat on my mother, but he felt an affinity with Francesca."

"How do you know all that? Isn't he dead?"

His mouth quirked in a soft smile. "We've been communicating since I was a boy." His smile faded. "I can't stay long. You felt one of the other Offspring remote-viewing you a few days ago."

"Yes. I think it's the woman."

"No, it was Nicholas Braden. What you told him piqued his interest. He wants to talk to you."

"We've tried that already. We nearly got killed in a trap at his house. Then we tried to talk to another Offspring and found the bastard who got inside Eric's head and made him shoot himself. Braden works for them, doesn't he?"

"He's doing contract work for Darkwell, but he has some doubts about the program. What you told him made him do a little digging. He doesn't like what he's found. He had nothing to do with what happened at his house. In fact, he's pretty pissed off that his home was violated. I told him I'd arrange a meet."

"How do you know all this? Can you get into his head, too?"

"I sensed his confusion. Checked him out. Then I talked to him psychically, told him a little about the Rogues—"

"How do you know what we're called?"

"Babe, I know a lot." His ghost of a smile, along with the endearment, sent her heart racing again. "Nicholas is okay. Nothing like the feeling I get when I try to get into Jerryl Evrard's head."

"You know he's the enemy?" She slapped the side of the car. "I wish we'd talked to you first."

"I tried to warn you that he was trouble, but you were too wiped out after you saved Eric's life."

Her eyes widened. "That *was* you warning me! I convinced myself that it was a dream."

"Remember what I said about mortal wounds? You're tearing yourself down. You did too much too soon. "

She nodded. "I know, but he's my brother. And Lucas . . ."

"Someone you love, too."

She narrowed her eyes at him. "It's not fair that you know so much about me, and I know hardly anything about you."

He shrugged, a deadpan expression on his face. "Who said life was fair?"

She planted her fists at her waist but couldn't really muster much ire. "That suggestion thing you do to me . . ."

"Yeah?"

"Just how far can that go? Like, if you told me to, uh, take off my clothes . . ." Her finger involuntarily went to the strap on her pajama top.

His eyes flared with lust for a second. "I couldn't get you to do something you didn't want to do."

"What if it's something I want to do?"

His eyebrow arched. "I wouldn't have to suggest it." He banked the fire in his eyes. "I'd better go."

"Come down to the shelter, meet everyone. At least meet Lucas."

"I'll help where I can, but I can't get involved. And I'll keep an eye on you." He studied her, her eyes, then her mouth.

He stroked his thumb over her lower lip and stepped back. "I'll be in touch to see how you want to proceed with Braden."

She let out a breath she hadn't even realized she was holding. "All right." When he reached the door, she whispered, "Zoe said you changed into an animal. Is that true?"

He opened the door a few inches, and she thought he wasn't going to answer. Then, before her eyes, he morphed into a black panther and vanished into the night.

She ran to the door and looked outside. He was gone. Zoe had described his transformation as liquid darkness. Petra could see why.

She stepped out into the night and locked the door behind her. She felt him watching her—watching over her. With a shiver that tingled through her body, she walked to the shed.

As soon as she entered the tomb, Eric's harsh voice jarred her out of the magical moment.

"Petra!"

She jumped, slapping her hand over her heart. "Eric, stop yelling! You scared me to death."

"What are you doing sneaking out?" He looked behind her as the door slid closed, probably expecting another Offspring.

"I met Cheveyo again."

He looked at her face. "Oh, yeah, I can see that now, Miss Dewy Gooey." He leaned against the counter and crossed his arms over his chest. "Why didn't you get me? You shouldn't be wandering out there alone at night. We don't even know this guy."

"I didn't want you along, and I trust him."

"Didn't want me along? Why the hell not?"

"For all I know, you'd shoot him, then ask questions." She hated to admit it, but Eric was becoming more and more unpredictable.

"What did he want this time?"

Lucas and Amy walked out of the hallway, no doubt drawn by Eric's voice. "What's going on?" Amy asked, rubbing sleep from her eyes.

Petra threw her arms up. "Might as well wake up Zoe and Rand, too. Then I'll only have to tell it once."

She walked down the stairs and knocked on both their doors. With the chemistry sizzling between the two of them, she couldn't be sure if they were, in fact, in separate rooms. They emerged from their respective rooms, though, and Petra had to admit to a tinge of relief. She had already endured Lucas falling in love with Amy; the last thing she needed was to watch another couple get hot and bothered.

"What's wrong?" Rand asked, mirroring Zoe's concerned expression.

"Town meeting." Her gaze dropped down from Rand's bare chest to the sheet he held in front of him. His eyes were alert, ready for trouble.

Zoe's eyes widened at the sight of him; she had a side view, which probably wasn't as covered. *Sleepy to awake in 2.2 seconds,* Petra thought with a smile.

"See you upstairs." She left them to get ready.

Zoe glanced over at Rand and shrugged. "Must be important." She tried really, really hard to not let her gaze drop to the swath of creamy white skin that the sheet he'd hastily pulled up didn't cover. The curve of his ass, the dusting of hair over his muscular thighs . . . *looking*!

Worse, he'd caught her. Instead of being arrogantly smug, though, his green eyes heated with desire. She'd thrown on a long shirt when Petra knocked, and she realized that much of her legs were showing, too.

"Have to . . ." She nodded back into the room and then closed the door. *Damn. Get a grip on yourself, Zoe girl. He'll be gone soon, and you do not want to get involved.* How she'd felt when he begged off from letting her ride back with him on Blue should be a warning. Besides, Eric was right; sexual distraction was dangerous.

She threw on hip-hugger cotton pajama bottoms and a tank top with a swirly design that camouflaged skulls, then went into the bathroom to throw on some makeup. When she went upstairs, everyone was waiting around the dining table for her.

Rand raised an eyebrow at her. "You put on makeup in the middle of the night for a meeting with *us*?"

"I don't go anywhere without makeup, so get over it." She took a seat and tried not to notice that he'd only thrown on a button-down shirt, leaving it open in front. "So what's up? Did you find out more about Wallace?"

They'd searched on the Internet and found that he'd authored several papers on fungus and slime molds. They knew where he'd been a professor, but none of that helped.

Eric sneered. "Petra had another rendezvous with Cheveyo, our mysterious ally."

Petra narrowed her eyes at him and looked at the group. "Remember when I felt someone remote-viewing us a few days ago and I told her stuff? It was Nicholas Braden."

Lucas stiffened. "The Braden who works for the enemy?"

"Yes, but he's got doubts about the program. I think I convinced him that Darkwell's the enemy. He wants to talk to us." Petra looked at the group. "Look, we know he's a good guy. He volunteers to search for remains so families have closure, and Cheveyo's been in his head; he senses that Nicholas is okay. He probably has no idea what Darkwell's really up to. Now that we have him questioning, he's done some digging."

Amy said, "If he does come over to our side, we'll find out more about the new program. And he's the one who can find people." She looked at the group. "Like Robbins."

Eric didn't look convinced. "What if he's a plant? We bring him here, he learns more about *us*, where we're hiding out, and it's all over."

Lucas planted his elbows on the table. "He wants to talk to us, so we make the rules about the meeting and what we tell him. We assess him, see if he's being truthful. He plays by our terms. And we test him. The test: give us Robbins."

Eric leaned back in his chair, his arms crossed over his chest. "This is all based on what some guy who won't even talk to us says. You trust him because you have that dewy-gooey thing going, but we don't."

Rand scrubbed his hands through his red hair, making it stick out as it had when she'd first met him. "I can arrange a meeting that will minimize our exposure. We have the advantage here because, like Lucas said, *he* wants to talk to *us*. We'll make him jump through some hoops to do it." He looked at each of them, excitement glowing in his eyes. "We set up a relay in Baltimore. I have some boys there who will help us. Braden meets with one of them, who takes him to another location where another of my boys takes him to another location. From there, I take him to some location where we won't be disturbed. Lucas, you can follow us in the car, make sure everything goes as planned, then participate in the meeting. Petra and Zoe can be lookouts and work on keeping up the shield so the others can't remote-view us."

His expression tightened. "We keep them out of it other than that. Out of sight." He looked at Amy. "You, too. And before you get all 'I'm as tough as you' about it, remember what happened to Zoe. They'll grab you because they know we'll do whatever we can to get you back. You're our vulnerability." He looked at Eric. "You are, too. We can't trust you to not tear in and shoot the guy if he so much as blinks the wrong way."

Eric shot to his feet and jabbed his finger at Rand. "You are not in charge here."

Lucas pressed his palms on the table's surface. "Neither are you. Rand's right; you've put us in danger twice."

Eric knocked a glass off the table, spewing cold milk across Zoe and Amy and sending the glass crashing to the floor. "You don't decide to cut me out of the action."

"It's a group decision." Lucas remained calm, though his jaw ticked, giving away his tension. "We can't take the risk until we think you're rational enough. This time you're backup, remaining close by if we need you but out of the relay." He looked at the rest of them. "I say we give it a try."

Zoe shot to her feet just as Eric had done. "Don't pull that old 'protect the girls 'crap. I escaped an assassin, and even though Jerryl did grab me, I got away from him. He wouldn't have taken me off guard if Eric hadn't gone all Rambo."

Amy stood, too. "I agree. Besides, Lucas, you can't take Nicholas to the meeting place."

"Because I might have an episode," he said darkly.

"Well that, too, but Darkwell thinks you're dead. In case Nicholas is setting us up, it's to our advantage if they keep thinking that."

Lucas nodded. "You're right."

Zoe turned to Rand. "I'll be the one to follow you."

Fury suffused Eric's face. "You're risking us all by trusting some guy we don't even know."

Petra said, "Cheveyo is Lucas's half brother." She turned to Lucas. "He confirmed it. He wanted me to tell you that his father loved your mother very much."

Eric narrowed his eyes. "Obviously being related to someone doesn't ensure loyalty. Look at you."

Petra turned to the group, ignoring him. "I say we vote. How many in favor of Rand's plan?"

Everyone's hand went up except Eric's.

Lucas said in a low voice, "How many agree that Eric stay out of the direct action?"

Slowly, the same hands went up.

Eric stomped out of the room and slammed his door. Petra winced.

Lucas shook his head but turned to Rand. "Tell me about these 'boys' you mentioned."

Rand glanced at Zoe as she dabbed at the milk across her shirt, then to the group. "These are street dudes. They know the ins and outs of the city and where the abandoned buildings are."

Lucas stood. "I'll print out a map of Baltimore. You're sure these guys will help us?"

Zoe nodded, as Rand said, "Yeah, I think they will. The plan has to protect them, though. No one will be in contact with Braden for very long, then they're gone."

Over the next hour, they worked out an elaborate relay system. Lucas raised his eyebrow whenever Rand brought up another nickname as he worked through his plan. Rand again glanced at Zoe, the tiniest smile at the corner of his mouth.

She smiled back. It was nice to know his secret. Nicer yet that he trusted her with it.

Rand stood and stretched, raising his shirt

to expose his narrow hips. "I'm going to crash. Tomorrow I'll head into Baltimore, see if they're game. We'll take it from there."

Tomorrow. Her mother would be at the revival. As though he were reading her mind, Rand looked over at her. "I can take you to your mother if you want."

She smiled, swallowing a knot in her throat. "Thanks."

Damn. It was easier when he was being a jerk. Then it was just the lust factor tearing at her. When he revealed that he cared, even just a little, her feelings for him tore even deeper. And her heart was too fragile to let him in.

Amy walked into the bedroom, closing the door behind her as she turned on the light. Arms grabbed her around the waist and spun her into a hard body. Before she could even think, a warm, soft mouth covered hers.

She smiled beneath the kiss and threaded her fingers up into the soft waves of his hair.

He made hungry sounds as he devoured her, his hands trailing over her body, trying to make up for the lost time and agony they'd endured. After kissing her crazy, he tilted her off-balance, and they fell onto the bed. He stripped off her clothes, and she let out a soft moan when she realized he was already naked. Hard and naked.

He growled as he nuzzled her neck and licked along the shell of her ear. She growled when he whispered, "When I come tonight, I'm going to wail like a banshee."

CHAPTER 22

*Z*oe's arms tightened around Rand's waist as he maneuvered the bike through the traffic going to the revival. She didn't have to hold on to him, but she wanted to. The revival was being held in a large auditorium that had seen better days. He found a spot at the end of a row for an easy escape . . . just in case.

They'd already met with Rand's boys and gone over the plan. Every one of them had signed on, even without knowing what they were really involved in. The fact that there was a possibility of danger actually excited them. Their loyalty had touched her, and though Rand didn't let it show, she knew it touched him, too. She had found Sly's slide show on Taze's MySpace page. Rand's painting, showing a boy falling in a forest, formed a lump in her throat even now.

She'd also sneaked into her tattoo shop and grabbed her equipment and several blue tubes of ink. She'd fought not to sit and absorb the shop . . . or to cry at the thought of never seeing it again.

Rand killed the engine and lifted off his helmet, taking in the crowd with amazement. Vendors were set up to sell food and drinks, filling the air with sinful scents of sausages and fried dough.

"Crazy, isn't it? My mom dragged me to one of these when I was sixteen. In protest, I wore a sweatshirt that said TEASER across the front. I didn't let her see it until we got there, and I wore nothing underneath it so she couldn't make me take it off."

He shot her a grin. "You *were* a she-devil, weren't you?"

She stared at the crowd streaming into the convention center like ants to a morsel. "Sometimes I wanted to act like the terrible person she thought I was."

"And now you want her to see you as what you are—just a normal woman with extraordinary abilities."

"Yeah." She hung up her helmet. "I'll be back as soon as I can. This won't be a long, drawn-out reunion scene."

He looked at her. "Nervous?"

She rocked her hand. "Ish." With a deep breath, she turned.

She merged with the crowd, wearing some of Amy's more ordinary clothing to blend in. As she'd gone through her clothing, Amy had admitted she'd worn drab clothing most of her life and no makeup to blend in, making up for the fact that she felt like such an oddity. That was before Petra had gotten hold of her. Zoe thought it was amusing that she had used the opposite strategy: dress a bit outrageously to put distance between her and other people.

Her curls were soft, though probably flattened by the helmet. This was the most normal-looking her mother would have seen her in years, though the black hair might surprise her. She was going to go back to her natural color as soon as she could.

She kept her gaze down, her arms wrapped around herself, and walked to the back where equipment was being unloaded and carried into the cavern of the building. A security guard stood near the doors, eyeing her approach. She obviously didn't belong there.

"I need to talk to Anne Withers. Please tell her that her daughter wants to see her."

A few minutes later he returned. "She said now is not a good time."

"I'm sure she did. Tell her that now is the only time I have." She met his gaze second for second as he contemplated whether he wanted to bother the preacher's wife again. With a sigh he walked into the back again. When he returned, he waved for her to come.

With a breath of relief, she followed him down the hall, where people bustled as though the revival were a Broadway production. He led her to the side of the stage where a heavy red curtain blocked the view of the stage and half-filled auditorium.

Anne was giving someone directions, her arms moving in concert with her words. Zoe had taken after her dad. Anne was petite, with silver hair she kept in an efficient and simple hairstyle and large-rimmed glasses. When she looked up, her face became pinched the way Zoe often saw it where she was concerned.

Anne walked over, looking around as though she hoped no one would see her talking to this lawless street urchin. "Are you trying to ruin our revival? Do you know that you're wanted by the police?" Her whispered voice got shrill on that. "Are you trying to drag us into your moral morass?"

"Moral morass? *Moral morass?* You've got to be kidding me." Zoe lowered her voice, relieved that no one was working nearby. "Mom, it's a setup. I came here to tell you the truth. About Dad, about me." She took hold of her mom's arms. "Just hear me out. That's all I ask."

"Your father has nothing to do with—"

"He has everything to do with my situation. You need to hear this."

Her mother held in the protest with tightened lips. "Fine. Talk."

Zoe nodded for them to walk off to the side. "You remember when you said I had probably inherited what made him crazy? Do you know what that did to me? It scared me. I began to worry that I'd walk into my shop and shoot my employees. So I started looking into what Dad was involved in before he . . . before he killed those people. Do you know what he was doing?"

"He said it was classified, and that's all he told me."

"It was an experiment that brought in people who had psychic abilities to help in the war against terrorism."

"That explains a lot."

"What do you mean?"

"If your father was psychic, he had the seed of Satan in him."

"Psychic abilities aren't evil. It's all in how a person uses them. We're just tapping in to a part of our brain that most people don't use. God made our brains this way."

"Sacrilege!"

"Mom, listen to me. Dad didn't do that horrible thing, not really. The shooting was a result of a substance the government was giving him to boost those abilities. That's what made him crazy. Before Granddad dies, you have to tell him his son wasn't an awful person, that something that was put in his body made him do that. I inherited Dad's psychic ability. That's why things fly around when I get emotional. It's called telekinesis. And now that I've found out about what they did to Dad, the man behind that project wants me out of the picture. That's why he planted drugs in my apartment."

Zoe squeezed her arm. "I have never done drugs. I have never sold drugs. I've never even *touched* drugs. I need you to believe me, to know that I'm not evil or bad." That need grew inside her chest. "Please. I'm sorry we haven't been close, but I'm your daughter. And right now I need a mother." Those last words had come out, surprising Zoe by the depth of emotion behind them. She thought she'd convinced herself that she didn't need a mother.

Anne looked at her, really looked at her. For a moment, Zoe thought she might believe, or at least consider it. Her body tensed at the thought, straining toward her mother.

"Zoe, turn yourself in to the police. Get help. Once they clear that stuff out of your system, you can get counseling. And though I can't publicly be involved— the Lord knows Harry can't have that kind of scandal attached to his reputation—I will be there to support you as much as I can. I'll pay for rehab and the counselor *if* you begin to attend church once you've served your sentence, and . . ."

Zoe tuned out her mother, feeling her chest cave in and her eyes water in anger and disappointment.

". . . the judicial system may be lenient since it's your first . . ."

Zoe backed away, unable to hear another word. She spun around—and right into Rand.

Rand, who'd been standing there listening to her pour out her heart. "Damn you." She pushed at him and stalked away, her cheeks burning in humiliation.

She sensed him behind her as she wended her way to the parking lot. It took everything in her not to turn around and deck him.

She stopped only when she reached the bike, where she stuffed the helmet onto her head. He grabbed her arm to turn her around, but she pushed him away.

He gave a quick glance to the heavens. "I just wanted to make sure you were all right."

"No, you were intruding on my space, my private moment. I told you I wanted to go in alone."

"It's not safe for any of us to go off alone."

She narrowed her eyes at him. "That coming from mister leave-me-alone, ride-off-into-the-sunset-by-myself. Perfect, just perfect. Let's go."

"Look, what your mother said—"

"Go!" she shouted, climbing onto the bike without him. "I don't want to talk about it, especially to you, mister don't-want-to-be-involved."

Shaking his head, he climbed on the bike. She didn't hold on to him. What total, freaking humiliation! Not only to be dissed by her mother after admitting to the woman that she needed her—*dumb move there, Zoe*—but to have Rand witness it. Shame washed over her again.

For once she was glad to be on a bike, where conversation was limited. If she never spoke to Rand again, that would be fine with her. Maybe he'd leave soon, today, tomorrow.

Thirty minutes later, he pulled into a parking lot of an apartment building. She remembered the place. He lived there, next door to the woman with the sick daughter. Great, a stop for more supplies.

He pulled the bike behind the Dumpster, parked it, and got off. She reluctantly climbed off, too, jamming her hands under her armpits and looking everywhere but at him. When she sensed him waiting for her, she said, "Go ahead and get what you need, or say hi to your girlfriend or whatever."

What? Why had she thrown in the girlfriend part?

He took her hand and pulled her toward the back door. He knocked, and a man inside waved in recognition and let him in.

"Thanks, dude. Anyone been looking for me? I've been out of town."

"No, man, not that I've heard." He gave Zoe an odd look. She hadn't removed her helmet yet.

With a death grip on her hand, Rand dragged her up a set of stairs. He studied the door, lifting a hair he'd strategically left behind to indicate if someone had gone in. Then he felt along the top of the frame and snagged a key, which he slid into the lock.

She tried to free her hand. "I'll wait here . . . or not," she added, when he tugged her into a small apartment with minimal furniture. It looked more like a hotel room, beige and browns, no colors or personal touches.

He tapped on her helmet. "Take it off."

She did as he ordered, getting more annoyed with every passing second. "Look, I'm not going to freak out or anything. I just want to go back to the tomb."

A glass on the coffee table fell over, spilling water onto the carpet.

She crossed her arms over her chest. "Can we just go now?"

"I'm sorry your mother did that to you back there. I'm sorry you're embarrassed that I saw it." He shifted uncomfortably but still met her gaze.

Her eyes widened. "You're apologizing?"

"Something like that."

Then it hit her. "You're . . . trying to console me?"

"Closer." He looked down for a second, rubbing the bridge of his nose. "I'm not good at this stuff. But I know you were upset"—he looked at the glass—*are* upset. And that thing you did for me the other day, with Sly . . . well, it was good. So go on, vent, scream, cry, whatever. Get it out."

She was so stunned, her anger and humiliation fled . . . replaced by something a lot more dangerous. "I'm fine. We should go."

She started to walk to the door, really she did. But she stopped, turned back to Rand and saw what she feared most—tenderness in his sea-green eyes. Dammit. Her lower lip began to tremble. So did the lamp on the end table. When was the last time someone had showed her real tenderness? Rand had in small ways, like painting her wall, but he hadn't even let her thank him, saying it was nothing.

"It doesn't matter." She wiped the tears forming in her eyes. "I never had a warm, loving mother. I shouldn't have expected . . . definitely shouldn't have said . . ."

In one swift move, he stepped closer, cradled her face in his hands, and covered her mouth with his. Soft kisses shivered through her body, so sweet they nearly made her teeth ache. He kept kissing, sucking her lower lip into his mouth and trailing his tongue over it.

Her chest hurt, and she realized she wasn't breathing. *Slowly, breathe, Zoe.* She heard something fall behind her and reined in her emotions.

"Don't worry about it," he murmured between kisses. "Remember, all this stuff belongs to a guy who skipped town. Let it fly, doll."

Doll. And the words before that all melted her. She shook her head, fighting it. Oh, God, she wanted to let go. She'd been holding back too long.

He pulled her body against his, and felt his erection pressing into her stomach. His hands toyed with her ears, sending chills washing over her and a soft moan out of her mouth.

Control yourself.

Let go . . .

Her sensible self and her wanton self argued in her head, the words lost in the daze he was creating. His fingers moved over her scalp, touching spots that ignited her body. She tilted her head back, then snapped it forward again.

His tongue now played inside her mouth, scraping along her teeth and tracing designs on the surface of her tongue. If he was that creative in her mouth . . .

Don't go there.

It had been so long since she'd had sex, and she'd never had fulfilling sex, that she felt the hunger ignite between her legs and rise into her chest.

She thought the lamp jumped off the end table behind her but couldn't pull away to look.

"Don't worry about it," he said again, moving down her chin and her throat, nibbling and licking at her skin.

Her voice was breathless as she said, "Are you . . . still consoling . . . me?"

He unbuttoned her blouse. "Does it feel like I'm consoling you?"

"Yes . . . no. I don't know."

"How 'bout I seduce you instead?"

He dipped his tongue between her breasts.

That did it. She put her hands on his shoulders and wrapped her legs around his waist, kissing him fully.

His hands, now holding her behind, tightened. She felt him carrying her into another room. She opened her eyes as they entered a bedroom lit by a shaft of late-afternoon sunlight coming through the broken blinds. He knelt and dropped her the last few inches onto the softest bed she'd ever felt. The light glinted off his silver eyebrow spike. His mouth covered hers, his breath coming faster, kissing her as he unbuttoned her blouse and helped her wriggle out of it.

He undid her bra with one hand and tossed it away. He sat back and watched his hands slide over her breasts, his eyes dilated with desire. She reached up and pulled his T-shirt over his head. Before she even threw it onto the floor, she was kissing the contours of his chest, tracing her tongue around his nipples and nibbling them when they hardened. She kissed around to the soft, pale skin on his sides, then up to the hollow beneath his armpit. His silky hairs tickled her nose.

She kissed along his rib cage and around to the front again, across the ridges of his stomach to the golden hairs just above his waistband. She unbuttoned his jeans, pulled down the zipper, and helped him out of them. Bright white briefs adorned the body she'd been dreaming of ever since she'd glimpsed him in the bathroom. His shaft was huge and rigid beneath the soft material, and she ran her hand over the length of it. He tilted his head back and let out a soft groan that spiraled right to the center of her stomach.

She loved the way a man sounded when he felt pleasure. Something else fell down behind her. She paused. "St. Barts. Fiji. Marquesas Islands."

He pressed his hand over hers. "Let go, Zoe."

"It's hard . . ."

"Yes, ma'am, it is."

They laughed, but it died down as their eyes met.

He took her hand and pulled it to his mouth. "Let go. I don't care if shit's flying around. It means you're hot and bothered, and that's how I want you." To illustrate, he flicked his tongue between her fingers.

She rolled her eyes, imaging, as he'd intended, that tongue being somewhere much more intimate.

Her chest expanded at the prospect of letting go. For once in her life, just totally letting go. Even more exciting, her heart filled with the precious gift he was giving her.

He kept tracing his tongue over her palm in circles, watching her with an intensity that released that last bit of resistance. She smelled smoke and saw it curling out of the clock on the nightstand. Crazy, wonderful, crazy energy.

She knelt and touched her tongue to the tip of him

that was peeking out of the waistband of his briefs. She peeled back the band and explored farther. She took him in her mouth, at least most of him, and stroked him with her tongue, and, very gently, the edge of her teeth. The sound he made was a combination groan and her name.

His body contorted in pleasure, his hand mindlessly kneading her hair, and she smiled when his toes curled. When he seemed about to explode, he flipped her onto her back and returned the favor. He pressed her bent legs apart, kissing the soft skin of her inner thighs the way she had cherished the skin on his side. He took his ever-loving time making his way toward the part of her that throbbed with wanting. He touched her with his tongue, then gave attention to the fleshy part of her while just barely touching her clitoris. By then *her* toes were curling. He had her so worked up that only a mere teasing touch sent her over the edge. Her body shuddered, and her bra flew past.

Rand wasn't finished. He flicked his tongue over her, and the pleasure was almost painful, until she felt the pressure build and spin her off again. The blinds shuddered, sending sunlight shimmering across the bed.

He chuckled, a soft, sexy sound that proved he indeed liked that she was sending things flying. That alone sent her roaring into a third orgasm. Oh, she did love . . . loved the way he made her feel. He kissed his way up her stomach, circling her breasts, then kissed her again.

She'd never kissed a guy after oral sex, and that Rand had no problem with that intrigued her. How erotic, the taste of their mingled sexuality. He reached over to the nightstand drawer, and she heard the crinkling of a condom wrapper. "Hope you don't mind orange flavored. That's what the guy who lived here preferred, I guess."

The condom went flying out of his hand. She gave him a sheepish grin. "Sorry."

She wasn't sorry, though, when he leaned over to retrieve it, giving her a luscious view of his tight ass. He sat back with the condom again, tearing it open. She took it and rolled it down over the length of him. He gently pressed her back to the bed, and with her legs bent, leaned close and teased the tip against her, sliding across her folds and sending another spasm through her.

The empty wrapper went this time, zinging over the bed.

He slid in slowly, giving her body time to expand, touching her with both his thoughtfulness and restraint. When he filled her, she sucked in a breath. Nobody else had ever *filled* her, not just physically but emotionally. She wrapped her legs around him. He locked his gaze onto hers as they moved together. Though his face was red and muscles tight, he kept going longer than anyone else ever had. She felt a different kind of pressure building inside her with every thrust, then she experienced her first internal orgasm.

From the smile on his face, he must have seen her surprise. Waves of pleasure washed over her from the inside. She rode him harder, tightening her muscles around him, and felt him throb inside her when he came. And still he moved, still hard, bringing her to another heart-rocking orgasm before collapsing on top of her, careful not to crush her with his weight.

"You're still hard," she said in disbelief a few minutes later.

He shrugged, and his voice was muffled because his face was nestled in the crook of her neck. "Yep. Want to do it again?"

She shook her head, unable to hardly manage even that movement. "I'm mad tired." Tired and sated and . . . she was afraid to name the glow that lit her from the inside.

He rolled her over so that she lay on top of him, their bodies still connected. That he obviously wasn't ready to pull apart intensified that glow.

He rubbed her "wedding ring" tattoo. "Feel better?"

Another kind of wave washed over her, this one cold and yanking her from the daze he'd left her in. "What's that supposed to mean?"

His expression became wary. "If I said something that can be taken two ways, and one pisses you off, I meant the other way."

She shifted to the side, feeling him slide out. "No, seriously."

He sat up. "I only asked if you were feeling better."

"Was this"—she waved to include the bed—"consoling me? Like . . . oh, my God, like a pity fu—"

He pressed his hand over her mouth. "Don't even say that. Of course it wasn't."

She got out of bed. "Oh, what an idiot I am. Of course it was. You brought me here to screw me so I'd feel better." She searched for her clothes, even more humiliation crashing down on her.

He grabbed her from behind, pulling her against him. "Zoe, stop. It wasn't like that."

She pushed away and faced him. "Then what was it?"

The challenge took him aback. He paused. "Great sex. Something that's been brewing between us since the beginning."

She wasn't sure what she wanted him to say, but when her heart fell, she knew that wasn't it. Great sex. She grabbed up her panties and stalked to the door. Somehow, being angry felt safer than what she'd been feeling when they were making love—no, having great sex. The digital clock launched, jerking when it reached the end of the cord and dropping to the floor.

She paused by the door. "Did you have pity sex with your neighbor, too?"

"That's just ugly."

It was ugly, but that's how she felt inside. "Is that a yes?"

He shook his head. "No, I never had sex with her. I don't go around screwing every pretty woman I can."

"Then who do you screw?"

"Women I . . . like."

"Ooh, you like me. Yippee." She went into the small bathroom and slammed the door.

"Zoe," he said from the other side of the door. "What do you want me to say?"

After dressing she snatched open the door. "Nothing. You made me feel better." She patted his shoulder, making the move as condescending as possible. "Happy now?" Then she walked to the door.

When she pulled it open, a man stood there, and he certainly didn't look happy. But he *was* holding a gun.

CHAPTER 23

Amy snuggled in Lucas's arms while they lounged in bed. They had been making up for lost time, staying up half the night, dropping off to sleep for a while, then making love again. She would have been in heaven were it not for the people hunting them down, and Lucas's episodes.

And Orn'ry, walking sideways from one end of the perch to the other, making whirring noises and trying to get her attention.

"You drifted off again." She gingerly touched the healing cut at his temple.

"In the middle of . . . ?"

She nodded. "Lucas, I'm scared. The storm of images, and now these spacey spells . . . it's the Booster, isn't it?"

He twirled a lock of her hair around his finger, his gaze on nothing in particular. "I think so. There might be a time when I lose it."

She sat up. "I know about your pact with Eric. I overheard you telling him to take you out if you go crazy. But that's not going to happen. We're going to find Wallace first. Do you understand?"

He sat up, too, his eyes haunted. "I'm sorry you heard that. But I'm not taking any chances. I bet the last thing Zoe's dad ever thought he'd do was kill innocent people. And Wallace, well, we don't know if he's alive or if he'll help us. He worked side by side with Darkwell."

"He's been hiding, afraid that Darkwell would kill him, I bet. Lucas, it's our only chance. Eric's becoming more volatile. Sometimes I'm afraid of what he'll do, and that's probably from the Booster, too. I'm glad you told him to stay out of the relay tomorrow." She took his hand in hers and kissed his palm. "I don't want to lose you."

"We'll try to find Wallace. First, though, we've got this other Offspring to deal with. One thing at a time." He stroked her face with his fingers, and she was overwhelmed by the love she saw in his eyes. "Amy, we know we're not related. Have you thought about what that means? Not for us, but for you."

She shook her head. "I haven't gotten beyond the relief yet."

"Cyrus said there were two men and two women. We know that Eric is an Ultra, so his father had to be one of those men. Since Kee probably wasn't his father, that leaves . . ."

"Dad." Her eyes widened. "Eric could be my half brother." The weight of that hit her like a wrecking ball. "My father was blond, like Eric. He had blue eyes like Eric." Her hand went to her mouth.

"Now might be a good time to talk to him, while Rand and Zoe are out. No need to involve them in our personal matters right now."

They dressed in silence, Amy deep in her thoughts.

She dug into her purse and pulled out a picture, then lifted her arm to Orn'ry, who climbed aboard. When they emerged, the scent of coffee still wafted in the air. She parked Orn'ry on the perch in the living area, ignoring Eric's snarl. She nodded to Petra, who was watching one of those obnoxious celebrity reality shows. Accusations flew, fingers pointed.

"It's nice to watch other people's problems," Petra said, as though defending the fact that she had been watching.

Eric sank farther into the couch. "People who haven't lost their powers and regained them when they should have."

Petra gave them a chagrined look. "You two were sure noisy last night."

"Sorry," Amy said, even though she wasn't.

Orn'ry screeched. "What the fluck!" Then he started crowing like a rooster.

Eric twisted around, his hands in position to strangle something. Orn'ry tucked his head down close to his body, and quietly said, "Kill the bird, kill the bird."

Amy crossed her arms in front of her. "Maybe if you were nicer to him—"

Eric mirrored her action. "Maybe if it was dead . . ."

Petra held out her hand, her gaze on the television. "Shh! She's about to pick the guy who gets to wax her pube hairs."

Amy walked into the living room and clicked off the television.

"Hey!" Eric said. "Didn't you hear what Petra said?"

Amy sat on the coffee table facing Eric, and Lucas

perched behind her. She took a deep breath. "We have something to tell you. The last time I spoke with Cyrus—when it *was* Cyrus—he told me that my father had gotten another woman in the program pregnant. For a while Lucas and I worried that we were related."

Petra put her hand to her mouth. "Oh my gosh, how terrible! Wait. That's why you were acting so strange."

Amy nodded. "But our visit to the SPP and what Cheveyo told Petra ruled that out. Kee is definitely Lucas's father." She turned to Eric. "Which means that you and I are very possibly half siblings." She forced a smile, teeth bared.

His face went white, then flushed red. Was he remembering how he'd looked at her before they rescued Lucas? How he'd kissed her once?

"You . . . and me . . . related?"

She nodded. "As far as we know, there were only two men who got the Booster. There was a second stage of BLUE EYES, but because of the sexual side effects, Darkwell kept them separate from the first stage. And you do have some of my father's features." She handed him the old photograph of her and her father. "You and I look nothing alike, but I took after my mother."

After being an only-child orphan for so long, it was strange to suddenly have a half brother. She wasn't sure how she felt about Eric being that brother, but it was a hell of a lot better than its being Lucas.

Eric studied the picture, and his tight expression transformed to wonder. "Maybe a little around the eyes." He looked up at her. "What were his skills?"

"Don't you want to know what *he* was like?"

"Sure. But I already know he must have been charming, smart—"

Amy rolled her eyes. "You'll be happy to know he was one of the best in the program. But Cyrus never got around to telling me what his skills were. Everything was so rushed when he told me about the program, and we . . . well, we didn't have time to get to that."

"Find out. Talk to Cyrus. Better yet, talk to your—our dad."

"I never considered talking to Dad. I'm not sure what I'd say to him." The thought of making that connection again made her shiver. "I'm not really comfortable taking a chance of Gladstone being the one who talks to me. But I'll think about it. Don't bully me."

"You bullied me, too. You—" His eyes lit as he must have realized they were bickering like siblings. "Oh, jeez, you are my sister."

She and Eric laughed as they remembered how they'd butted heads since they met. She said, "Let's just forget about all that other stuff." She gave him a meaningful look, which he seemed to understand.

He tilted his head. "Does this mean I have to be nice to you now?"

Amy laughed. "I don't think you have nice in you." Except she remembered when he had painted Petra's toenails once.

"You're probably right." He walked over to the bulletin board above the desk. "If it's all right with you, I'd like to pin this here." He put the photograph on the board with the ones of the five of them when they were children. "What *was* he like?"

"From what I've heard, a good man. A good dad. He taught me the constellations. At least the basic ones. After he died, I studied the globe he'd gotten me every day, like I was trying to hold on to him."

Lucas screamed out in pain and fell off the chair.

"Lucas!"

Tremors shook his body as Amy tried to bring him back. His eyes rolled back in their sockets.

Fear washed over her . . . for what Lucas was going through and for the reason he was getting the storm.

Five minutes passed before he struggled to open bloodshot eyes, much longer than before. He took a halting breath as she and Eric helped him sit up.

"What happened?" Eric asked at the same time that Amy asked, "What did you see?"

Petra hovered, her forehead creased in worry.

Lucas looked at them, disoriented. His voice was slurred when he said, "A bunch of images. Too fast. Faster than before. I saw Rand. Zoe. And I saw Steele."

Zoe recognized the man holding the gun: the guy who'd chased her down in Key West. Who'd hunted them at hospice. Steele. He still had four faint scratches on his cheek. He stepped inside and closed the door.

She turned to Rand, her anger vanished. He was only half-dressed, his jeans still unbuttoned, no shoes or shirt. Apparently he hadn't seen Steele yet, because he picked up the shirt on the floor.

"Rand." The word came out a muffled whisper.

Rand's face went sheet white. He dropped the shirt and raised his hands. "Whoa, dude, there's been a mistake. If you're looking for George—" His eyes widened in recognition.

Steele smiled. "No mistake." He aimed the gun. "You freaks are making me look bad. I had a perfect record until I was assigned to you."

She focused on the gun with all of her energy.

His finger tensed. "Say goodbye."

The gun flew out of his hand, spinning through the air. It hit the coffee table and fell to the floor. Rand was on it. She could tell by his pupils that he'd shot ahead and knew exactly where the gun would land.

Steele reached behind him. A backup weapon?

The gunshot was quiet, a *thwump* that threw Steele backward against the door. He hit hard and slid down, leaving a bloody smear. His body slumped into a heap, his eyes still open.

Agony over killing another human being etched itself on Rand's face. "Let's get out of here." His voice was thick, his gaze riveted to the man.

He pulled on his shirt, shoes, and grabbed her helmet. She followed him down the stairs and out the back door to where he'd tucked Blue.

"This is bullshit," he said. "I'll help bring in this Nicholas dude, then I'm outta here. I'm not doing this anymore."

They tore out of the lot. Despite her earlier anger, the thought of his leaving left her empty inside.

She had faced death again, and she had used her ability to cheat it. But fear tempered her triumph: how many times could they cheat death?

Rand needed the forty minutes it took them to make one stop and return to the tomb to sort through his thoughts. Seeing Zoe get trashed by her mother and the hurt in her eyes had torn right through him. He knew exactly how Lucas felt when he looked at Amy: that rip-your-guts-out-need-to-protect-and-love-your-woman thing.

Scared the hell out of him.

Taking her to his apartment *had* been about consoling her, giving her private time to vent or cry or whatever. The sex had been all about giving in to something they both had been wanting for a while. He still wasn't sure why she'd gotten all upset when he'd asked if she felt better. Maybe she wanted a deeper reason for his jumping her bones. Like that he wanted her, that he couldn't live without burying himself in her, that he'd never felt like this before, and it had him so tripped up that he took a step closer instead of racing off in the opposite direction.

And look what it had gotten him. Nearly killed, for one thing.

They pulled down the alley and into the garage, then made their way through the tunnel. As soon as the door slid open, the other four anxiously took them in.

"Did something happen?" Rand asked.

"That's what we were wondering," Amy said. "Lucas had another storm."

Lucas sat at the dining table, looking like the victim of a tequila hangover.

Rand started to head into the kitchen. "We got everything set up for tomorrow, the boys are in, then we made a quick stop at my apartment, where Steele found us. Zoe tossed his gun with her telekinesis. I shot ahead and saw where it was going to land, grabbed it, and took him out." He held up the gun. "It's got a silencer."

Eric held up his hand. "Whoa, wait a minute. 'Took him out'? As in killed him?"

Zoe answered for him. "Steele won't be a problem anymore."

The four let out whoops of triumph. Zoe looked at Rand, her face as sober as his. Eric walked over and raised his hand in a high five. "Good job, man."

Rand stared at his palm for a second, then finally gave him a halfhearted slap. "Thanks."

He wasn't as bloodthirsty as Eric. Like Lucas, though, he'd kill when necessary. Especially to protect someone else.

His gaze slid to Zoe, but he trained it away from her. "Get out the map and I'll fine-tune the plan." He looked at Petra. "Have you heard from Cheveyo yet?"

She nodded. "I gave him the message to give to Nicholas."

"I told the boys to be ready for tomorrow, but that it might be later." He grabbed a pen, put a mark on the map, and readied himself for the fight. "Eric, this is where you're stationed."

CHAPTER 24

Zoe and Rand dyed their hair back to their normal colors Saturday morning. She gelled her curls into waves and smiled at her reflection in the mirror. She felt like herself again.

She was about to head upstairs when he emerged from his room, his hair dark blond. "No light blond tips?" she asked.

"My hairdresser does that. God knows what it would look like if I tried."

"Yeah, that's why I didn't do my black streaks." She tilted her head, taking him in. "You didn't spike your hair."

He looked different. More grown-up, less prickly. She resisted the urge to touch it or tell him she liked it.

"Figured I'd go with a different 'do, so I don't look like they remember."

She started to head upstairs but paused. "I'm doing the blue eye tattoo on everyone today."

"You think I'm going to let you near me with a needle after yesterday?"

She narrowed her eyes at him. "I'm a professional. I never let my personal pissed-offedness affect my performance."

"No, thanks." He turned and went up the stairs.

She spent the afternoon tattooing the blue eye on everyone . . . everyone except Rand. She had set up a chair in the middle of the living room.

Eric admired the large version on his biceps. "Rand, you're the only one not getting the eye."

"I'm not a tattoo person." Rand watched Zoe finish the eye on the back of Petra's neck.

Eric propped his feet on the coffee table. "You have piercings, though."

"Yeah, but they're not permanent." He gestured to the staircase. "I'm going downstairs, burn off some of this nervous energy."

Amy, perched on the edge of the table, gave Zoe a sympathetic smile once Rand was out of earshot. "He'll come around."

No, he wouldn't, but Zoe wasn't going to relay what he'd told her the day before. She shrugged, concentrating on her work.

Amy stood. "Lucas, you ready? We're going to get the 'Cuda." She'd called Ozzie that morning and found out it was done. "We'll meet you in a few hours." She twisted around and tried to look at her tattoo though she couldn't see it well.

Lucas lifted her shirt and traced around the Saran Wrap that covered the raised, red area on the center of her back. "I like it."

Zoe smiled, filled with pride and satisfaction. "It feels so good to be doing this again. I can't believe I forgot the chicken diapers, though."

"Chicken diapers?" three of them said at once.

"They're like those little pads they put under the chickens you buy at the store that soak up the blood. We put them on the tattoo right after it's done." Even the buzzing sound was comforting. She finished Petra's tattoo. "Go check it out in the mirror." She savored the weight of the machine in her hand. "I feel bad, though, taking the shop's equipment. Even though it's mine, RJ's going to be surprised to find my note and my stuff gone. I promised I'd get it right back."

Petra ran back into the living room. "I love it!"

Zoe smiled. "I'm glad you like it. I'm going to go down and get ready for the mission."

She did her best to ignore Rand at the gym on the way to her bedroom. She wore black pants and a blue tank top. She touched up her makeup and headed toward the open area.

Rand was draped over one of the bars. "Hey, Zoe. About what happened—"

She held up her hand. "Look, it was a mistake. A mad, dumb mistake, and it won't happen again. Like you said, it was something brewing between us, and we got it out of our systems, so it's over."

She kept on walking, hearing an annoying voice in her head: *You should have waited to see what he'd say.*

An hour later they gathered around the table, and Rand went through the plan one more time. She had to admit it was pretty ingenious. Taze would take Nicholas on a motorcycle to another location across the city, where two more of the boys would be waiting. Nicholas would transfer to another bike in a dark tunnel, and if anyone was watching, he'd see two bikes emerge with two riders heading off in different directions. Both passengers would be wearing black.

The second relay would wind through the back alleys and deliver Nicholas to Rand, who would take him to an abandoned building. Amy and Lucas would be the lookouts there. Petra would watch the first stop, Eric the second, and Zoe the third stop.

"Let's roll." Rand grabbed up his black duffel bag. She knew it now contained his gun and not his spray paints. As everyone else got ready, he said in a soft voice, "You ride with me. We'll go over your route together. There's one change that no one but Lucas knows about."

She raised an eyebrow but said nothing about that intriguing tidbit.

The group walked to the garage, but Rand held Zoe back. "I know you're pissed at me, but hang on tight. We're going to be riding into some pretty rough neighborhoods, and I want to feel like you're secure back there."

"Fine," she said in a clipped voice.

He paused. "Thank you for not telling them where I know these guys from. You're an honorable secret keeper."

"You wouldn't tell them about that whole thing with my mom. So we keep each other's secrets well." She shrugged, no big deal.

He regarded her thoughtfully. "Zoe, we've seen each other naked. And I don't mean just physically."

She thought of the raw moments they'd shared, when she'd run down that path at Truxtun Park, when he'd fought to hold in the pain over Sly's death. "Yeah . . . I know." She knew that killing Steele, no matter who he was, had torn Rand apart. She had a feeling he was still haunted over shooting the guy who'd posed as Nicholas Braden, too.

"I didn't mean to hurt you," he said in a soft, low voice. He reached out and touched her cheek.

She felt a rush of so much at that tender touch, need and affection and, crazy as it was, love. Before she could kill it, he kissed her, a soft kiss that quickly deepened. Had he felt it, too? His hand came up to brace her face, fingers grazing her skin. Gawd, what he could do to her! Just a kiss, a stupid, simple kiss, and her heart was hammering and hurting and wanting and aching all at once.

She moved away. "It's a lot easier to be pissed at you, Rand. We'd better go."

An hour and a half later they reached an area of town she normally wouldn't be caught dead in. Graffiti was everywhere. Before Rand, she probably wouldn't have given it much notice. Now she did, and even recognized Taze's name on a piece depicting a beautiful array of tropical fish. Rand rode past the relay points, giving a thumbs-up to his boys as they waited in position. These guys thought a lot of Rand. As much as he wanted to deny it, he thought a lot of them, too.

He showed her where she would park and where her target was. A guy named Pith waved at them. She would follow Pith to where Rand would pick up Nicholas, then she would follow them to the old building, where they would have their meeting. Her heart pounded as she thought of the other times they'd tried to contact a new Offspring.

He tucked the bike behind the Dumpster next to a

building that was about to get demolished. Lucas and Amy were to lurk one floor above where Rand and Zoe would talk to Nicholas.

Never would she have thought she'd go into a building that looked like one good sneeze would bring it down. Mice scurried as they stepped into the vestibule. She tried to hide her shudder.

The building smelled of things she didn't want to take the time to identify, all disgusting. Bugs—she couldn't bear to think they were roaches—scattered, hiding beneath the debris. She and Rand moved aside some of the broken furniture that littered the floor to make a pathway should they need to escape quickly.

Lucas and Amy stepped out from the first apartment. "Everything in place?"

"Yep. Everyone's ready. Now we wait."

Zoe could see why Amy had fallen for Lucas. With his intense eyes and thick, wavy hair, he was gorgeous. And he loved Amy in a way that was painfully obvious and passionately deep. The way she thought she'd never love anyone. She found her gaze drifting to Rand, who was talking to Lucas. He'd taught her something, though: to let go. The problem was, who would she ever get to let go with besides him?

The cell phone rang, and Rand answered. "Yeah? Cool." He hung up. "The game is on."

Zoe and Rand walked out, he to the bike, she to the 'Cuda. The four original Rogues sighed sadly every time they looked at the brown, tricked-out car.

Zoe watched the second relay trade-off, then followed to see Nicholas get off Pith's bike and on Rand's. She followed at a short distance. As they approached the building, Amy gave a thumbs-up sign from the upstairs window. Nicholas was an Offspring. But that didn't mean they were safe.

Rand parked Blue, and both men got off the bike. Nicholas wore black, as instructed, so that he'd match the decoy rider. Zoe bet Rand's grandmother would think he looked a bit like Matt Dillon. He had a thick shock of dark brown hair, brown eyes, and pale skin. His body, though, had the long, lean look of a swimmer. Zoe took a deep breath and walked over to join them.

Nicholas looked around. "Is all this really necessary?"

"Afraid so." Rand stepped closer. "The last time we tried to contact you, we nearly got our heads blown off. Call us a little paranoid, but it keeps us alive."

They were keeping their guns out of sight, though.

Nicholas's thick brows furrowed. "The shoot-out at my house. That was the second thing that got me thinking. Made me suspicious. Darkwell, Director for Science and Technology at CIA, is my temporary boss. He told me to tell the police I had no idea why someone used my house, which is true. He said you guys—the Rogues, he calls you—were going to kill me. But he never gave me a good reason why."

"Because he wants you to fear us. And he sure as hell doesn't want us to tell you what's really going on or get you suspicious."

"What's really going on?"

Rand said, "You wanted to meet with us. Tell us what you know."

He looked as though he were about to argue but decided against it. "A month ago I was contracted to use my skills in a classified program called DARK MATTER. I've got an uncanny ability to find things."

Zoe tilted her head. "And you found out that your *skill* is actually a psychic ability."

"Yeah. And that I inherited it from my father." He tested the strength of a table nearby and leaned against it. "Darkwell promised to teach me to develop my skills so that I could help locate hostages. I liked that idea. Plus he offered me a wad of money to do it, enough so when I'm done with my contract, I can start my own business. He taught me how to remote-view, psychically see distant places, explaining that it was an extension of my location skill. But before I can find any hostages, I'm ordered to find these bad-ass Rogues—all of you.

"You're supposed to be terrorists, but you seem like ordinary Americans like me. He told me he wanted to question you. Then you guys break into the hospital and"—he rubbed his hand over his face—"that was some hairy shit, but what bothered me as much as anything you did was seeing one of our guards holding two women at gunpoint. I knew he would have killed them.

"When it was over, Darkwell told me it was an un-provoked attack, but I overheard him talking about a prisoner being rescued. I had no idea there *were* any prisoners. Darkwell denied it when I asked him. I knew he was lying. That was the first thing that had me suspicious. I haven't been comfortable since, but I've got another month on my contract."

Rand stood rigid, ready for anything. "Lucas Vanderwyck and I were being held at the asylum.

Darkwell was using us as guinea pigs, shooting us up with drugs to see if they would boost our abilities."

The horror of that colored Nicholas's expression. "Earlier this week I was told to try to find the women again. When Petra told me I was on the wrong side, it jibed with my suspicions. She said something about the classified program my dad worked in twenty years ago. That he died because of it."

Zoe nodded. "Darkwell created a program that put people with psychic abilities to work finding hostages and terrorists."

"Darkwell mentioned the program but never said he'd created it."

They filled him in on the original program, the Booster, and what it had done to their parents.

Rand crossed his arms in front of his chest. "How many of you are working in the DARK MATTER program? We met with Jerryl Evrard, who pretended to be interested in what we had to say, then nearly took out Zoe."

"What did he do?"

Zoe felt the anger of those terrible minutes all over again. "Grabbed me, put a gun to my head, then jumped into the water with me."

"Jerryl." Nicholas shook his head. "He's a Marine. All he ever talks about is serving his country and killing people, like both are a privilege and pleasure. There are three of us. Fonda's the third, and she's tight with Jerryl. Little thing, but fierce."

Only three. And if they could bring Nicholas over . . .

Don't get too excited yet. This could still be a trap.

Zoe leaned against the wall so she could face Nicholas. "What is Jerryl's psychic ability?"

"He remote-views, but I think he can do more than that. He and Darkwell spend a lot more time together than they do with me. They're like coconspirators, both with that killer gleam in their eyes."

"Jerryl can mind-control," Rand said.

Nicholas's eyebrows furrowed. "As in, getting into someone's head and making them do something against their will?"

Rand's expression hardened. "Exactly."

"And I thought this Cheveyo guy getting into my head was freaky enough."

Zoe narrowed her eyes. "Were you the one who found me in Key West?"

Nicholas scrubbed his fingers through his hair. "That was me."

"Darkwell sent an assassin after me. And he's come after Rand and me twice."

"In an apartment in Baltimore. The two of you were, uh . . ." Nicholas's cheeks actually flushed.

"Yeah," Rand said. "Talk about killing the after-glow."

Of course, that had already been squashed.

Nicholas rubbed his mouth. "I'm sorry. I didn't know."

Zoe checked her watch. "And the thing at your house, that was a setup. Darkwell knew we were going to contact you—contact, not kill—and he put one of his thugs in there to pose as you. The goal was to take all of us out, no questions first."

Nicholas massaged his temples and closed his eyes for a second. "This confirms the bad feeling I've had about this for a while now." He opened his eyes. "This . . . Booster stuff in us . . ."

Rand said, "We don't know what it is. Our parents were told it was some kind of nutritional cocktail, but it was obviously more than that. And it's a good bet that it could make us crazy, too."

That was something she didn't want to think about.

"Why is Darkwell out to kill you?" Nicholas asked.

Rand stuffed the tips of his fingers into his front jeans pocket. "He would have approached us the same way he did you, but we got suspicious and started digging. No way would we work for the dude who caused our parents to die. He can't take the chance that we'll expose him."

"Is that what you want to do?"

She said, "We want to shut him down. He's hurt a lot of people, and he's going to keep on hurting them. Some will be terrorists. Others will just be people in his way. Like us."

Rand asked, "Where did Darkwell move the operation?"

Nicholas met their gazes. "Not until I understand more about what's going on. You're not going to storm the place, are you? Innocent people work there. How do I know you *are* the good guys?"

Zoe pushed away from the wall, the signal to wrap it up. "Find out for yourself. Ask about your dad, what he was doing before he died. Talk to Jerryl and find out what he's up to. Ask questions about what's really going on there. You already know they're not being straight with you. You decide who the good guys are. But be careful. Darkwell kills curious cats."

Rand handed him one of their untraceable cell phones. "We'll be in touch. It's set to vibrate. We'll call once, disconnect, then call back in thirty minutes. That'll give you time to get someplace where you can talk."

Rand crossed his arms in front of his chest. "There's something you need to know. If you stay on Darkwell's side, you may not get out alive."

"You'd kill me?"

"If you're the enemy, and you help him find us or set us up, we'll have to. Or you may get hit in the cross fire. This is a war between Darkwell and us. And like in any war, people are going to get killed. We're going to make damned sure it's not one of us."

Zoe said, "But if you join us, you'll be a target like we are." She walked toward the hallway. "We'd better get you back to your car. If Jerryl remote-views and sees you with us, you're toast. Unless you're a setup."

"I'm not." Nicholas met their eyes. "Either you or Darkwell is lying. I'm going to find out which one."

He shoved the phone in his pocket and followed Rand out of the building.

At the creak on the stairs behind her, Zoe turned to find Lucas and Amy coming down.

"What do you think?" Lucas asked.

"He may be legit. If he is, he'll be a huge asset. And he'll lead us to Robbins."

They walked outside and got into the 'Cuda, Zoe now in the back. They drove to Eric's location. He yanked open the passenger door and jabbed his finger at them. "Bastards! There was no relay stop here. You cut me out of the loop, *and* you lied about where you were meeting Braden."

Amy pursed her lips. "So you went there?"

He dropped into the seat and slammed the door closed. "I don't like being left out of the action."

"Which is exactly why we left you out," Lucas said. "You're like a spark in a house filled with gas. We couldn't take the chance of you sending the whole operation up in flames. Figuratively speaking, not literally."

He narrowed his eyes. "Since I *still* can't start any fires, I figured that. So, what happened?"

Zoe gave him a bright smile. "No one got shot. That was nice for a change. Amazing what makes me happy these days. Seriously, I think Nicholas may work out. We've got him digging now. He'll find out that Darkwell's a sack of lies, then he'll be ours."

Rand saw the 'Cuda drive up at the same time that Taze returned on his bike. Asia, Pith, and four other graffiti artists who'd been watching the area for them all waited, too. Rand's body tightened as Zoe approached. The female Rogues were the strongest women he'd ever known, besides his gram. Zoe's hair was in the familiar wavy 'do, her full lips dark red against her pale skin. Damn, she was beautiful. He hadn't meant to kiss her back at the tomb. He hadn't meant to do a lot of things he'd done with her.

Everyone converged outside another abandoned building. Nearby construction workers banged away at a renovation project.

Eric's scowl was no surprise. It was worth angering him to protect the operation. And the Rogues. He wasn't going to let that hothead put anyone in danger again.

Taze extended his hand to Rand in their particular handshake. "Everything work?"

"Yeah, thanks. You guys are dope."

Taze looked at the Rogues. "Who are these people?"

Lucas said, "We're his family."

Those simple words struck Rand in the chest. He'd never really had much of a family, only his gram.

Taze wasn't convinced, but he said, "That's cool. All right, dude, we'll see you on the street?"

"You bet."

The guys filed out, and once they were gone, Lucas asked, "So, who were *those* guys? You hang out in the streets a lot?"

Rand looked at the group, at Zoe's knowing smile . . . and he told them what he did for fun.

Petra squealed as though he'd just revealed he was Jon Bon Jovi. "Oh, my gawd, I love Freedom!" She turned to Amy. "Weren't we just talking about him?"

Lucas grinned. "We have quite the artistic contingent in our group. Me, Zoe, and you."

No one said that graffiti was vandalism, a nuisance, or chided him about hanging with guys he knew only by nickname. Damn, for just this moment, he wanted a family. It gnawed at his belly like hunger pangs.

"We'd better get going."

Danger always lurked, and that danger reminded him how easily he could lose these people who considered him family.

CHAPTER 25

Sam Robbins paused outside of Darkwell's door and listened. He could barely hear through the thick wood, but what he could hear made the hairs on the back of his neck stand up. Darkwell was making arrangements to transfer Sayre Andrus out of prison.

In rare instances, CIA could transfer prisoners who had specific value to the government into their custody. That meant Andrus was willing to work with Darkwell.

Sam had read some of Andrus's file. The prison warden would probably be happy to see his troublesome prisoner go. Several accusations had been filed against Andrus, ranging from "voodoo spells" to unexplained deaths. None could be proven.

The door opened, and Darkwell stopped at the sight of Sam hovering there.

Darkwell's voice was terse. "Come in."

"You wanted the statistics report . . ."

Darkwell snagged the folder out of his hand. "I suppose you heard my conversation."

"Not intentionally. You're trying to get Andrus out of prison? He *murdered* a woman."

Darkwell sat at his massive desk. "He never admitted to that. The evidence was circumstantial at best. Besides, that has nothing to do with what I want him for. If he *has* murdered someone, then he's not squeamish. We already have one subject who's opposed to violence, and frankly, that's a hindrance."

Sam couldn't believe his ears. "You know Andrus is a cold-blooded psychopath."

"Yes, I do." Darkwell's black eyes glittered "But he'll be *our* psychopath."

The truth hit Sam like a wave of ice-cold water: he'd been working for a psychopath all along. He didn't want to let on how repulsed he was by both Andrus and Darkwell. Instinct said to play along. "I suppose you have a point. But I thought Andrus wasn't interested."

"I must have piqued his interest. He called to set up another meeting. He wants out of prison. I just got off the phone with a judge I know in Florida to find out what the process entails. I need permission from the court, and a judge authorizes the release. Should be easy enough. Andrus will work here with us for four months, and I'll let him think it could go on longer. He'll have to go back, of course. I'll blame it on red tape, regulations, whatever. If he escapes, or if word gets out to the public that he's been released, it'll create a media frenzy."

Sam approached the desk. "Does the director know?"

"I'm not involving him unless and until I have to. He's very impressed with the information I've already given him. We just got word that Jerryl's information led operatives to a terrorist cell in Afghanistan. If I need to approach the director, I don't think it'll be a problem."

Sam rubbed his balding head, nervous at the thought of that man here on the grounds. "Will he be kept secure?"

"Of course. He'll have a guard posted to him at all times."

"What is he capable of?"

"You know his heritage. There are several possibilities." Darkwell smiled with satisfaction. "I'm going to give him a test assignment. Andrus is going to be the turning point in DARK MATTER. He's going to get rid of the Rogues. That should make you happy." His smile faded when he didn't see agreement on Sam's face. "Was there anything else?"

It was useless to warn him. Sam shook his head and left. Bringing in Andrus would be Darkwell's biggest mistake yet. Sam wasn't going to stick around for the fallout.

He paused outside his office door, remembering the subtle warning he'd been given when he'd wanted out before. He had no doubt that Darkwell would eliminate him to protect the program. The man had had his own brother killed, for God's sake.

Sam went into his office and searched his computer for any relevant files. He printed them out and looked them over. Sensitive, but not enough. He needed security: files he could hold over Darkwell's head should anything suspicious happen to him. He didn't think Nicholas would harm him, but Darkwell's protégé, Jerryl, would take him out.

As he stepped out of his office, Darkwell headed down the hallway to the winding staircase. Sam followed at a distance and watched his superior get into his black Mercedes and pull away. He turned and went back upstairs, waiting until the hall was clear before trying Darkwell's door. It was locked.

Olivia, Darkwell's assistant, stepped out of her office, startling him. "He's gone for the day."

"I gave him a file earlier, and he set it on his desk. I just realized I gave him the wrong papers, and you know how he gets when we make a mistake."

She nodded in a knowing way. "Hold on, I'll get the key." She returned a minute later and unlocked the door. "Go ahead."

She followed him in, though. He grabbed up the file he'd just given to Darkwell. "Let me get the other file. I'll be right back."

Unfortunately, she was waiting when he returned. He set the same file on the desk, reached around the doorknob, and made the appropriate motions. "I locked it. Thanks. You saved me a browbeating."

She smiled as she pulled the door closed. "No problem."

Four hours later, after he thought Olivia had gone home, he walked the long, paneled hallway to see who was around. One guard always wandered the hallways in addition to the two patrolling the grounds. He doubted the interior guard knew that he had no business in Darkwell's office, but he couldn't be sure. Not enough to risk his life.

He passed Evrard's room and heard him and, presumably, his girlfriend, going at it as usual. He remembered the first round of subjects in BLUE

EYES, how they'd been consumed by lust. He passed Braden's room, too, but it was quiet.

His heart thudded softly as he stood outside Darkwell's office. He reached out, turned the knob, and slipped inside.

He knew the computer would be password protected. His only hope was to find something in his physical files. He pulled open one of the drawers, found nothing relevant. He tried another, then another. Finally, he found a drawer in the credenza that looked interesting: partial notes on BLUE EYES. Something, at least, that might keep Darkwell from dispatching him.

He turned on the copier. He was halfway through copying the pages when he heard a noise. Adrenaline shot through him. If Darkwell found him, he'd be killed immediately. He had no legitimate reason for being there, and Darkwell wouldn't believe anything he might dream up.

He shut off the copier and cracked open the door. He heard the echo of conversation in the grand foyer, one man's voice getting louder as he ascended the stairs. The office offered no place to hide. If he didn't lock the door, and that *was* Darkwell, he'd be suspicious, especially with Sam loitering in the hallway. Reluctantly, he turned the lock, his file tucked beneath his arm, and closed the door.

He headed toward his office, fighting the urge to look back.

"Robbins, what are you doing here so late?"

Cringing, he turned to face Darkwell.

"Just heading home." He pressed the folder closer to his body as Darkwell's gaze fell on it.

"What are you working on?"

The blood drained from Sam's face. "Different ways to look at the statistical data."

"Really? Let me have a look." He reached for the folder.

Sam swallowed hard, trying to find some excuse to refuse. That would only pique his suspicions. How would he explain having the data in his possession? He pulled out the folder and his trembling hand dropped it on the floor, spilling the papers. "Damn." The word fit the situation. He knelt and pulled the papers together. "They're all out of order now. I'd better get them sorted."

Another sound caught Darkwell's attention. His eyes narrowed at Olivia and Nicholas Braden walking down the hallway in a serious discussion. "I'll talk to you about it later." He walked up to the two. "Olivia, can we speak in private, please?"

Sam scooped up the last of the papers, shoved them in the folder, and headed down the stairs, afraid his wobbly legs would give out and send him tumbling down.

Did he have enough to give him some security? All he had to do was send Darkwell a copy of a couple papers and tell him that he'd gotten everything. Yes, he had enough. He would get them to his attorney. Then he would make arrangements to disappear.

Zoe leaned against the wall as Eric unplugged the computer and dialed Nicholas. The UPS started beeping. Rand stepped in front of the microphone, shooting Eric a warning look: *Shut up.* When Nicholas answered, he said, "It's Rand. Have you had a chance—?"

"Yeah, I'm interested." He sounded edgy, as though he were worried someone might hear.

Rand said, "You were able to sniff around?"

"Enough to think you're onto something. And that I don't want to be part of the program anymore."

"You need to be very careful about letting on. If Darkwell suspects, you may be taken out. You'll have to play along until we can get together and talk."

"When will that be?"

"After you've proven that you're not setting us up."

After a moment of hesitation, he said, "What do I need to do?"

"You're the master locator. Give us Sam Robbins's home address."

Another pause. "What do you want with him?"

"We just want to talk. He knows a lot about the program, then and now, and I think he'd be willing to part with that information."

Nicholas's voice lowered. "If I give it to you . . . I don't want him hurt. I won't be part of your violence."

Petra gave them a *See, told you* look. Zoe hoped she was right.

Rand wasn't completely convinced. "He won't be touched. Lucas and I were prisoners, he was the only person who was nice to us." He let out a soft breath. "And I understand your antiviolence stand, but you are going to find yourself in a kill-or-be-killed situation one of these days. You'd better be ready."

"I'll work on Robbins's address. Give me a few minutes. He left a half hour ago, so I'll try to do a locate on him."

They disconnected and waited ten minutes. Then they went through the unplugging and dialing procedure again.

Nicholas answered with, "I have an address for you. I'll give it to you on one condition: you tell me when you're going to talk to him. I want to remote-view, see what's going on."

Rand looked at the others, who, other than Eric, nodded their agreement.

"Deal."

Nicholas recited it to them.

So he believed. Maybe.

Eric leaned in front of the microphone. "If this is a trap, know that we're coming for you."

Nicholas asked, "Who is this?"

"Eric Aruda."

Rand pushed him aside. "We'll be in touch. And remember what I said: be careful."

"And remember what you said about not hurting Robbins."

"You have my word."

The phone disconnected. Lucas looked at Petra. "How much do you trust this Cheveyo guy's judgment?"

"Implicitly."

"Then we go in."

Three days later, on a drizzly night, Lucas and Rand crept to Robbins's car where it was parked in a pub's lot. Using a tool borrowed from Taze's brother, Rand unlocked the car door, and Lucas slid into the backseat to wait. The most dangerous part was staying in one place for a period of time.

Zoe waited nearby, focusing her energy on putting the golden shield around the car. Rand glanced over at her silhouette near the line of trees at the back of the parking lot. A voice whispered, *There are better things to do with a beautiful woman on a dark, drizzly night.*

Rand, just get that thought right out of your head. Both your heads.

He'd kept his distance from her as much as possible considering they were often in the same enclosed space belowground. But he'd caught her looking at him, which meant *he* was looking at *her* way too much. Every time their gazes locked, his body reacted. His hardened cock he could understand, since he knew every curve on her body, the smell of her, the taste of her . . .

He shook his head. *Yeah, all of that.* He could write off the physical reactions as typical male physiology. What he couldn't explain, and didn't want to explore, was the strange tightening in his chest.

He'd been working on his skills as Zoe had—she seemed to like practicing on him—and thought he'd gained a few seconds. He continually shot ahead. This time he saw that Robbins was about to come out. He rang Lucas's phone once, knowing he would feel the vibration.

Robbins appeared, looked ragged, and got into his car. Rand held his breath and waited for the signal from Lucas. When his phone rang once, Rand called Zoe. "He's got him."

The car started, and Robbins pulled around to the darkest edge of the lot as Lucas had instructed him. Zoe and Rand were there to meet them. Amy came from the left, and Lucas told Robbins to get into the backseat.

The man's face was sheet white as he stumbled out of the car. "Please, don't hurt me."

Amy slid into the driver's seat as Robbins got into the back with Lucas. Rand held the gun to Robbins's back as he followed, so that he and Lucas flanked their target. Zoe got into the front seat, and Amy drove away.

Lucas faced Robbins. "As I said, we're going to take a drive, and you're going to tell us everything you know. If you cooperate, we'll get out of your car and let you go."

Staying on the move seemed the best idea. Eric and Petra followed in the 'Cuda at a reasonable distance.

In the passing streetlights, Rand could see the fear on Robbins's face.

The man's expression transformed to disbelief. "Wait a minute. You're Lucas. But you're supposed to be—"

"Dead?" Lucas said.

"You were shot in the chest. And . . ."

"Because of whatever you were injecting into me."

"I never wanted to use that stuff again."

"What was it?"

"I . . . I don't know. I never knew what was in it."

"It's the same stuff our parents got, isn't it?"

"Yes. This time we extracted from the blood of the Offspring in the new program, though they don't know the real reason for the blood test. Lucas, I'm sorry for what Darkwell has done. I never wanted to be part of this. He is mad, mad with what he calls justice and a cause he considers noble."

Rand then asked, "What's the purpose of DARK MATTER?"

"Political assassination. Like what Lucas did."

Amy turned. *"What Lucas did?"*

"Killing through his dreams," Robbins said as though he assumed they knew.

Rand hadn't heard about that, and, if Amy's shocked expression was an indication, neither had she.

Lucas pinched the bridge of his nose. "That's what I had to do to keep you safe, Amy. I killed two terrorists. And that bastard had me kill his brother."

Robbins worried his trembling hands. "That was the beginning of the end for me. He knows I no longer support the program, that I want out. I've got papers about the first program. I can give you copies. Then I have to disappear."

Rand's heartbeat stepped up as he heard the words "My father?" come out of his mouth.

"Yes, some of the notes on Paul Brandenburg and Zoe's father. God, I'm sorry about that. He was a good man before . . ." Robbins could only shake his head.

Rand felt something shift inside him. All these years it had been easier to believe his father was a cowardly thief so he could forget him, not care. But . . . maybe he wasn't. As Zoe so desperately needed to believe, maybe his father, too, was possessed by madness caused by the Booster.

Rand shot ahead, and what he saw stunned him. *No, it can't be.*

Though Robbins's voice still quivered, he didn't look as much afraid as he was nervous. "I'm on your side. I don't like what Darkwell's become, what he's doing. I think he's onto me, though. I'm pretty sure he's having me watched."

"Will you help us?" Zoe asked.

"Take me back to my house, and I'll make you copies of the papers. What I can tell you is that Darkwell is gunning for you, and he's getting desperate. He's working on bringing another Offspring aboard, and he's the reason I'm finally leaving. The last straw. He's evil, he's powerful, and there's something you need to know about him."

Rand thought his brain had to be warped. No way would Lucas shoot Robbins. He was the one who'd adamantly ordered that he not be harmed. That's why Eric was separated from him.

Have you ever been wrong?

Rand held out his hand. "Give me your gun, Lucas."

"What?"

Zoe's voice mirrored the fear in his. "What's going on?"

"Give me your gun, Lucas!" Rand shouted, snatching in the dark for it.

The voice that came from Lucas was low and controlled . . . different. "No."

They drove under a streetlight, and in that second of illumination, he saw Lucas's blank expression as he raised the gun. Rand tried to grab it.

Robbins said, "Sayre," as Lucas shot him in the chest.

Blood sprayed everywhere. Zoe screamed. A map went flying. Robbins slumped forward. Amy slammed on the brakes, and the car fishtailed to a stop. She twisted around, fighting with the seat belt. "What happened? *What the hell happened?*"

Rand tore the gun from Lucas's hand. He went slack, his head falling against the glass with a *thump*.

"Pull off!" Rand shouted. "Over there, in that empty parking lot."

Zoe's voice was empty, shocked, when she answered Amy. "Lucas shot Robbins."

"What?" Amy said in a squeaky voice. "No! He wouldn't have done that."

Rand fought the urge to throw up. He was covered in blood, the car reeked of the coppery scent of it, and his brain still couldn't comprehend what had just happened.

Lucas's phone was ringing. Amy threw the car into park. They heard Eric screech to a halt behind them and car doors open. Eric yanked open the door on Rand's side, lighting up the interior and the grisly scene.

Lucas opened his eyes and looked around as though he were seeing everything for the first time. He blinked in disbelief. "Oh my God, what happened?"

Amy stared from the front seat. "You shot him. Lucas, you shot Robbins."

He looked down at his hands, covered in blood. "No. *No.*"

Rand took Robbins's arm and pressed his finger to his wrist. He looked dead, but he had to check. Rand shook his head. "No pulse."

Eric said, "He got into your head, didn't he? That son of a bitch said he was going to get into all of our heads."

Lucas couldn't take his shocked gaze from Robbins's body. "I . . . I don't remember doing it."

"Did you hear his voice?"

"No, only Rand demanding my gun. I felt a cold feeling, like an ice cube on the back of my neck. I don't remember anything after that." His face reflected his terror. He looked at Rand. "You must have seen me shoot him before I did it."

Rand nodded. "But it didn't make sense. I thought I was losing it."

"*I'm* losing it."

The phone rang again. Lucas was too shocked to even acknowledge it. Amy grabbed it up. "It's Nicholas." He had their number because they'd called him just before they'd begun their wait for Robbins. She punched in the speaker button. "Hello."

"Who is this?" he asked.

"Amy. Nicholas—"

"You weren't supposed to kill him!" The emotion in his voice stretched his words taut. "I remote-viewed you to see what was going on. You lied—"

"Lucas never meant to kill Robbins! Someone got into his head. He just blanked out. He has no memory of shooting Robbins, and he's torn up over it. How do we know it wasn't you?"

"Because I can't get into someone's head and because I'm not a murderer."

She paused, weighing his words, weighing hers. "Somebody did and somebody is. If you had anything to do with this . . ." She looked at the phone display. "He hung up." She got out of the car, nudged Eric aside, and put her hands on Lucas's shoulders. "It had to be Jerryl."

Eric shook his head. "It doesn't sound like Jerryl's MO. I can feel him in my head, hear his voice. But I remember every damned second of the struggle. I'm never out."

Rand said, "Something changed in your face, Lucas. When I saw you in advance and when it happened, your eyes looked blank. It was like you were possessed, dude."

Lucas's face was frozen in fear. "What if it was one of my episodes, only now they're different." He looked at Eric. "I'm going crazy."

Amy's fear was just as intense. "No, it isn't that. Robbins was telling us about another Offspring. What did he say right before . . . ?"

"He said 'scared,' I think," Zoe said.

Eric said, "Jerryl might be able to get into your head in a different way than mine. It has to be them, bro. You're the last person who would kill this guy. Or maybe it was Braden. Maybe this was part of the setup."

Rand looked at Robbins's body, slumped between the front seats. "We've got to get out of here. About a mile back we crossed a river. Let's get Robbins into the front seat, wipe the gun, put his fingers on it to leave his prints, and send the car into the river. It might look like suicide. We've got to wipe off our prints." He rubbed his forehead. "She-it, I can't believe I'm saying this. Come on, let's move."

They used Eric's shirt to wipe every surface they might have touched, along with the gun. Lucas was still in shock, moving robotically.

Eric nodded toward Robbins. "I can't really feel sorry for him. He was one of them."

Lucas's voice sounded empty when he said, "He wanted to help us. Give us papers on the program."

Petra eyes widened. "Oh, no, I've got the *feeling*. They're watching."

"Put up the shield!" Rand said.

She slowed her breathing as she rocked back and forth, her eyes closed. A few seconds later she opened her eyes. "They're gone."

Zoe twisted her fingers together. "They know. We've got to get back to the tomb."

Everyone's voice was shaky, even Rand's. They worked silently, getting to the bridge, waiting for a break in traffic to transfer Robbins to the driver's seat, then driving the car through the railing.

Zoe rubbed her face, pulling her hand away and letting out a garbled whimper. "I've got . . . his blood . . ."

In the moonlight, Rand could see her eyes shiny with tears. He took her hand and led her down the embankment toward the water. "We need to wash this stuff off so we don't get it in the 'Cuda. Evidence."

Amy and Lucas followed. They splashed the cool water all over themselves. Rand washed Zoe's face and dipped her trembling hands into the water. She kept saying island names over and over. Lucas kept whispering, "I'm sorry, I'm sorry," as he washed off the blood.

They piled into the 'Cuda and drove back to where Rand had stashed his bike. When he looked at Zoe's haunted expression, he wanted to take her with him. "It's going to be a cold drive. Wet body and wind isn't a good combination, and you're already chilled."

But it wasn't just to comfort Zoe that made him want her holding on to him as he rode back to the tomb. As much as he hated to admit it, the feel of her arms around him would have comforted him, too.

"Rand, that thought has *dangerous* painted all over it in ocean blue."

Zoe's skin was still scorched from the hot shower. She curled up on the couch, hugging a throw pillow. The rest of the group were scattered around the room, their drooping shoulders and long faces reflecting the shock still clinging to them. For a while no one said anything or even looked at each other. Zoe figured that, like her, they needed time to absorb what had happened. A possible ally killed. Hope of getting information lost. And one of their own acting totally out of character.

Eric finally looked at Lucas. "Why didn't you tell us about the dream assassinations?"

Lucas pressed his fingers over his eyelids. "I was ashamed."

Amy put her hand on his back. "But you did it to save me."

"That wasn't the first time I'd killed someone in my dreams." He looked up. "That's why Darkwell knew what I could do, based on my mother's dreamweaver ability and the fact that three local scumbags had died mysteriously in their sleep. He used that, and Amy, to get me to cooperate. I wasn't going to say anything to you guys unless I needed to."

Zoe could see that Amy was hurt over Lucas's secret, but her hand remained on his back in comfort. That kind of love touched Zoe so deeply her eyes watered.

Rand sat on the floor where Zoe usually sat. "So the question is, did Nicholas set us up?"

Lucas shook his head. "I don't think so. Given his background, his concern that we not hurt . . . Robbins." He took a ragged breath.

Amy said, "And he was pissed about Robbins's death. I could hear it in his voice. Guys can't fake that kind of emotion."

Zoe hugged the pillow tighter. "They can't even *feel* that kind of emotion most of the time." She gave Rand a quick glance, catching him narrowing his eyes at her.

Eric crossed his bare feet on the coffee table. "But we can't trust him because we don't know for sure. Anyone can act, you know. Remember Jerryl's charade?"

Zoe nodded, remembering too well. "Robbins mentioned another Offspring who is evil, powerful, and there was something he was going to tell us about him, something important. He died before he could tell us."

Lucas blanched again, even though she'd tried to couch it as neutrally as possible.

Rand rubbed his chin, still in the habit of stroking his goatee, no doubt. "He said he had papers on the first program. He was going to get us copies. We could check his house."

Eric shook his head. "Too risky. We have to assume that, since Petra felt someone viewing us, they know we were with Robbins. And we can't be sure it was Braden." He looked at them with narrowed eyes. "Next time I will not be left out."

Amy said, "Eric, you're a liability with Jerryl being able to get into your head."

"Well, so is Lucas, if that's what happened. So we're down to four of us being in the action, and that's not acceptable. We got rid of one of them, whether he was actually bad or not," he added, looking at Lucas. "But now it looks like we've got another one to deal with, and if he's more dangerous than Jerryl, he's going to be a big problem. We've got to deal with Jerryl and Darkwell *now*. That means we need all of us."

Amy asked, "What about Nicholas?"

Eric cut his hand across his throat. "Take him out."

Rand said, "We leave him out of the equation for now until we know for sure if he's the enemy."

Zoe let out a long breath. Kill or be killed. Either one scared her.

Zoe woke early the next morning, her gaze going to the clock: 7:15 A.M. Her heart hurt and her eyes were wet from a terrible dream. Her granddad had come to her bedside, telling her goodbye. She kept trying to tell him the truth about his son, but no words came from her throat.

"I have to tell him."

She started to get ready. She'd borrow the Camry, head out first thing. Quick in and out, not long enough for them to find her. Would the nurses call the police?

She looked at her face, all made-up, and frowned. They wouldn't even begin to believe the truth.

A knock at the bathroom door startled her. "Come in."

Rand stepped in, wearing only a pair of sweats and looking like a sweet boy with sleepy eyes and tousled hair. Well, except for the piercings and muscles. "You're up early."

"Sorry if I woke you. I had a bad dream. I'll be out in a minute."

He looked at her with tilted head. Just when she thought he was going to make some smart-assed comment, his expression softened. "Bad dream about yesterday?"

She shivered, at both the memory of that and his concern. "I had nightmares about that earlier, but this one was about my granddad. He died. I'm going to drive into Baltimore and check on him."

He nodded. "I need to call my gram, make sure no one's been around. I'll take you. Give me ten minutes."

She was so surprised she stood there dumbstruck for a few minutes. Blinking, she grabbed her brush and returned to her room.

Exactly ten minutes later, they walked upstairs. No one else was up yet. "I'll leave a note." She found paper and pen at the desk. The picture of five children caught her eye. Rand, as a child, blond and adorable. She was the only one of the six who hadn't been physically connected when they were children, and she caught herself wishing she had. But they were her peeps, as Rachael would say. She smiled. She'd never had peeps before. Lucas had told Rand's boys that they were family, and he'd meant it.

"Ready to go," Rand said from behind her.

Her smile faded. He *was* ready to go . . . to leave them behind. And in a way she understood. Caring about people made you vulnerable. She'd felt that vulnerability when they'd nearly been killed. She'd seen the effect of it in Rand's eyes.

She pulled the photograph down and faced him. "We are family, Rand, even if you tell yourself you're a loner. I happen to know that you do care, maybe a little too much. That won't change when you leave, you know. We'll still care about you. And you . . . you'll still care about us." She pinned the picture back to the board and walked to the door.

In the cool morning air, they rode to the edge of Annapolis before he took the side road to the place where he'd parked before so they could make calls. A breeze whipped in from the creek, raising frothy whitecaps on the water's surface. Thick clouds moved like gray molasses, some heavy with impending rain.

"Call your granddad, see if he's lucid." He didn't say *alive*. He stepped to the side and called Ruby.

"Tell her I said hello."

She stared at her phone, afraid to make the call. The cold, clamminess of the dream still clung to her. Rand laughed at something Ruby said. Zoe closed her eyes, absorbing the sound of it.

"Zoe says hello," he told her. "No, Gram. . . . Just get that out of your mind." He glanced at her, and she knew Ruby was asking if they were getting married yet.

She rubbed the tattooed flowers around her ring finger, took a breath, and called hospice.

The woman's voice didn't harden when Zoe identified herself. Not good. "How's my granddad?"

For a moment all she could hear was the sound of traffic on the highway. Then the woman's voice. "I'm sorry. He passed this morning."

"What time did he go?"

"Seven fifteen."

Zoe's hand went to her mouth to keep the gasp from escaping. Just when she'd had the dream. Or was it a dream? She couldn't tell him the truth now. She'd never see him again. She muttered a thank-you and hung up.

Rand said, "Gram, I gotta go."

She turned away, not wanting to cry in front of him.

He stepped up beside her. "Is he . . . ?"

She nodded, wrapping her arms around herself to keep in her emotions. "Just give me a few minutes. Alone."

She knew that wouldn't be a problem. He'd get as far away as possible.

So it shocked her when he turned her around and put his arms around her.

"Don't," she whispered.

"Why not?" he asked in an equally soft voice.

"Because if you touch me, I'll cry, and crying makes you uncomfortable."

He didn't loosen his hold on her. He pulled her closer.

If only he hadn't touched her. If only he'd walked away. Instead, he said, "I'm sorry."

The first sob escaped, despite her efforts to hold it in.

He rubbed her back. "Let it go, babe."

She gave in, just a little, resting her cheek against his shoulder. "I know it's for the best. He's not in pain anymore. It wasn't like I didn't know this was coming. But I wanted to see him one more time, to tell him about my dad. His son." She took a ragged breath. "Do you believe in heaven?"

He nodded. "Right now I do."

She unfurled her arms and wrapped them around

his waist. She curled her fingers against him and let the tears come. She'd wanted to mourn alone. The need to be comforted, to be held, washed over her as strong as her grief.

He held her, never giving her any indication that he was getting antsy or that they should not linger much longer.

Finally, she pulled back and saw the wet stain on his shirt. She tried to rub it, but he stilled her hand. "Don't worry about it." He reached out and touched her tear-washed cheek.

"I think my granddad came to me right after he died. The dream, only it wasn't a dream, was him coming to say goodbye." Her voice cracked on that last word. "Does that sound crazy?"

He shook his head. "I've heard of visitations. Gram claims that my grandfather came to her right after he died."

They walked to the bike, and he pulled out some paper towels he probably kept for his graffiti. She dabbed at her face and blew her nose. "I want to see my mom."

He raised his eyebrows. "Why?"

"I don't know. The words just came out. Do you mind taking me there, just for a minute?"

"Remember what happened last time."

"Yes. But this time it'll be different."

They rode into the tidy Baltimore neighborhood where the Witherses lived in their tidy brick house.

He pulled into the driveway and cut the engine. "I'll stay here this time."

She started to walk toward the door but paused and turned. "No, come with me."

"If you need me—"

"I don't need you. I just want you to come."

With a nod, he walked to the door with her, though he remained a step behind. She knocked, and a minute later her mother opened the door.

Her dismay and surprise were evident. "You've decided to turn yourself in?" She took note of Rand, and her expression hardened even more.

"No. I've come to forgive you."

"Forgive me?" She laughed in that humorless way Zoe knew so well. "I didn't do anything wrong."

Of course, because her mother was perfect. Several smart-assed replies jumped to Zoe's tongue. *Don't go there. Go on, get it out.*

"You live in fear. Fear of what you can't explain or what you believe God condemns. But sometimes people just assume that something they don't understand is evil. It's an easy label. You fear my psychic ability because you don't understand it. Now that I've faced fear, I kind of get that. But your fear doesn't give you the right to condemn me. My God is merciful, and He accepts and loves us exactly as we are. Last time I came to you, I desperately needed your acceptance, and I wanted your love. I now have acceptance and love from my other family." She glanced at Rand, who looked both surprised and proud. She turned back to her mother. "And most importantly, I have them from myself. I forgive you, Mom. Not for you, but for me."

She turned to leave, stopped. "Granddad died this morning. I won't be able to go to the funeral, since the people who are trying to kill me have set me up as a wanted felon. If you're half the decent person you pretend to be, you'll go. And throw a lily in the grave for me." She didn't wait for a response but walked away.

Rand followed, and when they reached the bike, he silently clapped. All right, his approval did fill her with a rush of emotion, but mostly because she didn't need it anymore. His or anyone's approval. As they pulled away into the sunny spring day, for the first time in her life, she liked herself. She really, totally liked herself.

Once back in the garage, they hung up their helmets and started toward the door. Something stopped her, and she turned to find Rand standing near the 'Cuda.

"What?"

He tilted his head. "You seem different."

"Well, I'm sad."

"No, not just that. Something changed when you talked to your mother. Like you let something go."

She walked back, feeling a curious heaviness flowing through her veins. "I've let a lot go. I let go . . . with you."

"Take off your makeup."

She blinked. "Why?"

He opened the motorcycle bag and pulled out a paper towel and a bottle of water, dampening the towel and stepping up to her. Gently, he wiped her face, circling her eyes, sliding it over her mouth. He stepped back and nearly laughed.

"You just smeared my makeup, didn't you?"

He gave her a sheepish smile. "I thought it would come off."

She reached into her bag and pulled out a makeup-remover pad. Leaning in front of the bike's mirror, she removed the last of it. "Okay, what was that about?"

"It's time to stop hiding behind all that makeup. That's not you. It's your shield. You don't need it anymore."

Her heart shifted as her gaze locked with his. "Now you've really seen me naked."

"Oh, yeah." His smile faded into something much deeper. "Thanks for including me in that scene with your mom."

She shrugged.

"No, that was . . . that you wanted me there, during that moment . . ." He shook his head. "Dammit, Zoe, why do you have to be so incredible?"

She nearly laughed at that, despite the agony she saw on his face. "Thanks . . . I think."

He ran his fingers through his dark blond hair, still unspiky. She liked it that way. "That wasn't a compliment. Lucas, Petra, Amy, even Eric, they're great, you know. Good people stuck in a bad situation. I could have walked away, though. From them, I could have saved myself and walked. But you . . . you had to be this sexy, brave, sassy, tender, beautiful person. You had to be the one person I couldn't walk away from."

His words filled her with warmth and giddiness and heat and . . . love. She slid her arms around his neck and in a flirty tone said, "It was when I started throwing things at you psychically, wasn't it? The towel, the pillow . . . you couldn't resist me, could you?"

His arms circled her waist and turned her so she was leaning against the car. "No, it was all the things flying when we had that fantastically crazy sex. *That* made me wild." He kissed her, and out of the corner of her eye she saw the paper towel he'd used on her face fly across the car.

She could also feel him smile beneath her mouth. She tugged his shirt out of his jeans, and he tossed it over his head. He tore off her tank top, unclipped her bra, and kissed each nipple with such tenderness, she groaned.

He kissed her stomach, dipping his tongue beneath the waistband of her jeans as he unbuttoned and unzipped. She slid out of both those and her panties. She ran her fingers through his soft hair and around his ears, halting him momentarily as he rolled his eyes in pleasure.

He stripped out of his jeans and lifted her onto the hood of the 'Cuda. He spread her legs and ran his finger through her folds as he plunged his tongue into her mouth.

"Now," she whispered.

He pulled a condom out of the back pocket of the jeans that were lying on the floor and slid it on before positioning himself between her legs.

"I want to make myself perfectly clear." His hands slid up and down her sides. "I know you're sad, but *I am not* comforting you."

"You already did. I just want you. Just . . . want . . . you," she said again on little breaths, as he teased her folds again.

"Okay, then." He pulled her to the edge of the hood and slid inside. He filled her perfectly, and he filled her soul, too. She moved with him, her arms around his shoulders, her mouth kissing his.

"We need to do this in the tomb so we can stay longer," he said breathlessly.

"We can do that," she said in the same way. "Again. As soon as I . . ."

She felt that delicious swirling pressure build inside her, exploding and shaking her body.

He let himself go then, ramming into her with a groan that sounded like a mix of pleasure and pain. His fingers dug into her as his orgasm rocked him. She held him close, her face buried in his hair, eyes squeezed tight.

He held her for a few minutes. Then he leaned back to look at her. "You know the most hair-raising thing I've faced since those guys grabbed me at the casino?"

"Being shot at? Running for your life?"

"Falling in love with you."

Those words swept through her, stronger than the orgasm. "I love you, too." A grin broke out on her face.

"What?"

"It's just funny. There you were, pretending to be a good guy with Ruby, not even realizing that you really are a good guy."

"We'd better get down." He pulled out and wrapped the condom in the paper towel she'd sent flying. He picked up her clothing and handed it to her, then got dressed.

Just before he opened the door, he turned back. "Oh, and be gentle with me, okay?"

"Gentle?"

"This will be my first tattoo, you know."

"You're going to get the Blue Eye?"

He rolled his eyes. "Can't be the only one in the family without one."

EPILOGUE

That night the Rogues lit a candle in honor of Zoe's granddad. They stood in the living room around a white candle that was sitting on the floor. The flickering flame cast undulating shadows on the artwork that covered the walls. The rose scent of the candle filled the room. One by one, they linked hands. Eric hesitated but finally took the hands that were outstretched to him.

On his perch, Orn'ry sang the chorus of "Fire," sounding more like Elmer Fudd than Bruce Springsteen.

Amy put her finger over her mouth. "Shh."

Zoe whispered a prayer and blew out the candle.

Eric was the first to release his hands and move out of the circle. "This whoo-whoo stuff is too weird for me."

Petra slid her arm around Zoe's shoulder. "I'm so sorry." Even in this sacred moment, though, she obviously couldn't resist smoothing a lock of Zoe's hair.

Eric eyed Zoe's and Rand's linked hands, but he

hadn't said anything—yet. He would, though, when the timing was better.

Amy walked over and took Zoe's hands. "I want to try to talk to him, tell him about your father."

"You'd do that? After what happened with Gladstone?"

Amy nodded. "I need a picture."

Zoe went to her purse and took a photo out of her wallet. "Roger Stoker."

She, Rand, and Amy walked into her bedroom. Lucas followed, protective of his love. Zoe glanced at Rand. Now she had someone to protect her, too. Someone to protect as well. She gave his hand a squeeze.

Amy lay down on the bed, patting the surface to indicate that Zoe sit next to her. Amy studied the photo, a soft smile on her face. "He was a handsome man."

"A good man."

Holding the picture, Amy laid her hands on her stomach and closed her eyes. She shifted, getting comfortable. Rand sat behind Zoe, sliding his arm across her collarbone. Lucas smiled at the gesture, though his smile didn't reach his haunted eyes.

Several minutes went by. Petra started to crack her knuckles but stopped immediately. She began braiding her hair instead. Amy's eyes twitched beneath her closed lids. Her mouth moved slightly, though no sound came out. Then it curved. She nodded.

Zoe could hardly breathe. Was Amy talking to her granddad? Sensing Zoe's excitement, Rand tightened his arm around her. She shared a smile with him, but her gaze went back to Amy.

Several minutes later, Amy's eyes opened. Lucas

helped her to sit up. "I tried really hard not to slip into REM," she said.

Zoe leaned forward. "Did you . . . ?"

Amy nodded. "He sends his love."

"What about my father? You told him—"

"He already knows. He's with your father, Zoe. And your father was there, too. He said he's been watching out for you." Amy looked at Rand. "And he approves."

Zoe put her hand to her heart, an overwhelming feeling of joy washing over her. She leaned forward and hugged Amy. "Thank you!"

She turned and touched the place over Rand's heart, where his new tattoo was hidden beneath his shirt. She knew that whatever happened, she was surrounded by family and by love. Along with her telekinesis and, oh, a few guns, that was all she needed.

ACKNOWLEDGMENTS

I'm always humbled and grateful for those who take time to help me get it right. My sincerest thanks to the following:

On tattoos:

Fellow author Julia Madeleine for answering my many questions about tattoo artists and helping me to not call them tats—God forbid!

David and the others at Blue Devil Tattoo in Ybor City, Florida, for letting me hang out and ask questions. You guys were great!

The guys at Cherry Hill Tattoo Company in Naples, Florida, for answering some of my technical questions.

John Case, for answering weapons questions . . . and being a good friend, too (you, too, Nanine!). And thanks for the ride on the Harley Road King!

Ride, cool graffiti artist, who helped me get a handle on a fascinating world. I'll never look at graffiti the same again.

Antonio "Tony" Sanchez, MSM, CLET, Captain, Biscayne Park Police Department, for answering all of my silly and not-so-silly questions.

My husband, Dave, who helped me brainstorm this series, and for all the wonderful things you do.

Turn the page for a sneak peek
at the next thrilling installment
in Jaime Rush's Offspring series

Touching Darkness

Available May 2010 from Avon Books

Nicholas returned to the estate, his head buzzing with what Zoe and Rand had told him. He'd been shocked at seeing the faces to match the pictures he'd been working on finding for weeks. More shocked because they hadn't looked or acted like terrorists. They were in their twenties, like him, and aside from their obvious distrust and wariness, a lot like him.

He knew something for sure: Darkwell had lied about their intentions. If they'd gone to his house to kill him, why had they not taken him out then?

From the beginning, Darkwell hadn't lived up to his side of the agreement, making excuses and promises. Dishonesty was usually a deal-breaker, but he understood that the government sometimes had secrets it couldn't share with the general public. This program was one of those secrets. But now . . . now he knew he was being lied to personally. He'd walk, screw the money and his obligation, forget that he always saw a job through to the best of his ability. Before he could do that, though, he had to find out the truth. Not because it involved him; it involved his father, a man he had no memory of. A man whose death had shattered his mother's heart.

He waited until the armed guard opened the gate. The mansion was a hell of a lot better than that creepy asylum. Darkwell had paid him a lot of money to participate in this program, more to reside on-site. Nicholas wanted control over what jobs he worked, whose stuff he retrieved. He wanted more time to help Bone Finders, a nonprofit that pulled mostly law-enforcement resources to find the remains of the missing. He could only do so many of those missions a year, though. Finding lost ships, equipment, even the remains of classified experimental aircraft was simple. The more emotions that were tied to the missing article, the more of a toll it took on him. Finding a child's bones, for instance, sucked out his energy for a week. It was worth it, though.

He nodded to the guard at the front door and walked inside. The place had the smell of old wood and older money. Rich mahogany paneling and trim, a winding staircase, leather accents. He couldn't imagine living in a place like this permanently. He'd take his place in the Eastport section of Annapolis any day, three bedrooms, two bathrooms, and a nice little yard where he could work up a sweat mowing and trimming.

He sprinted up the enormous staircase that wound up, then split halfway to the right wing and the left wing, where the offices and his suite of rooms were. He spotted Olivia in the hallway and felt that odd ping in his chest he did whenever he saw her. Since they'd moved to the estate, and she now lived there, too, he saw her a lot more. Her face, a perfect oval framed by long, shiny dark hair, transformed into a smile when she saw him. She tamped it down, though, and he suspected that had something to do with Darkwell spotting them talking in the hallway the other day. The man had glowered.

Nicholas paused a few feet from her. "I'm surprised to see you here on a Saturday." Their first weekend here, she'd gone back to her apartment.

She gave him a soft smile. "I had things to do here."

"Can we talk? Alone?"

Her mouth moved without sound for a moment, conflict on her face. "I, uh . . . maybe it's not such a good idea."

"Is that because of Darkwell? He say something to you?"

She nodded, her mouth tightening. "He doesn't want us, uh, socializing."

He felt both gratification that the order seemed to bother her and annoyance. "This is about work."

"Oh." Her face flushed in the sweet way that told him she had been way too sheltered as far as men were concerned. An intriguing thought in itself. "Of course."

He wondered if she'd been sheltered by her parents. Maybe she'd lived in a remote house for the first several years of her life. He knew the feeling, and being stranded out in the boonies for his first twelve years had left him more comfortable being alone.

He leaned in close, inhaling the faint scent of her rose perfume. "I'd love to *socialize* with you, but I don't want you to get into trouble. Where can we talk?"

Her face flushed again, but she quickly turned. "Come this way."

He walked beside her, their hands accidentally brushing. He stole a glance at her as they passed a large, framed mirror in the hallway. They passed Jerryl Evrard's room, where he and Fonda were noisily going at it, as usual. Olivia studiously avoided his gaze. Oh, yeah, he'd love to socialize with her, to make her moan and cry out, too, but he respected her adherence to the policy prohibiting staff/contractor relations.

Besides, Olivia was too classy for a one- or ten-night-stand relationship, and he wasn't into being tied down. He liked being alone, in his home, or in the middle of a forest tracking down bones, or a hundred feet down in the ocean looking for shipwrecks, without having to feel obligated to call the little woman and promise he was thinking about her every minute.

And the fact that he was probably going to die sometime in the near future made getting involved with anyone even more wrong.

They walked into the room at the end of the hallway where he and Jerryl undertook their missions and closed the door behind them. A look of both trepidation and anticipation crossed her face at that. The balcony had been closed in as a sunroom, but Darkwell had installed a heavy, dark curtain to block out all light. Olivia pulled it open, letting the sun stream in to burnish her straight hair with red highlights.

She was dressed nearly as conservatively as she did during the week, wearing black pants and a yellow, button-down shirt. It was unbuttoned just low enough, though, to show a hint of cleavage and the creamy smooth skin of her collarbone. She had incredible hazel green eyes, the kind that made him forget he was there on business and not pleasure. He walked to the curved glass that overlooked the courtyard. Across the way was where Olivia stayed.

He placed his hand against the warm glass. "Darkwell signed me on to DARK MATTER with the promise that I would be helping the government by locating hostages. So far all I've been doing is finding this group of what he calls Rogues, who are supposedly terrorists. What do you know about them?"

A shadow crossed her face. "He hasn't told me much about them, either. I . . . I took care of Lucas Vanderwyck when he was at the asylum. He had a fever, and I talked Peterson into putting him into a tub of water to cool him down. I remember thinking that he must have done something pretty bad to be there. But you saw what the Rogues did when they broke in. They shot our people. They're ruthless."

He didn't even know he was going to reach out and touch the side of her temple where one of them had coldcocked her two weeks ago. The bruise was gone, but there was a faint scar where she'd been cut. Eric Aruda was a bastard, no doubt about that. Her eyes widened at the touch.

He dropped his hand. "He could have killed you."

"I know." Her voice quivered, and the shadow of the violence still haunted her eyes. "Look what he did to Carl."

"No, I mean, he could have killed you. Easily. But he only knocked you out. They broke in to rescue their friends, not to attack. Carl was holding Eric's sister at gunpoint." Then he realized just what she'd said. "So there *were* prisoners."

Now her face paled. "I wasn't supposed to tell anyone. Please don't say anything to Darkwell."

"I overheard him talking about the prisoners right after it happened. You only confirmed it. He denied that there were prisoners at the asylum. I don't like being lied to."

"We have to trust that he's doing the right thing. He has his way, but he's a good man."

Nicholas narrowed his eyes. "You're not . . . involved with him, are you?" He did seem a bit territorial about Olivia, and she seemed both reverential and obedient toward him.

A half laugh, half bark erupted from her mouth, which she covered. "No. God, no. He's just . . . been my boss for a long time." She tilted her head. "Please don't let him know that I told you about the prisoners."

He moved closer, his voice lowering. "Only if you tell me what's really going on here."

Next month, don't miss these exciting new love stories only from Avon Books

Midnight Pleasures With a Scoundrel by Lorraine Heath

On a quest to avenge her sister's death, Eleanor Watkins never expected to fall for the man following her through pleasure gardens and into ballrooms. But soon nothing can keep her from the sinfully attractive scoundrel—not even the dangerous secrets she keeps.

Silent Night, Haunted Night by Terri Garey

Unwilling psychic Nicki Styx survived a near-death experience to find herself able to see and hear the dead, but she only has eyes for Joe Bascombe. But when a devious demon begins haunting Joe's dreams, Nicki realizes this Christmas could be her and Joe's last.

What the Duke Desires by Jenna Petersen

Lillian Mayhew is desperate to expose a devastating secret about Simon Crathorne, the Duke of Billingham. Yet from the moment she meets her rakishly handsome host, she begins to question whether she can destroy his world so callously.

To Love a Wicked Lord by Edith Layton

Phillipa Carstairs is all alone, waiting for a fiancé who disappeared many months ago. She's long forgotten why she loved him, and she's nearly given up hope...until a handsome spy for the Crown comes to her aid.

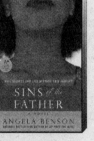

Unforgettable, enthralling love stories,
sparkling with passion and adventure
from Romance's bestselling authors

Visit www.AuthorTracker.com for exclusive
information on your favorite HarperCollins authors.

RT 0609

Available wherever books are sold or please call 1-800-331-3761 to order.

At Avon Books, we know your passion for romance—once you finish one of our novels, you find yourself wanting more.

May we tempt you with . . .

- **Excerpts** from our upcoming releases.

- Entertaining **extras**, including authors' personal photo albums and book lists.

- Behind-the-scenes **scoop** on your favorite characters and series.

- **Sweepstakes** for the chance to win free books, romantic getaways, and other fun prizes.

- Writing **tips** from our authors and editors.

- **Blog** with our authors and find out why they love to write romance.

- **Exclusive content** that's not contained within the pages of our novels.

Join us at
www.avonbooks.com